T0165190

THE SECRETS AND LIES OF
Yooper Girls

THE SECRETS AND LIES OF
Yooper Girls

BY T. D. CROEL

iUniverse, Inc.
Bloomington

THE SECRETS AND LIES OF YOOPER GIRLS

Copyright © 2011 by T. D. Croel.

All rights reserved. No part of this book may be used or reproduced by any means, graphic, electronic, or mechanical, including photocopying, recording, taping or by any information storage retrieval system without the written permission of the publisher except in the case of brief quotations embodied in critical articles and reviews.

This is a work of fiction. All of the characters, names, incidents, organizations, and dialogue in this novel are either the products of the author's imagination or are used fictitiously.

iUniverse books may be ordered through booksellers or by contacting:

iUniverse
1663 Liberty Drive
Bloomington, IN 47403
www.iuniverse.com
1-800-Authors (1-800-288-4677)

Because of the dynamic nature of the Internet, any web addresses or links contained in this book may have changed since publication and may no longer be valid. The views expressed in this work are solely those of the author and do not necessarily reflect the views of the publisher, and the publisher hereby disclaims any responsibility for them.

Any people depicted in stock imagery provided by Thinkstock are models, and such images are being used for illustrative purposes only.
Certain stock imagery © Thinkstock.

ISBN: 978-1-4620-5188-5 (sc)
ISBN: 978-1-4620-5190-8 (hc)
ISBN: 978-1-4620-5191-5 (ebk)

Library of Congress Control Number: 2011915950

Printed in the United States of America

iUniverse rev. date: 10/10/2011

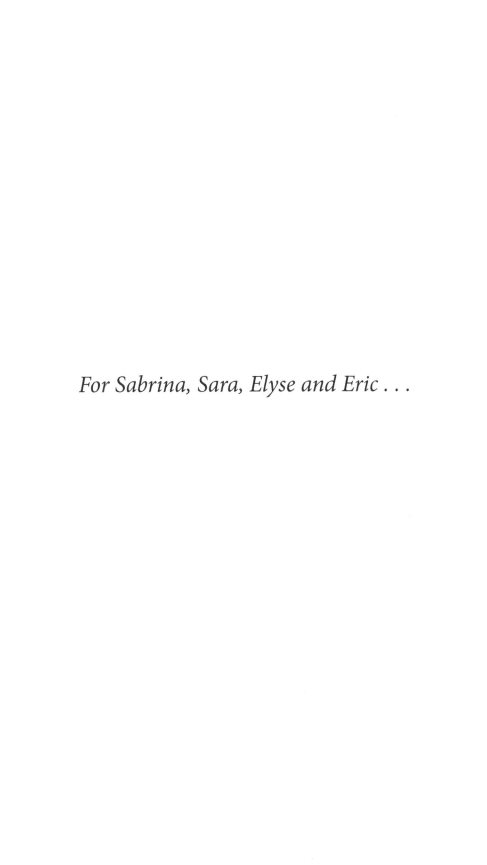

For Sabrina, Sara, Elyse and Eric . . .

ACKNOWLEDGEMENTS

No book is possible without significant help from so many others. I am very fortunate to have had some very good people help me along the way. I owe a great debt to Miranda Paul for editing my book and helping me learn so much about what it takes to write a good novel.

I would also like to thank Veronica Sweeney and Elsa Widmaier for being two of the first people to read The Secrets and Lies of Yooper Girls and giving me their feedback. The folks at iUniverse were also especially helpful. Special thanks to Michelle Koss who was an incredible help and great friend during this journey. Thanks to Anthony Bowers for his beautiful cover.

Like most books, The Secrets and Lies of Yooper Girls is heavily influenced by real people and real places. There is a real Rapid Junction, Robin's Inn and Four Seasons Motel that exist on a lonely stretch of U.S. 2 in the middle of the Upper Peninsula of Michigan . . . just with slightly different names.

And finally, thank you Wendy, Laurie, and Jim for introducing me to the great wonder that is the U.P.

CHAPTER ONE

August, 2010

Wendy La Claire, weathercaster for WTTL in St. Louis, pointed to various cloud fronts and magically made them disappear with a swipe of her hand. Her flaxen brown hair, cropped to her shoulders, framed her tanned oval face perfectly. It complimented a smile that charmed the Gateway to the West.

"And there it is, St. Louis; hot, hot, hot. Back to you, Ben."

Hot, hot, hot, is right. Ben whirled away from the beautiful weather 'girl' he'd be sleeping with later on that night and back to the main camera which zoomed in on his flawless face. "Thank you, Wendy. When we come back, the sports with Rich Dominquez. Did our Cards make it eight in a row?" He shuffled his papers and looked over at Rich and Wendy as the off-the-air light flicked red. "Hey, Dominquez, you going to make it?"

Rich Dominquez, the popular sports anchor, sweated profusely as the poor make-up artist desperately scrambled to reapply foundation that just seemed to slide down his face.

"Hell no, I'm not. Jesus, it's so damn hot. It doesn't even get this hot in Guadalajara. Can't we turn up the air conditioning?" He looked around for a producer to honor his request. He turned back to Ben. "How in the hell are you staying dry?"

"I don't sweat, Dominquez. I'm a trained television journalist." He smiled coyly at his friend and co-worker.

"He doesn't even sweat during sex, does he?"

About to walk off the set, Wendy didn't miss a beat. "Well, you know Dom; you actually have to exert some energy to sweat. Ben just lies there."

"Ouch!" Ben responded playfully.

Wendy didn't care who knew that she was sleeping with the Channel 11 anchorman. Ben was good looking, and despite his reputation, quite the gentleman. She had no intentions of trying to make him her husband; that might be a little awkward since she had no qualms about taking his seat one day. Ben was just like the others: companionship and sex. After six years of station hopping, she'd learned her lesson. Be careful who you sleep with if you want to be a prime anchor, and be willing to do whatever it takes—even if that includes playing a meteorologist.

Grinning at Ben, she walked up behind him, threatening to ruffle his hair. He could see her in the television monitor and waggled his finger like a parent warning an eight-year-old not to take another cookie. Instead of ruffling his hair, she grabbed him by the chin, turned him toward her, and gave him a quick peck on the lips.

*　*　*

Wendy awoke to an annoying ring tone set for unknown numbers. She decided to pick up on the last ring before it went to her voice mail.

"Hello," she let out with a rasp. There was no response on the other end at first, but she could hear someone breathing. She cleared her throat. "Hello," she repeated.

Still only the breathing. Wendy dangled her finger over the end call button, but pulled it back when a voice finally spoke. "Your mother is dead."

*　*　*

The next morning Wendy got on a flight from St. Louis to Green Bay, Wisconsin. It would be a two and a half hour drive from there to Rapid Junction. Ben drove her to the airport. He awkwardly offered to go with her the night before, and was beyond relieved when she rebuffed him. He knew where he belonged and where he didn't. A small town in the Upper Peninsula was not where he fit in. There would be talk of fishing, hunting and the flow of cheap beer. He would want to drink heavily to get through the ordeal and knew that no one would have his premium scotch of choice.

"Beverage?" the perky flight attendant asked.

"Huh?" Wendy responded, trying to regain her senses. She wiped her eyes, which were free of any mascara, and showed her true exhaustion.

"Beverage?" the platinum blonde repeated, losing none of her previous enthusiasm. When Wendy still hadn't responded, she felt the need to clarify. "Coffee . . . tea . . . soft drink?"

"You have any of those little whiskey bottles stocked in that compartment of yours?"

"We generally don't have those available for flights this early." The attendant's smile was finally beginning to wane.

"Too bad." Wendy turned away and looked out her window. She traced her finger along the glass, pretending to touch a cloud and move it out of the way just like she had done the night before. The real clouds did not move on her command.

CHAPTER TWO

January, 1992

Mike La Claire got in his expensive Cadillac Coupe de Ville and drove from his 3,000 square foot home in Birmingham, Michigan to a small rundown trailer park in Flint. Mike tripped on an extension cord that ran from the trailer to a neighbor's. He walked in and found his brother passed out on the couch in only his underwear—draped by a beach towel. He found his sister-in-law, Marie and ten-year-old niece Wendy, huddled together in a chair, trying to get warmth from a tiny space heater. He took the beer out of his brother's hand and poured it over his head. Paul woke up and immediately began to shiver. He looked around and tried to regain his senses.

"Get your clothes on, you're moving."

"Where?" Paul mumbled as he reached down for his pants.

"Rapid Junction, that's where."

Wendy was ecstatic at the news, jumping up and hugging her uncle. She looked over to her parents, who did not appear to share her joy. She couldn't understand why her parents weren't equally as excited.

"How about lending me some money to start up a bait and tackle shop?" Paul asked, as he awkwardly pulled his pants up over his legs as he stretched himself out on his recliner. Mike looked at his older brother for a quick moment; decided not to say what he was really thinking and instead walked out.

Paul looked at his wife; "What else can we do?"

"We could get a divorce, that's what!"

Marie began to pack their belongings.

* * *

Wendy stepped out the front door of her new home; her little ten-year-old body bundled in a black snow suit. Her mother had pulled her hood so tight on her face, that it was difficult to make out anything more than her bright blue eyes. She trudged her way to the end of the parking lot and looked up at a sign that named her new home; Four Seasons Inn. She turned to her mother, who stood by the door, trying to ignore the freezing temperatures. She gave her a wave, letting her mother know it was okay to go back inside and get warm.

It was twelve degrees and the snow was piled up higher than Wendy. Despite her well bundled appearance, Wendy was freezing her tail off. She hopped up and down trying to get a look over the snowplowed drifts to see if the bus was coming. She looked across the street and read the road signs; US Highway 2 and T Road. She had been in the UP for less than a week and couldn't get over the names of the roads. Most of the streets she saw were named after numbers or letters. She wasn't sure if these people were lazy or just lacked imagination.

The bus finally arrived and she gladly got on, just to remove herself from the cold. She walked down the aisle and felt the stares. Although no one actually came right out and said, "You caint' sit here" or "Seat's tayken"; their stares said it all. For whatever reason there is an unwritten code among children. *I can't be nice to you new kid, not until you prove to me that you are worthy.* It is the same in every big city and every small town. Maybe even more true in small towns; the microscope on people seems to be a little more intense.

School had started with the usual introduction. "This is Wendy La Claire, she's from Flint."

Like all true Michiganders, Mrs. Stewart, held up her right hand in the shape of a mitten and pointed to a spot just above the puffy part of her palm. "Flint is in the lower peninsula, right here." She smiled to the class, extremely proud of her geographic skills.

A particularly pudgy boy named John Frederick hollered out, "Troll!"

They get Yoopers and we get Trolls, that doesn't quite seem fair, Wendy thought to herself as she wished for her shabby existence back in Troll-land.

The gawky fifth grade teacher, with the Sally Jesse Rafael glasses, shrugged off the non-sense from John Frederick. "John, you know better than that."

"John Frederick," he grunted, as he corrected her.

"Anyhoo . . ." She stared at him for a few seconds and considered referring to him as *Ogre*, a nickname given to him by his peers. She resisted and maintained her professionalism as she turned back to the class. "Please, make our newest Rapid Junction citizen welcome." Wendy didn't expect it, and became even more uncomfortable when her new teacher put an arm around her.

Mrs. Stewart directed Wendy to a seat behind Maggie Fonduluc. Maggie smiled up at Wendy as she passed. Wendy wanted to smile back, but was caught off guard by the dimpled blonde's damaged face. She couldn't take her eyes off the thick, discolored scar above her lip or the way her left nostril caved in. Wendy had never seen anyone with a cleft lip before. Completely distracted, her butt nearly missed the seat. Maggie, used to stares, shrugged it off and continued to smile. *I don't think I could ever smile, not with a face like that.*

Wendy looked down, feeling immediate shame for her thoughts. Maggie finally turned around. Wendy's attention went to the girl sitting directly next to Maggie. She was tall and lean, nearly a head bigger than most of her peers. Savannah Sanders gave Wendy the most menacing glare she had ever received. The sound of Mrs. Stewarts voice finally got Savannah to refocus her attention; much to Wendy's relief.

*   *   *

"What's wrong with your face?" Wendy asked, peering over from her seat on a swing. There was a stony toughness about her, but also the rude innocence of a 10-year-old girl. She simply asked what was on her mind and did not think there was anything wrong with being inquisitive.

Maggie didn't seem insulted in the least. She let her feet slow her down on her swing and then placed both of her hands on her face and looked cross eyed down at her nose. "Goodness, I hope nothing," she said in her nasally voice. The *s*'s of goodness came with a whistling sound.

This made Wendy laugh. The confidence and humor that Maggie demonstrated made Wendy immediately like her.

"What's wrong with your face?" Savannah bellowed. Wendy didn't have a chance. Before she knew it, she was flying out of the swing backward. Due to nearly a foot of snow and the thick padding of her snow pants, she hardly felt it when she crashed to the ground. She sat in the powder white snow looking up at what she most certainly felt would be her nemesis for as long as she was going to be stuck in the shit-for-saken town of Rapid Junction.

Savannah put her fists up like she was a prize fighter. "Let's go, Sacajawea!"

Wendy gulped and touched her medium brown braided hair. She figured that and her coffee-colored complexion made her only a pair of moccasins and a feather headdress away from the nickname being spot on.

"I don't want to fight," Wendy lied as she stared up at the much bigger girl from the ground. She wanted nothing more than to fight, but also didn't want to face her mother and father at home if she got in trouble on the first day at her new school. She wanted to hit Savannah right in her perfect little nose and pull out her blonde hair from its roots. She wanted to cause someone else some pain; believing she had suffered enough in her short life time.

"You may not want to fight, but I do!"

Savannah rushed at Wendy and tackled her just as she had stood up. Savannah's father, the town's football coach, would have been proud of her fundamentally sound and viciously tough hit. The larger girl's shoulder hit Wendy squarely in the stomach. The air sailed right out of Wendy. She desperately gasped for air—the wind being knocked clean out of her.

"Savannah, don't!" Maggie cried as she hopped up from her swing. Her plea came out weakly.

Wendy could hear the gathering of fifth graders cheering on the toughest girl in their class. She couldn't blame them, knowing a good playground fight didn't come around every day and she had done nothing in her half day to prove that she was worthy of cheering for.

Wendy finally got her breath back. She refused to cry, but was still no match to get the heavier, stronger girl off of her. Savannah pinned Wendy's arms beneath her knees and gently smacked her face with her grandmother knitted mittens on. The pain Wendy felt in her arms was nothing compared to the pain she felt at her complete and utter inability to do anything about her situation.

T. D. Croel

"What's wrong with your face? Huh, huh? What's wrong with your ugly little face?" Savannah kept repeating as the mittens came down on one cheek and then the other.

Wendy could only close her eyes and try to get her arms unpinned. Finally, Savannah stopped. Wendy opened her eyes to see Savannah looking across the snow covered field. She followed the eyes of her nemesis. In the distance was the shape of a bundled figure pushing its way through the snow—Mrs. Thomas, the playground lady.

Like all great fights, there is a turning point when the underdog makes believers out of everyone. Wendy made her move. She knew she couldn't do anything with her arms. They now hurt something fierce and felt more like gelatin than anything else. She looked up at Savannah, smiled, then hocked up all of the phlegm she could muster. Before it could register in Savannah's mind what was about to happen—it happened. Wendy let it fly. The yellowish, sticky deposit from her mouth went directly into Savannah's right eye. She barely had enough time to blink and keep it from entering and stinging her retina. She threw up her right hand to wipe away the nasty phlegm that was stretched between her eyelash and cheek.

"Oh, grossss!" one of the spectators bellowed.

"Hey, Sasquatch!" Wendy hollered from her position in the snow.

Just as Savannah looked down, Wendy punched her square in the nose. As ten year-old punches go, it was a good one. There was enough force behind it to cause a little bit of blood to trickle to the edge of Savannah's nostrils. Wendy pushed her off as Savannah let loose a cry of pain. Savannah took off her right mitten, which now had the remnants of Wendy's spittle and yellow goo on it and then her left. Wendy had never been more frightened in her life. Her father, drunk off his ass, never put fear in her like that. She stumbled back a little, but otherwise held her ground. She wanted to run, but knew that in doing so she would lose all credibility with the masses that were assembled.

Fifty yards. The fat-ass playground lady rumbled toward the chaos. "Break it up! Break it up!" she bellowed as she huffed away.

Savannah put her bare hand up to her nose to see what the damage was. Due to the cold, however, it had already dried and flaked around her nostril. Wendy could see the anger raging through the taller girl's body. She knew the dangerous girl was done with text book tackling and mitten smacks that made the others laugh.

Savannah Sanders landed the haymaker with all the might she could muster in her youthful frame. Her balled fist crashed into the side of Wendy's left eye. Sacajawea spun to the left like a top, and then went down clutching her face. Her rival had also gone down.

Mrs. Thomas had cut through a half dozen fifth graders like a fourteen pound bowling ball on a mission. *Strike.* She tackled Savannah a split second too late to save Wendy's eye. All 200+ pounds of her landed on the tall girl. It was Savannah's turn to gasp as the air escaped her lungs in one giant *whoosh.*

The two Yooper girls proved their toughness to their peers. Neither shed a tear as they were being led to their doom. Wendy held her swelling eye which was becoming numb from the frigid temperature. Savannah kept putting her hand up to her nose, checking for blood.

"You girls should be ashamed of yourselves!" Mrs. Thomas barked as she led each girl by the back of their hoods. Both girls struggled to get through the snow at the pace they were being led; especially Wendy, whose legs were much shorter than Savannah's. She went down twice only to be yanked up by the burly Mrs. Thomas. Maggie ran alongside the threesome, telling Savannah that everything was going to be alright; but she looked at Wendy when she said it.

They finally reached the back doors of the school. The emotion of the situation finally got to Wendy and she began crying. "I think you're really pretty," she sobbed, before being yanked through the door.

"I think you're pretty, too," Maggie beamed.

Savannah and Wendy sat outside of the principal's office. They heard Mrs. Thomas explain what had happened in Mr. Stainforth's office.

He listened intently; then asked the only question he had. "Where were you?"

Wendy, having smelled the cigarette odor on the lady as she was being dragged through the snow, had her guess.

Wendy decided she had better get on the good side of Savannah right then, or else it was going to be one long hellish year. "That was one helluva good punch, my eye's throbbing."

Savannah finally turned to Wendy and admired her handy work. "Man, that's going to be one heck of a shiner!"

"I know!" Wendy managed a smile.

"Is there a lot of blood?" Savannah turned her nose so that the side with the dried blood on her nostril could be seen by Wendy. The truth was there were only a few remaining flakes of the dry crusted blood.

"No," Wendy said, somewhat disappointed.

"Huh . . . still that was the best punch I've ever gotten," Savannah responded with pride.

Wendy and Savannah had bonded, but there would be as much hate between them as there would be love throughout their relationship. They always had Maggie as their peace maker, their go-between—their stability. Maggie would always be the glue of their friendship.

*   *   *

"I miss my friends," Wendy said to herself as the flight landed. She hadn't realized she had said it aloud and the man next to her asked for clarification. "Nothing," she sighed.

CHAPTER THREE

Wendy had forgotten how busy US 2 could be during the summer. She faced tremendous traffic driving through tourist towns like Escanaba and Gladstone. She pulled up to a stop light and looked at the grey minivan in front of her. *I'm Proud of My Honor Roll Son.* She chuckled at the stereotypical bumper sticker from some family trying to escape their suburban lives downstate and trade it in for a week in the great outdoors of the Upper Peninsula. These vacation treks always made Wendy laugh. Most of these people spent their time on the beach, shopping, eating fudge, or playing miniature golf. Putting their ankles into the cold water of Lake Michigan was as close as they got to 'real' nature.

"Trolls!" she laughed to herself. The people who really wanted to experience the beauty of the Upper Peninsula and all Mother Nature had to offer stayed at places like Four Seasons Motel in Rapid Junction. There, guys like Paul La Claire with his thick Upper Peninsula accent took the nature enthusiasts to the best hunting and fishing sites and gave them the 'real' Yooper experience.

The burgundy colored Taurus raced along US 2, finally out of the insane summer traffic and onto the relatively wide open four lane highway. Wendy had tried several times to call back the number that had reached her the night before. Each time she was greeted by, "This is Marie, but obviously I'm not here, so do whatcha gotta do."

Wendy felt a shame burn through her pores. She always thought that there would be that chance to go back home, to finally swallow her pride and forgive and forget. But every time she picked up the phone a vision of what was stolen from her came to her mind and she promptly changed her mind. Even after twelve years, the pain still lingered.

With her mind on her dead mother, she hadn't even noticed that the air conditioning in her rental car had stopped working. She looked in the rearview mirror and saw sweat on her forehead. Wendy fumbled with every knob and button she could reach, desperately struggling to get cool air to emerge from the vents. Her legs were stuck to the vinyl seats and she pulled the white blouse off her back. Frustrated at the lack of results, she pounded the dashboard.

"Fuck me!"

She angrily rolled down the window, letting the 90 degree air roll past her face, which did not help in the least. Distracted, she almost missed the familiar sign and jerked the steering wheel to the right and into the parking lot, spraying gravel on the car behind her. She heard the blasting of the man's horn, and could only assume there was a middle finger pointed in her direction as well.

"Please, be here," she said to herself.

Wendy didn't bother to lock her car. She let out a quick sigh and then walked toward the doors of the Robin's Inn. There were two bars in Rapid Junction; the Robin's Inn and the Rapid Junction Tavern. In both places patrons can expect to be stared down as they walk in; but at the Rapid Junction Tavern the stare is both longer and more menacing. Out-of-towners quickly find that the Robin's Inn is the place to be. Karaoke on Thursdays and Sundays, Trivia on Wednesday and live bands on Fridays and Saturdays made it as hip as a second tier tourist town bar can get.

The Rapid Junction Tavern had a twenty-inch television, a juke box player that no longer worked, a lopsided pool table, and booze. The booze and quiet were the main attraction for the regulars.

Wendy pushed the door open and welcomed the coolness of the air conditioner. Like creatures of habit, the few patrons at the bar turned their necks as automatically as they took sips of their tap beer. Wendy didn't recognize two older men sitting with their necks craned in her direction. Being attractive, their stares lasted a little longer than normal. A tall woman came out from the kitchen area carrying a case of beer. It had been seven years since Wendy had last seen her in person.

Savannah, with her sheen blonde hair pulled back in a pony tail and toned, lean frame; was just as she had remembered her. Wendy sat down at the far end of the L-shaped bar. Savannah had her back to her as she knelt down and placed each of the beers into the bar refrigerator.

"What's a girl gotta do to get a beer around here, eh?" Wendy said, allowing her Yooper accent to come back.

Savannah paused as she set the last beer in the fridge. She smiled as she stood and turned to her friend, "Little Troll bitches have to wait."

She walked over to Wendy from her side of the bar with a beer in hand. "How are you, friend?" Her smile turned to compassion.

"Things are a little surreal right now." Wendy managed a slight smile.

"I bet." She opened the can of beer and set it down in front of Wendy. "Tell me the glamorous life of a news reporter hasn't turned you into a prima donna who now drinks chocolate martinis or fancy scotches I can't pronounce."

"Aw, hell no; that would be my prima donna boyfriend, I still love beer." Truth be told, Wendy had acquired a taste for the fancy scotches Savannah was talking about. But on a hot day there was nothing better than an ice cold beer. She took a huge chug and then put the can next to her sweating forehead. "Ahh, that feels good."

"Hotter than a mug out there, ain't it?"

"Yes, it is."

Savannah walked back around the bar and crossed through a little swinging gate that let the patrons know where they were not welcome. She walked past an older couple who were vacationing in Rapid Junction. The woman stopped her conversation with her husband—trying to eavesdrop. The man didn't notice and continued to gape at the television screen showing sports highlights. The other two gentlemen were done gawking and resumed their drinking.

Savannah reached her friend and held out her arms. "God, I miss you!"

Wendy, sitting on the stool, was near eye level with her friend. On her feet, she would have been a head shorter. She put her arms out and clutched her old friend a little harder than she would have normally. Past memories and current guilt swept over her.

"I miss you, too."

"Your mom was a good woman," Savannah said solemnly, pulling back from the quick embrace. Neither woman was particularly sensitive or sentimental. The moment was somewhat awkward and out of character for both of them. Neither knew what to say next.

One of the older men tapped his glass on the brass bar counter interrupting the silence. Savannah rolled her eyes. The man rattled the empty glass again.

"God damn it, Charley. Can't you see were having a moment, here?"

Charley stared blankly at the two women.

"Just get up off your old ass and get it yourself," Savannah said as she took a stool next to her friend.

"Does this mean I don't have to pay?"

"No, cheapskate, you don't have to pay, but ya still better tip me dare just the same. And get Lou a beer too while you're up."

She turned to the couple who had one bar stool in between them and her. "How about you folks, you okay?"

The lady spoke first, "Oh, we're fine, thank you." Her husband gave her a dirty look for turning down a drink on the house.

"I could use another," he said, then quickly guzzled what was most likely half of a can of beer.

"And a Bud for this gentleman," Savannah said.

Charley filled Lou's glass and set it in front of him.

Lou raised his glass and nodded his head in appreciation.

Charley turned and reached for a beer, pulling out a Miller High Life. He reached into the next cooler and grabbed a Busch. He grumbled.

"Jesus be, Charley. How long you been coming in here? Last cooler."

Charley grumbled some more before finally finding the right cooler. He grabbed a Bud and set it down a little harder than was necessary in front of the out-of-towner. He didn't bother to open it.

"Two more down here, Charley," Savannah ordered, snapping her fingers.

Charley grabbed two Bud Lights and put them in front of Wendy and Savannah. "Anything else . . . ma'am?"

"No, that will do. You know with your good looks and winning personality, you would make one heck of a bartender," Savannah teased.

Silver haired Charley, with the bushy white eye brows, never changed his expression. He went back to his seat and waited for the next person to walk through the door.

"So, how did she die?" Wendy asked. A million different scenarios had raced through her mind since receiving the phone call from her father.

Savannah was about to answer Wendy's query, when Charley piped in, "T'was murder, eh?"

He looked to Lou for confirmation. Lou looked straight ahead and took a sip of his beer without acknowledging his barstool neighbor.

"Jesus, Charley! It was not," Savannah hollered.

"There was blood. Heard it straight from John Frederick's lips, eyup."

He looked to Lou again for confirmation. Lou took another sip of his beer and adjusted his worn out green baseball cap. It had the outline of the Upper Peninsula on it and the word *Yooperland*.

Wendy couldn't help but look somewhat panicked. The man from out-of-town, annoyed by all the clatter reached for the remote to turn up the volume. His wife slapped his hand before he could press the volume button up. They exchanged dirty looks.

Savannah turned back to Wendy. "Wendy, your mom had a heart attack. I also talked to John Frederick." She turned back to Charley and gave him a dirty look.

"Oh," Wendy said softly. She knew she should be happy that murder wasn't involved, but also knew that no manner of death would bring her any comfort.

"Explain the blood, Vannah." Charley chirped in one last time.

"Shut the fuck up, Charley," Lou grunted, before turning back to his beer and taking another sip.

Wendy had to smile at the silent man's first words of the day.

"That's why you're my favorite, Lou," Savannah said. "You don't say much, but when you do; it's pure poetry."

Charley gave a quick *hmmmf* and returned to his beer.

"I'm really sorry about your mom," the lady tourist said with as much sympathy as she could muster.

"Thank you."

"Poor dear," she added. She looked to her husband for some support, but got nothing as he was busy trying to make out the scores on the television.

Wendy was desperate to change the subject. She slapped her hand down on Savannah's. "Tell me about this lawyer guy of yours."

Savannah sighed and rolled her eyes. "I don't know, I just don't think he's my type."

"Not good looking? No charm?"

"No, he's good looking . . . and he can be charming." Savannah fanned her face.

From the tone, Wendy wasn't so sure that it was the hot summer day that initiated the fanning.

"So, let me get this straight. He's a lawyer who makes a ton of money, he's good looking and charming . . . and?"

"Then again, maybe he is my type," Savannah joked. "So, my mom is married again."

"Oh, yeah?" Wendy took a sip from her beer, knowing the topic had been changed on purpose.

"Yep, she found an old geezer who was as attracted to her fake boobs as she was to his money."

Wendy laughed but wondered if Savannah had become too jaded by her past to ever truly love a man again. If so, she could completely understand and relate. Wendy hadn't come to relive either of their hellish pasts, only to bury her mother and then go back to the lonely sanctuary of her current life. She was very careful to avoid any mention of the past. Instead she caught Savannah up on her latest comings and goings and her relationship with the handsome Ben Alderson. She talked of her apparently stalled career, of her guilt for having turned her back on her mother and ultimately knowing this was how it would end. Savannah nodded empathetically as Wendy talked about having wanted to come back so many times, or just call and tell her mother she loved her. As easy as that, she was talking about the past and forgetting her own pledge to avoid such conversation.

" . . . he ruined my life . . . and she let it happen," Wendy finished up.

"She could only do so much, she wasn't Superwoman."

"But, isn't that what a mother is supposed to be? Superwoman?"

Savannah had resumed her bartending duties, chopping fruit as she listened to her friend. "That's why I don't have kids. I'm no Superwoman." Savannah opened another can of beer and set it down in front of her.

"Bull shit! If you aren't Superwoman, I don't know who is."

Wendy pointed to a picture over top of the cash register. In the picture Savannah was in a softball pitching motion. Her purple and gold uniform had *Rockets* written across the chest. There was a look of intense grit and determination on her face. Her right arm was pointing toward the sky, yellow ball firmly gripped by her long fingers. Her left foot was kicked toward the batter. Although the batter was not in the picture; Wendy could still imagine the look of fear that they all seemed to have when they faced Savannah "Foudre" Sanders. Foudre is the French word for lightning, a nickname given to her by Steven Fonduluc, Maggie's father.

"That, my friend, was a long time ago." Savannah carefully turned the white dry towel back and forth in the beer glass before placing it on a rack with others. Her expression changed slowly and a cocked grin crept across her face. "State Champs, baby!"

"State Champs!" Wendy raised her glass in a toasting gesture. Savannah took the beer glass she was drying and filled it with a shot of tap beer, before meeting Wendy's glass.

Wendy finished her beer, glad she had caught up on old times with her friend. She knew, however, that it was time to face the inevitable. "I've got to scoot. Gotta face this now or never."

"You staying at the motel, then?" Savannah asked. "Cause you can stay with me if you like."

"I'd better stay there. Who knows how my dad is handling this."

"Well, let me know what I can do to help."

"Oh, I will." Wendy smiled, then placed a five dollar bill on the bar and left.

CHAPTER FOUR

Wendy rolled into the little motel on the western side of Michigan's Upper Peninsula a few minutes after leaving the Robin's Inn. What once was considered a nice, clean and cozy little hole in the wall motel; was now just another rundown, dirty little place that existed on a cold, lonely stretch of US Highway 2. A rusted out truck sat in the driveway. She knew it belonged to her father. He had owned one beat up truck after another ever since she could remember. Like all truck owners, he had his loyalties. Paul La Claire was a Ford man, through and through.

Next to the truck was his fourteen foot fishing boat. In some ways the place hadn't changed at all, but she picked up on the subtle differences right away. The glass on the sign that read *Four Seasons Motel* had a hole in it; probably thrown by some teenage boy from a passing car. Garbage was strewn all around the parking lot; fast food bags, empty plastic water bottles, cigarettes and the like.

Wendy sighed for what seemed like the thousandth time in the previous sixteen hours. She forced herself to take the first step, and then her body took over after that. She contemplated knocking, but somehow thought that would be ruder than barging in. Daughters don't knock on the door of their own home, even if they renounced its existence as a teenager. She got out a key that she had never thrown out. The key slid in with ease and the door opened. Part of her thought she might find him passed out on his bed, drudging up memories of a horrid childhood in a far away trailer park in Flint.

Wendy walked through the entryway that separated her bedroom from the rest of the main unit of the small motel. There were five units to the right of their dwelling and a bait shop to the left of her bedroom. She walked into her old room and realized that nothing had changed. Her bed was made, just waiting for her to climb in it as if she had never left. She had expected the bedroom to be turned into a storage area.

Wendy set her bag on her bed and gave her childhood home a quick tour. The place was stuffy and reeked of cigarette smoke. Worst of all, the place felt like a tinder box. Wendy examined the thermostat. *88 degrees!* She quickly found the air conditioner and hit the on button; it sputtered to life. Her parents had always smoked, so she was used to the aroma. There was another smell, however, that she couldn't quite make out.

She threw her hands on her hips when the déjà vu feeling became clear. It was the pungent smell of stale beer. She looked on the kitchen counter and her eyes confirmed what her nose had already told her—her father was drinking again. She wondered if this was only a onetime thing, brought on by the tragedy of her mom's death; or if he had been drinking for some time. Wendy grabbed a garbage bag from under the kitchen sink and began the arduous task of cleaning up the sty.

She despised cleaning her own apartment at home and hired a cleaning lady twice a week. She had spent her entire youth cleaning up after drunken hunters and fishermen and tried to avoid the task whenever possible. Being single and relatively neat, the cleaning lady thought she was taking the lady's money. Cleaning now came automatic. She changed the dirty water that contained dishes she could only imagine her mother had meant to finish. She completed her mother's job and then found the vacuum cleaner. She turned it on; but it did not move as her mind went back to the first time she'd vacuumed that very room.

* * *

January, 1992

"Paul, we need to talk, eh?"

The man at the door was a towering beast of a human. He stood six feet five inches, had dark brown hair and a scruffy beard to go with his piercing blue eyes. He was extremely handsome in an outdoorsy, Paul Bunyan kind of way.

"I know, eh, but there isn't anything I can do about that. We're staying." Paul began to shut the door in Steven's face; but his lumbering buddy put his big paw out and stopped the door.

"I don't want you to leave," he said. "But, Melissa, well that's different, ja know?"

Paul opened the door the rest of the way. Wendy spied on the two from behind a washing machine.

"Just give it some time, eh?"

Paul nodded.

Wendy wanted to know who the guy with the funny accent was. Her father could sometimes slip into his Yooper accent, but nothing like this guy. She stood up from behind the washing machine to get a better look. The man caught her little eyes from around the corner.

His smile beamed. "Hey, you!"

Paul turned around and caught his daughter darting around the corner and back to the living room.

"Get back and finish vacuuming like your mother told you! You are in enough trouble, little girl."

Wendy had been suspended for fighting on her very first day at her new school.

"She's cute, eh?" Steven smiled. "You want to see a picture of Andrew and Maggie?"

Paul didn't, but knew eventually he would see what practically amounted to his own nephew and niece in person. Paul smiled politely at the picture. He never actually looked at Andrew, instead focusing on Maggie and the scar above her lip. He sighed.

"Love those two little monkeys, ja know?"

Paul did know. Steven suggested they go down to the Library, the clever name for the bar that would later become the Robin's Inn. Paul informed him that he had given up drinking. He was now officially two weeks sober.

"Too bad, eh?" Steven chuckled.

Paul nodded again and then shut the door.

Wendy was in love. Like so many other girls of various ages, Steven Fonduluc would be the object of her first crush. She turned the vacuum cleaner on again. She didn't actually get much accomplished; she simply pushed it forward and pulled it backward in the same three foot pattern. She was too busy trying to figure out what her father and his friend were talking about.

*   *   *

Eighteen years later Wendy pushed and pulled a different vacuum cleaner in the same three foot pattern. Eighteen years later she still couldn't figure out what that conversation meant. Steven Fonduluc, Uncle Steven, had been right. It didn't take Melissa long to cave into a reuniting of their friendship with Paul and Marie La Claire. Wendy could never remember a time in Rapid Junction when the Fondulucs and La Claires weren't together. Unlike so many years ago, Wendy no longer thought Steven was a 'red hot fox'.

Realizing that she hadn't accomplished anything with her vacuuming, she turned it off. She didn't hear the door open.

"You still stink at the vacuuming, I see," Paul La Claire said.

Many years ago this statement probably would have come with laughs from both of them. They could only stare in awkwardness; neither knowing what to say or do next.

CHAPTER FIVE

Paul was the first to break the silence. "You hungry?"

"Starving."

They got in the rusted out Ford and drove down to Scotty's, the local diner. There was no hesitation when the waitress came to take their order.

"The perch, mashed potatoes and gravy," Paul ordered. "Water's fine."

"Ham and cheese omelet, wheat bread, extra butter . . . and home fries," Wendy fired to a young redhead that she didn't recognize. The waitress began to ask her what she wanted to drink, but Wendy beat her to the punch. "Water is fine also."

The waitress closed her mouth, smiled and retreated back to the kitchen.

"So, it was a heart attack?"

"Yes," Paul answered, looking down at the table and playing with the paper ring that held the silverware snuggly inside the napkin.

"I heard there was blood." Wendy pressed for the story of her mother's death and not just quick yes and no responses to her questions.

Paul lifted his head up and for the first time in over twelve years, looked his daughter in the eyes. He wasn't sure if he was prepared to give her every truth she wanted, but he could at least give her this one.

*   *   *

"You going to be back early?" Marie asked, with hands on hip.

"We'll see." Paul tried to make his escape without an argument, but could see from his wife's expression, that was going to be a difficult task.

"Damn it, Paul; I can't clean the rooms, take reservations and take care of customers in *your* bait shop. And when the hell are you going to fix something around here?" She held her hands out in exasperation.

Paul heard the water running in the bathroom. "You better get into your shower before the hot water is all gone."

Marie looked back toward the bathroom, began to say something but was stopped as Paul's lips met hers.

Paul turned quickly and headed toward the bait shop to get the desired lures and worms that were sure to net him a great catch that morning.

"You're not off the hook!"

"Hot water's going down the drain," he hollered back. He heard a loud groan and felt a mixture of guilt and humor. He silently pledged to fix the hot water heater when he got back from fishing.

A customer came into the bait shop before he could make his getaway. The man, dressed in a fishing jacket and a hat on his head that contained hooks and lures, was from down state and was making a trek to the great UP for some outdoor excitement. Paul would normally humor the 'wannabe's' and try to sell them some expensive fishing rod or fish finding device that they would never use again after that weekend, but instead was quick and curt with the man.

"So, what do you think about this rod?" the man said holding it out and pretending he was casting out.

The phone rang. Paul listened to it ring three times before it stopped. He also heard the sound of the shower. He looked down at his watch. *She's been in there for ten minutes. She must really be pissed.* "I'm sure what you have out in your boat will be just fine. So, just the worms?"

The man, realizing he was not going to get his banter with a local, put the rod back on the rack and reached into his wallet. The phone rang again.

"Marie! The phone!" Paul hollered, then looked at the man and gave him a quick look of apology as he took the fifty dollar bill from the man. He looked at the man and thought about pointing to the sign on the counter that read, *No fiftys or hundreds, please!* Fifties was misspelled. Instead, he reached into his wallet and made change. The phone stopped ringing; but the water did not stop running.

"Marie? Marie?" He sauntered to the other side of his home. After walking through Wendy's bedroom, the kitchen and the living room, he peered just inside the bathroom. Neither he nor Marie had bothered to close the bathroom door since Wendy left. He made out his wife's hand sloped over the side of the bathtub—the shower curtain covering her body.

He rushed into the bathroom and pushed the curtain and rod out of the way and dropped to his wife's side. Waves of guilt poured over Paul as he reached in and grabbed a hold of her limp body. He didn't scream, call out her name, or sob. He tried to lift her up, but knew that she was dead, and quickly let her body slide back into the tub. His upper half became drenched in the cold water that he knew should have been warm had he just done one thing he said he was going to do. He held his wife in that water for ten minutes wondering how he was going to live without her. He shivered uncontrollably and the initial shock of the situation slowly faded.

He got up, dried himself off, and called 911. Paul took his wife out of the tub and dressed her. No one was going to see his wife that way. He could at least do that for her. When the paramedic asked him where he found her, he started to lie. He looked over at the state police officer. The cop, he recognized as a former classmate of his daughter's, did not take his eyes off of his dead wife. He realized that lying was silly and dangerous.

Her body was laying in the living room in her favorite chair with her head hunched forward, her eyes closed and her heart stopped. He didn't want to admit that he had moved the body; he didn't want to be lectured for 'breaking the rules.' He decided that her wet hair gave away where he had found her; and how would he explain the cut on her forehead?

"The shower, she has a weak heart . . . I'm sure she probably had a heart attack."

The paramedic didn't question this at all. People did much stranger things to dead loved ones than dress them and put them in their favorite television watching spots. He looked over to the Statie for confirmation to continue on. The policeman nodded. He took off his navy blue police issued hat and placed it under his left arm.

He held out his right hand to Paul. "Mr. La Claire, I'm Trooper Anderson. I'm terribly sorry for your loss."

Paul looked up at the much larger police officer and blankly nodded his head in acknowledgement.

As her body was on the way to Marquette General Hospital, Paul went to tell the three motel guests that they were going to have to leave; *emergency in the family*. Then he went fishing and broke eighteen years of sobriety. At 1:09 in the morning he stumbled into the motel, picked up his wife's cell phone and found the number for Wendy. Savannah had always given Wendy's number to her mother. After years of getting only her voice mail and no call back, Marie had finally given up hope. It had been six years since she last tried to make contact. Paul waited three rings, almost hung up then heard his little girl's voice.

"Hello?" He couldn't bring himself to say anything. "Hello?"

"Your mother is dead," he finally got out. He sounded remarkably sober, given the amount of alcohol in his system. He hung up—then passed out.

*   *   *

Wendy had wanted at some point in her father's story to reach out her hand and take his hand in hers. But, like a nervous teenage boy on his first date, her hand had only made it a few inches across the table.

"I . . . well, I'm sure you know I drank," Paul confessed.

"Dad, seriously, you don't owe me an explanation."

She felt a bitter taste reside in her mouth and took a drink of her water. The water did nothing to dispel the bitterness she both tasted and felt.

"Well, I just want you to know, little girl, I don't plan on drinking again. Eighteen years of sobriety is way too long to throw away."

"I know, Dad," she said with little emotion and even less conviction. She sat back and crossed her arms, wishing she had some food to quell the uneasiness in her stomach. The waitress, as if on cue, set their meals down in front of them.

They ate in relative silence; neither were big meal time conversationalists, although Wendy had learned the art of doing both thanks to a decade of dating.

With his mouth full of mashed potatoes, he finally broke the silence. "I saw that Who-Tube video of you." He meant to say YouTube. He laughed and then choked on his food at the thought of it. Wendy turned beat red as her father threw his arms back in the air as if he were falling backward.

"Shit!" She nearly spat out her eggs as she joined her father in laughter.

The infamous YouTube video, that had over 200,000 hits, followed her everywhere. She had been on assignment in Flint and was covering the Buick Open, a PGA golf tournament. Doing a fluff piece during a rain delay, she interviewed a member of the grounds crew near a small pond on the 13th hole.

"You guys have been out here all morning trying to get the course ready. Do you feel defeated by Mother Nature?"

Before the man could answer, a giant gust of wind imploded Wendy's umbrella sending her flying backward. With one hand still on the umbrella handle and the other on her microphone, she swung both arms backward in the air trying to regain her balance. Being barely a hundred pounds, the wind won. Wendy fell backwards into the pond and splash landed in foot deep water. Sitting in the pond, and having lost neither broken umbrella nor mike, she answered for the man. "Never mind, Mother Nature is a bitch!"

The producer loved it and decided to air the piece along with a 'beep.' As with any good video, it quickly went viral and made her a minor celebrity for a while.

"Hey, you don't know how cold that water was!" she cried, incapable of holding back the tears. Everyone in the place turned and stared at the two. Neither noticed.

"Christ, girly, why didn't you just let go of the microphone and reach out for the guy?"

"I ask myself that every time I see that God damned video." The roar of laughter came back.

If she got anything from her father it was a good sense of humor. Both had no problem laughing at themselves. She wished she could return to being 12 again. Her father wished the same. The laughter slowly faded away as they resumed their eating.

"You remember that fat prick, John Frederick Anderson?" Paul asked as he pulled out of Scotty's.

"Yeah, good 'ol Ogre. Why you bringing him up?"

"Well, he aint so bad, I guess. He's a state cop, now."

"Yeah, that's what Savannah told me." Wendy wasn't sure why her father was bringing up a kid who used to torture her in elementary and middle school and later stalk her in high school.

"He picked me up today and drove me to Marquette General. I had to sign the death certificate and begin making funeral arrangements and the lot." Paul pulled the truck into the driveway and put the truck in park. He turned to his daughter and licked his lips. "Do you think you could help me pick out a casket?"

"Yeah, sure."

Wendy closed her car door and followed her father into the empty motel. She looked at the parking lot void of guest's cars and wondered if anyone would ever be able to call it that again. She knew that her mother had always taken care of everything. Her mother couldn't be expected to take care of matters relating to her own death. That would fall on Wendy.

"Okay, tomorrow we can go over to the funeral home in Escanaba. Her body will be there by the morning." He choked over the word body.

They walked into the living room and spent the rest of the evening reminiscing about the woman they both loved so much. Paul sat in a beat up recliner that had called their living room home for over twenty years. Wendy sat Indian style on the floor against an equally beat up couch with a leftover beer in her hand. She didn't know if she should feel guilt over it or not, but knew she needed it. She wondered all night long how this man in front of her was going to survive without his wife. How long would he go before opening the motel and bait shop back up again. How long *could* he go?

"Dad, I would like to pay for the casket and head stone."

"No," he quickly replied.

"Dad, I know you and Mom have always barely gotten by with this place. Please, let me do this. I have some money set aside. Shit, I'm a single chick with very inexpensive tastes." She chuckled. "Please, you have no idea how guilty I feel for being gone so long; for not being here when this happened."

"Okay," Paul responded, never taking his eyes off of the television, except briefly to gaze at the two empty beer cans that sat next to his daughter on the carpet.

Wendy put the beer can to her lips and realized it was empty. She set it down next to the other two cans on the floor and propped herself up. "Well, I'm going to bed."

Wendy didn't know if her father would get up to embrace her or not. She waited a few seconds, realized he was not moving from his chair and began her trek to her bedroom.

"Night." He grabbed the remote and turned the volume up on the TV. The weatherman's voice traveled all the way to Wendy's room.

CHAPTER SIX

Summer, 1995

"Steeeeeeeeeeven, ice cream!!!" Savannah shouted.

The other girls joined in. "Ice cream! Ice Cream! Ice Cream," they chanted.

Paul, sitting next to his friend in the front seat of the extended cab, looked at Steven and shrugged his shoulders. He knew where this was going and there simply was no way out of it.

"Settle down; there girlies!" Steven smiled to his friend.

Being an adult, he could contain his giddiness for having completed a perfect season in softball; but barely. Savannah had just pitched her seventh no-hitter of the season. Paul and Steven had coached the girls softball team for the past three years.

Melissa and Marie rode in the La Claire's truck; a 1990 mostly red Ford Ranger. The front panel on the passenger's side was blue. They never missed a game. For three years, following their daughters' softball teams during the summer became a way of life. Marie looked in the rearview mirror and saw the big black F-150 turn into the parking lot of Gladstone's very own Ice Cream Heaven. The place was in the shape of a huge ice cream cone. The ice cream, vanilla; was the roof of the place. The cone was the building itself.

"Nice of them to see if we wanted any," Marie said to her friend.

"I could use a little peace and quiet, however short it may last," Melissa replied. "I have to deal with these three chicks all night." She smiled at her friend. "Besides, I have our treat waiting for us."

"Is it twelve ounces, cold, and calling my name?"

"Yep."

"I love you, man!" Marie said, quoting the famous light beer advertising campaign of the time.

T. D. Croel

* * *

The fire raged from the pit. Embers snapped and crackled and cast a billowy glow across the three 13-year-old's faces. The moon hid behind the clouds and thirty foot tall White Pines that guarded the Fonduluc residence.

Savannah, Maggie and Wendy sat in folding chairs, wearing shorts and sweatshirts. Near the coast of Lake Michigan, like they were, it could still get pretty chilly at night, even on the hottest of days. Andrew came out from the darkness and entered the glow like an actor under a spotlight.

Wendy, who had her chair facing in that direction, was the first to notice him. Growing up, they had never taken any real interest in each other. Maggie, Andrew and Wendy would play together occasionally, but most of the time he left the girls to do his own thing. He was a quiet kid who kept mostly to himself. When he did talk to Wendy, he usually said something mean. Wendy could give back as good as he gave, however; usually better.

"What's up, Lerch?" This was her nickname for him, given his height. He was fourteen and six foot three inches tall. He also had bangs that were cut across the middle of his forehead. He somewhat resembled Lloyd Christmas, Jim Carrey's character from the movie *Dumb and Dumber*. He tried to get the part in the middle, which was the style of the day, but it always came back together no matter how much gel he put in there. Kids at school called him Lloyd or Christmas; but Wendy preferred Lerch; the butler from the Addams Family.

The other two girls immediately turned around. Maggie threw a marshmallow in his direction which he promptly caught in his mouth. "Hey, big bro, nice catch."

Andrew didn't swallow the marshmallow. He walked toward Wendy and spat it in her face. He smiled. Wendy tried not to smile back.

"Jerk, you're so gross."

"Nice shot," said Savannah.

Andrew was always Maggie's brother to both girls and neither showed him any physical interest. Savannah simply had not been interested in boys at all. Wendy became interested in boys in the seventh grade when Carl Beaudean dared her to kiss him at a boy-girl party. It started as a peck and ended with his tongue in her mouth. She started to resist, but decided she liked it. They made out in a closet for five minutes.

When Savannah finally opened the door, she couldn't believe her eyes. "You're a slut!" She yelled to her friend, hoping she would stop mauling the boy's face.

Wendy's lips didn't budge.

"I'm telling your dad!"

That line worked; Wendy stopped immediately.

Although neither girl had outright said it, they both now liked Andrew and were competing for his attention. He was well liked by both boys and girls at his school. Despite his goofy haircut, he was a very attractive kid. He had his father's full crimson lips and smile, but his mother's soft blue eyes and high cheek bones. His hair was light brown and turned blondish in the summer. He was still rail thin, but was developing a chest—slowly, but surely.

"Thanks," Andrew told the tall beauty. He walked over to where she was sitting and held out his hand for a high five. When she put her hand out, he purposely missed it and smacked her in the head instead.

"Asshole!"

Savannah jumped out of her chair and chased the cute fourteen-year-old who would soon be a high school freshman. He cackled and Maggie laughed along with him.

"Nice shot!" Wendy said sarcastically, mocking Savannah's last comment when she was the butt of his silliness.

Although hating sports, Andrew was fairly athletic. He darted to his left and Savannah was left grabbing at air. He ran to his right and she skidded right past him, slipping to the ground.

Savannah, not being a quitter, continued to chase after him. Andrew raced over to a position directly behind Maggie's chair. Savannah stared him down six feet away on the other side of her friend.

Maggie got up, "Don't put me in the middle of this!" She laughed as she ran out of the way.

Andrew threw the chair down and ran to his right. Wendy, still sitting, put out her foot out and caught Andrew's leg just as he ran by. He went straight to the ground. Only his hands kept him from going face first into the grass. He rolled over just as Wendy and Savannah pounced on him. Wendy licked her finger and put it in his ear.

"Agggghhhhhhh," he grimaced.

"That's what you get for the marshmallow!" Wendy yelled. She was loud, but definitely not menacing. They were young teenagers having a good time. Savannah pulled his shirt up and twisted his nipple.

"Purple nurple!"

"Owwwwwwww," he screamed as he laughed.

He rolled over and took the first person he could with him. It was Wendy. In the process he knocked Savannah over to her side and sat on top of Wendy.

He smiled down at her. His facial expression quickly changed as his eyes wandered from hers to her swelling chest. Wendy could feel the rhythmic beating of his heart and recognized the intensity in his eyes. She looked up at him longingly. In her mind, Savannah and Maggie did not exist. Internally she begged him to lean down and kiss her. *Am I crazy, or does he want me?*

The intensity of his gaze was too much. She turned and looked over to Savannah. Her arms were crossed and she wore a scowl. Wendy couldn't help but feel a deep sense of satisfaction. She turned back to Andrew.

A string of phlegm hung from Andrew's mouth inching its way toward her nose. Wendy screamed, and no matter how much lust she may have been feeling at that very moment, it was ruined by the thought of the yellowish line of saliva landing on her nose. She easily tossed Andrew off of her. She remembered when she was on the giving end of spit back in fifth grade. Andrew sat up and looked at Wendy as she stormed off.

"You really are an asshole!" Wendy screamed as she made her way to the house.

"I was just kidding. I wasn't really going to let it land on your face!" He hollered out to her. He wiped the phlegm from his face and smeared it on his shorts.

She ignored him and stormed the deck steps and up to the back door of the two-story Cape Cod home nestled in the woods.

Wendy wasn't mad because he was going to spit on her. She knew he would never do that. She was upset because maybe he really didn't look at her like she wanted him too. Maybe that look she thought she saw really didn't exist. *Damn it, I know what that look meant.*

Melissa sat at the kitchen table with her reading glasses on. She sipped on a beer as she read a trashy romance novel. Her head flew up instantly when the sliding door slammed shut.

"Whoa! Easy on the door!" She was instantly angry, but softened when she saw the look on Wendy's face. Wendy had her arms crossed. "What's the matter with you?"

"Nothing!" Wendy saw the sharp look in Melissa's eyes and softened the response. "Nothing."

Melissa took off her reading glasses. "Okay?"

"Your son is such a jerk!" Wendy sat down next to Melissa who laughed at the comment.

"Tell me something I don't already know!"

Wendy looked up at her 'Aunt' Melissa. "How do you get a boy to notice you?"

This threw Melissa for a loop, first her son was a jerk, now this girl was asking how she could get him to notice her. It also frightened her. No romance, no matter what age, could be good when friendship was involved, especially the one that existed between the Fondulucs and the La Claires.

"Okay, first off, you aren't talking about Andrew, are you?" Her steely glare held Wendy's eyes.

Wendy guffawed. "No!" She moved her eyes away from Melissa's and looked down to the black and white marble tile.

"Good. You're too young to be thinking about boys, anyway."

Melissa watched Wendy walk dejectedly up the stairs to Maggie's bedroom. She desperately wanted to go after her and give her a different answer; one more comfortable and palatable. Instead, she looked out the window at her son and daughter and sighed.

* * *

Wendy walked down the aisle of her first hour class. The smells, sights and sounds of the first day of school always made her a little uneasy. However, being in Rapid Junction for three years, she was long past the feeling of being the 'troll' from down state. She had been accepted as one of them. She plopped her books down on a seat next to some of the cooler eighth grade girls and joined them in summer gossip. Her jaw nearly hit the floor when a girl named Tamara dropped a tidbit of scandal that hit a little too close to home.

"Hey, did you guys hear? Savannah Sanders and Andrew Fonduluc made out this summer."

Tamara said it to the group, but was looking at Wendy the whole time. Wendy knew she wanted her to react, but didn't bite. She raised an eye that suggested she didn't buy it. Beneath the desk, her clenched hands suggested otherwise.

For the first time ever, Savannah and Wendy didn't share any classes together; but they did have a common lunch. Savannah, Maggie, Wendy and many of the other 'it' girls, as they referred to themselves, sat at their table. Wendy said nothing as the other teens chatted about everything that had happened during the summer.

Finally, Wendy turned to Savannah. "So, what did *you* do this summer?"

"*You* know everything I did this summer, we weren't apart at all." Savannah stabbed her plastic spork into her peaches and was about to take a bite when Wendy shot the next question at her.

"So, you didn't make out with anyone?"

Maggie looked nervous. "Guys, what's going on?"

Wendy pressed on. "You know, like maybe Andrew?"

Savannah shot a glare of death toward Tamara. Tamara crossed her arms and smiled. Before Savannah could turn back, the spork was flying out of her hand and peach juice splattered her in the face.

"You and Andrew?" Maggie asked, bewildered.

Wendy seethed. "How could you make out with your best friend's brother?"

"I know I could," Sarah Stephens joked, "if he looked like Andrew Fonduluc." She kissed her hand. "That boy is hot. H-O-T, sizzling!"

Everyone, except for Maggie, Wendy, and Savannah laughed.

"Did you really make out with Andrew?" Maggie asked.

Savannah didn't answer.

"You did, didn't you . . . . bitch!" Wendy screamed.

The assistant principal, a woman in her late 40's who was on lunch duty, walked toward the fracas. Before she could get there, Wendy reached into Savannah's peaches and threw a handful at her. Savannah gasped. A few chunks of peaches landed in her hair and peach juice dripped down her nose.

Savannah bellowed back. "I'm so sick of you! You're nothing but a jealous little slut, anyway!"

Before the AP, Mrs. Huttle, could reach the table; Savannah lunged over the table and tackled Wendy. Her weight was enough to knock Wendy off of the little round plastic stool attached to the large table. Savannah landed on top and began wailing away. She landed three good shots to Wendy's head before Wendy was able to turn Savannah on her back. Wendy grabbed as much hair as she could and pulled. When Mrs. Huttle finally managed to pull Wendy off of Savannah, she had a handful of blonde hair to go with her own bloody nose.

Unlike their first fight, they did not end things by comparing battle wounds outside of the principal's office. The middle school and high school were in the same building and shared the same principal. Mrs. Huttle walked into Mr. Spivey's office and filled him in on what was going on.

Wendy sat stewing in her seat, believing that the physical fight was over. *Oh, it will be a long time before I talk to this bitch again!* Before she had a chance to finish the thought, Savannah had a handful of her hair. Wendy tried to fight off Savannah without much success.

"Girls!" Mrs. Cantro, the office secretary, yelled in dismay.

She was stuck behind the counter, but two football players on Savannah's father's team were not. The two looked at each other for a quick second and then took action. Tony, who was an all-conference linebacker, grabbed Savannah. He carefully removed her hand from Wendy's hair before the poor girl became bald. The other, Johnny, took hold of Wendy. He picked her up under her arms and accidentally held her under her breasts. He held on to her in this position a little longer than Wendy thought was necessary. Both girls tried to lunge after the other; arms and legs flew everywhere.

"Ladies," Mr. Spivey, a serious looking man in his late 50's, said in an amazingly calm voice.

The girls stopped fighting and the boys let them drop. Wendy fell to the ground, she had to push her t-shirt back down as she picked herself up and stood to face the principal. Neither boy tried to contain their laughter.

"Back to class, men," Mr. Spivey said without taking his eyes off the combatants.

"You're dad is going to be ticked!" Tony laughed as he walked out.

Wendy looked through the glass and saw Johnny holding out his hands above his chest as he explained to his friend how he managed to cop a feel on the feisty girl.

"You," Mr. Spivey pointed to Wendy, "sit."

Wendy's attention was firmly on the intimidating man who was only a few inches taller than she was.

"You . . . my office."

Savannah followed him in, but managed to give Wendy one last dirty look as she entered the principal's office. Wendy thrust out her middle finger. She quickly reeled it back in when she saw the secretary looking at her.

"I saw that," Mrs. Cantro said softly, but with a smile that suggested to Wendy that she had no intention of telling Mr. Spivey.

CHAPTER SEVEN

"Hey, sorry I haven't called you sooner," Wendy said, apologizing to Ben. Wendy had promised to call as soon as she got in.

"No problem, you hanging in there?" Ben asked.

Wendy looked at the ancient clock radio that had been sitting on her parent's kitchen counter for as long as she could remember. The three black plastic pieces with white numbers clicked and flipped at the same time; it was 8:00 a.m. She knew Ben only had a few rules in his life; one of them was never to get up before nine unless it was absolutely necessary. She figured answering a call from a grieving girlfriend counted as just such an occasion.

Wendy didn't bother to contemplate the future of their relationship, but she did know that she didn't want it to end any time soon. She hoped he had the same notions. In most ways he seemed to be an older, male version of her. Like Wendy, he had started off as an eager young reporter lobbying and preparing himself for the position of an anchor. Now 40, he had been in that seat for five years. He often reminded Wendy of just how long success can take whenever she sounded impatient with the prospects of her career. He also joked that he would be sleeping with one eye open, knowing her 'eagerness' for advancement.

"Yeah, but it just feels so strange. It's been so, *sooooooo* long; yet I feel like I left yesterday."

"You realize that you have never really talked about your childhood?" He asked rhetorically. "I just realized that. You know everything about me, you've met my dad, I gave you the grand tour of Hazlewood, Missouri . . . and yet, I know next to nothing about you."

She toyed with him. "You want my life story, now?"

Wendy never told anyone anything other than the basic facts of her past. *I grew up in a small town in the UP, my parents run a little motel and bait shop; had to get out of there and see the world.* She had escaped her past, and did not need to go back to it in any sense of the meaning.

"No, I can wait, but I really do want to know about things, you know."

"I know and I appreciate it. I just don't have the greatest memories of this place." Wendy changed the subject back to why she was there. "We're going to pick out a headstone and casket today. Her funeral will be on Friday."

She knew it came out as, *you will be at the funeral, right?* Both of them had always struggled with adult parts of life. Neither had been in a truly committed relationship in their lives, even when they had shared the same domicile with another person. Ben had never asked a woman to marry him, and Wendy had never been asked.

Wendy heard her father turn the shower off and decided that she didn't want to share this part of her life with her father quite yet.

"Well, I've got to go. I love you." The words slipped out so easily that she didn't have any time to edit herself. She cringed; *where in the hell did that come from!* Awkwardness filled the radio waves of their suddenly dead conversation.

Wendy had really only told one man in her life that she loved him and that was when she was sixteen. However, she had told almost everyone she knew that she loved them when she was drunk; including Ben. After six shots of tequila the night of the station's 50th anniversary party, it came out, "I luff you . . . now give me that cock-a-yers!"

"I love you too, kid," he finally got out.

More silence. Wendy cringed again. She wished that he would have just skipped over the response and said goodbye.

"I'm sorry. I don't know where that came from."

"Don't be, it was nice to hear," he replied back.

Wendy tried not to hear his words as condescending, but it was impossible. *Then why did you add, kid at the end, asshole?* "Okay," she said pleasantly, erasing all ill feelings that crept within her. He was too good of a guy to get caught up in what he might have meant behind those words. If she ever really wanted to know, she would ask him straight up. "I'll talk to you soon."

"Okay, if you need anything give me a call."

"I will," she responded, then hung up.

Her father walked into the kitchen; the hair left on his balding head askew. He had a little shaving cream just beneath his left ear and his shirt was only halfway tucked in. He was a sloppy little man. *This man is a tin cup away from being a bum on the street.*

"Your boyfriend?" He raised an eyebrow and gave her the fatherly look she was so familiar with.

"Something like that," she responded as she took a paper towel and dabbed the remaining shaving cream from his face; the first physical contact she had had with him since their reunion.

"It's not like you need my permission, you know." He smiled as he said it.

"Finally!"

They spent some time looking through Marie's closet for the right dress. They decided on a black one with white buttons down the front. It was simple, but just elegant enough. They both knew this was the type of dress she would have demanded to be buried in. She was not a showy woman and never had a need for material possessions. Paul pulled out a pearl necklace that had belonged to Marie's mother and was passed down to her when she passed.

"The guy said to bring underwear and stockings, these?"

He held out a pair of underwear. A huge pair, the kind a woman wears when she is on her period and has no reason to exude any amount of sexiness.

"Think about it, Dad. Eventually you will die and have to spend an eternity with this woman. Do you really want her bitching at you the whole time for making her wear these bloomers? I'll pick out her underwear." She took them from him and put them back in the top drawer.

"Good."

Wendy looked through the drawer and finally settled on a plain pair of cotton briefs. They were white and had a small little flower on the front; simple, yet just enough elegance to satisfy Marie La Claire. When she picked up the cotton panties, she saw a familiar item lying beneath them—a faded grey jewelry box.

*   *   *

December, 1991

The Christmas before Wendy and her parents moved to the UP was among the worst times of Wendy's life. Her parents were fighting all the time. Her father drank away what little money they had, their electricity had been turned off and they were relying on a space heater that was plugged into an extension cord that ran from a generous neighbor's power.

Although Wendy didn't know it, her mother had written her Uncle Mike asking for money for a lawyer. Despite these more serious issues, Wendy's biggest problem was buying something for her mom for Christmas. Her mother meant everything to her. She decided that her father was not worthy of a gift and therefore was not worthy of worrying about.

At her school they had what was called Santa's Workshop. As a fundraiser for the school, they sold cheap gifts that their students could purchase and give to their siblings and parents. The kids loved this and the parents didn't mind either. Most of them loved getting the 'shitty' little dollar store gifts because of the joy they saw in their child's eyes when they opened up their useless presents. Dads opened up cheap plastic screwdriver sets and told their child just how much they really needed the gift. Later they would put them in their tool box right next to the fifty other cheap screwdrivers. Mothers opened up their pathetically wrapped gifts to find a whisk or some embroidered knickknack. They smiled and told their child how thoughtful they were. This was a time honored tradition that Wendy looked forward to every year.

That year, however, she did not ask her parents for fifty dollars and then settle for ten. That year Wendy decided that she would not burden her mother with the begging, she knew what the response would be already. "Honey, there's just no money." She had heard it a thousand times. *Mom, can I get this candy bar? Mom, can I buy this book from the book fair? Mom, can we get McDonalds?* The answer had been the same for over a year.

As Mr. Coswell's class took their turn shopping at Santa's Workshop, Wendy eyed what she was going to take. She didn't consider it stealing, because she really needed it and would gladly give the money *if* she had it. Santa would surely understand this logic. However, she was smart enough to realize that the angry, little PTA mother running the shop on behalf of Santa, wouldn't see things the same way.

She heard, "Alright, Mr. Coswell's class; time is up, you need to bring up any items you have to me."

Nervous and lacking valuable time, Wendy did not give her 'gift selection' any thought. She quickly reached down and grabbed a little grey box from the jewelry selection. She had no idea what was inside. She balled her little hand around the felt box and walked toward the rest of the class. Wendy was the only one not to bring any money.

She walked past the line of kids eagerly waiting to pull out their cash and pay for their precious gifts that would earn them so much praise, to join the others who had already made their purchases.

"Miss La Claire, the line is over here," Mrs. Stanley, the PTA Gestapo mom bellowed.

Wendy froze in her tracks before turning around. "I'm not getting anything."

Mrs. Stanley discontinued her cashier responsibilities and walked toward Wendy. Wendy licked her lips and prayed to God. *God, make this box disappear.* When the ugly, sweaty Mrs. Stanley grabbed Wendy's hand and pulled back her fingers the box was still there. God had failed her.

"You are nothing but a little thief!" she screamed. All of the other children, including the class that had just walked in, gawked at Wendy, like pedestrians at the scene of a terrible car accident.

"Relax, Mrs. Stanley," the young fifth-grade teacher said, smiling as he tried to reduce the tension.

"If you would keep a better eye on your class, we might not be having this problem." The two stared at each other for what seemed like an eternity to Wendy.

Mr. Coswell lost the stare down. He turned and looked down at the brown haired little girl with the spunky attitude. "Wendy, you know I have to send you to the principal's office."

Wendy sighed, "I know."

Wendy's feet swung back and forth above the elementary school office floor; not coming close to touching the cold tile below. Her feet came to a sudden halt when she saw the office door slowly open. She looked up and saw the look of disappointment on her mom's face. She squeezed her eyes shut and prayed, *please, God, make me disappear.*

She opened her eyes and saw her feet dangling, but no longer moving. God had failed her again. Her mother shook her head, then turned to the secretary who instructed her to come back to speak to the principal. Five minutes later her mother came out of the office. She snapped her purse shut and yanked Wendy up by the arm. "Let's go!"

Her mother didn't say a word to her all the way home; which Wendy felt was more tortuous than if she had pulled her pants down and given her a spanking right there in the school office.

That night Wendy lay in bed and heard her mother tell her father what had happened. Her father, who had been at the bar at 1:30 p.m. on a Tuesday when his daughter had been busted, could not have been reached at home even if he had been there. The phone had been shut off six weeks earlier. Marie assured Paul that she had taken care of matters with Wendy and that it was never going to happen again. She made Paul promise her that he would not dole out anymore punishment.

Paul broke his promise. The next day when his wife was at work, he took out a belt and whipped Wendy's hind end with it. Three quick lashes and Wendy's little butt was swollen and red. She refused to cry, which made her drunken father even angrier. She could see her father's face turn crimson and perspiration form on his forehead, despite the cold temperatures. She ran to her bedroom, before her father could change his mind and go for a forth swat. She jumped on her bed and began kicking the walls as hard as she could.

Paul stumbled down the hall. He had spent another day cursing God and trying to drink his life away at a dive bar down the street from the trailer park. He threw open her door in a rage.

Wendy immediately stopped kicking. She sat up and looked her father in the eyes again. "I hate you."

Paul froze in his tracks. "Join the club. Tell your mother I spanked you and it will be twice as bad next time."

Wendy closed her eyes and prayed for her father to disappear. She opened her eyes. *Finally, God!* Paul walked to his bedroom and passed out.

That Christmas Eve Wendy had no trouble falling asleep. There simply wasn't much to be excited about. Her mother read her *Twas the Night Before Christmas*, a family tradition. Her father sat in his underwear and drank beer in the living room.

Wendy didn't get up at 5:30 in the morning to wake her parents up like so many other kids did. Instead, at a little after nine on Christmas day, her mother woke her up. Her father, hung over, was also forced up. He sat in his recliner and tried to get his senses back by drinking some coffee. He didn't say one word during the opening of presents. His wife handed him a present. "This is from Wendy."

Wendy, who was opening one of her three presents, a cheap Barbie lookalike; looked up quickly. *I didn't buy him anything!* Her father obligingly opened up the present, a cheap coffee mug that said 'World's Greatest Dad.'

World's Greatest Drunk! Wendy figured her mother must have purchased it at the drug store her mother worked at. One of the few perks was a twenty-five percent discount.

"Isn't that nice," Marie said, smiling at Wendy first and then looking at Paul.

"Thanks, sweetie; it's real nice." In one hand he had a generic coffee mug; in the other he held a mug with the biggest lie in the world on it. He set the 'lie' down and took a drink of coffee from the other mug.

Wendy opened up her other two gifts. One was a packet of coloring books. They were very generic, but she appreciated the gesture. The third and final gift was her favorite, and she knew it had cost her mom more money than she had—more than Wendy felt she was worth. She felt guilty for every bad thought she had ever had toward her mother; and maybe even her father if in fact he had anything to do with the gift. She stared down at Felicity Merriman, a doll in the 1991 American Girl collection.

Wendy had seen the doll advertised in a magazine that she was reading in the dentist's office in October. She immediately fell in love with the doll. She looked up at her mom, who was reading her own magazine and dreaming of her own things she couldn't afford.

"Mom, can you . . ." She stopped; she knew what the answer would be. *Honey, you know we can't afford . . .*

Wendy couldn't handle this kind of no. The doll was special, too special. Hearing no would be too painful. It wasn't like being told no to a candy bar, or even some stupid book she wouldn't even finish reading. She decided she had been forced to face enough disappointment in her life. She made up her mind that she would forget about Felicity. While she was sitting in the dentist chair agonizing over a cavity being filled; her mother picked up the magazine that her daughter had been looking at. She looked around, then tore out the ordering form and stuffed it in her purse.

Wendy jumped up and ran to her mom. Marie was on her knees admiring her handy work. For Marie, she could gain no better satisfaction as a parent then buying a gift for her child that brought out true and complete joy. There couldn't possibly be a material gift that Christmas that could have given Marie more pleasure.

Wendy nearly knocked her mother over, but Marie managed to get a hand out behind her just in time not to topple over from the force of her daughter's collision. Wendy said nothing, just squeezed her mother's neck.

"You're welcome!" Marie laughed; then kissed her little girl.

Wendy would keep that doll forever, and even though she would end up with nearly every doll in the series, no other doll could compete with Felicity.

"Don't forget about your father, he helped buy it, too."

Wendy slowly recoiled from her embrace and looked toward her father, who was only six feet away. She thought she saw softness in her father's eyes that she had not seen in forever. She leaned in and hugged her father as hard as she had her mother. She sobbed, and blubbered "Thank you, Daddy."

Wendy felt the strength of her father's arms around her, something she desperately missed. It was short lived, however. He pried her from the embrace and softly pushed her away.

"You're welcome." He returned his attention to his new scope.

Wendy didn't notice the tears welling up in his eyes.

She turned to her mother for comfort and reassurance. Her mother had her eyes locked on her husband. She shook her head in amazement.

Marie refocused her attention to her daughter, brought the smile back to her face, and reached under the tree for one last gift. She pulled it out and read the card, "To Mommy, from Wendy."

Wendy, who had gone back to her spot on the floor, looked up from her doll; her mouth agape, her eyes bulged.

Marie smiled slyly at Wendy. "What do we have, here?"

She pulled the wrapping paper away from the little gift. Wendy gasped when she saw the familiar grey felt jewelry box.

Marie opened the box and gasped herself. "Oh, Wendy! They're beautiful!"

She pulled out two dolphin earrings.

Wendy scooted over to her mother on her knees and looked down at the earrings. They were beautiful. Wendy had no idea how the earrings ended up under her tree, but said a private thank you to Santa, just in case it was his handiwork.

Marie grabbed a hold of Wendy and held her. She whispered in her ear, "Thank you so much, honey. These will always be my favorite earrings."

Wendy closed her eyes, *thank you, God.*

*   *   *

Wendy opened her eyes; she looked down and saw the earrings that she had not thought about in so long. They were not real gold, of course; and like so many people, Marie had allergic reactions when she wore them. She only donned them a handful of times, but each time brought about a greenish-grey tint to her ears and an agonizing, itching sensation that ultimately led to scabbing. The last time was so bad that she had to visit the doctor to get a prescription. She never wore them after that, but never dared to throw them away, either.

Wendy turned to her father. "Daddy."

Her father turned around surprised. Wendy rarely called him Daddy, even when she was very young. He was always, Dad.

"Do you mind if Mom wears these?"

She opened her hand, revealing the dolphin earrings that were now silver color; the gold painting having chipped away long ago.

"Of course not."

Wendy moved toward her father and reached out to him. Unlike eighteen years earlier when she had reached out to him, he finally knew how to reach back. They embraced and both broke down in tears. Wendy finally gave into twelve years of spite and justification for her absence. She knew the time had come to begin the process of forgiveness; even if it meant never getting her answers.

Paul was unaware of the symbolic meaning behind the earrings, but he did know that his dead wife treasured them. "But, if she bitches about how itchy her ears get wearing these damn things . . . I'm blaming you."

Wendy pulled away from her father and struggled to control the conflicting combination of crying/laughter that was coming from her. Her father joined her in laughing. "I love you, Dad."

"I love you." The words were soft and barely audible. He pulled out a handkerchief from his back pocket and wiped his eyes, before leaving the room.

*   *   *

They pulled up into the parking lot of Henderson's Funeral Home, once again in Paul's beat-up truck. Death is a full time business, but even in a small town like Rapid Junction, there simply is not enough death to turn a profit. Escanaba, to the south along Lake Michigan, was a much bigger town, and therefore worthy of not one, but two funeral homes.

Paul and Wendy sat stone faced across from the funeral director and his assistant. They listened as the man went through the litany of papers to sign, procedures to follow and next steps.

Wendy hadn't heard a word, she finally interrupted. "Can I see her?"

"She's not ready for viewing, Miss La Claire." Mr. Henderson responded calmly with his hands folded.

"Please, I haven't seen her in over twelve years. I can handle it."

The funeral director exchanged a look with his assistant, Miss Adams. It was the assistant who turned to Wendy. "Of course, just give me a minute to get her presentable."

Wendy could never have been more ill prepared for anything in her life. Seeing someone as important as her very own mother in a lifeless state for the first time was as unreal and out of this world as it got. Paul stood behind Wendy and stared at his shoes. Wendy looked at her mother and became transfixed on the bruising above her temple. Her immediate inclination was to vomit. Her father had told her of the blood, but she still was not prepared to see the actual wound. Covered in a sheet, Wendy was spared from seeing her mother's ribs laced together by stitches. Wendy wanted so bad to cry, but was incapable; her emotional tap had been drained earlier.

Wendy turned to the assistant. "Will these make her ears turn green?"

She held out the fake, once gold colored, dolphin earrings. The assistant did not laugh.

"No, not at all. They must have been very special to her." The woman was a true professional.

They returned to Mr. Henderson's office where her father resumed signing every form that had ever been created. It took more signatures to 'officially' end a person's life than it did to bring them into the world. The funeral director took the dress, stockings and elegant, yet simple underwear from Paul.

"Sir, her lower half won't be seen; but it is customary for the deceased to wear shoes. Would you like to bring a pair back, or have us supply them?"

"Oh, shit, how much?"

"Dad, we can bring back a pair."

"Actually, I think she would appreciate a new pair of shoes. She's been wearing the same two pair of shoes for a long damn time."

The female assistant came back with a pair of new black flats. "These are probably a size too big, but I think they would match the dress well."

Paul and Wendy looked at each other and nodded. She would like the shoes. Wendy knew that they would both be shopping for shoes forever trying to find just the right pair, only to come to the conclusion that the ones offered to them at the funeral home were exactly what she would have wanted.

Wendy made sure that Miss Adams, the assistant, was taking care of the visitation and funeral service aspects with her father while she took care of finances with the funeral director. She didn't want her father to see her expression when her jaw dropped after hearing the cost of the burial service. She had been a pretty good saver in her time; but even she had no idea how much a death could cost.

When Mr. Henderson said, "Eight thousand five hundred and sixty-two dollars for everything," Wendy didn't bat a lash. She simply got out her credit card and handed it to the man. Inside, she thought to herself, *fuck.* Most of her savings were gone, but a certain piece of mind temporarily replaced any thoughts of financial woe.

Their time at the funeral home lasted a little over two and a half hours; but to both it seemed like an eternity and wiped them out.

Paul walked toward his room and said, "I need a nap." Wendy, who had been up since 5:30, did too. The business of death was exhausting.

Paul, never one to pray, kneeled beside his bed and clasped his hands together. "God, please give me the strength to tell Wendy the truth."

Wendy stood outside her parent's bedroom with her hand ready to knock. She closed her eyes and moved her hand down to her side. She whispered her own prayer. "God, please give me the strength to accept the truth."

CHAPTER EIGHT

Halfway around the world an expatriate finished up his normal morning routine; two cups of coffee, check the e-mails and since it was Wednesday, go to the online version of his hometown newspaper. He skimmed through a few stories; one about a fire that burned over 2,000 acres in the Hiawatha National Forest, another about a woman who was found guilty of embezzling from the local Boy Scout organization. He continued to scroll through *The Daily Press*, but didn't find much of interest until he got to the obituaries.

Fifteen minutes later he came back to his computer. He left the URL page of his hometown rag and switched to a discount travel site. After reaching the confirmation page he paused. He turned and looked at the blonde woman with the fair complexion. She sat on the edge of the bed and raised her eyebrows. *I'm not changing my mind . . . and I know you won't either.* He loved the woman, but not with the passion or the completeness that was needed to sustain it. She had always known that he was a wild flower that should not have been picked; so she let him go. The tall, lean man with long sandy blonde hair, pulled back in a pony tail stroked his beard once then struck the key confirming his one way ticket back to the United States.

CHAPTER NINE

1980-1981

"I'm leaving you, Steven." Melissa sobbed into her hands. She had said it a thousand times before and he never believed her because she never left. She looked up at Steven, her eyes were blood shot and her hair disheveled. "And I will get as much child support as I can get. You better believe that, ass hole!"

"Of course, I'm going to marry ju . . . Don't ju worry bouta ting." His blend of French-Canadian and Yooper accent could make him as endearing as it could annoying.

She didn't believe him, but she smiled and kissed his forehead and told him how much she loved him—and she did. However, love and reality were two different things. One half of Melissa's mind would never allow herself to believe in a 'happily ever after' with Steven Fonduluc. She knew for the teenage girl who had managed to snag him, he was the ultimate catch. But, for a woman in her late twenties? No. Steven Fonduluc was the kind of guy who would break your heart in a new and inventive way each and every day. Melissa was a realist; a stone cold realist; she knew she would be pursuing the man's heart like Ahab pursued his white whale and most likely the whale would win again. She just wondered whose casket she would be floating on when it was all said and done.

*　*　*

"He's so beautiful!" Marie exclaimed. It was a cold January day in the Upper Peninsula. Marie and Paul had driven to the hospital to visit Melissa who had just delivered Steven Andrew Fonduluc Jr. Steven Sr. was nowhere in sight. Melissa allowed him to be named after his father, but had no intention of ever calling him by Steven, Steve, Stevie . . . or Junior. He would be called Andrew.

At that moment Steven, not a huge drinker, but one who knew how to mix it up as good as the next Yooper, sat in a bar next to his girlfriend of the month. She was a pimply-faced teen who filled out a sweater nicely. He had absolutely no feelings for her. She laughed at his jokes, worshiped his existence and bragged to her friends about his penis. She was simple and she was stupid; she was worth forgetting about—worth hurting without feeling bad. However she was not his pregnant girlfriend; and that made her worthwhile.

He sat in the bar listening to her go on and on about absolutely nothing and he realized, that no matter how angry that 'woman' could get, how 'pushy' she could be, how 'God damned' right she always seemed to be, he loved her. He had had more beautiful women, more adventurous women . . . but no one made him want to escape his immature existence like Melissa.

She sucks, she really sucks. He told Paul this all the time; every time Marie had talked him into 'getting Steven back.'

Paul was not Plato, but he put it in words Steven could understand, *no one else is going to put up with your shit . . . . at least not anyone who you actually respect.* And Steven knew this to be true.

Paul wanted kids, there was no denying it. However, it was more because that's what you did. He and Marie had been married for eight years and had tried to have kids as hard as Steven had tried to avoid them. Melissa lay back in her hospital bed with the newborn wrapped tightly in a pink blanket and seemed to glow in a way that neither Paul nor Marie had ever seen. She actually appeared happy. Paul sat in the hospital room chair with his legs stretched out and looked at his wife fuss over what he considered to be a small version of complete 'monstrosity;' the kid was hideous. He had a cone head, a prunish face and the most bizarre discoloring. Paul saw nothing beautiful about the child. However, it was a child, and even Paul knew that the child would not always be ugly; probably not even by the next day. He knew that the child represented all that was good about life; hope, dreams, and possibilities that had drifted away for a previous generation. He was envious of his absent friend, and suddenly furious.

"I'll be right back."

Paul drove down to where he knew his friend would be; the Library. He decided that he would play hardball with his friend, not little boy games. He strutted right up to the little tramp sitting in the seat next to Steven.

"Hi, you gotta a minute?" he asked the girl.

She flung herself around in her barstool. She looked him up and down with a sneer that suggested that gaining her attention better be worth her while.

"Yeah?"

Paul seethed. "His woman just had a baby, you know that?"

The nineteen year-old with the rotting attitude began to soften. She knew that Steven, the muscular lumberjack with the funny laugh, had a woman. She also knew that she was pregnant, but somehow, until just that moment, she never seemed to care. Now she did; now she could think of nothing but her future. She saw one in which she walked up to Steven and dropped that same bombshell on him.

"*Steven, I'm pregnant.*"

"*So.*"

That was an answer she couldn't accept. She was young, immature and even uncaring; but to be pregnant, hell to be having a baby and your man is in a bar with some other woman—nope. She didn't have many scruples, but she did have those ones.

"What the fuck, Steven?" She got up and walked out.

"Thanks, asshole." Steven stumbled out of the bar and straight to Paul's truck.

*   *   *

Some days Steven would act excited about being a dad. He would pick up his baby boy and plant a hundred kisses all over his face. But most days he would sulk; babies demanded more attention than he ever dreamed. Since he had made it crystal clear that he would change no diapers, heat no bottles, nor get up in the middle of the night with the child; Melissa's attention was more often than not on little Andrew.

Paul became more and more disgusted with Steven's attitude about being a father. At first what he thought was just a normal desire to be a father started to be overtaken by a 'need' to be a father.

"Shit, cry . . . . eat, cry . . . . shit, cry . . . . shit, shit, shit. I swear da kid's a little shit monster, eh?" Steven turned off his power chain saw and looked over at his diminutive friend. The two stood in the midst of a thousand white pines. They were in a sea of green.

Paul pulled his safety glasses up over his head and slowly walked over to Steven. Steven knew the look and had to take a step back. He couldn't move fast enough as Paul cold cocked him. Paul leaned over and jabbed a finger at Steven's nose.

"Shut the fuck up, I'm so sick of your shit. Do you know what I would give to be a dad? Do you?"

Steven picked himself up. He had never thought that Paul might actually want to have kids. He never talked about it, thought it was kind of strange that Marie hadn't gotten pregnant, but just figured his friend was lucky enough to dodge so many bullets. He never realized that his burden could actually be another man's treasure.

"Sorry, Paul. Jeez, Louise I never knew you wanted kids so bad."

Paul picked up his chainsaw and started it up, ignoring his friend. He suddenly stopped, turned around and pulled the kill switch on the seven horsepower beast. "We're moving downstate. Marie's uncle has a construction business and I can make a whole hell of a lot more money down there and not have to put up with your ass anymore."

Steven rubbed his jaw and tried to take in the information. "You two would really leave and break up the Fantastic Four?"

"Jesus fuck, Steven!" Paul put his right hand on his hip and shook his head in disbelief. "We're almost thirty years old. I can't be babysitting you anymore. I don't have the energy to keep you out of trouble, to drag you away from one whore after another and back to your girlfriend and child. Don't you think it's time you grew up?"

Steven contemplated the question. He knew he would never be able to survive without Paul or the group. "Do you think he would hire me, too?"

Paul rolled his eyes and dropped the chainsaw, then walked away. Steven quickly turned his attention to a squirrel that sat perched on a fallen tree. The furry creature wiggled his nose and looked quizzically at Steven.

The logger smiled, then took a pistol out of a holster beneath his coat and fired it at the poor rodent; sending it tumbling backward over the frost covered fescue grass. Steven curled his bottom lip under his teeth and felt an immediate sense of calm. He turned to see if his 'babysitter' was coming back.

CHAPTER TEN

Thanks to her husband's new job downstate, Marie had health insurance for the first time as an adult. She decided to find out why she hadn't gotten pregnant.

Marie shook her head in violent denial. "Chlamydia? That can't be. I've only slept with one man, my . . ."

She snapped her mouth shut. Tortured memories swamped her brain as the doctor rambled on about her condition.

"Your chances of getting pregnant are pretty slim. The damage to your fallopian tubes is just too great."

She looked into the doctor's eyes and saw a monster from her past. She shook with rage. Sixteen years of repressed memories flooded back like the waves of a tsunami.

The doctor mistook her condition as that of a woman who was only just learning that she was incapable of reproduction, not refreshing memories of a previous rape. He tried to console her, placing a hand upon her shoulder.

"Don't touch me!"

His hand recoiled as if her words were 10,000 volts of electricity.

Paul brought up the subject of children in one subtle way after another. Marie knew that the subject had to be broached before she went crazy with guilt

"So, if we were to have a little girl, what would you want to call her?"

Paul put his head on his hand and leaned on his elbow as he waited for an answer from Marie. Marie, lying beside her husband on their bed, turned to her side and faced Paul. She rested her hand under her head in the same fashion as he had done. She smiled gently; then ran her free hand over Paul's increasing receding hairline, smoothing out stray hairs that were flying in every direction.

"Sweetheart, let's not play what if. Okay?"

"Alright," Paul sighed, as he fell back on the bed and put his hands behind his head.

Marie followed suit and began staring at the same light bulb as Paul. *Wendy, I would want to call her Wendy.*

CHAPTER ELEVEN

Steven and Paul sat at the Fonduluc's kitchen table and poured over numbers that Paul had written down. In the living room, Marie and Melissa sat on the couch with coffee mugs in their hands. Andrew sat in a high chair eating cake with blue frosting. Being one, he had no need for a fork.

"Tweedle Dee and Tweedele Dum," Melissa cracked.

Marie ignored her comment as did the men. Andrew also ignored them, shoving more cake in his mouth. Melissa turned to Marie for a response. She caught Marie glaring at her child. *What the hell is that look for?*

Paul and Steven had been in the Lower Peninsula for nearly a year and although they didn't hate their jobs pouring concrete and laying bricks, they both dreamed of something more. Both Paul and Steven enjoyed the building aspect over the destruction aspect of the logging business. Being good with their hands, they decided to use their skill as craftsmen and planned for a side business refurbishing kitchens, bathrooms and in the spring and summer building decks.

The little birthday party/business meeting subsided. Both men went to sleep, resting for a long, hard day to come. Marie sat on her knees and picked up wrapping paper that was skewered around the Fonduluc's living room. Little Andrew bounced up and down on his mother's lap; laughing away. He wore a little party hat that had *Birthday Boy* on it and still had leftover blue frosting from his birthday cake on his lips.

"Marie, stop."

Marie ignored Melissa's request and continued to pick up the litter.

"Marie, stop!" Melissa barked good naturedly.

Marie stopped picking up. She froze and continued to stare at the fibers in the carpet.

"I'll pick everything up later. You're not my maid, girl." Andrew bounced harder on Melissa's lap trying to trigger her knee back into action. Melissa ignored his attempts and observed Marie. She was still frozen, still staring at something. "Marie?"

"Yes," Marie answered, but still didn't move.

"Are you okay?"

"No." Marie set herself back on the floor with her legs bent at the knees and covered her face as she quietly sobbed.

Melissa didn't know what to say, so she sat there with her child bouncing on her motionless knee.

"I can't have children."

Melissa closed her eyes. The reason for Marie's recent strange behavior became crystal clear to her. "Are you sure?"

Marie nodded. "My fallopian tubes are all messed up."

"How?"

Marie shook her head and let out a nervous laugh. "Let's just say from something that happened a long time ago."

CHAPTER TWELVE

Winter, 1965

"Fine, fine; just go."

Helen Fenwick, put the cold washcloth back on her forehead and waved her thirteen-year-old daughter away. Marie didn't wait for her to change her mind. She snapped the top button on her navy blue wool petty coat and threw on a snow hat that didn't come close to matching.

Marie's mother managed to get herself up to a seated position and wiped her nose on her sleeve, no longer caring what anyone thought. She was that sick. "Just stay out of that man's way."

"Yes, ma'am." Marie waved goodbye as her mother plopped herself back on the couch and moaned.

Marie trudged her way through the thick snow, crossed the street to Melissa's house and used the faded brass knocker to announce her arrival at the old but meticulous Victorian house. Marie admired the perfectly applied navy blue paint that matched her winter coat. She turned and looked at her home, although nearly a football field away, she could still see the faded dull yellow. Everything seemed better at her friend's house—almost everything. Melissa answered the door.

"Wow, I can't believe your mom is allowing you to spend the night."

"I know, this is a first."

Melissa's mother, a stay at home mom, made the girls cookies as they listened to *Can't Buy Me Love*. Melissa's little brothers taunted the girls as they bantered about who was the cutest Beatle.

"Oh, Ringo, I love you." Her ten year old brother kissed his hand. The seven year old rolled on the ancient wooden planks, laughing at his brother. Melissa got up and stepped down on his stomach until he howled.

"Melissa, get off your brother!"

The little boy kicked Melissa in her shin as he got up and ran off. She pointed a finger at him, letting him know that she would get him back later. Marie looked around and admired her friend's family. Her mother was so much more domesticated than her own mother, who worked long hours and never seemed to have time for her. Her father was like so many of the other loggers in the UP, he spent as little time as he could at home with his family and as much as he could at the bar with his friends.

It was not hard for Marie to avoid the man her mother had warned her about. Melissa's stepfather wasn't home. He was at a local bar and usually didn't come home until after the bars closed on Saturday nights. He was a paper salesman and was on the road a lot. His wife didn't mind him coming home at this time, or his demanding travel schedule during the week. It kept him away from her. The bills got paid, they had a nice home and he never hit her. That was more than she could say about Melissa's real father. "There are worse things in life than having a man like him in your house," she would often tell her own mother who had never trusted her new husband.

The girls downed their cookies and milk and then talked and laughed about anything and everything until they were told to 'hush' and go to sleep for the tenth time by Melissa's mother. Before long both were sound asleep.

Marie, a chronic snorer, woke her own self up with a loud ripple snort. It wasn't the yellowish hue of his eyes that made his presence known to Marie, but the aroma of his foul alcoholic breath and the stench of a body odor that seemed to fit the man's nasty personality. Marie stared into John Peterson's sinister eyes and opened her mouth to scream. She didn't get anything out as his hand quickly clamped down over her mouth and nose. She struggled to breathe and reached up to pull his hand away from her covered nostrils. He allowed her this much, but did not release his grip from her mouth.

"I'm going to take my hand off your mouth. If you scream, I will kill you like I did Melissa. Do you understand?"

Marie nodded her head and used her free hand to reach over to touch Melissa. She wasn't there. Marie didn't know if she should believe the man, but was resigned to accept her fate. She wanted it to be over as quickly as possible, not knowing of the immense pain or lasting effects her rape would have on her life.

She squeezed her eyes shut as she heard the man's zipper being jerked down. Within seconds of his pants being lowered to his knees, he reached down and yanked Marie's panties off. He wasn't gentle in the least and they cut into her thigh. She let out a short yelp. Peterson smacked her across the face. It wasn't hard, but enough to let her know that she better not emit any more sounds—at any noise level. He pulled up her blouse and put his hands on her nubile breasts. He shuddered. Marie felt his thing push into her belly. She squeezed her eyes even harder, wishing she could squeeze out the feel and smell of the man as well.

The penetration brought on a pain that Marie had never experienced in her life. She bit her lip and let the tears slide through the miniscule slits of her eyes, making their way down her cheeks and forming a pool above her upper lip. The blood created by the breaking of her hymen produced the only lubrication. Fortunately for her it was over within a few minutes. He did not make a sound as he succumbed to orgasm. When it was over he let the weight of his body fall on top of Marie. She had trouble breathing and pushed him off of her. He didn't resist. He rolled out of his step-daughter's bed and pulled his pants back up.

In the darkness she could barely make out his image, but she did see his finger pointing at her in the glow of the moonlight. "I will kill you." He placed his index finger over his lips and gave her a silent 'shhhhhh' as he shook his head. Marie, glad to have the ordeal over, had no intentions of ever telling anyone.

The man left and Marie closed her eyes and sobbed softly; eventually falling asleep. Her sleep was short and restless. Before the sun was even up, she got herself out of bed. She saw the streak of dried blood that ran from her crotch to her right knee. Marie limped to the bathroom and let the water run over a towel.

She pulled back the covers on her friend's bed and gasped as she saw the amount of blood. She placed the wet towel on the bed and began scrubbing furiously, trying in vain to scour away the stains both on her bed and in her mind. Marie placed the ruined towel in her carry bag along with her ripped underwear and equally destroyed pink night gown.

She had to hold on to the railing of the stairs with each painful step, fearful that she would tumble down the staircase. As she reached the bottom, she saw Melissa sound asleep on the couch. She let out a huge sigh, relieved that John Peterson had lied about killing her. Marie assumed it was her snoring that forced her friend to come downstairs and sleep and ultimately led to her doom. She leaned over Melissa and whispered, "I had my period last night. I tried to clean it up."

Melissa looked up and yawned. "Huh . . . oh, that's okay?"

Marie slept away the rest of the day. She threw the blood stained towel in the garbage and buried it with the previous night's waste. She knew she would have to tell her mother what happened to her nightgown so she divulged her 'menstruation lie.' Helen Fenwick promptly gave her a womanly lecture about going out in public prepared for such an occasion.

CHAPTER THIRTEEN

Wendy held her hand up to shield the blinding light coming from the early afternoon sun. She looked down on the rippling water of Lake Michigan and longed to be twelve again. Her father, standing twenty feet behind her on the long dock, looked at his daughter and wished for the same thing.

Paul brought over a pole and held it out in front of Wendy. "You remember what to do with one of these things?"

"Please, mister," she responded as she took hold of the pole. She reached into a small foam cup and took out a slimy earthworm. It wiggled in her fingers, but she easily controlled it and placed it squarely on the end of the hook, puncturing it as it released yellowish goo. She folded it in half and securely placed both ends on the hook so that any biting fish would not easily tear away a piece of the food it craved.

"Still a pro," Paul chuckled.

The two took opposite sides of the dock. Paul cast out first. With a quick flick of the wrist the line sailed out toward the sun, splash landing into the cool summer waters of Lake Michigan. On the other side of the dock, without looking; Wendy emulated her father. She stared out at her bobber and without turning around, asked; "You ever wish I was a boy?"

"No, I've wished you weren't such a pain in the ass . . . but not a boy."

"Thanks!" Wendy reeled her line back in and then easily guided the line back out into the royal blue water. *Splash.*

Paul did the same. He looked down into the water and saw his wife's face rippling right along with the waves looking back up at him. *I know, Marie, I know . . . but not now . . . this moment is . . . too perfect to end.*

"Your mother and I were perfectly happy with our little girl."

On the other side of the withering dock Wendy smiled out of one corner of her mouth; her trademark. Then she felt the violent tug on her line; it jerked her forward.

"Ohhhhh!"

She quickly pulled herself back before she tumbled right into the water that was well over her head. She pulled back on the rod, reeling in as much as she could as she went. Paul set his pole down and stood next to her.

"You got yourself a big one, girl."

Paul watched the bowing of the rod. He encouraged her to keep reeling. Wendy continued to struggle with the great fish. She reeled in ten feet and it pulled back fifteen. She was losing the battle, and Paul saw from her expression, that doubt was creeping in.

"You want me to take over?" Paul asked innocently enough.

"No," she snapped back before he could even finish his sentence. "Sorry," she said, briefly turning around to smile at her father.

Paul put his hands on his hips and grinned.

After a five minute battle, the angler finally won. A sixteen-inch silver colored perch lay flopping under the glistening sun. Wendy bent down and with her left hand took hold of the fish in its midsection, and with her right she skillfully moved the hook down and twisted slightly to the right, removing it with ease. The fish squirmed in her grip. Wendy dropped it in the white five-gallon paint bucket.

Paul clapped his hands in mock applause.

Wendy bowed, then looked in the bucket. "Sorry, fella . . . but you're going to taste good!"

"You want a pop, Dad?" Wendy asked from the kitchen.

"Sure," Paul replied.

Wendy leaned out around the corner of the archway that divided the kitchen and the living room and could not contain the smile that pursed her lips as she witnessed her father.

Paul sat in his recliner and took in the smell of the perch and salmon grilling in the kitchen. He held the remote control in his hand and thrust it out at the television as he pushed the channel up button; as if that were the only way the radio waves would magically reach the television set.

Wendy walked in with a beer battered piece of perch in one hand and a diet cola in the other. She handed the cold beverage to her father and stuffed the golden brown piece of fish into her mouth. "This is good," she said with her mouthful.

It dawned on Wendy that waiting on Ben at home had been a give and take relationship. He was just as likely to offer a beverage as she was. But, here in the UP, the relationship was different; she did it out of obligation and duty. Her mom had gotten the man thousands of beverages from the fridge for over thirty five years; Wendy had gotten him her fair share in her time as well. It wasn't that Paul wouldn't get them something out of the fridge if they asked, but it wasn't the culture in which he was raised to actually ask. It was one of the things Wendy had wanted to escape when she left. She had vowed as a little girl that she would never be in a relationship in which she was not the equal of the man in every manner.

When Wendy was twelve she became fully aware of the inequality in the subservient behavior of her mother. She decided she would enlighten her mother by keeping track of the 'polite' things that her mother did for her father, and vice versa. She drew a line down the middle of a page and wrote 'mom' above the left column, and 'oppressor' above the right. Wendy had recently added that word to her vocabulary after a seventh grade social studies lesson in which her teacher discussed the Civil Rights movement. Wendy saw a few parallels.

After a week of observing her parents, she came up with some interesting, although not surprising, data. For every kind gesture or action, Wendy marked away. After one week, she had tallied 72 instances in which her mother had offered to change the channel when the remote had gone missing, bring her husband a glass of milk, or put his shoes where they belonged. On the right column, one kind gesture; Paul had opened a bottle of pickles for Marie. When Wendy showed her mom her scientific proof of her father's selfish male ways, her mother laughed and said. "You wasted a lot of time, honey. I could have told you how the study was going to come out."

"Doesn't it bother you?"

Her mother shook her head, although truthfully there were times that it could be frustrating.

"We could have a sit-in, you could go on strike; we've got to do something!"

Her mother laughed some more and then finished the ironing. Wendy only sighed.

Paul and Wendy ate in relative silence; both dreading the impending evening ahead of them.

CHAPTER FOURTEEN

Wendy and Paul arrived a half hour before the viewing was scheduled to begin. Wendy couldn't get over the way in which her mother looked. It was completely surreal. It was not her, but it was. She was sure that her mother was going to get up at any moment and complain about the borrowed shoes. Wendy had to give the make-up lady credit; *she done did good*, as her mother would say.

Mom, I'm so sorry . . . so, so sorry that you died before we got the chance to make things right again. I think you would be proud of me. Please, forgive me, I love you so much.

Although, tragedy and her father's intolerable ways were the major reasons for her leaving; in many ways it was her mother who she had been the angriest with. She had stood by and allowed everything to happen. She could expect her father to be stubborn, but it was her mother's stubbornness that gave Wendy no choice but to leave. *I forgive you.* She hadn't thought it would be the case, but those would be the most difficult words to get out.

She turned to her father and noticed that he could not bear to look at his wife. Although, she had only been to a few funerals in her life, she knew that he needed to look at her. He needed to say goodbye, and he needed the alone time to do it.

"Dad, I know this is hard, but I think this is the time you really should say goodbye to Mom. There will be people all around in a little while. This might be the last time you get to talk to her face-to-face."

Paul nodded. Wendy put her hand on her father's shoulder for the briefest of moments and then turned to find Miss Adams to thank her for her professionalism.

Paul spoke his words aloud. "Marie, you know I'm not so good with words, but let me say it's so good to have Wendy home. She's turned into such a beautiful woman; and successful too. But, you already knew that."

Wendy stopped when she heard her name, believing he was calling after her. She stood a few feet away and observed the rest of her father's goodbye.

Paul stood silent for a while, simply existing with his wife—something the two of them knew how to do so well together. Slowly the tears came, then they filled his face and the sobbing began.

"Oh, Marie, what am I going to do without you? I'll be lost. Please, forgive me for every bad thing I ever done, for never quite being the husband or father you needed me to be."

He reached down and touched her hand; briefly. He pulled it back. He wiped his eyes with the sleeve of his suit coat.

Wendy, wanting to honor her father's privacy, stifled a laugh. She knew how mad this would have made her mother.

He pulled out a handkerchief and wiped away the rest. "Good bye, my love."

Marie was an only child and her parents had passed away. Her mother, however, had many cousins; most living in the UP. She and Paul did not have a lot of friends, but they did have loyal ones. There was a steady flow of traffic for the two hours. The visitors said all of the things you expect to hear at a viewing. *"I'm so sorry for your loss." "She was a wonderful woman." "If there's anything I can do, anything; just let me know."*

Paul and Wendy's responses were also just as typical. *"Thank you." "Yes, she certainly was." "Thank you, we will."*

Mike arrived about half way through the viewing. He embraced his older brother; the guy who had taught him how to throw a football, shoot a rifle and later the man he would have to bail out and create a new life for. Mike was three years younger than Paul, but looked twenty years younger. He was now 54, but looked better than most men in their 30s. He was in great shape; he ate well, worked out and was an avid marathoner. He was actually one of the top long distance runners for his age group in the state of Michigan. He had completed the previous year's Boston Marathon in 2 hours and 43 minutes which was good for 17th place in his age group.

"I really loved that woman, you know?" Mike said to Paul. "Don't know what she saw in you."

"That is a question for the ages, eh?"

Wendy stuffed a cracker with cheese in her mouth and left her uncle to reminisce with her father. Savannah was cornered by her crazy Aunt Sheila. She decided to save her friend who loyally suffered through nearly two hours of her mother's funeral visitation.

"That mouse—or rather rat, scared the holy living shit out me. I must have jumped a mile when it dashed out of the dryer."

Sheila nearly clipped Savannah in the nose as she waved her arms in the air, accentuating her story.

"Hey, Aunt Sheila, I need Savannah's help for a sec."

Sheila nodded. Savannah mouthed the words, *thank you.*

They eventually made their way over to an isolated area in the main entryway to the funeral home. Wendy positioned herself so that she could still see people walking into the visiting room of the funeral home.

"God, I could use a drink," Wendy confessed, before being distracted by two familiar faces walking in the main entranceway. "Oh, my God; there she is . . . and Conner."

Savannah turned to see Maggie and her husband walk into the main entrance.

"Damn, he still looks good enough to eat."

Wendy walked toward the two; but still had a word for her friend. "Savannah, you dirty thing."

Savannah smiled and followed her friend toward the remaining member of their childhood trio.

CHAPTER FIFTEEN

February, 1998

"Hey, let's go up to Northern Friday night," Savannah said to the others at the lunch table. She stuffed a fry in her mouth and waited for a response. She got none. "Well?"

"Count me out," Wendy said.

Savannah scoffed. "Why? Can't miss one of Todd's games?"

Wendy stuck her tongue out and made a farting sound.

"I don't know if I really want to drive an hour there and an hour back," Maggie added.

And Maggie knew she would be driving. Maggie was given a Jeep Cherokee for her sixteenth birthday. It was a couple of years old, but she definitely was parking one of the nicer vehicles in the school parking lot each day. Wendy drove a piece-of-shit Cavalier that none of them trusted to get them anywhere. Savannah didn't drive anything since she failed to take driver's training. Softball, volleyball, and basketball had taken up all of her time; there simply wasn't any left for driver's ed. If she needed to get anywhere, she always had Wendy or Maggie, or whatever boy she was dating. Being licensed simply wasn't a top priority.

"Come on, guys, let's live a little. I'm so sick of this little shit town." She dipped her fry in catsup and shoved it in her mouth. "Carla Johnson invited us up there."

"No, Carla Johnson invited *you* up there." Wendy pointed a finger at her.

Carla's boyfriend made the mistake of talking to Wendy after a game the previous season; congratulating her on having the winning hit. Wendy had made the mistake of smiling, and later on at Savannah's place allowing him to kiss her. In addition to Carla's alleged 'oral' skills, she also had an incredible temper and the fighting skills to back it up.

That night Carla confronted the two after someone had spilled the beans on them. She wasn't the type to cry and she sure as hell wasn't going to allow some sophomore girl to get her guy. She jabbed her finger into Wendy's chest and asked her, "Who the hell do you think you are?"

Wendy grabbed her breast and felt the bruising already developing. She was sure the fiery girl's finger prints were actually imbedded.

"I'm sorry, I . . . . I . . ." Wendy had nothing else to say. She felt guilty, but was in more fear than actual remorse at that moment.

The guy, Wendy couldn't even remember his name, just stood there. He was from neighboring Gladstone. He seemed to be as afraid as Wendy was at that moment. Carla balled her fist up and cocked it back. Wendy closed her eyes and thought, *Savannah Sanders has got nothing on you.* She clenched her face tight, awaiting the blow that she knew she deserved. Instead, when she opened her eyes and looked down, she saw the good looking guy from Gladstone on one knee holding the side of his face. Carla stormed off.

Wendy sighed. The guy tried to reach up to her and say something, but his jaw was swollen. It came out, "Sobby bout dat."

Wendy turned tail and headed home. "Yeah, yeah, me too." She spent the rest of the season trying to avoid Carla Johnson. If Carla was at one end of the bench, Wendy was at the other.

Savannah stuffed another fry into her mouth. "Oh, she's so over that," Savannah lied.

Carla's actual words were, "If you have to bring the little slut, fine; but don't think I'm going to be talking to her."

"She's going to get us tickets to the Wildcat's hockey game," Savannah added. She raised her eyebrows and looked at Maggie, then tossed another catsup soaked fry into her mouth.

Maggie knew it was bait, but didn't care. She was crazy about Wildcat's hockey. Steven had taken her to several games in the past, but only one during that season.

"We're going to Marquette." Maggie looked at Wendy, who only shrugged.

"And, Wendy; stay away from whoever she's blowing, okay?" Savannah added.

"It's *whomever* she's blowing; and yes, I think I can manage that."

*   *   *

"Come on, bitch; swallow already!" Savannah griped.

Savannah and Maggie, bundled in their warmest winter wear; sat in Maggie's Jeep Cherokee with the music cranked. Wendy finally emerged from Todd's house with a brown paper bag clutched firmly in her gloved hands. She got to the vehicle and turned back toward Todd, who was leaning in his door jamb with a shit eating grin. She blew him a kiss with her free hand. Todd grabbed at air and planted the imaginary token of affection firmly on his groin.

"What do you see in that moron?" Maggie asked, just as Wendy made her way into the vehicle.

"Well, for one; he has a fake ID!" Wendy reached into the bag and pulled out a can of Busch Light. She handed one up to Maggie who took it readily. She pulled another one off the plastic stem and held it out to Savannah; who shook her head rejecting the offer. Wendy pulled it back and cracked it open, taking a huge gulp.

The girls pulled out of Todd's driveway and were off to what they all had hoped would be a night to remember.

"Hand job or blow job?" Savannah casually asked without turning around.

"Are you kidding? Blow job!" Wendy took another sip of her beer. She wiped some foam from her lip and continued. "I'm missing his last game, he bought us beer . . . . yeah, he wasn't going to be satisfied with me just jerking him off again!"

Maggie looked in the rearview mirror at her friend.

Wendy's face was contorted in a curious expression. "Guys, I think there is something wrong with his dick."

"What do you mean?" Maggie asked.

She had a hard time explaining what it looked like to Maggie, who had only seen one penis in her life and that was her brother's. They were alone and bored and played truth or dare when they were twelve. Andrew said dare and Maggie said let me see 'it.' He sighed and then showed it to her; Maggie wasn't impressed. She simply had no point of reference.

"How do I say it . . . the skin just keeps getting narrower." Wendy held out her hands and turned her right index finger and thumb into the okay sign and dragged it across the air in front of her. The okay sign got smaller as she dragged, eventually closing completely. It dawned on her what it looked like. "It looks like an anteater's snout!" She was finally satisfied with her description.

Maggie and Savannah exchanged a look of disgust.

"I think he's deformed." Savannah told her.

"Well, it looks normal when he's hard. It's just that the, you know . . . helmet disappears when he's limp."

Savannah threw her hands in the air. "Jesus Christ, girl, he's not circumcised! Dumb ass!"

"Fuck you!"

Maggie, who had never seen an un-cut penis in person, had seen one in a picture her brother had shown her. She thought Wendy's anteater analogy was a good one.

"Do you know what that means?" Maggie asked.

"Yes," Wendy lied.

"What is it, then?" Savannah said as she turned to the backseat to stare down Wendy.

"It's . . . shut . . . fuck you." Wendy stammered as she folded her arms. Without realizing it she had begun to crush the can of beer in her hand, losing some in the process.

"Hey, don't be mad, she's just messing with you." Maggie said, alternately making eye contact through the rearview mirror and keeping an eye on the road. She decided to give her friend a scientific lesson about circumcision. "When guys are born, their cockles look like what you described. But, because it is considered unsanitary, doctors recommend that they have it circumcised. They cut a little flap of skin, so that the skin doesn't fold over the head. I guess it stays cleaner that way."

"Man, I'm glad I have a vagina," Wendy responded.

Even Savannah laughed at this reaction. Deciding she had had enough of penis talk she turned up the volume on the radio and the three teenage girls sang along with the hard rock that was blaring from the speakers. Wendy settled in the back seat; her back propped against the driver's side door and her feet lying across the back seat. Her crossed feet swayed in rhythm to the music as she continued to drink her first beer.

Savannah leaned over Maggie and looked at the speedometer. She was flying at a 70 mile per hour clip, despite snow coming down in large clusters.

"Slow down, Maggie," Savannah demanded.

Maggie didn't want to miss one minute of the Wildcats hockey game. She didn't care about meeting some dorky engineering student, or one who was pre-med, pre-law, business or anything else—unless, he also happened to be a hockey player. She was bound and determined to meet one on their excursion.

Maggie had always been realistic about how most boys viewed her; but she still believed that she was worthy of nothing but the best. She had never had a boyfriend, not because there weren't guys interested. There were guys like Bobby 'Stork' Wright and Shrek. However, she saw herself as beautiful; in the same league as Wendy and Savannah. Those two got the best looking, coolest guys; so she wasn't going to settle for anything less. It was going to take the right guy to be able to see through exterior flaws.

She didn't expect a hockey player, who could probably have any 'college' girl on campus, to be interested in her. However, that didn't mean she wasn't going to try. She knew that her personality always won people over; maybe she might make a friend or two. Maggie had two favorite players. One was Tomas Petersen, a Junior from Oslo, Norway. Unlike many Norwegian players, he liked to hit, and hit hard. He could also score goals. His nickname was 'Nordie Howe' which was a play on his homeland and the great Gordie Howe, who could also hit and score with the best of them. Her other favorite was a freshman goaltender from Prince George, British Columbia.

It was only 5:30 when they left Rapid Junction and turned north on US 41, but between the darkness and the flurries that were beginning; travel had become a little hairy.

"Slow down!" Savannah cried.

Maggie's large vehicle began to fishtail. She quickly got it under control. Savannah grabbed onto the 'oh shit' grip above the passenger's door with both hands. As Maggie corrected her fishtailing, the open beer can between her legs flew to the floorboard, spilling Busch Light everywhere.

Wendy, onto her second beer, howled, "Yeeeeeeee . . . . haaaaaaaaaa!"

"Oh, beertender, thoust need a fresh one," Maggie said, reaching her left hand back toward Wendy. Wendy pulled another beer from the plastic stem and set it in her friend's hand.

"You should have let me drive if you are going to act this way," Savannah said, finally letting go of the handle.

"Yeah, right, you don't even have a license," Maggie responded.

They had all told their parents that they were spending the night at each other's house. Savannah informed her mother that she was spending the night at Maggie's. Her mother thought Steven was a cretin. Wendy told her parents, who would never have allowed her to stay the night at a college dorm; that she was spending the night at Savannah's. She knew there would be a good chance that her parents would be in communication with Steven and Melissa. Maggie also told her parents that she was spending the night at Savannah's for the same reason. Neither the La Claires nor the Fondulucs cared for Sharrie Sanders and therefore weren't likely to call.

The snow flurries turned into a flat out blizzard.

Maggie looked down at her hands gripping the wheel of her vehicle. They were as white as the snow coming at her. She shot a quick glance at Savannah, who looked green.

Maggie didn't feel so well, herself. She was dizzy and somewhat disoriented. The snow seemed to be coming in sideways. Driving in a near white-out, she felt like she was in a snow globe that had just been shaken.

Wendy lay her head against the back driver's side door with her legs stuck out, bent at the knee. She finished her third beer and let out a loud belch.

Maggie set the full beer sitting between her legs into the cup holder and left it alone. Although extremely excited at the beginning of the trip, her nerves were completely frazzled. She had never driven in conditions like that before.

The black Jeep Cherokee pulled into the parking lot of the Northern Michigan dorm. Savannah flung open the door, slid down the seat and onto the pavement of the visiting parking lot. She leaned over and put her hands on her knees. The urge to vomit passed and she stood up straight. Maggie unclenched her hand and set her St. Christopher medal back on the dashboard. She sighed and looked at the imprint of the patron saint of travel on her palm. Wendy opened the back door and hopped out ready to go.

"Les do it, eh? Yooper style!" She grabbed the six pack ring that only had one beer left on it; hanging like the last grape on the stem.

The smile returned to Maggie's face. The snow continued to come down hard, but they were at least done driving. They confronted the wind that blew the snow hard into their faces, stinging as it came in. Maggie and Savannah pulled their scarves tighter around their faces. Wendy, wearing an ushanka that she had picked up at a thrift store; stuck her tongue out trying to catch the white fury.

The girls scurried to the dorm entranceway and stomped their feet off as they took in views of the lobby. Maggie and Savannah looked around in awe; *so this is college?* Wendy yawned; then belched, causing a girl walking past them to give her a dirty look. She took off her Russian hat and dusted the snow off it. To their left an acne-faced forestry major manned the reception desk. He threw envelopes into the mails slots, a job which he was supposed to have done when he first got on duty at 3 p.m.

Savannah strutted confidently up to the desk and slapped her hand on the counter. It was just hard enough to be annoying to the receptionist. He turned around with letters still in his hand, but he didn't stand up all the way. His sneer quickly vanished when he stood fully erect and noticed Savannah. "Hey ya, ladies, what's going on?"

"We're staying with Carla Johnson. We supposed to sign in or something?" Savannah said, looking at everything around her except him.

The receptionist turned a pad of paper on a clip board around so that it was facing toward Savannah. "All ya gotsta do is sign in, you're all 18, right?" He licked his lips, which really disgusted Maggie.

He took turns staring at Wendy and Savannah. Maggie was used to not being the center of attention, and in this case was glad of it. He shifted his attention to her. Like most people he was caught off guard by the scar above her lip. He wasn't to the point of rudeness, but his eyes did stay on her mouth longer than Maggie cared for. Savannah glared at him.

"Fuckin-A, we're over 18, want to see some ID?" Wendy bellowed, throwing her identification on the counter. It was actually her high school ID. Her eyes were shut and she looked like a dork. The kid didn't pay any attention to it. His eyes were fixed on Savannah's. He pushed the card back toward Wendy and looked down.

"Just asking, she's in 307."

"Thanks," Maggie said sweetly and smiled. She knew how intimidating Savannah could be and almost felt sorry for the college kid.

"You're welcome," he muttered, then turned back to his letter sorting duties.

The girls stepped onto an elevator. Savannah pushed the silver button marked 3. She crossed her arms and leaned against the wall of the elevator.

"Hey, guys, I don't want these people knowing we're just high school peons. If anyone asks, I'm a Secondary Education major." She looked to Maggie. "What are you going to be?"

"Savannah, this is silly."

Savannah unfolded her arms and held them out to Maggie. "C'mon?"

Maggie sighed as they reached the third floor. The elevator door opened and they stepped out. "Fine . . . I'm a . . . an Electrical Engineer-to-be from Michigan Tech."

Maggie smiled, satisfied with her made-up major.

"That's fine," she turned to Wendy, "and you?"

Without missing a beat she responded, "I'm a philosophy major with a minor in African studies."

"Good."

Wendy winked at Maggie. She giggled realizing that Wendy had pulled one over on Savannah.

They passed a couple of guys, who Maggie figured had to be on the football team. They were way too mammoth not to be. She gave them a big smile. They awkwardly smiled back, but they *did* smile. Maggie sighed in relief.

"I'm a philosophy major from Lake Superior State; eat that, jocks!" Wendy bellowed after they walked by and were almost to the elevator.

"High school kids," one jock sneered to the other. They were both six months removed from high school themselves.

"Are you going to be this belligerent all night?" Savannah asked as she stopped in front of room 307.

Wendy pulled the last beer off the ring and popped the lid. The can began to foam over. Wendy put her mouth up to the lip to stop it from spilling. She ended up with suds on her nose before pulling her head up to answer. "What was the question?"

Savannah knocked on the door then folded her arms and gave Wendy the look an unpleased parent gives a kid after bringing home a bad report card. Carla opened the door.

All three girls were taken aback. Carla, who had been an artificial blonde in her previous existence in Rapid Junction, had jet black hair with a long purple streak through it.

"What's up, bitches?" she rasped in her deep husky voice. Her hair had changed, her personality had not.

"Hey, Carla," Savannah managed to get out before Wendy opened her mouth.

"Wuzzup, hookah?"

Carla rolled her eyes and moved back from the door motioning them in. She lived in a quad apartment with three other girls. The apartment was actually two separate units, with a bathroom shared by both sets of suite mates. Her suite mate was a Goth girl from a Detroit suburb, who like Carla, reinvented herself for college. She stared up from what Maggie thought was the strangest contraption she had ever seen. There was smoke coming out from a clear red plastic tube. At the bottom of the tube was a piece that came out at a forty five degree angle. It had a hollowed out metal piece on the end. The center tube was filled with water.

Maggie, never one to be shy, asked. "What's that?"

Theresa, the newly converted Goth girl, put her mouth over the end of the tube and took a lighter out and lit the marijuana packed in the chamber. She breathed in the smoke out of the tube, pulled her head back and closed her eyes. After a few seconds, she exhaled. Theresa opened her eyes and looked at the girl without staring. "It's a bong, want a hit?"

Before Maggie could even answer, Wendy jumped in front of her and said, "Oh, hell yes." She sat down next to the girl, who smiled at the high school kid's enthusiasm.

"You ever smoke from a bong? You ever smoked period?"

Wendy answered honestly in her drunken state. "Just once and it was a joint. Teach me, dark spirit; I'm an excellent student."

The girl laughed and looked up to her suite mate. "I like this girl, Carla. I don't know why you think she's such a bitch."

Carla raised an eyebrow.

"Hey, we going to the hockey game?" Maggie piped in, definitely not wanting to miss a second of the game.

"In good time," Carla answered, "You guys want a beer? I see La Claire brought her own."

"Sure," Maggie said, somewhat disappointed. She plopped down on a beanbag chair and tried to force a smile.

"Yeah," Savannah added. She grabbed the open bottle from Carla. She closed her eyes and put it up to her lips. She hesitated as if it might be poison, before tipping the bottle back so that the foul liquid went down her throat.

As they sat drinking their beers, Carla caught the girls up on what college life was like and Savannah and Maggie filled her in on all the small town gossip from back home. Wendy, on the other hand, was content to spend time with her new friend—the bong. She sat back and smiled with her hands behind her back. Savannah leered at her in disapproval. Wendy put her middle finger up to her forehead and scratched; a smile plastered on her face.

After a half hour of catching up, Maggie looked down at her watch again; which she had been doing every two minutes.

Carla noticed, "Alright, kid, you can stop looking at your watch. We'll go." She grabbed her coat, hat and gloves and turned to Theresa, who stood up. "Okay, we'll be back after Northern gets stomped by Michigan."

Maggie was about to protest the last comment, but stopped in her tracks when Carla leaned in and pushed her lips to Theresa's. It was wet and passionate. Maggie could not hide her surprise. Her mouth flew open and she looked to her friends who had similar shocked expressions. She mouthed, 'lesbians.'

Carla broke off the kiss and gave Wendy a dirty look. "Kinda makes you wonder why I was going to kick your ass last year, huh?"

"Yup," Wendy responded.

"Well, there's always the fact that I think you're a little bitch."

"Yep, there's that, too." Wendy put her tacky, bushy hat on and joined the rest as they walked out.

*   *   *

Wendy yawned and slouched in her hard plastic seat. Carla and Savannah jabbered back and forth about softball while Maggie moved rhythmically in her seat with every hit, pass and shot on goal. She looked incredulously over to Wendy who threw her hands up in the air suggesting that she just didn't get it.

"So, is there any chance of you coming to Northern?" Carla asked Savannah.

"Uh . . . ."

Carla put up a hand. "Don't say a word, if I had your skills I'd be thinking a little bigger than a D-2 school in the snow belt, too."

"But tell your coach, I'm still flattered."

Maggie stood and screamed "Come on, Tomas!"

Tomas Petersen had not disappointed Maggie thus far. He scored the team's lone goal and delivered one vicious hit after another. One poor Wolverine got rammed into the boards on a border line cheap shot that didn't earn the Norwegian a penalty. The opponent turned to retaliate, before deciding that wasn't the best idea.

Maggie's other favorite, the young goalie from British Columbia, was flat out standing on his head. He gave up a goal on a deflected shot early in the game, but since that moment had been unreal. The horn blew signaling the end of the second period. The goalie took off his mask and skated toward his bench. His hair, soaked with sweat, molded into the shape of the inside of the goalie helmet he wore.

Maggie stood and clapped. Deciding that wasn't enough, she put two fingers in her mouth and whistled. She began a one girl chant, "Conner! Conner! Conner!" No one joined her, but she didn't care.

"Hey, Mags." Maggie turned toward Carla. "You know he lives in my dorm?"

"Get the fuck out!" She climbed over both Wendy and Savannah to sit down next to Carla, who all of a sudden seemed like a much nicer person than she remembered. "I've got to meet him!"

"Easy, girl. I'm sure I can arrange it. He's actually a really nice guy. I hate to break it to you, but most of them are arrogant pricks who think they own the world; especially that Swedish meatball, Tomas Petersen."

"He's Norwegian," Maggie corrected her.

"Whatever, he's a dick."

"That's too bad, but Conner's a good guy, huh?"

"Yep, there will be a party at one of the frat houses that some of the players belong to. We'll go there tonight."

"Cool," Maggie said, her blue eyes beaming.

Normally sullen Carla smiled, Maggie was infectious.

The game stayed 1-1 for the rest of the third period. Tomas Petersen then changed the fortunes of his Wildcats, but unfortunately for the worse. He took a stupid penalty slashing a guy who had put a hit on him earlier in the game. He received a five minute major and put the Wolverines on an extended power play. Despite Conner's best efforts, he couldn't stop a slap shot that zipped past his left shoulder. Three minutes later the game was over.

Maggie screamed out, "It's okay, Conner!" He looked up in the direction of the voice, but quickly was distracted as several of his teammates patted him on the back. Tomas Petersen was not one of them.

The girls walked back to the dorm to get Theresa. From there they drove to the frat house which was off campus and parked quite a way down the street. It was a big game and despite the disappointment by many at the frat party, there was no time to be glum. College frat parties don't allow for sadness of any kind. There was beer to be drunk, chicks to be hit on and hockey players to rub elbows with.

The girls walked in, paid their five bucks, got their hand stamped and received a red 20 ounce plastic cup. Maggie bumped into one person after another, concentrating more on looking out for Conner or Tomas. Despite what Carla had told her, she still held out hope that she was wrong about Tomas Petersen. Most of the people she bumped into turned around somewhat agitated.

Maggie didn't notice Wendy disappear. Savannah stuck close to her, however; forever her guardian. Theresa and Carla ditched the high school girls for the time being and found a game of quarter bounce to join. Maggie was starting to fret that none of the hockey players would show up, but after an hour they began to slowly trickle in.

Maggie spotted a seldom used player; one of the few from the state of Michigan on the team. She pulled on Savannah's sleeve, "Hey, there's one of the players, Albert Jackson."

"How do you know that?"

Maggie didn't answer; she was too busy watching his every move. A few more players walked in and her excitement reached a new level. Each time she tugged on Savannah's shirt. After being told the fifth player, Savannah turned to her friend. "Yeah, Mags, I just don't care."

When Tomas Petersen walked in, she reached over to clutch Savannah. Her eyes bulged and she started shaking.

"Easy, girl." Savannah pried her hands off of her wrist.

Petersen was flanked by two fellow players; they looked more like bodyguards to Maggie. She decided to find out first hand if Tomas really was a jerk. She walked toward where he was standing.

The frat house was now a sea of people. Tomas was not one to say 'excuse me', he just kept pushing forward. One poor guy got between him and his destination, the keg. Rather than trying to walk around the guy; or say excuse me, Tomas just kept pushing the guy, knocking him into other people as he went. Tomas shoved the unfortunate college kid two more times before he was even able to get out a word. Finally he did. "What the fuck, man?"

The guy was much smaller than Tomas, who stood six feet two inches tall and was built like a brick shit house. Tomas held out his hands suggesting the two settle their differences with fisticuffs. "Dude, I'm not going to fight you. Just be cool and stop shoving me."

"Sure thing." With his Norwegian accent, it came out 'shoe ting.'

The smaller guy turned around to resume his conversation with a girl he was flirting with when Tomas leveled him from behind. If he was on the ice, Tomas would have received a ten minute major and been kicked out. In real civilization, he might have been arrested for such an act. But at a frat party where he was considered a God, no one said a thing. The guy flew into the girl; they both were knocked to the ground. The girl hit her back against the corner of a handrail that led upstairs. She ended up bruised and soaked; the bullied guy's beer all over her. She fought back tears. The freckled victim turned around red faced, ready to give Tomas a piece of his mind. He didn't get a word out.

Tomas held out his hand and covered the guy's entire face with his big mitt; muting the guy. He shoved him toward the stairs again. This time the girl managed to get out of the way. The guy fell into the stair case, landing hard on the third step and bruising his coccyx. Maggie couldn't believe what she was seeing. *Carla was right, Tomas Petersen is a dick.*

Tomas leaned over the sophomore whose name was Mike; just ordinary Mike who had played high school hockey and was in the school of business and most recently was trying to score with a cute girl at a frat party. Petersen took the beer out of Maggie's hand. "Here, have a beer on me." He poured the beer over the guy's head. Ordinary Mike did nothing but take it. The guy walked dejectedly toward the door, but not before Maggie came to his defense.

"What the hell is wrong with you?" Maggie squinted her eyes and shook her head; it came out more as disappointment than anger.

Tomas looked her up and down and then put his index finger on her nose and pushed it as if he were ringing a door bell. "What's wrong with me? What the hell is wrong with you, mush face?" Maggie pushed his hand off her nose, but he put it right back.

Savannah, who had always been Maggie's protector, jumped into action. She grabbed his finger and bent it back. The tough guy could have fought her off. As she bent his finger back, he laughed. The laughter became a roar as she tried to break his finger completely off.

"Hey, honey, easy. I was just having some fun."

Savannah threw down his finger and stared him down.

"Some fun, asshole!"

Wendy entered the scene and asked Maggie what was going on as she tried to quickly figure it out for herself.

Tomas put his arms around Savannah and lowered his hands so that they were resting on her ass cheeks. "Why don't we go up to my room and have some real fun."

Some of his cronies chuckled; most others just looked on. Savannah tried to push him off, but now he was no longer playing. He grabbed her ass a little tighter and squeezed hard.

"Get the fuck off me!"

"Oh, baby, don't fight what you know you want."

Wendy pushed her way past a person blocking her path and stood next to the hockey player who dwarfed her. She looked up and pointed her finger at him, "Get your God damned hands off her!"

Tomas made a motion to one of his 'bodyguards' to take care of Wendy. The seldom used winger tried to grab Wendy, but she smacked him hard across the face. He opened his mouth to protest, took a look at his teammate and clenched his teeth. He stood back. Wendy balled her hand back in a fist and punched Tomas in the cheek. Savannah threw his hands off of her.

Tomas gave Wendy his full attention. "Stupid little bitch!"

"What are you going to do, big guy; hit a girl?" Wendy bellowed.

"Damn well should."

Maggie shook, fearing the outcome of her friends' loyalty. There was something crazy in his eyes.

Neither saw Savannah lift her leg straight out and connect with Tomas' groin. He immediately went to a knee as he felt the immense pain and nausea of being hit in his balls. He stumbled to get up. Wendy belted him again, knocking him backward. He sprung to his feet like a jack rabbit and most assuredly would have thrashed both Wendy and Savannah, had the seldom used, recently humbled teammate not stepped in between them.

"I don't think so," he said with total conviction. Tomas tried to get around the player, when another teammate stepped in. The second player put an arm around him and turned him away from the trouble.

"Easy big guy, you don't want any trouble you can't get out of. These little cunts will get the police involved and then instead of being next year's number one pick, you'll slide down to number five."

The veins on the side of Petersen's temples pulsated. Maggie thought they were going to explode for sure. She never saw someone's face so red. He pointed a finger at Wendy and then Savannah. "You little whores need to leave, now! And take the fucking mutant with you." He stared directly at Maggie. He saved the most venom for her. Savannah darted toward Tomas, but was blocked by the morally changed teammate.

"Just go home, ladies," he said softly with his head down.

Carla stood next to Maggie and shook her head. "Told you he was a dick."

"You weren't kidding," Maggie replied almost inaudibly.

The girls remained quiet on the short ride home, each trying to figure out just what had happened. Wendy sat in the backseat between Maggie and Savannah. She turned to Savannah and looked up at her. She held out her right hand, Savannah gripped it quickly and gave it a little shake. *Nicely done.*

You too!

Maggie was beyond disappointment. She was mature enough to realize that athletes, college or otherwise, could be exceptional athletes and also exceptional jerks. It was how jerky the guy was that bothered her so much. She tried to focus her attention on the poor college kid who was shoved into the stairs, but her mind kept racing back to what he said to her. *Mutant! Mush face!* She knew she wouldn't feel any different if he were just another college kid. The words stung. She was used to people doing a double take when they saw her up close and heard her high pitched nasally voice; and had even heard people talking behind her back. But it was rare to actually hear the words *you're hideous;* or in this case *mush face and mutant.* As the words raced through her mind she instinctively put her hand up to her nose; she then traced the scar above her lip. She put her tongue on the inside of her surgically repaired mouth. For the first time in a very long time she had to resist the urge to cry. Wendy stared at her. She put her head on Maggie's shoulder and her hand on her knee.

"Love ya, Mags."

"Love ya, too," Maggie replied, but with little emotion in her voice.

They stopped at a party store before heading back to the dorm. Theresa had her older sister's driver's license and bought a case of beer. Each of the girls grabbed as many of the beers as they could and hid them in their coat. The elderly security guard on duty was too busy with his Fishing Life magazine to even notice the girls signing in. Not bothering to look up, he waved them on.

"Alright, time to party," Wendy said as she flopped on the old orange couch in Carla's room. "Where's that bong at?"

"She always this gung ho?" Theresa asked Savannah.

Savannah looked over at Wendy, who was trying unsuccessfully to find the bong, and made a face that suggested to Theresa that she was not happy with her friend's behavior. Theresa went over to a curio cabinet that was in the corner next to the ancient couch and pulled the bong from off the top shelf. She had to reach on her tippy toes to get it.

Maggie maintained her composure up to that point, but after going to the bathroom and looking in the mirror she finally broke down. She prided herself on being tough, on never allowing her appearance to get in the way of enjoying life. She refused to feel sorry for herself. She had great friends, *loyal* friends, parents who loved her, the best brother anyone could ever ask for and one day she would have a boyfriend, a man that loved her for who she was. It would be someone she could love back for the same reasons. He would be handsome because he was beautiful on the inside, he would have confidence but also compassion, he would be a hardworking guy like her dad, and he would adore her. He would put her on the highest pedestal and she would do the same for him. Maggie looked up at her face in the mirror. She wiped the tears away from her eyes and forced a smile. She no longer saw the scar or the mashed nostril; she only saw the inner beauty that the love of her life would see. "You're so stupid," she said to herself softly and then laughed. After splashing a little water on her face, she dried it off with a towel.

Maggie walked out with a fresh attitude and saw that their little party had grown. There were about a dozen people, including a couple of cute freshman guys walking in. Savannah sulked in the corner with her arms crossed. Wendy, on the other hand, sat on some random guy's lap with the bong in her hands. *Jesus, how long was I in there?* Amazingly, no one wondered what was going on with her, or actually had to go to the bathroom.

Maggie turned from her friends to the doorway. Carla handed a notebook to someone. Maggie couldn't make out the man's face at first, being blocked by Carla.

"Thanks, I'll get this back to you tomorrow," the person told Carla.

Maggie arched her head to the left and saw that the voice belonged to Conner Patrick. Her heart raced; she knew the night was going to improve significantly.

"Whenever," Carla replied. "You sure you don't want to stay? It's Friday, the only people who study on Fridays are the Chinese kids who fear they will be deported if they don't get straight As and . . . apparently you."

"Ah, I'm good. Just trying to take my mind off the game."

Carla pointed to the notebook. "This ought to do it, then."

Conner laughed just as Maggie made her way over.

"Conner Patrick! You were sensational!" She came across as an overzealous rock band groupie.

"Thanks," he told her with some hesitation. "I take it you're a hockey fan."

"Oh, yeah, the biggest. My dad and I come to as many games as I can drag him to."

He smiled at Maggie. Maggie melted. This guy could not be more different than the pompous, arrogant Tomas Petersen.

"I'm Maggie." She held out her hand.

Conner took it. "Conner."

Maggie giggled and repeated his name as if he were not actually standing there holding her hand. "Conner Patrick." She pumped his hand repeatedly. He finally put his free hand on hers and stopped the handshaking motion. "If you think I'm letting go, you're crazy." She giggled again. This time he joined her.

"Can we at least sit down, then?"

"Okay, but I'm not letting go."

Conner Patrick was a good-looking guy and had been a star athlete since he was young. He was never really into girls, at least not like his teammates were. He was raised by a single mother, who was his first coach and his biggest fan until Maggie came along. She raised him to respect women and to put them on the back burner until he knew what his future would be and how he was going to achieve it. She had no illusions of him being in the NHL, although she secretly dreamed of that kind of success as much as he did. She wanted him to get a good education and prepare for a life without hockey.

Maggie dragged Conner across the room to the hideous orange couch. Savannah sat on the other side of Conner. She still had her arms crossed and was being pissy.

"I want to go," she hissed.

Maggie laughed. "Not a chance, girl!"

Wendy walked over and handed Maggie and Conner a beer. Conner sighed but took the bottle. Wendy thrust another one in Savannah's direction. Savannah pushed it out of her face, gave her friend an evil look, then folded her arms. Wendy, seeing no other place to sit, parked herself on Savannah.

"Come on! Get up!" Savannah bellowed. Wendy put her arm around her, stared deeply into her green eyes and shook her head. Savannah sighed and rolled hers.

Both Maggie and Conner held a beer in one hand and each other's with the remaining one. "Okay, either were going to have to let go, or get real clever all of a sudden if we plan on drinking these things," Conner joked.

"You hold mine, and then I'll hold yours," Maggie suggested. "That sounded dirty!" They both laughed. She took a hold of his beer, steadying it, while he lifted the pull tab and heard the classic 'whoosh' of a carbonated can being opened. He grabbed a hold of hers and she did the same thing. They accomplished the task without having to stop holding hands. "Let's toast!"

They brought their cans to each other; Wendy joined her can to theirs.

"Okay, what are we toasting to, exactly?" Wendy asked.

"I have no idea," Conner said, trying to turn toward Wendy. He looked like he was in a bizarre game of Twister and was losing.

"To Yooper Girls!" Maggie finally said.

"That, I can drink to," Wendy said. Savannah groaned under the weight of Wendy.

"Me too," Conner added. They pulled their beer away from the triangular fusion of aluminum and each took a drink.

"What do you want to talk about?" Maggie asked.

"Anything . . . except hockey," he warned. Maggie had to think for awhile before she could think of anything to ask that didn't have to do with his athletic career.

"Who's your favorite Stooge?"

In addition to introducing his daughter to the great sport of hockey, Steven had also introduced her to the comical genius of the Three Stooges.

There was absolutely no hesitation on his part. "Shemp, of course."

"Oh, shit, here it comes!" Wendy leaned backward so she could see Savannah, who was now drinking a beer.

"Yep," Savannah responded then took a little sip.

Maggie set her beer down on the floor and then grasped Conner's hand with both of hers. "You're not just saying that are you?"

He began to laugh. "Um, no . . ."

Maggie got down on one knee and looked up at him, still holding his hand with both of hers. "Will you marry me?"

He looked to Wendy and Savannah for help.

"You think she's kidding, don't you?" Savannah asked Conner, peering around Wendy's head.

"At this point, I'm not sure what to think." He turned back to Maggie who was looking up at him from the floor.

"I've got to go to the bathroom, when I get back I expect an answer . . . if you're going to break my heart, just do it quick like ripping off a band aid." She got up, gave Conner her best smile; letting him know that she was kidding, and then walked to the bathroom.

"Hey, hockey boy; do you actually have any interest in her, or do you just see her as some crazed chick you can get a piece of ass from?" It was Savannah. She managed to get Wendy off her lap.

"Seriously, you heard what we did to Tom-Ass. We'll cut your nuts off." Wendy made a scissoring motion with her fingers.

"Easy, ladies; I don't plan on trying to score with her. She's nice, but she's just a kid. I was just having fun talking to her is all."

"Okay," Wendy said, then made the cutting motion again.

Maggie returned from the bathroom. She sat back down next to Conner, who now appeared nervous. Maggie picked up on the iciness that now existed between the occupants of the couch.

"You guys got quiet all of a sudden," Maggie said, staring down her friends. *What the hell did you guys tell him?*

Conner sighed, then stood up. "Maggie, it was really nice to meet you. I hope you come see us play again."

Maggie stood up and took Conner's outreached hand.

"You can count on it." She tried her best to hide her disappointment. She didn't really expect the guy to be anything but what he had been; a good sport and a gentleman. But, that tiny little speck of hope had gotten a little bigger with each second of holding his hand, or making him smile. The speck was shrinking fast, and she let it. He was a nice guy, so much more than she could say for Tomas—or Tom-Ass as Wendy had referred to him.

This time Conner was the one reluctant to let go. He looked into her eyes a little longer then Maggie expected. That speck of hope, nearly extinct, found new life and grew exponentially. "Can I show you something?" He didn't let go of her hand, just readjusted it so that he was now holding it like a sixth grade lover.

"Sure."

"Better not be your penis!" Wendy hollered after them.

They ignored her and walked out the door.

"Our little girl is growing up," Savannah said, taking Wendy's hand in hers. Wendy put her head on Savannah's shoulder. "She's going to get her cherry plucked, isn't she, Pa?"

"Yes she is, Ma . . . yes, she is."

Conner led Maggie to his room to show her a picture of his sister. A photograph of Conner, aged fourteen and his sister, Samantha who was a year younger, sat on his dresser. In the picture, a sweaty Conner stood in his goalie equipment while his sister leaned into him with both hands wrapped around his waist. Maggie noticed a sadness in Conner's eyes in the photo. It was also quite obvious to her that the girl standing next to Conner, who he had already 'introduced' as his sister, had a wig on. Maggie rightfully assumed that the shoulder length hairpiece was to cover up baldness created by cancer and chemotherapy.

"She was always my biggest fan," Conner told Maggie, still holding her hand. "Maybe until, now, that is." He looked down at Maggie and smiled.

"She's beautiful."

"Thanks." They both continued to look at the picture that meant so much to Conner.

"I take it she died shortly after this picture was taken." Conner only nodded his head. Maggie put her other hand on his and rested her head on his shoulder. "I'm so sorry."

Conner turned his body and took hold of her left hand in his right. He leaned down and she leaned up. He had never seen anything or anyone so beautiful in his life. He knew at that moment that this girl, who stood inches away from him, who was holding his hands, who he introduced to his 'dead' sister, was the one. He had no doubts. Maggie let a single tear drop run down her face, trekking its way down past her high cheek bone, around her 'bad' nostril and finally resting above her lip, directly on her scar. He was beautiful in every way she could ever hope a person could be; she refused to think *why would this guy be interested in me?* She just thanked God that he was.

Conner saw the tear resting on the scar; he took his thumb and wiped it away. He paused just before his lips met hers. He wanted to make sure there was no hesitancy on her part. There wasn't. His top lip met hers, then his bottom one connected. Maggie let go of Conner's hands and put them behind his neck. She pressed her lips against his a little harder and intensified the kiss. He put his hands on the back of her head and ran his fingers through her hair. Before he knew it, they were heading toward his bedroom. She was incredibly talented as she led him toward the bed. The back of his legs hit the side of the bed, and they buckled so that he ended up sitting upright. Maggie did not allow his lips to leave hers. She fell on top of him and continued the deep kissing.

The kissing continued for another ten minutes, before he pulled back. He lay back on the bed and pulled Maggie to his chest. He stroked her hair. Maggie felt his breath and his love.

"Tell me a story about Samantha," she said.

He told her many stories that night; most happy, but a few sad, including how she had died holding his hand.

She told him stories of her brother, of the fifth grade fight between Savannah and Wendy, of her lumberjack father, etc. Eventually they fell asleep. On a couch two floors below, Savannah and Wendy also fell asleep in each other's arms.

CHAPTER SIXTEEN

Savannah leaned in and kissed Paul on the cheek. She was a few inches taller than he was, making it appear as if she were a mother kissing her son before sending him off to summer camp.

"If there's anything else I can do, please don't hesitate."

It was the fifth time that evening that Savannah had made the offer.

"Savannah, just allowing us to have the funeral reception at the Robin's Inn is more than enough."

Wendy cocked her head at her father; he looked exhausted. "Dad, do you mind if I go out with the girls? I can . . ."

His response was quick. "No, you probably have a lot of catching up to do."

Wendy knew immediately what her father would be doing that evening and where he would be doing it. He was going fishing on Little Bay de Noc.

Outside the funeral home the ladies figured out who was riding with whom. They giggled about past fights between Wendy and Savannah as to who would be riding shotgun. Conner, who was invited to come along, decided that Maggie was in need of a girl's only night out.

"Hey, you ladies don't seem like you need a fourth wheel for your tricycle. I think I'm going to head back to the motel."

"Oh, baby, come on; we'll all have a blast like the old days."

Wendy and Savannah chimed in too, but with less conviction. They both wanted their friend to themselves. They liked Conner a lot, but both also had a little resentment. Conner represented all that they didn't have in a relationship.

"Tricycles tip over rather easily; maybe we need a fourth wheel to make us a sturdy cart, eh?" Savannah joked.

"Nope." Conner smiled. His mostly fake pearly whites shined through the impending darkness of the evening. "You ladies need some girly time, and I don't want anything to do with it."

"Wimp," Wendy added.

Conner grabbed a hold of his wife and pulled her in quickly. "Why don't you get a ride back with Wendy and I will see you later tonight, okay."

Maggie squinted, looking up at her husband as if considering it. "Okay, call the kids for me, alright?"

"Sure thing." He leaned down and kissed his wife.

Conner opened his eyes and saw Wendy and Savannah staring at them like they were exotic animals on display at the zoo. He broke off the kiss and spun Maggie around, almost making her dizzy. He gave her two quick pats on the butt as if he were sending in a football player to the huddle with the next play. "Have fun." It came out as an order.

Maggie saluted her husband. "Yes, sir."

"Hey, Conner, are you a Mormon?" Savannah asked.

"Nope," he responded.

"Cause if you ever want to convert, we would love to make it a harem," Wendy said, finishing the joke that began twelve years earlier.

"Somehow, that never stops being funny," Conner replied without laughing. He had only the slightest smile.

Thursday evening at the Robin's Inn meant Karaoke Night. There would be as much singing to please the ears as there would be to offend. Either way it was always enjoyable for the patrons from Rapid Junction and the tiny burgs of Ensign and Trenary. The ladies sat at a table in the back, away from the speakers. They would be able to hear both the wannabe singers and each other without much effort. John Frederick moonlighted as the karaoke emcee on Thursdays at the small town pub; his wife was always at a table up front. It was their one night out; he mostly had to work the weekend shifts, being low on seniority. Neither of them drank. His wife sipped on tonic water all night, and he on diet cola; his one addiction. Being the karaoke king, he got things going with a song himself.

Wendy couldn't take her eyes off of him. He finished up *I'll Be* by Edwin McCain. The crowd of over sixty on lookers burst in applause.

Wendy clumsily clapped along, more in awe than in appreciation. "I can't believe Shrek can sing like that."

"I know, right?" Savannah responded. "All of a sudden, about five years ago, he starts coming in every night we have karaoke and just blows people away. He really is good."

"Good? He's fantastic," Maggie added.

"Thanks, let's welcome to the stage, Adam." John Frederick handed the microphone off to a skinny kid, who was home from college. The kid looked incredibly nervous as he watched John Frederick walk off the small portable stage. He stumbled with the first few lines of a Counting Crows song before coming into his own. John Frederick noticed Wendy and Maggie sitting next to his 'boss' and walked over to them as the college kid continued.

"Hi, Maggie; it's good to see you again." He held out his large hand. His wife, sitting a few tables from the gathering of women, craned her neck to see where her husband was headed. She was quick to her feet when she realized that he was at a table full of women.

Maggie took his hand and held on to it similarly to the way she first held Conner's hand. "Wow, you were sooooooo good!"

"Thanks," he replied, then looked at Wendy who was shaking her head in disbelief. "Wendy, it's definitely been a long time." His smile was ear-to-ear. Maggie finally released his hand and allowed him to extend it out to Wendy. Stephanie Anderson cleared her throat waiting for her introduction. It would have to wait. John Frederick looked down quickly at Wendy's hand; no ring. "Sorry to hear about your mom."

"Thanks. How the hell have you been, John Frederick?" She asked, taking in the man that he had become.

"Good, you can call me John."

"Are you sure? Cause you used to get pretty pissed when anyone called you anything but that."

"As long as you aren't calling me Ogre or Shrek, John is just fine." He chuckled. Mrs. Anderson cleared her throat again. This time it sounded painful. Everyone turned their attention to Stephanie. She was also tall, a little shorter than Savannah, but very large boned. She had a very plain round face that showed off her serious side more than it did her fun side, which usually was only seen by her husband. Maggie was the first to jump up. She offered out her hand.

"Hi, I'm Maggie an old classmate of John's." She was all smiles as Stephanie took her hand. The warmness of her greeting and softness of her hands immediately thawed the iciness that Stephanie came over with.

"Nice to meet you, I'm Stephanie." Her smile came naturally.

"Sorry, hon," John managed to get out, but no one noticed.

Wendy was next to stand up. "Hi. Wendy." Instead of offering a hand, she reached out both arms and Stephanie, who dwarfed her; awkwardly hugged the woman she had never met. Wendy, who was not a hugger, was just in that kind of mood. She looked up at John and shook a finger at him. "First that," she pointed to the stage. "And this." She waggled her finger at Stephanie. "She's beautiful. You, my friend; are full of surprises."

Stephanie blushed; unable to control a smile from forming on her mouth. "Thanks."

John shrugged his shoulders. "What can I say?"

"Hey, I want to thank you for helping my dad out like you did. That was really nice."

The mature, talented singer and reformed elementary school bully only nodded.

We're gonna be big stars . . . Mr. Jones ended. The nervous college kid let out a big sigh of relief. The karaoke crowd cheered.

"Well, I have to go, but I will talk with you later." He turned quickly and hustled his way up to the miniature stage just as the last beat of the song ended.

"Have a seat," Maggie suggested to Stephanie, patting a black chair that was currently empty.

"Umm, okay," Stephanie replied, sitting down.

"So, do you sing?" Wendy asked.

"Oh, no, no, no." She held up both hands waving her off. "I leave that up to John."

"Us either." Wendy looked at the other two who were agreeing with their friend by vigorously shaking their heads. "But, that's not going to stop us tonight, is it?" She looked at her friends, who began to give her disparaging looks.

She grabbed a song catalog that sat on the table and thumbed through it.

"You can forget about it, Wendy," Savannah said, crossing her arms. "I'm trying to increase my patronage, not lose customers."

Wendy looked up from the book toward Stephanie. "Whatcha drinking?"

"Oh, uh . . . just tonic. I'm not much of a drinker, I'm afraid."

"But, you have drank before?"

"Yes," she replied sheepishly.

Wendy reached into her purse and grabbed a twenty and slapped it in Maggie's hand. "Four shots of Hot Damn!"

"Hot Damn!" Maggie replied enthusiastically. It was the booze of their teenaged years; a cinnamon flavored schnapps that went down so smooth.

"I thought we agreed. No shots?" Savannah asked.

"That was before we made a new friend."

"She's been my friend for a while now, thank you."

Wendy knew this was a lie. Savannah had never been friends with women like Stephanie.

"You'll do a shot with us, right?" Wendy asked, turning her attention to Stephanie.

"Sure," Stephanie replied. "Big guy is going to have to drive home tonight, bring it on!" Her voice cracked, no one noticed.

Wendy put up a hand and Stephanie joined it completing the high five. "That's my girl!"

Savannah rolled her eyes. "Puke in my joint, you're cleaning it up!" She pointed a finger at Wendy. Stephanie gulped, before realizing the finger was not directed at her.

"I haven't thrown up in . . . a long time!" As a teenager, Wendy's drinking binges almost always ended with her head over some toilet if she could get to one. Wendy thumbed through the catalog a little longer, before finding the perfect song. "Here it is."

"So, what are we singing?" Savannah asked, resigning herself to the fact that she would be up on stage in front of her customers.

Wendy smirked. "You'll see!" She smiled at Stephanie, raised her eyebrows and took the slip up to John Frederick, who had just finished introducing a couple who were going to sing Sonny and Cher's *I Got You, Babe.*

At the table, Stephanie smiled nervously at Savannah, who now alone with her; had absolutely nothing to say. Savannah sighed in relief as Maggie came back holding the four shots.

"Here we go, ladies!" Maggie set them down, spilling a little on the back of her hand. She licked it off. Stephanie looked down at the shot as if it were poison. She looked at the others and blew out a deep breath. Maggie shot her a wink and nodded, before turning back to Savannah. "Where's Wenders?"

"Putting in a song request." She said it as if Wendy were activating a bomb. "You singing?"

"Hell yes! Aren't we . . . um, I'm sorry." Maggie said, looking apologetically at Stephanie.

"Stephanie. It's okay . . . and, uh, sure." She closed her eyes.

"John Frederick," Wendy hollered above the noise of the speakers. "John, I mean. Think you can work us up the list a little?" She cupped her hands over his ear as he leaned down.

"Absolutely." He smiled down at her. He took the slip, read it real quick as he raised his eyebrows a little, then put it in right after the top slip in his hand. "Classic."

Wendy punched him in the arm. "Smart ass!" She walked back to her seat and joined the ladies.

"Yummy!" She grabbed her long stem shot glass. On the side of her glass was a picture of a cartoon robin drinking a shot. Underneath was the label, *Robin's Inn.*

"Cool shot glasses, Savannah," Wendy said.

"They should be, they cost enough. And people keep stealing them, too."

Wendy's shot glass would end up in her purse before the night ended. "Alright, ladies, what are we drinking to?"

"How about to Marie La Claire?" Savannah asked, raising her glass.

Wendy's smile disappeared. She had nearly forgotten why this reunion was happening. She forced it back, choosing to remember her mother in happier times, rather than dwelling on her loss.

"To Marie La Claire!" She raised her glass to the air and looked up. "I love you, Mom."

She choked through the last word.

"To Marie La Claire," the rest of the group added, before connecting their glasses with Wendy's. They threw back their sweet, spicy red liquid with ease. Stephanie took a little sip. Everyone's eyes were on her. She smiled and then threw it back, Yooper style. It burned all the way down, but it did taste good.

Maggie gave Wendy's hand a little squeeze and mouthed *I love you*. Wendy leaned in and kissed her on the lips.

"I love you, too."

"Lesbos!" Savannah said, shaking her head.

"Says the college softball player," Wendy snapped back. "Pot black, kettle black."

"Your friends this crazy?" Maggie asked Stephanie.

Stephanie snapped her head in her direction. "Huh? Oh . . . no, not at all."

"Okay, ladies and gentlemen, let's welcome to the Robin's Inn stage; Wendy, Savannah, Maggie and . . ." He hesitated before saying the last name. " . . . and Stephanie!" John bellowed in his best deejay voice.

Maggie and Wendy jumped up. Stephanie hesitated, before Maggie grabbed her hand and helped her up. Savannah, shook her head, grunted and then stood up and followed the rest to the stage. There were only three microphones. Wendy commandeered one, Maggie shared hers with Stephanie and Savannah held hers out to her side. John punched a code into the computer generated machine and the title and artist popped up on the screen.

"You've got to be kidding me," Savannah bitched, before the music began and the lyrics started popping up . . . *The Spice Girls?*

"Oh, bite me, Sasquatch!"

"Don't make me kick your ass again, Sacajawea."

The words crept across the screen. Wendy threw a hand out dismissing Savannah and belted out. "Yooooo, I tell you what I want, what I really, really want." It was horrible.

Maggie, equally as bad, sang the next line, "Tell us what you want, what you really, really want."

Savannah sang her line with little enthusiasm. "If you want my future, then forget my past." She held the microphone down by her side

Maggie thrust the microphone in front of Stephanie's face and encouraged her to sing the next line. She was late for the start of it, but quickly caught up by singing the line twice as fast and twice as off key, "If you want to get with me, better make it fast."

John leaned against a railing with his arms crossed and laughed. His wife turned to him and held out her hands as if suggesting, *I have no idea what the hell I'm doing or why, but damn it, I'm having fun.* Her smile said it all.

The foursome looked funny; the two tall women were bookends for the little women in the middle. As the song continued, eventually all four were as enthusiastic as Maggie and Wendy. They were awful, but they were entertaining the crowd who cheered them on, and more importantly they were entertaining themselves.

To everyone's surprise, Savannah was the first to actually strike a Spice Girl pose; she jutted out her hip and threw a hand toward the crowd. The song eventually came to a merciful end, for those who actually took their karaoke seriously. The cheers they received, however, were the loudest of the night. Most people were there just to have a good time. Bad Spice Girls was definitely fun. Maggie blew kisses to the crowd, while Wendy repeatedly bowed. Savannah set her mike down and walked back to the table with a scowl. Stephanie went to her husband and gave him a quick kiss on the lips.

The women conversed at the table as John played the role of emcee the rest of the night. Stephanie told the others how she had met John . . . shot of Hot Damn. The girls shared the story of their first meeting, the infamous fight . . . another shot. A lot of laughing . . . then another shot. The night continued that way until it was 1:30 in the morning. Normally, they closed up at 12:30 and karaoke ended at midnight, but that night everyone seemed to be having the time of their life. Savannah made the executive decision to stay open an hour later and didn't have to twist John's arm too hard to get him to stay on an extra hour. Stephanie was far past wasted when John finally sat down for the night with the ladies. The bartender and wait staff said good night and walked out.

"I think I'm going to be doing a little driving tonight," he said.

The four women stared back at him with glazed looks.

"Yoll gona get a bloooooooo job," Stephanie howled. The others cracked up. Wendy spit out the beer she was drinking all over the floor.

"Sorry," she said to Savannah.

"Who cares," Savannah responded, waving a dismissing hand to her friend.

"I can't even give Conner blow jobs anymore. My jaw hurts too damn bad afterward." Maggie held out her hands, first showing his supposed length, and then holding out her arched hands showing the width, which if her hands were accurate would give him a two foot long penis with the thickness of a two liter bottle. Both were huge exaggerations, but his endowment was long a story of legend between the girls. Wendy grunted in disgust.

"I seriously hate you," Savannah slurred.

"You love me and you know it." Maggie slurred back.

"My boyfriend . . ." Savannah held out her fingers two inches apart; then held out her pinky.

"Oh, you poor thing." Maggie put a sympathetic hand on her friend's shoulder before belching. "Cuze me." She belched again; then laughed.

Stephanie took her turn at sharing dimensions. "Johnny isn't . . ." She held out her hands as far apart as Maggie had and then as big around as she had. "But he isn't . . ." Stephanie then held her fingers apart two inches; then lifted her pinky as Savannah had. " . . . either! But it's definitely a nice cock!"

"Honey, let's not talk about my . . ." John Frederick Anderson sighed.

CHAPTER SEVENTEEN

Ben finished Thursday's evening news and headed straight for the St. Louis-Lambert International Airport. He made up his mind that he was going to be the good boyfriend. He would be by his girlfriend's side during her time of need.

The connecting flight from Minneapolis arrived in Green Bay a little past ten. By the time he grabbed his luggage and picked up his rental, it was almost eleven. He made sure his rental car was equipped with a GPS. The last thing in the world he needed was to get lost deep in the woods of Michigan's Upper Peninsula; something that he could easily see happening.

Ben first called Wendy when he arrived in Minneapolis. He wanted it to be a surprise that he had shown up during her time of need. Then it registered to him just how stupid it was to arrive unannounced for a funeral. Something about this young woman always made him lose track of his sensibility. He left message in Green Bay and again on the road.

"This is Wendy La Claire; I am unavailable to answer your call. Please, leave a message," Wendy's recorded voice said to all callers who either legitimately missed her or she simply ignored.

"Hi, baby, it's Ben. I know you said I didn't need to be there, but . . . well, hell I'm on my way. But, I won't be there until very late, probably around 1:30 in the morning. Give me a call." Wendy was finishing up at the funeral home and was about to leave for the Robin's Inn when the first call came in. Her phone was home on a night stand.

"Hey, hon, I'm in Green Bay. Give me a call." Wendy was downing a shot with her two best friends and a woman she had just met. A few minutes later she would be on stage with a karaoke microphone in hand, pretending to be a Spice Girl. Her phone was still on the night stand.

"Hon, it's me again. I hope you're not mad, please call. I'm about an hour out." Ben stomped on the gas pedal, upping his speed to nearly 70 miles per hour. He snapped the phone shut, looked up, and gazed into the glowing eyes of a white tailed deer. He did exactly what they tell you *never* to do—he slammed on the breaks; then swerved. The deer, not wanting anything to do with the oncoming Lexus, darted to his right and ran into the woods just missing a certain death.

Ben tried to regain control of the vehicle, which he managed to spin around completely. It came to a resting spot on the side of the road, pointed in the wrong direction on the wrong side of the road. He also managed to take out a mailbox.

He got out, assessed the damage, and wondered if this woman was worth it.

He expected some hick with a shotgun to come running out of his house aiming it at him, but of course that never happened. He thought about walking up to the house nearby, but decided not to wake up a local over a busted mailbox after midnight. He took a fifty dollar bill out of his wallet, found an ink pen in the jacket of his suit coat and wrote on the bill, 'Sorry about your mailbox.' He pulled open the lid and stuffed the money in the mailbox that lay on the ground, separated from the wooden post that it once adorned.

After stuffing the fifty in the mailbox he sighed and headed to his vehicle. He thought about calling Wendy again; then decided against it. His next thought was that he should call the police. He decided against that as well. Ben decided that the damage to the back panel had been done by some reckless teenager in a parking lot and then drove off before he could get his license plate number. He thought about the extra car rental insurance that he had neglected to purchase. *Is that going to come back to bite me in the ass? Oh, screw it, I'm not Bill Gates; but, I think I can afford whatever the outcome is.*

He started the ignition, turned the car around without looking and was nearly clipped by a passing Bronco driven by an irresponsible teenager out way past curfew. He put his head down on the steering wheel and let out the biggest sigh of his life. He lifted his head, looked both ways and pulled back out onto US 2. "This woman is going to be the death of me," he muttered to the night.

He glanced at the fluorescent green lights of the vehicle's clock—*2:03*, as he pulled into the parking lot of Four Season's Motel. He sat in the car and contemplated going up to the door and knocking. He was desperate to lie in a bed, but didn't want his first meeting with his girlfriend's father to be at that time of the morning. He settled for the next best thing. He pulled back on a little silver lever and his seat began to recline automatically, then it suddenly stopped. He looked down at the lever and pulled it back again. Nothing.

"That's just great!" Frustrated and with the temperament of a naughty nine-year-old during a timeout, he threw himself a little tantrum. He thrust himself back as hard as he could; in the process breaking the seat. In an instant he was on his back and staring up at the roof of the vehicle. He closed his eyes and cursed Wendy one more time. He didn't realize just how exhausting the trip had been and before he knew it, he was a sleep. He woke up an hour and a half later with a severe cramp in his calf. He jumped out of the car to walk it off. He was prone to cramps, and this one was a doozey.

Paul heard the door slam shut and jumped off the couch. Wendy, who had her head on his shoulder, didn't hear a thing. She simply plopped back down on the couch. Paul was used to cars coming up to his driveway at all times of night. Sometimes they came to simply turn around; the parking lot was conveniently located and easy to make that particular maneuver. Some simply came at all kinds of hours and acted like someone actually 'left the light on.' At Four Season's if the light was on after midnight, it didn't mean shit. *Come back in the morning.*

However, after he saw a man with a dress shirt untucked, no shoes on, and hobbling around like he was drunk; he decided to get his shotgun. He grabbed an unloaded one; this guy might need 'some help' in leaving, but he certainly wasn't a thief or someone to fear. Paul quietly opened the door and walked out with the shotgun at his side, but not raised. He knew his mere presence alone would scare the man half-shitless.

Ben held on to the window ledge of Unit 2 with one hand. With his other hand he caressed the back of his calf and cursed softly. "Need more fucking iron, need more fucking iron."

"You need to get back in your car, eh; and roll on down the road. We're closed."

Paul got as far as 'You' before Ben snapped around and faced the grizzly looking man. The deer hadn't caused him to piss himself, his near death experience with the oncoming truck didn't either; but Paul La Claire, even with the shotgun to his side, did. He quickly got control of his bladder before he actually had a river of urine running to the feet of the man with the rifle. Ben ended up with a major wet spot. He prayed that Paul didn't notice this particular fact.

"Ahhhhh . . . . hi, sir, my name is Ben Alderson, I'm Wendy's boyfriend." He held out his hand, which had been covering his wet spot.

"I see," Paul managed to say. "Why didn't you just come to the door and knock like normal people do?"

Ben flashed his newscaster smile. "I didn't want to wake you up at this hour, so I planned on sleeping in the car." He pointed a finger over to his rental as if Paul couldn't figure out that the only unaccounted car in the parking lot didn't belong to the stranger. "Then I got a cramp."

"I see." Paul still hadn't smiled. "Well, come on in. I'll get you a key and you can sleep in Room 2."

Ben sighed, realizing his vision of having a rifle pulled on him had nearly come true. He hesitated before following the much shorter man with the wild grey tufts of hair.

Once inside, Ben leaned up against the washer which was located in the entrance way. Paul reached over the counter across from the washer and dryer and grabbed a key with a blue diamond shaped plastic piece attached to it. Ben thought he was a kid the last time he saw an actual *key* to a motel or hotel. The number two, which was once white, was now faded next to nothing. "Cash or credit?"

Startled, Ben uttered, "Uh, credit."

"I'm just messing with ya," Paul said, still not smiling.

"Oh, I don't mind paying," Ben managed to get out, trying to desperately save face. He had met many fathers in his day. This was by far the most intimidating man and situation that he had ever found himself in. As an adult he was used to meeting country club types—lawyers, doctors, even a U.S. Senator; but this man was without a doubt, the one who made him feel sixteen again. Paul shrugged off the gesture with a slight wave of his hand.

He handed the key to Ben. The two stared at each other blankly; neither knowing what to say next. Ben wanted to ask about Wendy, but couldn't bring himself to do it. He figured Paul's gesture of a smoky little motel unit, implied the father was not in favor of the two of them sleeping in the same bed. Ben, who was 40, also realized that the man might not approve of his age either.

"Oh, I'm really sorry to hear about your wife. Wendy told me what a great woman she was."

Paul ignored the gesture of sympathy. "Wendy's in the living room. She fell asleep on the couch."

"You mind if I go in and say hi?"

Paul pursed his lip outward and shook his head. Ben hiked a thumb to his right, asking for directions. Paul nodded. If Ben turned to the left he would walk straight into Wendy's childhood bedroom and then onto the attached bait shop.

Ben found Wendy asleep on the couch. Even in her current state, she looked beautiful to him. He knelt down and stroked her brown locks which hung down over her cheeks. He pushed them gently out of her eyes. "Hey," he whispered.

Wendy moaned something unintelligible.

Paul walked toward his bedroom. "The funeral is at 11 tomorrow. It was nice of you to come."

Ben turned around to tell the man, who showed his first sign of defrost, 'no problem.' Paul slipped into his bedroom and the door shut before Ben could get the words out. He turned his attention back to his pretty young girlfriend. He caught the strong aroma of alcohol on her breath. She continued to mumble things. He laughed to himself; Wendy always talked in her sleep when she had been drinking.

Finally, she said something that he could clearly understand. "Andrew, it's so beautiful!"

Who is Andrew?

CHAPTER EIGHTEEN

Spring, 1998

"Hey, der, Conner." Steven stuck out his huge paw and Conner took it. The kid shook his hand nice and firm; he passed the first test. He had managed to avoid the dreadful introduction to the family for the first two months of his relationship with Maggie.

Maggie beamed, her father's approval meant more to her than her mother's. She knew it would be next to impossible to get that anyway. Melissa looked on with her arms crossed. Conner went over to introduce himself with his hand out; Melissa didn't uncross her arms. Conner awkwardly pulled his hand back as all looked on.

Christ's sake, Mom! Maggie turned to Wendy who held her arms out, sharing in her disbelief.

"Hi, nice to meet you," Conner said, before safely placing his hands in his pockets.

"Yes," she replied, stone-faced.

Maggie turned to Andrew for help. He stood up from the table and offered his hand to Conner.

"Hey, man, hear you're quite the goalie."

Conner took his hand back out of his pocket and shook Andrew's. He looked around to see if there were any more siblings, grandparents, or others he would have to suffer through. "I wish I were a little better, I might not be here right now."

Melissa raised her eyebrows, *excuse me*. Andrew held his hand to his mouth to stifle his laughter.

Conner tried to regroup as quickly as possible. "I just mean, my team would be playing right now in the CCHA championship . . . that's all." His voice trailed off. He swiped his hand though his hair and sighed.

Steven, who had long since moved into his favorite spot, his black leather recliner; bellowed out from the living room, "Hey, taco boy, bring home some of those chalupees."

Andrew looked down at the embroidered Taco Bell logo on the purple shirt he wore.

"Dad, keep calling me taco boy, and I'm going to spit in your food . . . and it's chalupas; not chalupees."

Steven opened his mouth to say something, held his hand out toward his son and pointed it at him.

"Yes?" Andrew replied waiting for a response.

Wendy laughed aloud. "Trying to think of a witty comment, aren't ya, Uncle Steve?

Wendy regretted getting involved, as the attention shifted to her.

"Hey, girly; you going to come up to the gym tonight and work on your slap hitting?"

"Ahhhhhhh! I hate that stuff. Why can't I just hit?"

Steven got up from his seat and walked into the kitchen. "Hey, you, it's going to help us win a state championship." He stood with his hands on his hips waiting for a response.

Relieved that the attention was off of her boyfriend, Maggie took Conner by the hand and led him toward the door and to safety. Andrew made an exit as well.

"It's just boring," Wendy replied. She looked around and realized the others had all made their escape.

Melissa decided to make hers as well, picking up a laundry basket and hurrying out of the room. "You two are ridiculous."

Wendy had been an All-League player the previous year as a sophomore. She was a slick fielding second baseman who could also hit. Steven believed that she could take advantage of her speed better. She was one of the fastest girls in the UP and much to the chagrin of the track coach, refused to run for the team. Track was even more boring than slap hitting. Steven believed that he could take advantage of this speed by getting Wendy to bat left handed and slapping at the pitches so that the ball would bounce toward the left side of the field. She would then use her wheels to outrun the throw to first. In 1998 it was becoming en vogue; there were just too many good pitchers who were firing the ball past everyone. This was one way of combating it.

"Anyway, the answer is no, I have homework to do." She stuck her tongue out at him.

"You just be ready for tomorrow, first practice. I need you to be a leader, eh?"

Wendy grabbed her book bag and flipped it over her shoulder. She turned her head over her shoulder to say her final piece. "Anything for you, Uncle Steven."

"For the team, girl! For the team!" He hollered after her.

*   *   *

Andrew decided that he would make a visit to someone he hadn't talked to in a while. He parked his large F-150 in the driveway and let the vehicle idle. He knew it was wrong, but his libido was in charge at the moment. He inherited more than just his father's facial features.

He didn't bother knocking on the door; there was no vehicle in the driveway and he knew it wouldn't be locked. He walked right past the pictures that hung on the wall; the paint was discolored where a couple of the pictures had been taken off, but never replaced. *Divorce is a bitch; the poor guy has been erased.* He heard the shower running. He made his way into the bedroom and plopped himself down on the girl's bed. Andrew kicked his shoes off and put his hands behind his back as the steam from the shower entered the bedroom from the adjoining bathroom. He looked up at the canopy above him and couldn't believe a sixteen-year-old girl slept in the bed.

The water shut off and Andrew anticipated her arrival. She walked into her bedroom with a towel wrapped around her body as she was drying off her hair with another.

"I hear your breathing, mister."

Andrew's smile disappeared. "Oh, shit; busted." He hopped up to a sitting position.

Savannah dropped her towel and let out a slight gasp. This didn't go unnoticed by Andrew.

"So, what are you doing here?" She picked up her towel and wrapped it around her head. She stood in front of a full length mirror and eyed him in the reflection.

"You expecting someone else?"

"Maybe I was." She applied blue eye shadow; refusing to turn around.

"Ouch, so does this mean I'm now officially cut off?"

Savannah stopped her hand right before the brush touched the skin above her other eye. She turned around and pointed the blue dipped applicator at him. "You have a lot of nerve, jerk off."

Andrew stood up and walked toward her; he got within inches of Savannah's face. He knew she was trying to act cool and unaffected, but he could feel her temperature actually rise. He had always had that kind of effect on her. She arched her eyebrows and pursed her lips. *Well?* He leaned in a little closer; his nose almost touching hers. Savannah closed her eyes, unable to control her breathing. Andrew took the eye shadow applicator out of her hand and took a step backward.

"You wear too much makeup," he tossed the plastic thing onto her dresser and walked away.

Savannah opened her eyes and exploded. "Fuck you, Andrew! Fuck you."

He was half way down the stairs, but Savannah was still letting the expletives fly. Andrew felt incredibly guilty and thought about turning around and apologizing, but also knew she was more likely to pop him in the jaw than she was to accept his apology. They had been fooling around since the beginning of the year, but had stopped in January. Andrew had no interest in her other than the oral sex. He wanted a real relationship and began to feel guilty for taking advantage of her.

Savannah had not stopped lusting after him since the episode by the bond fire three years earlier. Much to her disappointment, he had made her swear the relationship to secrecy. She wanted nothing more than to rub it in Wendy's face.

Ten minutes later the guest she had expected plopped down on her bed as she finished blow drying her hair. When she turned around he had it out.

"Put it away, Todd."

She grabbed her glove and trotted downstairs. Todd Stephenson put his anteater penis back in his pants and followed her. Although she was not sworn to secrecy with Todd, she kept this dalliance to herself as well. He and Wendy had broken up only a month earlier.

"You need a ride home?" He asked as he watched her trot away.

"Nope," she answered without turning around.

*   *   *

"Finish your rotation!" Steven bellowed from his squatted position forty-five feet away in the Rapid Junction gym.

Savannah was having a bad day. Fifteen minutes in; she couldn't locate her fastball, her changeup wouldn't fool a blind man, and her riser kept rising to the point that it flew over the six-foot-five inch coach's head. Savannah was simply never wild. When she had a softball in her hand, finding the catcher's mitt was her only focus; but not on that night.

"I am!" She hollered back.

Savannah slammed the ball into her mitt and turned her back on her coach. Steven, who already had bad knees; stood up awkwardly and straightened out his stiff right leg. He took off the catcher's mitt and walked toward the door. "Time to go, girly."

"What?" She screamed; the sounds bouncing off the walls of the small gymnasium.

"You heard me," he said, holding his ground. "We're done. You don't want to be here. That's obvious, eh?"

"Fine!" She stormed past him and walked through the double doors into the hallway of the school. "I quit."

The words froze Steven. He followed her out to the parking lot, forgetting his own coat. Savannah was determined to walk the mile and a half home. Steven began walking after Savannah, but panic crept in and his fast walk became a jog and then a sprint. He caught her as she got to the school driveway leading out to US 2. He reached out and spun her around, grabbing her by her left shoulder. She immediately jerked back.

"Don't touch me!"

"Settle down, you." He leaned over to catch his breath, then put a hand up toward her. "You aren't quitting."

"Oh, yeah?" She raised her eyebrows and nodded her head in a challenging gesture.

"Yeah," he responded, meeting her challenge.

Savannah tried to come back with the meanest thing she could think to say, but when she opened her mouth she immediately began to cry; softly at first, then a complete sob. She turned her back on him, ashamed that she was behaving as a little girl.

"What is the matter with you?"

"Nobody loves me," she said as she threw her hands up in the air, suggesting this was obvious.

Steven looked down at his feet; his shoes were soaked, wet from tracking through the snow that had been melting on that particularly warm March day. He opened his mouth, but nothing came out.

"No one, Steven."

He opened his mouth again. "What about . . ."

Savannah cut him off. "My mother . . . . nope; whoring around at her bar."

"I was going to say . . . ."

She interrupted him again. "Daddy? Try again. He's got himself a whole new family to love!"

"I was going to say . . ." He paused, waiting for her to interrupt. " . . . me."

Savannah rolled her eyes. "Great, the coach loves his star player," she snapped back. "Going to win him a state championship . . ."

Steven interjected. "Believe it or not, girly, I happen to appreciate you for more than just softball." His voice trailed off as he finished the sentence.

Savannah sensed that he regretted having showed his softer side to her; but her attitude thawed, nevertheless. Steven was the one constant in her life; the one person who made her feel worthy and important. It may have only been for his own selfish reasons; but she felt it nonetheless. He needed her; someone needed her.

"Come on, let's go back in there and have you a good practice."

"Okay." She pushed some stray hairs that had escaped her barrette out from her mouth.

They walked back to the high school in relative silence. She felt silly for her meltdown, and assumed her coach felt relieved for saving his season.

As they got to the door Steven put his hands in his pockets and began fumbling around for his keys.

"Oh, shit."

"What?"

Savannah followed him around to the back of the gym. He peered in through the narrow window of the door.

He turned around as he said, "There they are . . . ."

Steven didn't get a chance to finish. Savannah leaned into him just as he turned and put her mouth on his. She took her lips off his for just a second to see what his reaction was; it was shock. She smiled and then leaned back in. Steven grabbed her by the shoulders and pushed her off.

"Whoa, there, girly!"

Savannah only smiled, she knew he wanted her. She mocked him. "Don't you love me, Steven?"

Steven's breathing became deeper. He looked directly in her eyes as she leaned her back against the brick wall of the school. His eyes traveled down to her breasts that were protruding through her long sleeved t-shirt. Her smile faded as she wondered if she was going to be rejected by two Fonduluc men in one night.

In an instant, he attacked her neck with his lips, his beard tickling her ears. His hands moved up to her breasts. She didn't hesitate to grope his manhood. *Junior's got nothing on you!* She unzipped his pants as he continued kissing her all over her face and neck. All of her fears were put to rest.

He grabbed her sweatpants with both hands and yanked them down. He pushed her up against the brick wall and then took her virginity. She was the second of the three Yooper girls.

Although finished in less than a minute, Steven still had all of his weight on her as he tried to catch his breath for the second time in the previous ten minutes. His bearded cheek rested against the side of her face. Savannah wondered if she should be disappointed. He finally pulled back from her and zipped up his pants; looking in both directions as he did so. Savannah reached down and pulled her sweats up from her ankles. She looked longingly at Steven and decided she felt anything but disappointed. She had someone's complete attention.

Savannah walked away with a newfound swagger. She could feel his eyes on her as she led the way back to the front of the building. Steven caught up to her and slid his hand into hers briefly.

A woman in her early twenties walked out of the front door.

"Hey, hey!" Steven hollered as he quickly pulled his hand from Savannah. Savannah didn't let this happen easily.

The woman, a first year teacher trying to get ready for the upcoming week, threw her hand back and caught the door just before it closed.

"Oh, thanks; we'da been in a real mess. I forgot my keys in da gym."

"No problem," she said, smiling. She didn't notice that he had also forgotten his coat.

Steven drove Savannah home that night and set the ground rules. He made it abundantly clear. They were to show no emotion, other than that of coach and player. If she deviated in any way, it was over. She assured him that she had as much to lose as he did, and did not want to jeopardize either her future or her relationship with him. He decided that he would walk her up to the house and say hello to her mom. He didn't want any suspicions of any kind.

"Hey, there; Sharrie, your daughter really has her fastball sizzling."

Savannah rolled her eyes and walked past her mom and told her she was going to bed. As she got to the top stair she turned and looked down at Steven. She licked her lips seductively then blew him a kiss. Her mother's back was to her. Steven felt a nervousness and excitement that he hadn't felt in nearly twenty years.

"Oh, yeah. Think we really have a shot at States?" Sharrie, owner of the Robin's Inn, asked. She stood up. Steven could see the resemblance to her daughter. They both had legs that didn't seem to end. She smiled and he saw yet another resemblance.

"Definitely, 'ol Foudre, up there," he pointed to the ceiling, where Savannah's bedroom was; "Is definitely going to lead us to da promised land."

"You don't come into the Inn much anymore. You need to stop in some time; beer's on me." She crossed her arms and took in her daughter's coach. She had always found him repulsive when she was the upstanding wife of the town's football coach and a PTA mother. But, now she owned a bar, something her husband did not want any part of, had lost thirty pounds, gained synthetic tits and was making up for lost time. *Fuck my ex.*

Steven returned her smile with a devilish one of his own. "Maybe, I take you up on dat offer."

CHAPTER NINETEEN

"Hey," Wendy whispered, lowering the volume on the TV where *Friends* was playing, "remember that pot we smoked last summer?"

Andrew frowned and put his finger over his lips, motioning his head toward the kitchen where his father was making a sandwich.

"Sorry," she threw her hands off her lap and then reached for her cola that was sitting on a coaster. "I think they call people like you bogarts."

"You're an idiot."

Wendy flipped him off and made a face.

"After my dad goes to bed, okay?"

"Yup." She smiled in appreciation.

Steven came into the room with his Dagwood sandwich and a Bud Light and plopped down in his leather recliner. He kicked up his foot rest and rocked away.

Wendy and Andrew were sitting a mile away from each other on the expensive black leather L-shaped couch that matched the recliner. They shot each other a look as they found Steven's interest in *Friends* more humorous than the show itself. Steven let loose with his trademark cackle, especially when Joey said something funny.

"Like the show, Dad?" Andrew asked his father with a slight tone of sarcasm.

"What? You don't think Joey's freakin' hilarious?"

"Yeah, he's great. But, I'm more of a Seinfeld fan."

"That idiot?" Steven took a huge chug of his beer to wash down his sandwich. "You got no sense of humor if you like that guy."

"I love Seinfeld!" Wendy piped in.

"You two would."

"What's the matter, Dad; Seinfeld too deep for you?"

"You gettin' smart over dare, eh?"

"Easy, dad; just busting your chops."

"I'll be busting your chops." He tossed a nearly empty can at Andrew. Remaining beer sprayed on the couch. "Get me a beer, funny guy."

"Mom would've kicked your ass if she saw you do that."

Steven laughed along with his son. "Well, your mama isn't here is she?" They both bolted upright when they heard the garage door open. "Quick, grab a rag and wipe that up. Hurry, eh?"

Andrew sprinted to the kitchen and soaked a hand towel, then came back to the living room and began dabbing at the couch. Melissa walked in and took in the sight of the three nervous looking people. Her hands went to her hips. "So, what's going on here?"

"Hey, Aunt Mel," Wendy said, trying to sound as cheery as she could.

"Oh, hey, hon . . . just watching Friends," Steven said, looking up from what remained of his sandwich.

"Hey, Mom." Andrew looked up from his knees; then went back to scrubbing.

"What did you spill?"

Andrew looked up again. "Me? Nothing, Wendy spilled her pop when she walked in."

Wendy's eyes bulged out and she shot Andrew a death glare. He held back his laughter and smiled back as he continued to scrub.

Melissa walked over and picked up the glass from off the coaster. "Well, at least you use a coaster. Drinks and food in the kitchen, lady."

"Sorry, Aunt Mel." She took the glass from Melissa and walked to the kitchen. She kicked Andrew in the shin on her way.

"Ouch."

"Ooops," she said with her back turned to him.

Melissa moved on to Steven who was beginning to cackle again. She stared at him, before he finally looked up.

"What?"

"Look at you. You got crumbs all over. I've got two kids to raise; I don't need a third." She leaned in and kissed her husband just above his increasingly graying beard on his cheek. "Good thing I love you people."

"I love you too, babe," Steven said. He went back to Phoebe, Joey, Chandler and the rest of the gang.

"I'm exhausted and I'm going to bed. I'll be seeing you in a little bit?"

Steven shot her a glance and smiled while he nodded.

"Goodnight, Andrew."

Wendy was still in the kitchen, deciding if she was going to make a clean getaway.

"Goodnight, Wendy. You should probably be getting on home soon, you do have school tomorrow," she hollered out.

"Goodnight, Aunt Melissa. Going home in a few minutes."

Wendy grabbed a beer and cracked it open. She took a big sip, before taking it to Steven.

"Feels a little light, eh girly?"

"Should feel heavier, I hocked a loogey in it," she said smiling.

"First game next week," Steven said, switching gears during a commercial break. "You been practicing that slap hitting?"

"Every waking moment, *Coach*."

"We're going to win States this year, with or without you, smarty pants."

She leaned in and gave her coach/uncle a kiss on the cheek in the same spot as Melissa. "Let's do it with me, then." She stood up and looked over to Andrew. "Alright, then, I'm off." She pantomimed batting left handed and slapping at the ball just as she had been instructed, then she ran in slow motion toward the kitchen.

"That's right, just like that, girly . . . going to make you an All-State player!"

"Bye, Uncle Steven!"

Wendy stood next to the shed and rubbed her hands together before blowing on them. It had been a nice spring day, almost 60 degrees. But at 8:42 p.m. it was barely 40. Andrew slipped a small key into the padlock opening and turned. He pulled the U-shaped piece away from the tumbler.

"C'mon in, mon," he said in his best Jamaican accent. He held out his hand and Wendy walked in. The shed was pitch-dark. Andrew reached up and pulled a string that gave the room a dull glow thanks to a forty watt light bulb.

He stood on a step ladder and reached up onto a shelf that was above a riding lawn mower. Wendy shivered and rubbed her biceps with opposite hands. He reached around, before his fingers finally found what they were looking for. He had two prized containers on that shelf. One was his shiny blue cookie tin. He had always liked it for some reason, and when his mom bought the cookies back when he was 12 he asked if he could keep it. He stored his baseball cards in it forever. Then one day, his baseball cards were evicted and replaced by his new passion—marijuana. In the much bigger box, was his 'business' supply and equipment. He had baggies, expensive scales and assorted paraphernalia. The tin was for his personal pleasure. He pulled out an already rolled joint and held it under his nose and inhaled. He put it before Wendy's nose to do the same.

"I don't want to sniff it, I want to smoke it. Light that bad boy up," she ordered.

He laughed and took a lighter out of the box, before setting it on the top of the step ladder. He inhaled deeply and stared at Wendy. She was in awe at how the paper burned backward, followed by the green crushed leaves. He also felt it was a beautiful sight. Andrew exhaled and politely blew the smoke to the right of Wendy. He passed the joint to her.

"Careful, this stuff is some shit, I'm telling you."

"Better than what you had last summer?"

"Oh, yeah."

"Alright!" Wendy took a huge hit and immediately began coughing. It took a while for her to get her bearings back. Andrew was impressed that she could still keep the smoke in as she contained her cough. She finally exhaled and her eyes were bloodshot and teary.

"I told you to be careful." Andrew took the joint from her, smirking.

She tried to speak but began coughing again. Andrew took another hit, before handing it back to Wendy. Before she placed it up to her lips for a second time, she managed to say, "I've smoked this stuff before."

Her second hit was much more successful. She sucked in the smoke more carefully and slowly. She let it settle in her lungs, before finally exhaling. Wendy told Andrew about her trip up to Northern Michigan and her second encounter with marijuana, which was indeed from the same source. They talked about Maggie and her increasingly more serious relationship with Conner. Andrew told her that he thought the guy was okay and that his dad liked him; but pleasing her mother would be impossible for either sibling when it came to bringing someone home. Wendy agreed with that assessment.

Half a joint was plenty. Andrew licked his index finger and thumb on his right hand and snuffed the burning joint as it sizzled beneath his touch.

"Does Maggie know?" Wendy asked, motioning toward the joint that Andrew set in his former cookie tin.

"I'm sure she knows I smoke it," he said as he placed the blue container back up in its place on the shelf next to various other articles that had no official home. "But, I don't think she knows I sell it."

Wendy nearly shrieked. "What?"

Andrew couldn't believe those words had escaped his lips. *Fuck! How could I be so stupid?* He grabbed Wendy by the shoulders harder than he wanted to. "*You* cannot tell a soul, do you understand?" He gave her a shake.

Wendy recoiled, caught off guard by the intensity in his eyes and behavior. "Yeah, Jesus, relax. I'm just shocked is all, don't know many drug dealers."

"Sorry, you just know what would happen to me if my mom or dad found out."

"Yes, I do." Wendy looked at Andrew for a while before asking, "I was just kidding about being a drug dealer, but are you really selling this stuff in serious amounts?"

"Large enough to get me in some trouble; but no, I'm not a kingpin if that's what you mean."

"Well, just be careful." Wendy shook her head. "So many secrets! Looks like I'm going to be getting free pot for a while, eh?" She shot him a smile.

"I guess so," he responded.

"I'm just kidding."

"I know; it's just that I didn't want anyone to know about this part of my life."

Wendy glanced at her watch. "Shit, I have to go." She started to head out before turning to Andrew.

"Don't worry, I won't tell anyone, especially Maggie."

Andrew looked toward his feet, still in disbelief that his secret was out. Wendy stepped up and put her lips to his cheek. He was not looking for or prepared for any kind of affection from her. It was her scent, however, that completely caught him off guard. He turned his cheek; the kiss missed and found his lips. He waited for her to pull away, but the gravitational pull was too much and she kept her lips on his until finally stepping back without saying a word. She pressed her top lip to the bottom, tasting Andrew.

She turned and walked jelly legged to her car which was parked down the street so that Melissa and Steven would assume she had already left. Andrew stood in the same spot with his mouth agape for five solid minutes; he tried to blame the pot, but knew otherwise.

He walked in and was grilled to his whereabouts. He told his mom he was just out in the shed thinking.

"Thinking?" She asked as she unfolded her arms. "Go to bed, I think you have a physics test tomorrow, don't you?"

"Yep," he answered as he walked up the stairs to his room. He couldn't take his mind off the kiss. He decided to hell with family loyalty, he was going to see where a relationship with Wendy could go.

Wendy walked in her home ten minutes past her curfew and ended up grounded for the next week. Her parents, who had called over to Steven and Melissa's, assumed she was still going out with the Stephenson kid. A ten o'clock curfew on weeknights wasn't a negotiable thing with either parent. She was ready for the chewing out and grounding as soon as she got in the house. Because she played it cool, her punishment was only one week and not a month.

She went to bed that night and touched her lips; the tingling sensation wouldn't go away. She also felt a sensation between her legs. *Oh, girl, this isn't good. He only sees you as a friend.*

CHAPTER TWENTY

Paul stood before Ben, leaning against the kitchen counter with a cup of coffee in his hand. He donned his favorite fishing hat, a beat up and tattered tan thing, that seemed to fit both his head and personality perfectly.

"Catch anything?"

"Yep."

"Is that Wendy making those sounds in the bathroom?"

"Yep."

"Girl can't hold her liquor."

Ben heard the birds chirping outside.

Ben hiked a thumb out toward the disturbing sounds coming from the bathroom. "I'm going to go check on Wendy."

Wendy pulled away from the toilet to slump against the bathtub. She'd vomited three times in the last three hours. *I'm becoming my father.* There was no denying one thing. She used booze as a crutch.

Ben walked to the bathroom door and looked in. "Hey, girl, this is like the Christmas party all over again."

Wendy covered her face. She didn't care if Ben saw her at her morning worst or even in the stupor of a hangover. He had already seen both. It mattered to her what he might think of her as a human being. If roles were reversed, would she find him in this condition hours before his mother's funeral? He moved toward her and put his arms out.

"It's alright, sweetheart."

She removed her hands and allowed him to put his arms around her. It felt good; he rubbed her back and said nothing. After a few minutes, Wendy pulled back and wiped the tears from her face. She looked at her fingers, mildly disgusted by the black streaks left over from her mascara.

Without looking up she said, "I really do love you, you know?"

"As you should, I'm fucking awesome." Ben responded with his Mona Lisa smirk.

Wendy smiled back, laughing slightly, before her face returned to being stoic.

"Thank you for not saying I love you back . . . and I'm being serious."

The smirk left Ben's face. "I know. Tell me again when all of this is over and see what kind of response you get."

"Now a girl's got something to look forward to."

Wendy turned Ben around and held him around the waist as she guided him to the kitchen where her father stood over the stove.

"How you like your eggs?"

"Uh . . . scrambled is good." Ben looked surprised.

"Scrambled it is; my specialty." Paul smiled at Ben. "You like cheese and ham in it?"

"Actually, I do."

"You look like you could use some coffee," Paul said to Wendy.

Paul's smile disappeared.

"Thanks, Dad."

Wendy saw the concern in her father's eyes. She looked away and poured herself a cup and automatically poured one for Ben. She put in two teaspoons of sugar in Ben's and handed it to him. She needed hers black, the stronger the better. She was starting to come around to the hot beverage the world had long ago become addicted to.

Mike, who had slept in room one, walked in with his cell phone to his ear. He closed his eyes and took in the aroma, before saying goodbye to the person on the other end. He set the phone in his pocket.

"Ahhhhhh, big brother's famous scrambled eggs with cheese and ham." He opened his eyes and looked at Ben, who had his mouth full. "Hi, I'm Mike, Wendy's uncle."

He held out a hand. Ben stood up and swallowed his eggs fast as he took Mike's hand and shook it.

"Ben, Wendy's boyfriend," he responded.

"Nice to meet you." Ben nodded in agreement. Mike turned to Wendy. "Boy, you really look like shit."

"Thanks, Uncle Mike."

Wendy ran her fingers through her hair like a comb, trying to detangle the mess.

The rest of the morning was spent in silence as each of the members of the breakfast table contemplated their day.

*   *   *

The funeral service was attended by fifty to sixty people. Many were family members, many others were simply local business folk who knew the nice motel operator. Neither Paul nor Marie had many friends in the past decade; they were acquaintances and people to hang out with on a dull Friday night. After losing their best friends in the world and their daughter in the span of days, making new friends just never seemed that important. For over a decade they relied more on each other than they ever had in the past.

A Methodist minister that had never met Marie delivered the memorial service at the funeral home. It was quick, lasting only twenty minutes. Mike and a few of the other healthy male relatives acted as pall bearers. Ben held Wendy's hand as she watched the body being delivered to the long, black hearse. There wouldn't be a burial service; the body would simply be buried without witnesses. This was their final good bye. Earlier, both Paul and Wendy had said their separate, private goodbye to Marie. There had been tears for both, but not near the emotion as with their first good bye. Acceptance had already started to creep in.

Wendy put her hands to her face and gasped as she walked into the Robin's Inn following the funeral service. In front of her sat two large poster size photographs on easels. In one picture, Paul and Marie were crashing into each other in bumper cars at the Upper Peninsula State Fair. The picture was taken the summer before everything fell apart. Both wore expressions of an intense desire to smash the other into oblivion. They looked much more youthful than their true ages. There was no escaping the love they held for each other—the picture captured the essence of their relationship. Under the two-by-four foot picture was a caption. 'When true love collides!'

"Oh, my God!" Wendy turned excitedly to Savannah. "Where did you get this picture?"

"Little Miss Maggie, here."

Maggie smiled and waved to Wendy from a few feet away. "You know she was always snapping pictures. I found them in some old albums."

"I love them!" Wendy cried out again, wiping away tears.

These ones were happier tears; ones cried in honor of a woman who had been happy at one time. Wendy turned to see her father standing beside her. He seemed to be in his own world. Wendy turned her attention to the second picture. In it, three twelve-year-old girls holding ice cream cones and wearing softball uniforms were huddled around Marie. Maggie and Marie, standing in the middle; smiled ear-to-ear. Wendy and Savannah, who clearly had been pouting, were on the outside.

"Oh, shit, I remember that day," Wendy exclaimed.

"Yeah, me too," Savannah said, crossing her arms. "You cost us the game."

"Woman, you walked in the winning run."

"Yeah, after you made two errors. It's a simple throw, Wendy." Savannah pantomimed throwing a softball.

"Whatever," Wendy responded playfully. "A good pitcher doesn't get flustered."

"Remember what your mom said when the picture was being taken?" Maggie interrupted.

"Yeah," Wendy responded. "Smile girls, ice cream makes all the pain go away."

Melissa, always the photographer, snapped the picture right after.

"Your mom was awesome," Savannah said, sobering the mood even more.

"Yes, she was."

Paul, who still hadn't said a word; finally opened his mouth.

"Can I have this?"

Everyone turned to him.

"Of course, Paul." Savannah told him. "I made them for you guys. I figured you would want that one and Wendy could take the other."

"Thanks," Paul responded, still a million miles and thirteen years away.

"Yeah, thanks, Savannah, this was really nice. All of this," Wendy added.

She looked around the place; people were mingling, smiling and sharing good memories of her mother. It was turning into a great final goodbye. She wondered how she and Savannah could ever have fought the way they did. She also wondered if she would have gone through all of this if roles were reversed. Wendy hugged her long time friend and rival.

"I love you."

"I love you, too."

It dawned on Savannah that that was the first time they had ever shared those words with each other. They probably had told Maggie 'I love you' a hundred times, but never each other.

Savannah pulled away first. She turned to Ben, who awkwardly stood to the side while people remembered a woman who he had never met.

"Hey, handsome, come help me out."

"At your service."

He smiled to Wendy and followed Savannah into the back where he helped carry out a couple of large metal trays of desserts. Her boyfriend, a man she had been dating for years, could not drag himself away from his legal practice to come and help her out for a day. During her conversation with him the previous night, right before she showed up to the funeral home for Marie's visitation, she had decided it was time to end things with him. He simply couldn't give her what she needed. She knew it was her fault and not his; she simply could not express her real emotions. She acted tough, independent and often non-feeling. The truth was she didn't know how to get close to anyone; but she desperately wanted a man who was strong enough to pull it out of her. Without observing too much, she saw the power that Ben had on Wendy. She wanted that type of man; he was out there waiting. *I'll find my Prince Charming.*

As Ben set a tray down he turned to Savannah. He hesitated before finding the words. "Who is this Andrew guy?"

Savannah couldn't contain her smile. "Are we jealous?"

Ben smiled back. "Should I be?"

"No," Savannah said as she returned to taking the desserts off of the tray and setting them down on the folding table. "Not at all."

"Okay. One more question."

Savannah turned to him and put her hands on her hips. "Shoot."

"Who is Steven and Melissa and why does everyone clam up when Andrew or their names are mentioned?"

She knew he had no way of knowing the pain that just the mere mention of their names elicited. She put her hand to his face and forced a smile. "That, my friend, will be a mystery that I will let Wendy resolve for you." She spun and hustled away.

He called after her. "You Yooper girls sure have a lot of secrets."

You don't even know the half of it.

*   *   *

The last of the mourners left at 3:30. Cousins, aunts, uncles and the like said their goodbyes to both Paul and Wendy; thanked Savannah for a lovely meal and went about their ways. Only Conner and Maggie remained along with Ben.

Maggie, Wendy and Savannah came out of the kitchen to find Ben and Conner acting domestically. Conner pulled a broom back and forth across the area of the floor that served as the dance floor the previous night. Ben leaned over and held a dustpan as Conner swept debris, dust and dirt into it.

"Jesus, ladies; you've both hit the mother lode." Savannah said; hands planted firmly on hips.

"Trust me, mine is only imitating what he sees. Monkey see, monkey do." Wendy teased.

"I don't know what to tell you, girls. My guy can be so sweet it's sickening."

Maggie was only slightly kidding. Since her earlier tragedies, she had often tried to challenge his love. Maggie would purposely be difficult; she would start arguments and fights and tell him to leave if he couldn't handle her. He never did, he never left her side. It was difficult for her to believe that someone could be so good to her. It was also difficult for her to give back to him what he had given to her. She often felt that the relationship was one sided.

*   *   *

After her mother was incarcerated, Maggie moved in with Conner; who had moved out of the dorm after his freshman year. She finished her senior year of high school at Marquette High School. Savannah tried to talk her into staying with her, but she left to be with the man she loved. Wendy tried to talk Maggie into leaving with her, but she refused. Maggie got court permission to be married at aged 17.

Her marriage to Conner caused a rift between him and his mother, and also one with his coach. Conner knew the coach believed that Maggie was a distraction and the reason the team and Conner never enjoyed more hockey success. Conner easily lived with his coach's disapproval. It was the relationship with his mother that made things difficult. She refused to attend his wedding.

"I'm sorry, Conner; but I just can't be there. I'm not going to watch you throw everything away."

Conner sat on his bed with the cordless phone pressed to his ear as his mother spoke. Maggie sat next to him wringing her hands.

"Mom, I'm not going to be throwing away my hockey career."

"Your career? I could give a rat's ass about hockey; it's your life I'm worried about. You cannot marry someone because you feel sorry for them. I feel for her, I truly do; but, how long do you think it will be before you start thinking about yourself?"

He only listened. He put his free hand on Maggie's. He knew she could hear most of what his mother was saying.

"How will you feel when you break her heart? Because that's exactly what's going to happen." She paused. "Conner, I won't be a part of this. I won't watch you ruin your life. Maggie has friends and family that can help her get through this. You don't have to marry her."

Conner finally broke his silence.

"I know I don't have to . . . but, I want to."

He knew his mother was a woman of her word. She didn't attend the wedding; only a few hockey buddies did. Savannah stood up for Maggie as her bridesmaid. Wendy was long gone, she learned of her best friend's marriage after the nuptials.

* * *

Conner and Maggie said their goodbyes and headed back to their motel.

Wendy sent Ben to the car with the large photos of her mother. Savannah raced around making sure everything was back in order and things were ready for what hopefully would be a busy, financially successful night. Fridays were live band night; they began play at nine.

"Savannah, slow down." Wendy chased her around as she placed salt and pepper shakers where they belonged and straightened out table tents that advertised whichever cheap domestic beer was on special.

Savannah stopped and sat down at a four top table.

"Sorry, always on the run."

"You always have been," Wendy smiled. "I need to talk to you for a few minutes."

"Okay, shoot."

Savannah knew that this wasn't another display of gratitude. Wendy wanted to discuss something more important; she wasn't sure if she was ready for it. So far, this had been about Wendy and Paul's loss; but she suddenly felt that she was about to revisit some horrific memories.

Wendy sighed and looked down. Savannah moved restlessly in her seat. The silence was getting to her. Wendy finally looked up.

"We have to tell Maggie about what happened between you and Steven."

Savannah wanted to yell, she wanted to choke her friend for even mentioning his name. But, she contained herself the best she could. Under the table, she clenched her hands, not realizing how hard she was holding them.

"Why do we *have* to tell Maggie? What will that accomplish? Other than her hating me, too."

"Savannah, we have lived a long time with these secrets. Everything needs to be out in the open. There's a woman in a prison down state who hasn't seen her daughter in over twelve years. She could have told Maggie everything, but she didn't to protect . . ." Wendy looked down again, not finishing the sentence.

Savannah tightened the grip on her hands.

"I didn't ask her to do what she did, Wendy." Savannah shook her head. "This is a mistake, I'm telling you." She stood up and walked away leaving Wendy to ponder the situation.

CHAPTER TWENTY ONE

Summer, 2001

Wendy waited in the visiting area of Robert Scott Correctional Facility in Plymouth, Michigan. She sat, nervously pulling on a curly strand of hair near her ear, letting it bounce back into place with every tug. She didn't belong here, then again neither did Melissa. There were people of all races, longing to see loved ones. Wendy looked to her left and saw a Mexican-American woman in her fifties with two young toddlers. The two sprung around the place carefree; unaware that their mother was being jailed for drug trafficking for a boyfriend who wasn't their father. They could've been in church, pre-school or a bounce house. They were oblivious to their surroundings.

Wendy fought back tears when she saw her Aunt Melissa walk through the gate. She appeared as she may have on any other day of her life. She wore blue jeans and a denim shirt, her hair was pulled back in a ponytail and a fake smile plastered her face. She looked just like Wendy always remembered her looking, except her hair was really graying. *Clairol is apparently not an option, here.*

They sat talking about absolutely nothing important for the first fifteen minutes before Melissa brought up what Wendy knew she would.

"When are you going to come to your senses and talk to your parents?"

Wendy sighed; Melissa was as cold as ever.

"Why did you do it?" Wendy snapped back, putting the focus back on Melissa and why she was there.

She had come for one reason only; it was not to get a lecture about having run away three years earlier. She was nineteen, halfway through college and in no mood to have 'Aunt' Melissa chastise or judge her. She wanted one adult in her life to finally give her some truth.

"You know why I did it," Melissa lied.

She knew that Wendy would never be able to understand the depths of her decision making that fateful day three years earlier.

"Let's just leave it at what it is . . . a terrible man deserved to die." Melissa turned the tables of guilt on her. "Maggie still hasn't come to see me. Do you know how painful that is?"

Wendy didn't know what to say; she clasped her hands together and looked down, before finally looking at Melissa, tears in her eyes. "Do you want me to tell her the truth?"

"I don't know," Melissa replied, before looking away.

Wendy left the prison feeling like a hypocrite. She expected so many people to be honest with her, yet she had kept so much from so many people herself. She got out her cell phone and dialed a number that had long ago been memorized.

"Four Seasons," came the voice from the other end.

Wendy froze; she was overwhelmed by a cocktail of emotions. She stared at her phone.

"Hello? Hello . . . . Wendy, is that you?" came the voice of her mother.

She snapped the phone shut.

CHAPTER TWENTY TWO

Spring,1998

After the *kiss*, Andrew and Wendy avoided each other as much as possible. The kiss had been wonderful, but that longing to know if it meant as much to the other person was killing both of them on the inside. Neither had the guts, nor wanted to face their own vulnerability, by approaching the subject with the other. Andrew was busy with his 'Taco Bell' gig. Wendy, grounded for a week for coming home so late on a school night and busy with softball, only ran into Andrew at school. Their reactions to each other were coy; a casual look then a smile or a wink. They played the game of cat and mouse, each pretending they were the cat.

Andrew leaned up against his locker with his arms folded and watched Wendy and Savannah walk down the hall toward him. He had a smirk on his face. Savannah was certain it was meant for her. She smirked back. *Hey, junior!*

"Hey, La Claire, come here," he said as they had almost passed him.

Wendy stopped and turned about face, and headed back toward the family friend. Savannah also halted for a moment and eyed her friend approaching the boy who had scorned her into an illicit affair with a married man. Her first instinct was to return to her past jealous ways. Instead, she turned back toward the direction she was walking in. *He's all yours, Wendy.*

"What's up, Fondlefuck?" Wendy tried to keep from grinning. She was sure he saw right through her, despite her attempt at being cool toward him.

"Fondlefuck? Clever," he responded. He made no attempt at trying to hide his smile. He looked at his feet for a few seconds, before regaining his composure and looking back up. Wendy stopped smiling. She was desperate to know what made him call her over. "Too bad about Owens and Jenkins, huh?"

There was no way of smiling now. Owens and Jenkins were, Sheila Owens and Ken Jenkins, two seniors in a class of only 45 who were killed in a car accident. Ken Jenkins was drunk and driving way too fast trying to impress a girlfriend who wasn't in need of being impressed.

"Yeah," Wendy said, feeling somber.

"I guess they are going to cancel the prom now," Andrew added.

"You seem depressed about that," Wendy said raising an eyebrow toward him.

"Well, I was going to ask Tina Carney," Andrew responded with a half cocked grin.

"Horse face?" Wendy asked with both eyebrows now arched.

"Shit, you seen her rack?" Andrew held out his hands in front of his chest, emulating her large breasts.

"Still got a horse face, my friend." Wendy was having a difficult time keeping up the game of acting like she didn't care, like she wasn't jealous; even though she knew he was teasing. She held her breath waiting for his next response.

Andrew hesitated before looking up again. "If I had asked you, would you have gone with me?"

Wendy burned inside; she thought she was going to explode in delight at finally knowing that the kiss had meant as much to him as it did to her. "I guess we will never know." She had the slightest grin on her face as she walked away. *I'm the cat in this game.*

The bell rang; they were both tardy for their next class. This didn't keep Andrew from smiling. He saw what he wanted to see in her eyes. He knew. *Meow.*

* * *

"You wanna hold it?" Steven asked as he lay naked next to Savannah in her ten-year-old girl canopy bed.

Savannah looked at his limp penis. "You seriously want to go again?"

She was ready, but so far in her experiences with him, he was only good for one ride.

"Not that, silly!" Steven cackled.

He reached over to the bed stand and grabbed onto a sheen solid black .44 Magnum.

Melissa was downstate to a cousin's wedding. Due to a weekend tournament, Steven couldn't go. Melissa didn't complain too much, needing a break from the man. She took Maggie, much to her chagrin, with her. After the softball tournament, Steven decided to get drunk and shoot things in his backyard. Bored, he took a visit to his young mistress's house.

When he first showed it to her she was not interested in it in the least, instead pulling him to her bedroom and clawing his clothes off. But as he handed the gun over and she saw the full power that she was holding in her hand, she became mesmerized. "Nice, eh?"

She pointed the gun at him mockingly, he didn't flinch. "Better be good to me, mister!"

"Yes, ma'am."

They cackled together. In his drunken stupor, he forgot to take the $500 gun with him. Savannah put it in her dresser drawer—for protection.

CHAPTER TWENTY THREE

Steven grabbed the trophy and hoisted it aloft for the small cheering section from Rapid Junction to see. The girls had just won a tournament in Frankenmuth, winning five games against some of the top competition in the state. Savannah won all five games, striking out sixty-one batters in thirty innings. Everyone left believing they had just witnessed one of the greatest softball pitchers the state of Michigan had ever produced.

After being handed the trophy, the team lingered around congratulating each other and also dreading the long drive home. They had gotten out of school early the day before, making the long drive downstate to Frankenmuth in a rented extended van. Many parents made the trip down early that morning and took their kid home with them. Savannah's mother was not one of them; although her father did make an appearance to see her, he only stayed for one game. His new wife and baby needed him at home. It made her want and need Steven even more. He would never treat her that way. He had always been there for her before and had foolishly made the promise that he would always be there for her in the future. They did not discuss specifics; Savannah would not allow her heart to trick her into believing in a 'fairy tale ending.' At the same time, she would not allow her brain to tell her to be rational, either. She just enjoyed their moments and viewed their 'future' as being there, even if that 'future' didn't have any discernible traits in her mind.

Dusk set in as the final cars left Memorial Park in the small Bavarian tourist town. The two remaining girls, besides Savannah, were in the van. Exhausted from playing so many games in one day, they were both plopped down on the seat benches, occupying the back two rows of the vehicle. Steven made a routine check of the area, looking for forgotten visors and gloves.

Savannah sat in the dugout; equally as exhausted as her resting teammates. She stared at the man she thought she was in love with. As he finished his inspection, he turned to Savannah.

"Ready, you?"

"Yep."

She pushed herself up off the bench and walked side by side with her coach to the van. In a rare display of affection, he put his arm around his star player as they walked.

A lone figure watched the two. *That girl was something*, the Frankenmuth athletic director thought to himself. He was collecting the bases and putting them in the storage shed. He thought nothing of a coach putting his arm around a player, even if it was a female athlete. He dropped second base and his thought process immediately changed when the coach slid his hand down from the tall, slender pitcher's shoulder to her bottom and gave it a little squeeze. The girl did not react at all. *What the hell?*

The athletic director made a call to Rapid Junction High School the following Monday. He spoke with the assistant principal, who also happened to be the athletic director. Mrs. Huttle, who had once had to pull Wendy off of Savannah in a cafeteria fight, listened intently as the man told her what he saw.

"Ma'am, maybe I saw nothing, it was getting dark. But, to be honest with you, I believe your coach was acting inappropriately."

She thanked him and assured the fellow AD that she would investigate the situation. Mrs. Huttle sat and tapped the phone with her index finger. She pondered her next move. There was always something she didn't like about Steven Fonduluc; but it was all based on a 'gut feeling,' never by what she actually witnessed or was reported to her. There had been complaints about his coaching style in the past. There are always complaints about coaches, but they were usually along the line of 'he doesn't play my daughter enough' or 'he yells too much.' She never had any calls that suggested he was abusing his role as coach in that way.

One hour later Steven looked down at his pager and saw the number to the high school scroll across the miniature screen. He immediately looked to the sky. It was a perfect day; sunny and absolutely no chance of rain. The only time his pager ever went off with that number was when it was Peggy, the athletic secretary, letting him know a game was cancelled. An uneasy feeling settled in his gut. He informed his supervisor that he was heading back to the office. Steven rarely worked alongside his loggers at that point, after thirty years in the business; his back could no longer take it. He spent most of his time in the office looking over numbers, making calls to distributors, or merely getting in the way of his supervisor, Tom.

"Hey, it's Coach Fonduluc, I got paged," he informed Mrs. Cantro, the secretary on the other end.

"Hi, Coach, let me transfer you to Mrs. Huttle."

Within seconds he heard, "Steven, we need you to come in as soon as possible, we may have a problem."

"A problem? Is one of my girls in trouble?" *Am I in trouble?*

"I'd prefer to discuss the matter in person," Mrs. Huttle responded. Her tone was too serious for Steven's liking.

"I'll be right there." *Shit, shit, shit.* Steven drove slower than usual.

Mr. Spivey had been with the district in one capacity or another for over thirty-five years; the past fifteen as principal. He was a diminutive man, but still had a certain intensity and intellect that made many men and women crumble in his presence. He decided to have Savannah be in the office when Steven arrived.

"We'll know if there is anything to this by his expression . . . or hers," Mr. Spivey informed Mrs. Huttle.

Savannah received a pass to see the guidance counselor at 1:30. She wasn't sure what she was being called down for, but didn't think too much about it. She grabbed her algebra book and notebooks and headed down to the office. She looked up at the clock every two minutes. She shook her head continuously as her right foot tapped the floor harder and harder with each motion.

"Mrs. Cantro, what's taking so long?"

"He's on the phone, dear. I'm sure it won't be too much longer."

Mrs. Cantro wasn't in on the sting operation; she was too much of a gossiper. Mr. Harris, the guidance counselor, was told to keep his door closed and his phone off the hook until further notice and that he would be informed of why later. He didn't question Mr. Spivey; he was one of the many who feared the man.

As Steven slowly moved his new Hummer down US 2 he tried to review in his mind where he may have gone wrong. Half way there, he finally convinced himself that he was just being paranoid. He drove past the purple rocket. A few minutes later he walked into the office and his heart nearly stopped. Steven's survival skills immediately went into overdrive. He quickly regained his composure as the principal walked out.

"Don't tell me this one here is in trouble?"

He poked a thumb back at his ace pitcher and mistress. Steven's cackle did not elicit even a smile. Steven put his hands in his pockets.

"I'm not in trouble," she snapped. She put a finger in her mouth and tried to find any remaining nail to chew away.

"No one is in trouble, Savannah." Spivey walked up to Steven, who was nearly a foot taller than him. It was Steven, however, who could not hold the man's steely glare. He held out his hand and Steven took it. "Coach, good to see you again."

"Good to see you, too." Steven's eyes were square on the man's red and grey striped tie.

Steven wanted to pull his hand back, but the man would not let go. He seemed to be feeling for his pulse. Steven knew the man could feel his *sin* oozing through his pores.

The principal finally released his hand and invited him into his office. Steven took a seat in a chair that was lower than the ones in the reception area, the kind Savannah currently occupied. Steven felt very small. He knew exactly how every troublesome student or obnoxious parent must have felt sitting in the hot seat as they were being interrogated by the 'professional.'

The Assistant Principal followed them in.

"Hi, Steven," she said as she took a seat next to Steven.

"Hey, Barbara. I've got to admit, you guys got me nervous. What's going on?"

"Probably nothing, Steven," she began. "However, I got a call from the athletic director from Frankenmuth . . ."

Steven jumped in. "Barbara, my girls were on their best behavior . . ."

Spivey held up a hand, and without having to say a word, Steven stopped.

"Mr. Fonduluc, no one is questioning your players' behavior. The Frankenmuth AD believes he saw you place a hand on one of your player's buttocks in a very inappropriate way." He did not hesitate when he said 'buttocks' like some people might have. "We just need to know if this happened."

Steven desperately fought to keep control of every part of his physical condition; from his facial expressions to his body language and even pulse. It was easy to blurt out words of denial, but he also knew that his body and face needed to match his words.

As calmly as he could, he said; "Never . . . I have never touched any of my players in that kind of way."

He sat back and crossed his arms. He quickly thought that a mild air of disgust was in order; too strong a denial would only make him look panicky and guilty.

"Do you have any recollection as to what the athletic director may have seen?" Huttle asked him.

"Well, when does he claim to have seen something?" Steven knew exactly when and what he saw. He made a promise to kick himself later for being so careless.

"After the final game when everyone had gone. He was picking up bases . . ."

On cue, Steven interrupted. "Oh, I know what he musta seen. I had my arm around Savannah. I was just telling her how proud I was, then I probably moved my arm back down and he musta thought he saw it come into contact with her . . ." Unlike, Spivey, he didn't know what the correct usage of 'ass' should be. " . . . you know, bottom. Yeah, that's got to be it. You can ask Vannah. She tell you."

"We will, Mr. Fonduluc," Mr. Spivey said, still expressionless. "But, I'm sure we will get the same answer. Thank you for coming in and I'm sorry we had to ask you these questions."

The words sounded good to Steven; he should have been relieved beyond belief. But, the tone and the man's eyes told him something completely different. *I know you're fucking that girl, and if I catch you I will make sure you rot in prison.*

"Oh, that's okay, eh? I know you guys are just doing your job." Steven got up; he looked at the man across from him as if requesting permission to leave. Spivey nodded. "See ya, Barbara."

"Bye, Steven."

He looked for Savannah as he walked out. She was no longer in the chair.

Savannah sat in the guidance counselor's office. He was talking to her about her upcoming ACT test.

"I waited out there for over a half hour so you could pump me up for the ACTs?"

"They're very important, Savannah."

"So is my grade in Algebra II. Right now I'm getting a C-."

Mr. Harris blushed.

Savannah stood up and walked to the door shaking her head. Her mind immediately returned to why Steven was at the office; she assumed he was just there to talk about some scheduling situation. She would not allow herself to believe it had anything to do with their relationship. They had been careful, extremely careful.

Mrs. Huttle looked at her boss for his assessment of the situation. "So, what do you think?"

"Doesn't matter what I think," he said, clasping his hands behind his head. "We've got a he said, she said situation."

"Maybe Savannah will break under the pressure; or maybe Steven is telling the truth."

"Doubtful."

Huttle wasn't sure which part of the question his response was to, but assumed it was for both.

Fifteen minutes later another office pass came for Savannah.

"What the hell," she muttered as her math teacher handed her the pass. He was as annoyed by the interruptions as she was.

She walked into Mrs. Huttle's office and took a seat in a normal size chair. Mr. Spivey was not there.

"Yeah?" Savannah said, agitated over her presence in the office for the second time in less than an hour. She never liked Mrs. Huttle, but for the same reasons anyone dislikes the assistant principal.

Huttle asked her point blank. "Has Coach Fonduluc ever touched you in an inappropriate manner?

Savannah looked disgusted and snapped back, "I'd kick his ass if he did."

"Watch the language, Savannah."

Savannah jumped out of her seat and walked toward the door. "Is that it?"

"Yes." Barbara Huttle sighed.

Savannah stormed down the hallway and kept up her pissed off appearance, scowling at anyone in her path, including a freshman girl who happened to be in her way as she walked into the bathroom. She looked into the mirror and her facial expression changed in an instant. The scowl immediately transformed to a look of terror. The air escaped her and she bent over falling into a panic attack. She couldn't control her breathing. *Shit, shit, shit . . . . oh, God, what the fuck!* She walked into a stall and spent the remainder of the day there sobbing. She received an unexcused absence for her 6th hour; a journalism class she shared with Wendy.

Savannah finally regained her composure and walked out of the bathroom and blended in with the rest of her schoolmates as they left for the day. Wendy saw her up ahead and sprinted to catch up with her.

"Hey, girl, what's going on?"

"Nothing."

Savannah kept walking without turning to look at her friend. She had one thing on her mind, talking to Steven. She needed to know that everything was alright.

The practice was a terrible one. Steven let Dr. Dedrick run practice. Dr. Dedrick was an ER doctor who also had a freshman daughter on the team. Steven complained of a migraine and sat on the bench trying to figure out what he was going to do. He looked up and he saw the principal standing by the outfield fence.

"That little prick has never stopped by a practice before," he muttered to no one.

Savannah took her batting practice swings and missed every single one that came out of the pitching machine. It was only set on 45 miles per hour.

Savannah didn't notice Spivey by the fence, but he noticed her lack of concentration. Spivey was not a fan of sports; he thought they had nothing to do with education and caused more trouble than they were worth. He knew this girl was supposed to be good, the best in the area. It didn't take a sports nut to realize this girl couldn't keep her mind on the sport she supposedly was infatuated with. *Nope, her infatuations rest somewhere else.* Spivey left; he would make his presence to the coach known over and over again. He may not catch the molester, but he would do his best to discourage the asshole.

As practice ended, some of the girls were putting the heavy pitching machine away.

"Leave it," Savannah barked.

The girls set the machine back down and walked away. They were used to the moody pitcher; and being freshmen, they knew not to mess with the cantankerous captain and star.

"Coach, can you work with me on my swing?" She stood with her hands on her hip and stared Steven down.

Dr. Dedrick turned around. "Sure, Savannah."

"No, I was talking to Coach Fonduluc. He knows my swing better than anyone."

Dedrick looked over to Steven.

"I got it, coach, you go home or to the hospital and stitch someone up, eh?" He managed a smile.

"You must be feeling better," the happy-go-lucky assistant coach said.

"Headache all gone." Steven didn't return the smile.

"Alright, come on, Allie," he said to his freshman daughter, one of the girls barked at by Savannah.

Wendy, who had just taken off her cleats and was now in her sneakers walked up to Savannah. "You want me to snag your balls?"

Savannah, realizing that she needed to deflect as much drama as she could, forced a smile to her face.

"Nah, I just need to get some aggression out. I'm going to pretend each ball is the face of this dickhead from Escanaba."

Wendy smiled, "I knew you had a guy! You dirty skank; why were you holding back on me?"

"It's over, now. I'll see you later, alright?"

"Sure, how you getting home?"

Savannah looked over to Steven who was plugging the pitching machine back in. "I'll get a ride from Coach Assmunch."

"Man, what is with you and him? I thought I gave him attitude. You take it to a whole new level." Wendy gave Savannah a concerned look. "You sure, that's all that's bothering you?"

Savannah didn't take her eyes off of Steven. "Yeah, I'm sure."

"Okay." Wendy walked away.

Savannah took one swing after another as Steven placed the yellow dimpled balls in the pitching machine. This time she didn't miss one. Every ball was hit solidly, and hit hard. Neither one of them spoke; they patiently waited for everyone to be gone. After a few minutes Steven broke the silence.

"What did they ask you?"

He casually placed another dimpled ball into the machine. Savannah smacked it into left field.

"The same thing they asked you," Savannah responded. She settled the aluminum bat back up on her shoulder; lifted it and then took a mighty swing as another ball came her way.

"What did you say?" Steven put another ball in. Savannah swung as hard as she could, the ball went sailing right back at him. He barely ducked out of the way.

"What the hell do you think I said?"

"Just asking, calm down." Steven put another ball into the machine. Savannah smacked another pitch, this time to the fence.

"We need to stop things for a while. You know this, right?" Another ball came toward Savannah. Her heart was being crushed. She swung and missed.

"No, Steven. We just need to be more careful. Someone saw you grab my ass, didn't they?" Steven ignored the question and walked toward her. "Just pitch!" she ordered.

Steven stopped in his tracks and turned back toward the machine. He put another ball in. Savannah turned her hips perfectly as she swung. Her Easton bat connected with the batting practice ball and it went straight up the middle. This time Steven, who was not wearing a glove, couldn't avoid the missile. He turned just as the ball struck him in the middle of his back. He swore in pain. He turned around and saw Savannah drop the bat and walk off.

She grabbed her equipment bag off the bench and headed for the parking lot. Steven allowed her to go. He quickly put the pitching machine away. He left the two dozen practice balls scattered all over the field. He could always come back later and pick them up. The disappearance of a $3,000 pitching machine purchased by the athletic boosters, however, might be hard to explain. He hastily locked up the storage shed, which was directly behind the first base dugout. He caught up to Savannah just as she reached the edge of the long school driveway.

"Hey, get in." Steven leaned out his cab to be able to see Savannah.

"Go home, Steven. You're right; we need to cool things for a while." She stopped walking. Steven stopped his truck, which was only moving a few miles per hour; Savannah glared into the vehicle. "But, we are not over!"

CHAPTER TWENTY FOUR

Wendy stood in front of home plate with an imaginary bat in her hand. She eyed the handsome young man in the distance. She resisted the urge to burst into a smile that she knew she would never be able to wipe from her face. She swung at an equally imaginary ball and sprinted down to first base.

Andrew, dressed in his Taco Bell uniform which lacked any stains, stench or other signs that he actually really worked there, stood by a fence with his arms folded.

One after another the rest of the girls followed, but much slower than Wendy. Savannah was last to run. She stood with her arms crossed and her trademark scowl plastered on her face. After completing the run down to first base, Wendy trotted back to where the line started. She swatted Savannah on the rear end and smiled, trying to relieve the tension she recognized in her teammate.

"Let's go girls!" Steven bellowed.

Savannah finished the first leg of the 'circuit.' The girls repeated the process, but the second time around they acted like they were legging out a double. On the third trip they would run as hard as they could to third base. This was something they always did and always groaned about. As the year went on they seemed to be merely going through the motions, rather than exerting every bit of energy they had left.

The team ignored their coach and ran even slower. The girl in front of Savannah even ran like a duck. Wendy had to stifle her laugh. The girl was not nearly as amusing to her as the look on Savannah's face.

"Listen up, if you don't start running harder, we can do these all night long," Savannah snapped.

Allie Dedrick made the mistake of saying what the other girls wanted to say. "You can't tell us that, you aren't the coach."

"Excuse me?" Savannah unfolded her arms and moved toward the freshman, whose father was not at practice.

Allie stumbled backward and into the arms of Wendy who caught her before she could fall into the fence.

"I'm your captain, damn it!"

Wendy couldn't control her laughter. "Easy, cap'n," she said in her best pirate voice. She stepped in between the two players as Steven watched, not saying anything. "Freshman, just run . . . and run hard." Wendy turned the girl around by the shoulders and patted her on the butt as if she were sending a mare back to the stable. "Run, freshman, run!"

Allie ran and ran hard. Wendy followed her and sprinted as hard as she could, almost catching the freshman from behind despite the girl getting a thirty-foot head start on her. The rest of the team followed suit and ran hard as well, with Savannah running harder than she ever had before. No one said a word as they completed their final leg of the circuit. Wendy caught Allie and passed her halfway between third and home.

Steven applauded each girl as they crossed home plate and reminded them, "You get back what you put in, girls. With that kind of effort no one can deny you a state championship."

To a player, each girl was either hunched over in near exhaustion, or standing up with their arms over their head trying to desperately catch their breath. Steven approached Wendy and put an arm around her.

"Nice job out there, you." He patted her on the back and walked back to the dugout.

Savannah and Wendy strung their equipment bags over their shoulders as they walked to the parking lot. Andrew stood by the fence immediately in their path. Wendy could feel the grime and sweat caked on her body and face. Her face flushed. She knew something like that would never bother Andrew; but she still wished he was seeing her in a better light.

"What's up, Andy?" Savannah asked.

"Nothing much, Vannah," he responded, using her equally hated nickname.

His eyes never left Wendy. She pulled at a strand of sweat soaked hair that plastered itself against her cheek. She tucked the sweaty glob of hair behind her ear.

"You guys certainly practice hard," Andrew said, breaking the momentary silence.

"Captain Hook, here, is a tyrant."

"Yeah, well, that little freshman bitch is just lucky you stepped in when you did."

"The girl is a little soft in the head," Wendy replied. She turned to mocking the girl. "You can't tell us that, you're not the coach."

Her impersonation of the slightly high pitched girl was dead on. Savannah couldn't help but laugh.

"Hey, I have to head to work, but I wanted to talk to you for a sec," Andrew interrupted.

"I'll wait in the car. Give me the keys," Savannah ordered.

Savannah held out her hand; Wendy tossed the keys to her. She walked to Wendy's car and hopped in the passenger's side. "So, they rescheduled the prom," Andrew said. He never took his eyes off of Wendy's.

"Yeah, I guess 'ol horse face will be very happy," Wendy smiled.

Andrew returned her smile. "So . . ." He bit his lip and smiled harder. Wendy, no longer caring about her current physical condition, knew what the pause was for.

She finally bailed him out. "Yes, I will go to the prom with you." She turned and strutted off toward her vehicle, believing for sure that her heart was going to explode right in her chest.

"Hey, meet me up at Gladstone High School after you drop off Savannah," Andrew hollered after her.

"Okay," Wendy answered coolly without turning around.

Her heart continued to flutter; no boy had ever made her desperate for one more second with him. This was unchartered territory for her. She was excited and scared at the same time. She wondered how her parents would react to her and Andrew. She remembered her mother's reaction to her fight with Savannah three years earlier. Wendy decided that her mom was probably just concerned about her because she was so young at the time. She was now a woman; she had to understand that love was not something you could control. Her father, on the other hand, was never keen to anyone she was dating and made it difficult for her to even get out of the house. She dreaded the thought of telling him about any guy, especially if the guy was Andrew.

Wendy got in the car and hadn't even shut the door before Savannah fired the first question.

"What's with you two?" Savannah had her arms crossed and her eye brows raised. If her foot was stomping the floorboard, she could've been someone's mother.

"Nothing, why?" Wendy gave her the best 'what are you talking about look' she could muster. She had been worried about her parent's reaction, scared to death about Melissa's reaction, and not concerned in the least about Steven's or Maggie's. She figured Steven would be oblivious to it all and that Maggie would be happy for them both. Savannah's reaction, however, she hadn't thought about. She didn't know anything about Savannah's sexual history with Andrew, but was sure that she still held some infatuation for him.

"Bull shit, just tell me." Savannah softened her tone. "I'm your best friend."

Wendy hesitated, but decided to divulge certain facts that were going to eventually become common knowledge.

"We're going to the prom together . . . as friends." She looked to Savannah, waiting for a response.

"Really, that's cool. Just friends, huh?"

Savannah did not act shocked in the least.

Wendy was caught off guard. Her response seemed sincere; something she could never remember Savannah sounding when it came to Andrew. The sincerity made Wendy want to bust open like a piñata horse smacked in the head by an overly-hyper eight-year-old boy. She wanted to spill the candy of her soul, but decided that she just couldn't. She still wasn't even sure if Andrew felt the same as she did. For all she knew, she could just be the latest cute girl to get his attention. Her inner voice told her that she should just keep quiet for the mean time.

"Yeah, just friends. I really don't want to go," she lied. "But, Andrew doesn't want to miss his senior prom and Tina Carney backed out on him, so . . ."

She looked over to her friend as she pulled into her driveway. "Andrew, of all people, wants to go to the prom?" She shook her head in bewilderment.

"Yeah, I was surprised too." She stopped the car in front of Savannah's house. "Maybe he's actually becoming like the rest of us!" Wendy joked.

Savannah opened her door and swung her equipment bag over her shoulder before peering back into the car. "I wouldn't count on it."

I hope your right.

"Hey, Mom." Wendy said as she plopped down on the couch.

"Wendy! Go take a shower, you're all grubby."

Wendy looked down at herself. Andrew had made her completely forget this fact. Her sweats and t-shirt were covered in dirt from making a diving stop of a ball during practice. She hopped up.

"Sorry." She strutted over toward her mother. "Give me a hug, Mommy."

Her mother set a dish into the rinse water, then turned to her daughter who had her arms outstretched like a mummy ready to pounce on a victim. "Don't you dare."

Wendy picked up the pace, moving toward her mother like a horny date who wasn't going to take no for an answer. "Give me a hug, Mommy!"

Marie backed up and pointed a wet finger at her. "I'm serious, go take a shower." She laughed, unable to control herself.

"Hug, Mommy." Wendy chased her mother around the kitchen. She completed the first lap around the table without any success. However, she caught her mother on the second time around. She held her mother from behind and rubbed herself up and down, leaving a trail of dirt all over her. "I love you, Mommy."

"Ahhhh, you brat!" She broke away from her. "Shower, now!"

"Fine," Wendy stuck her tongue out at her mother who continued to laugh. She turned around before entering her bedroom to get a change of clothes. "Hey, I'm going over to Savannah's to work on our Government project. Is that okay?"

"She can't come over here?"

Wendy lied; they had already finished the project.

"Mom, she came over here the last two times. Can I just go, please?"

"Yes, just don't be late or you will never be allowed outside of the house again."

"Go where?"

Wendy looked across the kitchen to where her father stood by the refrigerator. He pulled out a diet cola and turned for an answer. He and

Wendy had been fighting more in the past two months than they ever had. Wendy, desperate not to get on her father's bad side that evening; resisted her urge to be sarcastic or nasty. She wasn't sure why she and her father were going through the patch of miscommunication and dislike; but figured if he would just back off some they would probably be okay.

"I'm going to go over to Savannah's to finish up our Government class project."

"Okay, but be home by ten."

She thought about requesting more time, but quickly closed her mouth.

Andrew sat in the school parking lot. As he watched the clock tick, he began to give up hope that Wendy would show. His mood changed as he saw her red Cavalier with the dented blue door approach. He set his cell phone down in his console as she pulled up next to him so that they were facing in opposite directions. His truck sat up much higher than hers, so she had to look up at him as she rolled down her window.

"So, we going to hang out in a high school parking lot?"

"Nope, hop in."

Wendy put the car in park, rolled up her window and got out of her beat-up excuse for a vehicle. Andrew took the sight of her in as she walked around her jalopy. It was an unusually hot May evening. It was six and the temperature was still in the 70s. Wendy, in a hurry to leave the house, hadn't bothered to dry her hair. It hung on her shoulders; clumps of wet curls soaked her white, silky blouse. Normally, Wendy pulled her hair back in a schrunchy. In her hurry, she had forgotten. Andrew was glad; she looked like a woman and not a teenager. Her face was perfect; blemish free with a certain glow to it. She had a nice tan due to all her softball playing. Wendy pushed her knockoff Ray Ban sunglasses to the top of her head as she stepped up into Andrew's truck.

"Where to, Taco Andy?" She looked down at his uniform.

Andrew suddenly felt intimidated by Wendy's beauty. She couldn't look any hotter, and he looked like a dufus teenager who should be taking someone's order at that moment.

"Shit, I've got to change."

"I think you look nice," Wendy told him sarcastically.

He shook his head and looked away. "Whatever, chick."

He turned around when he felt the softness of her hand touch his. He turned his palm over and took in her hand. They took their time, simply taking in the prospect of each other. Andrew took the lead and moved closer, never taking his eyes off hers. Being much shorter, she had to lift herself up as she met his lips for their second kiss. They continued until the passion got to them both and they each closed their eyes. He put an arm around her and awkwardly tried to adjust himself in his truck seat. She removed her hand from his and put her fingers through his lush, sandy blonde hair.

Andrew hadn't stopped thinking of the taste of her lips. He remembered the smell of her hair and the texture of her skin. Some nights he couldn't get to sleep. They lingered in the air like the mist resting above a calm lake on a cool morning. On nights like that, he didn't want to sleep. He wanted to keep the memories of those senses alive for as long as it took before he could recapture their true sensation. The time was now; he never wanted it to end.

Finally, however, he did break off the kiss. He coolly put his truck in drive. "I have an errand to run first, then off to my special spot."

"Special spot? Hmmm, I'm intrigued."

Wendy picked up his cell phone and looked it over. "I so wish I had one of these."

"Honestly, it sucks. I can't get reception worth shit."

"Still . . . ," her voice trailed off.

Andrew drove into the parking lot of the Taco Bell. He looked down at his purple shirt and immediately felt silly for his attire; he pulled off the shirt and threw it in the back seat with the visor that he had also discarded. He could feel Wendy looking at his physique. The white t-shirt he wore molded perfectly over his lean, but muscular frame. There wasn't an ounce of fat on him.

"Welcome to Taco Bell, would you like our new Chalupa?" an uninspired teenage girl asked from over the intercom.

"No thanks," Andrew answered before turning to Wendy. "You want anything?"

"No, I already ate," Wendy answered, "I'll take a Pepsi, though."

"Two large Pepsis . . . and four soft shell taco supremes . . . beef," he ordered.

"Two large Pepsis and four beef taco supremes, soft shell," the girl repeated. "You're order comes to $5.83."

Andrew pulled up to the window with his wallet out. The girl's expression quickly changed when she recognized him.

"Oh, hey, I didn't realize it was you. I'll go get Tom."

She smiled at Andrew. Andrew had been making special deliveries to the restaurant for the past year. Tom, the assistant manager, was a med school dropout who was perfectly fine with his current existence of smoking his life away. Tom, who all the Taco Bell potheads liked, came to the window.

"Hey, Andrew." He leaned down a little to take in the person sitting next to his supplier. "Hey," he said to Wendy.

"Hi," Wendy responded.

Sarah, the oily-faced Taco Bell drive-thru girl who hated her job, but was infatuated with the 25-year-old assistant manager who shared his marijuana with her, came to the window and handed over a bag that was stuffed with more tacos than what Andrew ordered. She handed over the bag to Andrew who took it and handed it off to Wendy.

"I'll be right back with your drinks."

"So, nice evening or what?" the once promising doctor-to-be asked.

"Yeah, you can't beat this, that's for sure." Andrew reached under his seat and pulled out a brown paper bag. "Can you throw this away for me?"

Tom grabbed the bag. "Sure."

Sarah returned with the two large plastic cups containing their drinks. "Here, you go." Andrew attempted to hand her a ten. She waved him off. "You're all set, Andrew. Hey, I'm having a party this weekend, you want to come?" She leaned down to look at Wendy. "I'm sorry, I'm Sarah." She waved to Wendy, who politely waved back. "Anyway, if you want to come it's going to be a great time."

"Yeah, maybe," Andrew responded. He smiled then pulled out.

They both heard her shouting after them. "Bring your girlfriend!"

As the truck pulled away from the drive-thru, a black Impala facing the drive-thru window pulled away behind Andrew and Wendy. Two men sat in the vehicle.

"So, when do we move in?"

"Soon," the man's partner responded.

The two Michigan State Policemen had trailed Andrew, without his knowledge, for over a month. They were after his supplier, a chemical engineering student from Michigan Tech.

Wendy looked at the green digital glow coming from the trucks clock with mild trepidation. 7:35 p.m. stared her in the eyes. They left Escanaba over forty five minutes earlier. Her eyes gravitated away from the clock and to the speedometer. Andrew was driving over eighty miles per hour down the two lane roads. She knew from the signs they passed where they were headed.

"Pictured Rocks?"

"Yep," he answered, turning toward her, his hand still firmly in hers. "But not like you've ever seen them."

Wendy challenged him. "Really?"

"Really," he confirmed.

Wendy put her hand out just in time to avoid the evergreen branch from smacking her in the face. She regretted having worn a white blouse. The quick walk Andrew had promised had turned into a twenty minute journey through the woods.

"Hey, Romeo, how much longer?"

Andrew stopped suddenly causing Wendy to hit him from behind. He removed his hand from Wendy's and turned to her. "Close your eyes."

"Okay."

He pulled her to him, then turned her around and led her forward. Wendy took each step with trepidation.

"Alright, take a large step up."

Wendy did as directed. Andrew led her ten more steps then whispered for her to stop. "Open your eyes."

"It's beautiful . . . I can't believe how amazing this is," Wendy exclaimed.

Wendy looked down from the cliff that overlooked Lake Superior and the Pictured Rocks of Munising. Dusk approached and the transfer of power from the sun to the moon began. Within an hour, the last remnants of the dazzling orange sun would be splashing down upon the rippling waves; the moon sitting high in the sky ready to take over for its daytime partner.

The reddish orange glow that reflected off the murky green-blue water was mesmerizing. Wendy suddenly felt ashamed of herself for never truly appreciating the beauty that existed in the far reaches of Michigan. She sat with her arms wrapped around her knees which were pressed into her chest; only inches away from the edge of the fifty foot cliff that overlooked the majestic Great Lake. She had the strong arm of the man who would most shape her view of what true love was, around her. Every man was going to have to compare, and always unfavorably; until Ben, to him. Wendy felt the chill due to the departure of the setting sun. Andrew wrapped his arms around her a little tighter.

"Simply mesmerizing," she sighed.

"It sure is," Andrew agreed, but was looking down at Wendy when he said it. She met his stare. He pulled her back and kissed her passionately. They lay against the blanket he brought with them. He stroked her brown curls. After a few minutes, his hand traveled to her left breast. Wendy didn't resist. However, after she looked down at his hand and noticed his watch she suddenly jolted upright. It was 8:50.

She stood above Andrew. "Let's go!"

He looked up at her confused. "Sorry, I guess the romantic setting got the best of me."

Wendy shook her head and laughed. "You can touch my tit anytime you like. I have to be home by ten or it's my ass!"

Wendy took him by the hand and they ran back toward the car. Andrew led her along the same trail they came in on. She ran fast earlier at practice; this sprint rivaled that speed. It took them nearly twenty minutes to climb up to where they were. It took them ten going back; she jumped into the truck, Andrew right after her.

"Come on, come on, come on!" she snapped, both in voice and with her fingers.

Andrew sat feeling his pant pockets. "Shit," he said in a panic, looking at Wendy. "I think I left the keys up there."

"Fuck!" Wendy responded in equal terror.

Andew flashed a smile and pulled out his keys. "Gotcha!"

"Oh, you asshole!" Wendy sighed. "Drive, mister . . . and fast!"

Andrew turned over the ignition and pulled out, his tires burning rubber the entire way. The trip from Pictured Rocks to Gladstone High School normally would take an hour. Andrew made it in 40 minutes. It was 9:41 when they pulled up next to Wendy's car. She opened the door and was ready to fly out of Andrew's truck and into her car, but stopped herself. She turned back to Andrew and leaned over and kissed him. It wasn't as long as the kisses earlier, but was equally as passionate. The thirty seconds she lost was worth it. She gained enough willpower and pulled away from him. Wendy patted him twice on the face and sighed. "Gotta go, gotta go."

Andrew watched her as she got into her car. She rolled down her window. "Thanks for tonight; I'll never forget that sight as long as I live."

Wendy smiled before making her best attempt at burning rubber. Being an older Cavalier 4-cylinder with balding tires, she barely made a squeak.

Wendy passed her high school and the purple rocket at 8:56. Her home was only two minutes away and she had four minutes to spare. She breathed a sigh of immense relief as she pulled into the little motel parking lot. The sign welcoming guests was brightly lit. 'Welcome to Four Seasons Motel.' She felt welcomed. She took a final look at the little digital clock in her car. '9:58.' *Perfect.*

She grabbed her book bag from the passenger's seat and shut the door. She couldn't hold back the smile that creased the corners of her lips. She suddenly realized that wearing white was a mistake. She did her best to brush dirt off her shirt and jeans as she walked in. Thinking quickly; *we sat down in her back yard, if they even ask . . . hell, they're probably sleeping.*

Wendy strolled confidently into the kitchen; even whistling. She expected to find her mother sitting at the dining room table, sewing something and her father sitting in his recliner with his eyes closed and snoring away; the sound of the weather channel on. She immediately knew something was up when she found them both at the table. Neither returned her smile.

"Hi." She set down her book bag on the kitchen counter and waited for a sign confirming her worst suspicions.

That sign came quicker than she expected. Her father sprang from his chair like a jack rabbit and grabbed her by the shoulders. "I'm sick of the God damned lies!"

Marie jumped up. "Paul!"

Wendy swallowed hard. She felt the sharp edge of the kitchen counter press into her back. She wanted to cry, but fought back the tears.

Her father pulled his hands back, but still thrust an accusing finger in her direction.

"Where were you?" Paul demanded. He stared down his daughter and clenched his teeth.

Wendy put her hands behind her, placed them on the counter and pushed herself up. She felt like an animal trapped by its predator. Wendy's subconsciously prepared lie even surprised her as it came out.

"With my boyfriend."

"Who is he honey, and why didn't you just tell the truth?" Marie asked softly.

Wendy sat down at the table; her parents followed suit. Like an award-winning actress she put herself in someone else's body and became a new person. She was so convincing, she believed her own story.

"He's a friend of Conner's."

Her parents were aware of Conner and had even met him on one occasion. She knew they disapproved of the relationship between Maggie and Conner; but it still seemed like as good a story to give them as any.

"Well, that relationship is over, do you understand?" Her father said, looking up. His glare was intense.

Wendy continued her performance. A part of her wanted to get the truth out; it had to be better than this stupid lie she was telling. But, she had started and she couldn't stop herself.

"This isn't fair," she said calmly. "He's a good guy. Mom, tell him this isn't fair."

"Honey, lying to us isn't fair . . ."

Wendy cut her off. "What was I supposed to do?" It came off as a near scream.

"Don't raise your voice to your mother."

Wendy turned to meet the blazing glare of her father; but it was too intense, she immediately looked down. "I'm sorry . . . but, you both have to start letting me live my own life."

This time it was Marie who was unable to control her emotions. She started to raise her voice, but halfway in lowered it. "*You . . . you . . .* a sixteen-year-old girl . . . Honey, you don't know what life is all about, yet. Someday, you will. But, right now, your life is getting good grades and playing softball . . . not falling for some college guy who is just using you."

Wendy looked up at her mom. *If I tell you the truth, will you understand? I'm dating an eighteen-year-old boy who still has two weeks of high school left. So what if he's your best friend's son! Isn't that better than this bull shit lie?*

Her father stood up from the table. "You're grounded for another month . . ."

"No!" Her reaction was finally a completely honest one. One month would mean she wouldn't be going to the prom with Andrew.

Her father continued on, ignoring her outburst. "The relationship with this college kid is over. If you lie to us again, you will be grounded for three months and softball is gone."

He walked off to his bedroom.

Fuck softball.

She looked at her mother pleadingly.

"You shouldn't have lied to us, Wendy."

She joined her husband.

I hate him, I really hate him.

CHAPTER TWENTY FIVE

Wendy looked down at her feet and finished giving Andrew the bad news. " . . . I'm so sorry; I really wanted to go to the prom with you."

"Don't worry about it; I really didn't want to go to the prom. I was just looking for an excuse to be with you." He looked around to see if anyone was around before taking her hand. "Wendy, I really like you; not gee she's kinda cute, but you know . . . there's just something about you that I don't see around here in anyone else. I think you feel the same way."

Wendy didn't hesitate. "I do." It came out like she was accepting his hand in matrimony.

"Then we have to bite the bullet and tell our parents."

"You think your parents will take it well?" She leaned back against the pushed-in wooden bleachers in the gymnasium and sighed.

She listened to Andrew lie—a lie not to deceive another, but instead to soften the pain of what the truth really carries. It was a lie designed to deceive himself. Maybe if he really believed it, it might just be true. Andrew thought back to three years earlier. Steven had only raised his hand to his son once in his life and that was the day after Savannah and Wendy had tussled for his son's attention.

His body was easily lifted and his back slammed against the wooden planks of the shed; the same shed that now stored his growing enterprise. A long, thick finger waggled in the air right between his eyes. He could have counted the hairs on the first knuckle of his father's finger. His attention, however, rested on the fire in his father's eyes. His father didn't get mad often, and when he did it was usually more comical than it was frightening. This was definitely the scary version of his anger. There were no mixed metaphors or his father stumbling for the right word; the message was crystal clear.

"Stay away from that girl . . . she's like your sister for Christ's sake." There wasn't even a trace of his accent or Yooper lingo, and that's how Andrew knew he was dead serious.

*   *   *

That night after practice Savannah tried to get Wendy to talk. Wendy didn't take the bait. She really missed Maggie; Maggie was almost never around. Occasionally she would come to one of their games, but for the most part she was at work or with Conner. That second semester she had gotten a co-op job working for her father. She got out of school at 12:30, drove to his office in Trenary, which was a small town twenty miles to the north, famous for their Trenary toast. The UP delicacy was nothing more than small pieces of hard toast covered with cinnamon sugar. Next to the pasty, however, it was the most famous food of Michigan's great Upper Peninsula.

"So, you going to tell me about last night?" Savannah said looking at her friend from the passenger seat.

"Nothing to tell. I told my parents I was over your place, when I was out with Andrew . . . only I told them I was with a friend of Conner's. So, if that ever comes up, please cover for my lie."

"So, are you two . . ." Savannah couldn't think of the right way to phrase things. She didn't feel the need to be girly and say something like 'romantic' or practical and say 'going out', instead she chose the blunt and coarse manner. " . . . fucking?"

"No, we are not fucking . . . we're just friends. I told you that. The guy's cool, you know . . . plus, he's like a brother, you know that."

Savannah didn't buy the logic or calmness of Wendy's response. She knew he was cool, handsome, different and *like* a brother, but *not* a brother. She was actually happy for Wendy, if in fact there was something between the two of them. The longer removed from her infatuation with Andrew, the more she realized that he was not the guy for her. The idiosyncrasies that he embraced, his counter-culture thoughts, even his intelligence were things that would have driven her mad. She *wanted* to want a guy who challenged her, one who she could have sophisticated conversations with. But the reality—at sixteen, she just wanted a guy who worshipped her and looked good. She wanted someone simple, someone like Steven. The irony did not escape her.

"You're so full of shit; drop me off at Stan's."

"What are you getting so mad about?" Wendy asked, peering over at her from the driver's seat.

"Hey, I know you probably think I still have the hots for him, but we aren't in eighth grade anymore. If you want him you should go for it . . . if you haven't already. But, shit, we're supposed to be friends. I just don't know why you won't tell me the truth."

Wendy's facial expressions softened. "There's nothing there, Savannah."

"Fine, drop me off at the drug store."

"You're pissed at me, so you want to go to the drug store?"

"No, I'm pissed at you *and* I want to go to the drug store,"

Wendy took a turn past Robin's Inn. Savannah's mother had quit her job two years earlier as an accountant for a chain store in Escanaba and purchased the bar. She had taken money that she inherited from a wealthy grandparent for her down payment. The grandfather had actually died five years earlier. One of the reasons for Savannah's parents' divorce was the bone of contention over what to do with the money. Her father, the football coach, wanted to buy a cottage in Wisconsin, or simply put the money aside for their retirement. Her mom, however, wanted to quit her job and become her own employer. The reality was that they had fallen out of love long before. He wrapped himself up into his football and teaching duties; she into whatever collecting hobby to replace her desire for her husband. Sex had been replaced by a new Hummel; romantic dinners with some odd collector plate. She would slowly spend the small fortune if necessary. Then one day she saw the local bar, the Library, with a real estate sign in front. She walked in and asked, "How much?"

She signed papers a few months later, renamed the place the Robin's Inn and her husband walked out of her life and Savannah's.

"I'll get a ride home with my mom afterward, so you can just drop me off."

"Okay," Wendy responded, pulling up to the curb.

The family drug store had been in the town for fifty years. Up to that point it had survived the mega-drug stores that existed in both Gladstone and Escanaba.

Savannah watched Wendy pull away and then sighed. She closed her eyes before she took her first step into the dingy, dirty store that had the musty smell of a place whose doors had been closed since 1952. She had been in the store three times in the past week, each time scouting the joint. She looked for one thing and one thing only; and since she didn't want anyone to know, she had no intention of paying for it. The same older lady, with hair that was in desperate need of a comb and some dye, was at the register.

The pharmacist, not named Stan, stood in the back behind the raised counter of the pharmacy filling a prescription. His eyes were down. *Good.*

Savanna turned and looked at the sign above the entrance way. *Shoplifters will be Prosecuted! No exceptions.*

Savannah had no doubt that the seriously looking man in the back of the store was in fact the man who wrote the sign and stood behind the words.

However, she didn't plan on chickening out this time around. She gulped some stale air and casually grabbed things as she walked down the aisles. Her duffle bag hung over her shoulder, the zipper opened about six inches. She looked to the back and then over her shoulder toward the cashier. She tugged on the opening of her bag, making sure that a small box could easily be dropped into it. Savannah grabbed a stick of deodorant she didn't need; not even a scent that she would like; something with berries in the name. She grabbed some toothpaste. Her mom, one to always buy things they already had plenty of, had three unused tubes sitting in the bathroom closet at home. She grabbed a few more items she didn't need or want.

Savannah finally found the only item that had any meaning to her. She reached for it and dropped it casually in the opening of her duffle bag. The small box landed in her glove, landing right on the name of Jack Morris. The glove was handed down to her by her father. He was a huge fan of the Detroit Tigers; his favorite player happened to be one of the heroes of the 1984 World Championship team, pitcher Jack Morris.

She looked over to where the pharmacist, Thomas Feister, should've been standing. He wasn't there.

Shit.

Feister's look said it all. His outstretched hand said even more. She reached into her bag and pulled out the box and placed it in his hand.

"I'm really sorry," she said sincerely.

She tried to walk past him, praying like so many others that the sign out front was just for scare tactics. No one would really prosecute over a nine dollar item. He stepped in front of her path.

"No, young lady; the cops will be coming. We prosecute everyone."

He bent his elbow back awkwardly pointing to the sign behind him.

"Another one bites the dust," the unattractive lady behind the counter said.

"Follow me," the pharmacist told Savannah.

She was in shock, trying quickly to think of what to do or say. Something had to be done to get her out of this mess. Explaining the shoplifting to someone was the least of her worries, even to her mother or coach. But, having to explain the contents of what was stolen was an overbearing burden that was quickly sinking her sanity. Her heavy breathing turned quickly to hyperventilation.

Feister helped the girl up the step into his office. He still hadn't looked at what was in his hand. "Sit down, here. Try to calm down. This isn't the end of the world . . ."

What the fuck do you know!

She tried unsuccessfully to control her breathing, but the desperate gulps for breath were overtaking her. She sat in the chair he pulled out for her as he began to dial. Tears flowed down her cheeks.

There was no local police, not even a sheriff. The town was under the jurisdiction of the State Police. The same officers that were assigned to busting small fish like Andrew Fonduluc and finding his big fish supplier were also the ones who routinely had to answer the calls of the small town pharmacist with the overzealous moral code. Feister looked in his hand; the sweat moistening the box. He read the contents and set the phone down on the third ring.

"What do you need this for?" He stared at the early pregnancy test.

"Whhaaaaa . . . . ddddddooo . . . . you think?" Savannah sobbed. She wiped away tears from her eyes, but not fast enough to get rid of them. Her fist was like a wiper on low during a rainstorm; useless.

"Honey, stealing isn't right, no matter what the reason?" He closed his eyes and shook his head. "Do you have money to pay for this?"

"Yyyyyyeeesssss."

The useless wiper of a hand was still at work. However, this sudden change in tone from the insensitive pharmacist and the words he chose did not escape her. The speed of tears slowed down to a drip. *Hope . . . I still have hope.*

"Do you really need this other shit . . . . stuff?"

"No," she responded, finally looking at the man. "I'm just praying that I'm not in trouble, you know?"

He nodded.

"I should have just paid for the thing, but I didn't want anyone knowing my business."

"Understood," he said to the town's star. He walked over to the register and scanned the EPT kit. *$10.01.* "Ten dollars."

"I have the penny," Savannah said, trying to stop the smile of relief that wanted to spread across her face like an uncontrollable spider crack on glass. She lost the battle, the smile was there.

"That's okay."

Savannah walked down the steps of the pharmacy area with a small little brown paper bag that contained what she hoped would put her fears to rest; but knew deep down would cause her nothing but regret and heartache. She had no idea of the extent of the pain, or of the damage it would cause so many people. Savannah walked past the cashier, who suddenly stopped chewing her gum. Her mouth was agape. Seeing Savannah walk out was like watching a man on death roll just stroll out of prison as if he were on a leisurely Sunday walk.

The bitch musta gave him a BJ. "Son of a bitch!" she muttered loud enough for the little old lady standing in front of her waiting for her to ring the rest of her items up.

"Excuse me," the lady stammered, putting a hand to her chest to show her shock.

The cashier ignored the old geezer, her mind was on her nephew who did not escape the dickhead pharmacist's *We prosecute Everyone!* policy.

Savannah walked out of the bright sunshine and into the dimly lit bar, squinting and wishing her eyes would adjust faster. *Funny how life could send a "Daddy's girl" running for Mom.* There she was, on a bar stool, a half-empty rum and coke in front of her and flirting with a guy ten years her junior.

"Mom," Savannah said barely above a whisper. Her mom did not respond. "Mom," she said louder, finding her voice.

"Hi, honey." *She didn't even turn around.* Ignoring the stares of the bar patrons, Savannah perched next to her, glad to see the 'drinking heads' turn back to their beers as quickly and naturally as geese turning to bread crumbs.

Savannah leaned close. "Mom."

"In a second, honey."

Never mind. Savannah headed for the bathroom. Moments later she was still there, sitting in a stall, her sweats and underwear around her ankles. She hadn't been to church since she was a toddler, but squeezing her eyes shut, she prayed. *If you're up there . . . please. I need a minus.*

Sticking the little white stick between her legs, she let the urine flow, then pulled it up and stared at the little rectangle on the end of the stick. *C'mon, c'mon, c'mon.* The directions on the back of the box said to wait two minutes. It seemed to take an eternity.

Fuck. She stared at the little plus sign for the next half hour. *Guess I'm only allowed one miracle a day.* When she headed back into the bar, she saw her mother still flirting; too busy to pay any attention to a kid who might need her.

She strolled by just in time to see the young pharmaceutical salesman hand her a pen advertising a new birth control product. *Now that's fucking irony!*

CHAPTER TWENTY SIX

Wendy lay on her back reading when she felt a sudden vibration from beneath her pillow. She flipped herself over and grabbed the vibrating cell phone. Andrew gave it to her after she was grounded. They spoke nearly every night.

"Hey."

She spoke at a level just above a whisper as she crept to her door to see if anyone, especially her father, was in the kitchen. Her room was in the worst possible position it could be; right between the entranceway and the bait shop. Her father walked through her room more than a dozen times a day.

"Hey," Andrew answered back. "Can you talk?"

Wendy plopped herself on the bed, then adjusted the phone as she lie on her side. "Yes." She couldn't contain her smile. His voice alone could change her worst mood.

Their conversation went on for hours. She listened to him tell her of his plans once he graduated.

"I'm not going to be a drug dealer forever, you know."

"I know," Wendy responded. She did not know, but hoped that Andrew was smart enough to know that he couldn't beat the odds forever.

"My supplier wants me to take over for him next year. I'm going to go to Michigan Tech . . ."

"Where's he going?" Wendy pushed the hair back from her forehead as she interrupted him.

"He's going to Amsterdam for a year. Says he wants to live the life of an addict for a change instead of only supplying them. I swear the guy totally creeps me out, but the money is good . . . and next year I will make enough money to leave this shit-town forever."

Wendy's heart sank. "I see." She tried to sound as upbeat as she could. "Hey, I've got to get to bed. I have a Chem test tomorrow." She wasn't sure how well she hid her sudden dejection.

"But I'm not done with my story," Andrew responded.

Wendy smiled. His tone told her that she would like the rest of it. "Please, go on."

"Thank you," he chuckled. "I want you to come with me. You, me and my guitar. Anywhere you want. How does that sound?"

"I love you." Wendy pressed her tongue over her upper lip and tasted the saltiness of the tears that had made their way down past her cheek.

"So, you're in?"

Wendy moved her head up and down then laughed, realizing he could not *hear* a nod. "Oh, I'm in."

"Good . . . and I love you too."

"Play me a song," she demanded.

"What does the lady want to hear?"

"Surprise me."

Wendy laughed and cried the whole song.

"*. . . We gotta get out while we're young . . . Cause tramps like us, baby we were born to run . . . yes, girl we were . . . Wendy let me in I wanna be your friend . . .*"

*   *   *

Savannah told no one of her dilemma, actually blocking it out to the point of nearly forgetting about it. Her memory of the child developing inside her came back with a vengeance when she took a wild pitch from a girl who threw nearly as hard as she did, directly into her side. It hurt like hell, and left stitching marks from the ball. Her first reaction was, *oh, my God! My baby!*

She walked down to first base clutching her side.

Steven marched along side her. "Are you okay, are you okay?"

"Yeah, yeah. Go sit down, I'm fine."

She knew that Steven was only concerned about his potential state championship, not the life of a fetus he had no knowledge of. She stared back at the pitcher who plunked her and showed no remorse. *You think that hurts, bitch? Wait!*

The next inning, it was the other pitcher's turn to take a fastball to the body. Savannah threw a riser that just kept rising right toward the face of the opposing pitcher. Had she actually let the pitch hit her, she would have only suffered a nasty bruise to the shoulder. But, instead she held out her hand which deflected the ball up, smashing right into her mouth and knocking out her front tooth.

Wendy stood near second base and had a perfect view of the incident. She cringed. "That sucks," she said as she watched madness unfurl.

A girl from the other team stood on second base with her arms crossed. "If you ask me, she deserves it. Might actually shut her up."

Wendy smiled at her. She loved honesty.

Blood dripped in a steady flow from the girl's mouth. The other team's coach, a portly woman, ran out as fast as she could to check on her star player. She alternated between checking on her player's condition and thrusting out an accusing finger at Savannah.

"She did that on purpose! Kick her out, Blue! Kick her out," she screamed to the umpire.

"I don't know that she did it on purpose," the umpire lied.

He knew, but was old school. Tit for tat, the other girl had certainly plunked Savannah on purpose; she had already taken her deep for her fifth home run of the season.

While the clamor over whether to kick Savannah out or not went on, others tried to help the injured girl out. A trainer applied an ice pack to her mouth. No one noticed that the girl had lost a tooth, except for the girl herself and the catcher for Rapid Junction. The girl who had replaced Carly Johnson, was a sophomore named Henrietta Stanford; Hennie to everyone. She was a funny kid, the kind who says goofy things without realizing it. Everyone would laugh at her faux pas or butchering of the English language. She was high school softball's version of Yogi Berra.

While Steven argued with the other coach over whether Savannah should be kicked out; while Wendy and the girl on second base shared slap hitting techniques; while the pitcher for the other team sobbed and regretted her beaning of Savannah; Hennie was down on her knees sifting through the dirt for the missing tooth. She looked like a panhandler who found the illusive gold as she jumped up with the dirt covered nugget firmly in hand.

"Got it!"

She was ignored as the chaos continued. The little woman jabbed a finger into Steven's chest as he laughed. The umpire warned her that she was going to be the one who got tossed if she didn't calm down.

Hennie ran to the small bleachers and hollered out, "Duth anyone have any milk! Or onge juice, onge juice will do, too!"

The thirty fans that sat in the small set of bleachers or in lawn chairs; stared at the goofy kid with the braces and lisp. She spotted a seven-year-old, who had a juice box. *98% real juice*, it read. *That'll do*, she thought to herself as she snatched the box from the kid. She tore open the box and deposited the quickly drying, dirt-stained tooth into the 98% orange juice full of plenty of vitamin D. She ran back around the backstop to the regretful pitcher with the busted mouth.

"Here," Hennie said, grabbing the tooth out of the juice box.

The tooth was once again pearly white, and more importantly contained the much needed moisture and vitamin D that was provided by the orange juice. The girl took the tooth and stared at it, not knowing what she was expected to do with it. *What is this, some kind of souvenir?*

"Well, put it in!" Hennie's smile was a mile wide. She stood with her hand on her hips as the sun reflected off her braces.

"She's right," the trainer said, embarrassed that he hadn't thought of it.

The girl put the tooth into the freshly rinsed spot where it once sat proudly. She tried to smile as she felt her gums absorb the tooth. She grimaced; her mouth still hurt like hell.

She tried to thank Hennie, but it came out, "Tans."

The small crowd cheered the girl as she walked to her bench. Hennie, believing she was the one who really deserved the cheer, bowed to the crowd.

She grabbed her face mask and put it back on. "Play ball!" she screamed.

"Hey, that's my line," the umpire said, amused.

*   *   *

Andrew pulled the grey rippled tubing of the carwash vacuum cleaner from his truck. He set it back on the steel U-shaped latch, before leaning into his console and grabbing a fast food bag. He tossed the bag into the large rusted out garbage barrel. He didn't notice the sticky note stuck to the bottom of the bag.

He hopped up into his truck and pulled up to the exit. He looked both ways before pushing his foot on the accelerator. His mammoth glistening truck, the envy of his peers, darted down US 2. He headed back to his house to watch his sister leave for the prom.

The blue police car across the street didn't go after the speeder. Instead, it crossed over to the carwash and parked next to the barrel with chipped blue paint.

*   *   *

Conner pulled up the long driveway in a Purple Camaro. He hesitated before he opened the door. Andrew stood in front of his truck with his arms folded. Conner sighed, but knew that Andrew was the most sane, and least to fear of the Fonduluc clan. He opened the door and stepped out of the low riding sports car. The coolness of the air conditioned vehicle was immediately replaced by the sticky humidity of the warm May evening. Sweat seemed to jump out of his pores and on to his skin. He felt his undershirt stick to his skin.

Andrew approached him. "Dude, she's going to be a while, do you mind?" He motioned toward the door.

"No, hop in," Conner replied.

He hadn't had too many meaningful conversations with Andrew, but knew he was about to have one. Andrew sat behind the wheel; then motioned for Conner to hop in the passenger side. Conner smiled; the protective brother coolly controlled the situation. *This guy would make one helluva coach.* He walked around and opened the door and sat on the elegant leather upholstery. Andrew held out his hand and smiled; Conner put the keys in his hand and shook his head. *This guy is good.* Andrew put the key in the ignition and revved the engine. His grin expanded.

"Nice, eh?"

"Yep," Conner replied.

"Listen, we could sit here and bullshit about the amount of horsepower this bad boy has, or the size of the engine, top speed and all that other shit, but I really only have one thing to say to you."

Conner thought about stopping him and reassuring him that he was a good guy and had nothing but respect for his sister, but decided to let the guy have his moment.

"And that would be?"

"I think you love my sister as much as I do, so I won't be a dick about this. Just take care of her, okay . . . always."

"I can do that."

"Alright, then!"

Andrew backed the car up in an adjacent concrete parking space. Conner turned his head to see the car narrowly miss a pole that held a rusted out basketball hoop. Conner didn't bat an eyelash as Andrew thrust the gear shift forward into drive and slammed his foot down on the accelerator. The tires squealed and left their mark black and long on the cement of the driveway outside of the four-car garage.

Andrew slammed on the brakes when he got near the end of their three hundred yard long driveway. Conner saw the menacing eyes of Paul La Claire fixed directly on Andrew. Marie grabbed her heart, and sighed. Wendy pointed an accusing finger at Andrew and bit her lip as she smiled.

Andrew pulled alongside the truck and rolled down his window. "Sorry, Uncle Paul, I just gotta see what this thing can do. Hey, Aunt Marie."

"Just don't kill your sister's date, okay?" Marie joked.

"That would be bad," Andrew agreed.

Then he slammed his foot on the accelerator again and the Camaro fishtailed down the road. Conner put his hands behind his head and relaxed. The needle on the speedometer passed 120 mph as they careened down US 2. He was a goalie, and a good one; always ice water in his veins.

Maggie's prom was a family affair that rivaled only a woman's wedding in terms of pomp and circumstance. Steven snapped pictures of everything and everyone, as directed by Melissa. Wendy and Andrew waited by the kitchen, only inches away from each other. Wendy had her arms crossed as she bounced back and forth between extreme jealousy and agonizing anticipation. She settled on agonizing anticipation. It wasn't Maggie's fault she couldn't go to the prom. *It was his!* She glared over at her father, who sat out of place in Steven's expensive black leather chair. *Come on, Mags!*

Maggie's dress had only been described to her; she was dying to see what she looked like in it. The purple dress had ruffles on the sleeves that hung just over her shoulders, and black satin ribbon that traced the edges of the hem of the dress. Purchased from an Escanaba specialty store that designed wedding dresses, it came with a hefty price tag.

As much as it killed Wendy to wait, she knew it must have been twice as bad for Conner. He stood next to the kitchen island alone. Sweat beaded on his forehead. The corsage in his hand wilted in the heat.

Wendy caressed Andrew's arm without even realizing it. She looked down and saw that his hand was on top of hers. They exchanged quick glances. Wendy knew that it was too dangerous and removed her hand. Andrew made it difficult, hanging on just long enough to make Wendy's heart beat a little faster. Between the feel of his touch and the danger involved, she struggled to contain her breathing.

Everyone stopped their chatter as they heard footsteps, then their sounds turned to irritating annoyance as they saw it was only Savannah. Savannah returned their displeasure with a scowl and the middle finger. She stopped at the bottom of the stairs and spoke to Steven for the first time that evening.

"Your wife is insane."

Marie laughed, "Sweetheart, there are two days when a woman gets to be insane, her daughter's first prom and her wedding."

Wendy bit her lip as her mother looked her way.

Marie turned back to Savannah. "So, I would just stay out of her way."

"Oh, I am. Trust me." Savannah stepped over Paul, who rocked away in Steven's comfy recliner and sat down alone on the L-shaped sofa.

"Just cake it on, let's accent those baby blues."

"Get out!" Melissa was done with the advice.

Savannah, who despite her tomboy athletic ways, was always dolled up; even when delivering a 60 mph pitch. She refused to wear a visor, always had a new ribbon in her hair, caked on the eyeliner to make her green eyes 'pop,' and even added a little flair with the occasional glitter added to her thickly applied eye shadow. It was humiliating enough to walk back to the bench having struck out for the third time that day, but to have it done by a girl who could be walking down a runway? Throw in her attitude and she was by far the most hated player around.

Savannah stormed off.

Melissa took her time; she didn't want to share the moment with anyone else, not even Steven. As she looked at her daughter, who sat silently and stared back at her mother from a seated position on her bed; she couldn't help but allow her eyes to reveal rare tenderness. A track of tears slowly slid down her cheeks. Her eyes, watery and red, still showed extreme happiness.

"You've always been beautiful, but tonight . . ." Melissa wiped the tears from her eyes, unable to finish her sentence.

"Thanks, Mom." Maggie dabbed her eyes with a soaked tissue. "Don't make me cry again."

Melissa endured endless surgeries with Maggie and spent so many nights with her arms wrapped around her daughter in one hospital bed after another. She suffered through endless trips to speech therapists and hammered home what true beauty meant in one lecture after another to her daughter. Melissa's eyes wandered from her daughter's eyes to the scar that traced its way up like a snake to her nose. It was an unnecessary scar caused by a shoddy surgeon. Melissa touched the scar with her thumb, then leaned in and kissed her daughter gently on the lips, careful not to smear her lavender colored lipstick.

Moments later Maggie appeared at the foot of the stairwell. She walked slowly; first giving her lover a glimpse of her tanned legs, then of the beginnings of her satin dress and on up to the top where her breasts swelled under the soft, lacy material. She giggled as she saw his jaw drop along with the corsage.

He quickly picked up the ill flower and approached her as she landed on the final step. Neither of them heard the clamoring of the others. For the first, but certainly not the last time that evening, Maggie felt as if no one else existed. She looked down at the tender hands of her lover. They calmly and easily fastened the dying white corsage to her dress. Maggie looked up into Conner's pale blue eyes as he rested his forehead on hers, before finally kissing her quickly. Then he was pushed out of the way. Maggie jumped back.

"Move it, Romeo!" Wendy said. "You get her the rest of the night." Maggie took a deep breath as Wendy put her hands in hers. "You have never looked more beautiful."

"She's hot, idn't she?" Savannah added.

"Hey, little girl, smile perty, eh?" Steven held the camera out toward his daughter.

Maggie turned and stuck out her tongue. Click. Years later Maggie would stare at that picture for fifteen minutes, before returning to her mission of finding pictures of a dead woman.

Maggie received a dozen hugs from everyone in the room, including the unaffectionate Paul, before she and Conner left for their *Evening With the Stars*. They walked out to the rented Purple Camaro that Conner had for the evening. The vehicle would never be paid for; it was a gift from a Marquette Chevy dealer who happened to be a big fan of Northern Michigan's talented goalie. It also happened to be an NCAA violation; but Conner didn't care. Compared to guys like Tomas Peterson, his onetime infraction was small potatoes.

The festive mood ended after the happy couple left. Savannah made no attempt at joining the small talk exchanged by the remaining members of the diminishing party. Wendy was at the store with Andrew on an 'errand.' She realized that she was jealous of both Maggie and Wendy. Both were currently *free* with their lovers. Hers sat on his stupid recliner, flanked by his wife. She glared over at Steven. She suddenly felt old, way too old for a teenager to feel. She knew that she wouldn't be going to this prom or any other in the future. Her future lay inside of her; she no longer had the luxury of being young and carefree. She felt bitter. *You better make this alright, mister.* Steven held her gaze for a few seconds before turning to Paul.

*   *   *

"That girl looks at you like a scorned lover," Melissa accused.

"Oh, you crazy, woman," Steven guffawed, although his heart raced madly. He took a huge drink of his beer. "She looks at me like dat because she thinks I'm da big bad coach, that's all."

*   *   *

Savannah plodded up to her bedroom at nine. She threw herself onto her canopy bed and grabbed a magazine. She was not a reader, at least not of books. She finished a *Teen Beat* magazine, exposing an immature teenager that desperately needed to hang on to what was left of her youth. Afterward she masturbated. She had never even thought about doing something like that before she got hooked up with Steven. That, however, was something that turned him on more than anything else. She would pull down her sweats or shorts in the equipment shed and begin fondling herself as he unzipped his pants and took care of his own needs.

Since their sabbatical from each other began; masturbation became a regular part of her life. She pictured Steven and his magnificent penis looking down on her; within minutes she would have an orgasm, but never a fulfilling one.

She threw down the magazine, sighed heavily and then touched her belly. It was too early to actually feel life; she was only nine weeks pregnant, but she *could* feel it. She briefly contemplated aborting the fetus inside her and not telling Steven a thing. Those thoughts were short lived. While researching for her and Wendy's Government class project she stumbled upon an article about a female college basketball player who had a baby in high school, but was still recruited to play at a major college. She somehow managed to raise a child, go to school and play basketball. Savannah printed out the article, and the African American girl became her role model.

* * *

At ten o'clock Wendy told her mother that she was going to bed. Her mother tried to take her mind off things by playing two handed Euchre, one of their favorite games. Her mom always, always won. Wendy appreciated the fact that her mother had allowed her to win three straight times. She told Marie that she was tired and was going to try to finish a book she was reading; but truthfully she just wanted to get away from everyone and feel sorry for herself. Even her father had tried to be unusually cheerful, offering to take her out on the boat and do some fishing; something that had bonded them when she was younger. It was during these times that she learned to forgive her father for his earlier imperfections. But, now, she just wanted to hate her father like so many other teenage girls across the world. *I can always forgive him tomorrow.* She had no idea that it would be over twelve years before she would finally accomplish forgiveness.

Wendy picked up *The Stand* by Steven King and turned to a page near the end of the book. She read a lot since her series of groundings began. Her English teacher raved about the tale between good and evil. She was right; it was a great book and would become one of her favorites of all time, but she couldn't get into it that evening. She found herself reading and re-reading the same pages over and over again; picturing Flagg, the man who represented evil, as her father.

Tap . . . tap . . . tap. The sound at the window startled Wendy. The motel and adjoining house and bait shop had nothing but woods behind it. She put her hand to her heart, but knew exactly who had made the noise. She pulled the chord, raising the blinds. There he stood, peering in. He raised his eyebrows and waved, despite actually only being one foot from her.

"Nerd," Wendy said quietly. *I love you so much.* An immediate thought preoccupied her entire being as she lifted her window. *This night will not end well, there's just no way.* She had no desire, however, to slam the window back down and wave him away.

"Let's go," he ordered.

"Hold on," Wendy replied.

She turned and slowly opened her bedroom door, listening for sounds. She heard the sound of the television in the background, but nothing else. She tiptoed out toward the kitchen; she could see the glow of the television on in the living room. All the other lights were off; then came the unmistakable sounds of her parents alternating snores. Her father sat in his small and uncomfortable recliner. He let out a snort, then a soft snore. From her parent's bedroom came a much louder rattling type sound. Wendy didn't even know if you could call it snoring; it was a sound like no other. It was part chain saw and part rattle snake; a loud whinny sound, followed by a rattle that would send any desert animal running for its life.

She turned back and headed to her bedroom. Andrew lie on her bed with his legs crossed and the King book open in front of him. He moved the book from his face. "Great book, you ready?"

"Almost," she replied seductively.

He threw the thick novel on the floor as Wendy threw herself on top of him. She reached down and stroked his penis from outside of his cargo shorts. Instantly, it rose to full attention. She pressed her lips against his as if in attack mode. She had her way for about five minutes before he sat up. She fought his urges to push her off, but finally his strength was too much.

"Easy, girl." He stood and zipped up.

Wendy followed suit and pulled her frazzled hair back against her head, as she adjusted the rubber band that had kept her hair fairly neat before her sexual attack on Andrew. "I've got to change my underwear."

Andrew laughed. Wendy threw daggers his way with her own eyes. He threw his hand to his mouth to contain the laughter. Her eyes held no anger or real annoyance. The smile wouldn't leave her face if someone tried to pry it off with a crowbar. She decided to give Andrew a preview of what he had in store. She pushed him back down on the bed, and put a finger to her mouth shushing any possible sound he might want to make. She began a dance that involved no music. Her hips swayed and her hands wandered across her body. Her eyes, her incredible blue eyes, never left Andrew's.

Wendy put both hands on the bottom of her plain t-shirt and teased Andrew as she playfully pulled it up revealing the bottom of her bra, then pulling it down—all the time swaying her hips in perfect unison with a song that had no name, but existed in both of their minds. The teasing ended, and the shirt came off. She swung it around two times, then tossed it in his lap.

She wasted no time with her bra. She unsnapped it from the front and dropped it to the floor. She quickly put her hands over her breasts and her nipples quickly doubled their length and hardened in the excitement of being free and being the object of an 18-year-old's horny affection. Andrew swallowed hard. Wendy turned her back on him. The beautiful music still playing in their minds; she held her breasts with her back still to him. She turned around inches away from him and took his hands off of his lap and placed them firmly on her perfectly shaped tits. They weren't large and they weren't small—they were just right. Andrew's eyes locked in on his hands as they softly caressed the tender flesh of her tits. His thumbs and forefingers instinctively found her nipples.

Wendy let him fondle her as she continued her seduction. She closed her eyes and ran her fingers through her hair, causing her rubber band to come loose and fly across the room as it reached the last strand of her brown wavy hair. After a few more seconds, however, she pulled back a few feet and shook a finger his way. *No, no; naughty boy.* Her grinding continued as she stuck both thumbs inside the lining of her blue and white checkered boxer shorts, also catching the inside of her panties. She pulled them down slightly; first one side, then the other. Her left side exposed, then her right; then left, then right again. Finally, more soft white skin was exposed as her little boxer dance continued. She pulled the left side down far enough that her smooth ass cheek was exposed. She turned in a full circle, alternating which cheek he got to see; finally pulling down both sides so that he got a perfect view of her complete ass. It was every bit as perfect as her breasts.

Wendy could hear Andrew's breathing get heavier. He couldn't stop gulping as new parts of her anatomy were being introduced. She turned back into him and took his hands and placed them on her firm buttocks.

She played with his hair as he stared up at her tits and squeezed her ass. Wendy knew he wanted to take her right then and there. She could feel the heat from his hands. She backed away just as he was about to grab her and throw her on the bed. The 'naughty boy' finger came back out. She twisted, grinded and backed her way to her dresser, where with her ass half out of her underwear and boxers, she grabbed a pair of fresh panties, a pair of jeans, a t-shirt and a new bra. She set them down on top of her dresser. Wendy turned around and slowly wiggled out of her underwear as she lowered them to the floor. She followed Andrew's eyes, knowing they were in sensory overload. They took in her breasts; they begged for her to turn around and give him another glimpse of her sweet ass, although now her sweet womanhood stared back at him. The music came to a screeching halt. She grabbed her clothes and ran into the bait shop.

She laughed as she heard Andrew groan in the other room. He plopped down on the bed and covered his eyes. In the bait shop, with tadpoles as her only live audience; she slipped into her fresh clothes.

*   *   *

The DJ played *I'll Be* by Edwin McCain as Conner leaned down and kissed Maggie as passionately as he had the first time. Boys danced with their dates; but looked at Maggie, wondering why they hadn't seen her beauty before tonight. Girls looked over their date's shoulders and wondered why she was so lucky; some convinced that he was nothing more than a 'charity chaser,' others just jealous that she was with a 'man' and not a boy.

CHAPTER TWENTY SEVEN

Wendy put her head through the opening of the sunroof of Andrew's truck and felt the unusual warmth of the May air rush past her face. She loved the cool sensation. The carefree teenager stretched her arms out through the window and began another dance for her love. Andrew placed his hand on her bottom and stroked the back of her jeans as he sang to the tune on the radio.

"*Love is . . . it's what I got*," he crooned.

After, the *Sublime* song ended, Wendy pulled herself back into the cab and sat down. She turned her body and leaned against the passenger side door. She put her legs over Andrew's lap and gazed longingly at him. She took in everything about him; his smile, his scent, his physique. There was nothing about Andrew that didn't seem ideal to her.

"What?" Andrew finally asked, alternating his eyes between the road and Wendy.

Wendy shook her head, slowly; still taking in her idea of 'perfection.'

"I've got to take care of some business; then we are off to our spot," Andrew said.

Wendy reached over and took Andrew's free hand. "That sounds good." She knew exactly what *spot* he was referring to.

He was supposed to meet Todd Sexton, his supplier, at midnight. He wasn't planning on the seduction. He arrived at the Michigan Tech campus house at a quarter to one. He never noticed the headlights of the Impala that had followed him for the previous two hours, driving a nice, safe five hundred yards behind.

Once the big red F-150 passed any turnoff to Northern Michigan, the two Michigan State Police detectives working overtime knew where he was headed.

"Tech," Lieutenant Dan O' Reilly told his partner, Trooper Peter Mackey.

"Yep," he responded.

They were now less than fifty yards behind the truck as it entered the Houghton, Michigan campus. Officially being summer break, there was not much traffic or social life at nearly one in the morning. Andrew pulled up to the same driveway he had pulled up into nearly two dozen times in the past year and a half.

"Andrew?" Wendy asked, now sitting upright and leaning in toward her boyfriend. He turned and looked at her as he placed his vehicle in park. "Do you really think you will be able to quit?"

He did not answer right away. "Give me one year. Wendy, we will have enough money to do anything we want; or at least make a life for ourselves." He leaned in toward her.

Wendy loved the feel of his fingers as they combed through her hair. She loved the touch of his lips against hers even more. She had no idea that it would be the last time she ever experienced either sensation.

Andrew warned Wendy that Todd Sexton was a showoff, especially for pretty young girls. Sexton led her into his basement and turned on a light. "You've got to check this out; I guarantee you've never seen anything like this."

Wendy looked to Andrew, who gave her the 'it's okay look.' They followed him down the rickety stairs. She looked around very unimpressed. All she saw in the old basement of the Victorian house that once belonged to an engineering professor was dirty laundry and a bunch of junk that generations of people had not been able to get rid of. Sexton kept a steady gait toward the back of the dank cellar. He turned back once to look at Wendy. The guy freaked her out. She wasn't sure if it was his translucent skin or the severe acne that bothered her most. Mostly, she quickly decided, it was his eyes. They reminded her of the bugged out eyes of a lab rat that had had one too many experiments performed on it.

He put a key into a door toward the back of the musky basement, turned again and peered at Wendy. "You ready?"

"Yep," she smiled. She wasn't, she didn't know what to expect. Having never really been exposed to much in the way of illegal drug operations, she couldn't help but visualize a few tables with some pots on it and the unmistakable green marijuana plants sticking up.

When the door opened, she had to look away at first. The lights were so bright. Once her eyes adjusted to the brilliant lights, she couldn't help but blurt out, "Oh my!"

The sight of the 600-watt, high pressure, sodium lamps that lit up the room better than the lights of a major league baseball field; truly amazed her. The room was painted all white and oscillating fans whirred and turned in all directions. There were literally rows upon rows of marijuana growing in the room.

The room was a secret addition that was put in during the 1950s bomb shelter building era. In all, the room stretched sixty feet deep. There were over five hundred plants in all, with different strains of marijuana. She was right about what the plants would look like, but completely wrong about the size. She couldn't believe how high the marijuana plants grew. She pictured the little plants they grew in science class during middle school. She was so proud when the zinnia plant poked through the soil back in the seventh grade. Wendy could certainly understand why the Toad would be so proud of this science experiment.

"Oh, my; indeed," he exclaimed. He walked over to a black box in the corner next to an electrical panel box. "You see this?"

"Yeah," Wendy answered.

"This little transformer here scrambles the electrical meter," he smiled proudly. "Otherwise my electrical bill would be close to two grand a month, which obviously would alert old Consumers Power."

"Obviously," Andrew muttered.

Wendy knew he was antsy. He hadn't stopped checking the time on his cell phone since the moment they arrived.

"What's that?" Todd asked. He moved toward Andrew.

Wendy didn't like the way he stared down Andrew.

"This is all going to be yours next year. You don't want it anymore?" He threw his hands in the air. The Toad's smile was completely gone, replaced by a menacing snarl.

"Todd, we've just got to go is all. She's got to get back home."

"Alright, but let's smoke a little first." His grin was back.

Wendy sighed. There was something seriously wrong with the guy.

"Okay, but let's do it quickly. I'm tired, and we've got to go."

They walked out of the room. Todd was the last to leave. Wendy turned to see him look back at the room like a nostalgic boyfriend taking in his last glance of his 'true love.' He locked the door and followed the other two up the stairs.

Wendy jerked upright when she heard the sudden pounding on the door. Her heart stopped when she heard, "Open up, Michigan State Police!"

Wendy clutched Andrew's arm and closed her eyes as the Toad ran back down the stairs to his sanctuary. She heard the locks snap shut. She opened her eyes when she heard the front door bust open. Wendy's grip on Andrew tightened.

"Don't say a word to the police, not a word. Do you understand?" he said calmly.

Wendy nodded, but she didn't understand. She didn't understand anything that was happening. She just wished she had slammed her window shut, turned down the blinds and told him to go away. This was the kind of trouble that was going to lead to a lot more than a month-long grounding. She expected to be taken away in handcuffs.

They stood at the step of the stairway as the police rushed toward them. O'Reilly approached them first. "Put your hands on your head," he barked.

Wendy refused to let go of Andrew as he followed directions. Her eyes firmly set on Mackey and the .40-caliber Glock pistol the state policeman was pointing at them. *This is not a nice man.* Her opinion of him was confirmed when less than a second later he ripped her off of Andrew. She fell to the hardwood floor.

The Michigan State policemen ignored her temporarily as Mackey threw Andrew up against the wall and pulled his arms back behind his back and snapped the handcuffs onto his wrists.

Wendy pushed herself up against the wall and screamed. "You don't have to hurt him!"

"Where's Sexton!" Mackey screamed.

"Downstairs," Andrew responded through gritted teeth.

Wendy knew he was suffering. She couldn't tell if it was the mental or physical anguish that caused his current facial expression. "Leave him alone!" she screamed again.

"Is he armed?" O'Reilly asked more calmly.

"I don't think so," Andrew answered softly. "I think he locked himself in his nursery."

Wendy remained ignored as O'Reilly read Andrew his rights. What struck her was the first two words the Statie used. *"Andrew Fonduluc, you are under arrest. You have the right . . ."* This was no accident. It wasn't just a matter of being in the wrong place at the wrong time; his arrest was imminent.

Mackey and two sheriff deputies carefully scaled the stairs with pistols holstered.

Two different State officers took Andrew and Wendy out the doors. Wendy was not cuffed.

"Call my parents," Andrew began. "The number is . . ."

Why the hell are you telling me a number I have known since I was ten? Hey, that's not the right number.

Wendy cried out when they pushed her into a different police car than Andrew. She threw her hands over her eyes and sobbed uncontrollably.

By the time Mackey and the deputies got to the nursery, the unmistakable sound of a pistol went off. Wendy jolted upright at the sound. She continued to cry, but it was now a whimper.

Despite his best efforts, Mackey could not kick in the door. Five minutes later they were taking an axe to it. When they walked in they were nearly as impressed as Wendy was at the sight. Mackey immediately came up with a sum for the value of the illegal substance in his head; *quarter of a million.* He wasn't even close. The value reported to the papers was closer to a half a million.

It wasn't hard to find Todd. They all could easily see the red and grey matter splattered against the far wall. Slumped against the white wall was Todd Sexton, the brilliant son of a widower and professor. Long ignored and left to his own devices, he would finally have his father's attention.

A pleasant deputy sheriff managed to get Wendy calmed down to the point that she could even smile a little. The stout woman, who filled out her tan uniform to the point that she almost busted through the seams, told Wendy about her two-year-old son who had managed to get his head stuck through the bars on her stairway railing.

"We kept putting butter and baby oil, anything slick we could think of on that poor boy's head. He looked like a greased pig, I tell ya."

The woman had one leg up on a chair as Wendy sat in the visitor's room trying hard to smile, which was difficult. Between her impending doom and thoughts of what was happening to Andrew, she was nearly out of her mind. She sipped on the soda that the woman had bought for her.

"How did you get his head out?" Wendy asked, trying to express both real interest for the lady's sake as well as hopefully getting to the point where she might actually be truly distracted.

"My husband had to cut the, oh what do you call them," the woman was looking for the word baluster. "The posts, or whatever they are called. My son hadn't cried up to that point, but when he saw my husband coming up with a saw he started screaming bloody murder."

Wendy laughed with sincerity, more because of the storyteller's own uncontrollable laughter than the story itself.

"No, Daddy, no. I'll be a good boy." She wiped the tears from her eyes, she was laughing so hard. "Wendy?"

Neither heard the buzzing sound. Wendy's laughter came to an abrupt halt when she saw her father's face. She could barely make out her mother who stood only inches away from Paul. Her father's eyes had her full attention. *If looks could kill, I'd have coins on my eyes.*

Paul and Marie had been awakened by a call from Deputy Sheriff Sandra Collins at a little after two in the morning.

"That's impossible, my daughter is sleeping in her bed," Marie said, almost unintelligibly. Paul rose as if he had been awake for hours instead of only seconds. He bolted for his daughter's room and threw on her light. She was gone. Within minutes she and Marie were in their truck and on US 41.

"I'm going to kill that boy," he muttered. He was referring to a made-up college guy that Wendy had created. He just assumed when the lady said he was with a boy who had been arrested; it had to be 'that guy she was warned to stay away from.'

"You are not, relax," Marie replied. "Besides, we're going to kill Wendy. That boy is someone else's problem."

"You must be the La Claires." The deputy sheriff held out her hand.

Marie normally would have been embarrassed by her husband's current lack of manners. He ignored the woman's outstretched hand and set his eyes firmly on Wendy, who continued to stare down at an empty soda can. Marie finally accepted the portly lady's handshake and spoke for the two.

"Yes, I'm Marie and this is Paul." She turned her attention to her daughter. "And that one belongs to us."

"I know you're both mad right now, and rightfully so; but, I think she really is a good kid who just got caught up with the wrong boy. She'll straighten herself out, wontcha, Wendy?"

Wendy finally looked up and nodded.

Paul spoke his only words. "Is she free to go?"

"Yes."

"Who is this boy?" Marie asked.

Deputy Sheriff Collins did not get a chance to answer. Another buzzing sound went off. Steven and Melissa entered the county jail waiting area. Marie had her answer.

Melissa and Steven walked past their friends like they were ghosts straight to the desk where another deputy sheriff was working; the one who buzzed them in.

The shock of seeing each other in this most unexpected setting was nothing like friends who run into each other on vacations half way around the world. No one said, *oh my God, what are the odds?*

"Let's go," Paul ordered.

Wendy and Marie followed. Marie wanted to find out what was going on with Andrew; she wanted to be a good friend. But the empty feeling in her gut; put there by the thought of what might have transpired between her daughter and Andrew; or even had been going on between the two, was too much to deal with. She didn't even realize that her feet were moving.

Paul put the key in the passenger side door and opened it up to allow Marie and his daughter in. It was clear that Wendy was to be put smack dab in the middle of the two, with no possibility of escaping. Wendy started to step into the truck when she was suddenly jerked back by the back of her shirt. Paul held her by the collar and raised a fist.

"Paul, have you lost your mind?" Marie screamed.

She reached out to pull Paul off of Wendy, who was bent awkwardly over the side of the truck bed. Paul, still in an uncontrollable rage, pushed her away with his free hand. He had been a terrible drunk at one point in his life and smashed up a few things, but up to this point he had never raised a hand to either his wife or child. In a matter of seconds he had done both for the first and last time.

"You've lied to us for the last time!"

Marie and Wendy quietly stepped into the vehicle. Not one word was spoken between them on the long trip back.

*   *   *

They locked Andrew up in a cell with a couple of drunks. He was briefly let out to talk with O'Reilly. The State of Michigan police officer led him to an interrogation room that was nothing like Andrew had ever seen in the movies. He sat in a chair at a large table facing a window. Andrew figured he would be in a small, dark room with no windows. He also hadn't counted on paintings of former Houghton County sheriffs donning the room. The 'interrogation room' was also a conference room for official county business. State Trooper O'Reilly rubbed his chin, yawned and sat down across from Andrew. Andrew didn't show it, but he had never been more afraid in his life. His fear, however, was for what all of this meant to his relationship with Wendy.

O'Reilly slapped a yellow sticky note on the table in front of Andrew. Andrew looked down at his very own handwriting.

May 21Midnight. Pick-up 1 kilo.

Beneath it was Wendy's handwriting.

Now that's a lot of weed!

O'Reilly opened his mouth to speak at the same time Andrew did.

"You are probably going to want to get a lawyer."

"I'm not saying anything without a lawyer."

They both managed to end on the word lawyer at the same time.

"Listen, kid, we know you've been dealing marijuana, and in large amounts. Enough to put you behind bars. However, we got what we were after. If you cooperate with us, I'm sure your sentence will be light."

"Is Sexton dead?" Andrew asked.

"Yes, he is." O'Reilly stood up. "Listen, I'm exhausted, this has been one long-ass day and I'm going home. Good luck, kid."

O'Reilly led Andrew back to his cell. Andrew looked around the cell at the two drunks who were passed out and snoring. He envied them; he didn't know how he would ever sleep again.

* * *

It was nearly eight in the morning when Wendy got home. There were no more lectures, at least not at that time; her parents had plenty to discuss.

Wendy walked to her bedroom door and peered through it, opening it only slightly. Her parents were at the table. They were talking too lightly for her to be able to make out what they said; but she had a pretty good inclination that it involved her and Andrew. She closed the door all the way and tip toed back to her bed. She pulled her cell phone from beneath her pillow. She dialed the number she had memorized and mumbled to herself as the phone rang several times. On the seventh ring it went to some guy's voice mail.

"Trevor, leave a message," the voice on the other end said with a certain disinterest that only a teenage slacker could muster.

Wendy almost hung up, then after a few seconds spoke. "Ummm, hi. Andrew told me to call this number." She immediately wondered who Trevor was as she held on to the black Nokia phone. It suddenly vibrated, almost causing her to drop it, she was so startled. She flipped the phone up and quietly answered.

"Hello."

"They got Andy, eh?" Trevor asked.

"Yes, who is this?"

"Let's just say I'm in the same business as Andrew."

Trevor lived in Escanaba with his girlfriend. He was twenty and a high school dropout. However, the success of his current business venture made him want to flip his high school guidance counselor off. *No one ever told me about this option.* He wasn't the brightest guy, but he was smart enough to realize that his field of choice had pitfalls. His pal, Andrew, was currently experiencing the second biggest one.

"Tell Andrew to hang tough and everything will be taken care of." He hung up, looked down at his girlfriend and baby boy, leaned down and kissed them both. Stacy wiped her eyes and looked up.

"Wuh ya doing?" she asked groggily.

"They got Andrew," he said as he slipped on a pair of jeans.

"That sucks." She sat up and thanked God that it was Andrew and not Trevor.

Trevor drove up to the street that his buddy Andrew lived on. He parked his car on the side of the road and walked through the woods to the house. It was a long walk, but one he was glad to be taking. It meant that he wasn't the one who had been busted. He reached the shed and pulled out his keys; found the right one, one he had never used before and inserted it into the pad lock. He opened the door and reached up to a top shelf. He pulled the one time home of baseball cards down, and then the empty bag.

Trevor took the two steps off the step ladder and put it back. He bent over, and on one knee, swept the dirt around the ground. His fingers grazed across a rusty metal ring. He scraped the dirt away with his fingers and pulled it up, bringing with it a plank of wood. He reached his arm down below and pulled up a large metal box. He moved the combination lock and looked inside.

"That's a lot of money," he said to himself.

An immediate thought was to take the money and screw Andrew altogether. *What's he going to do, call the cops?* He laughed to himself; then let the selfish notion pass. He knew Andrew wouldn't even entertain the thought.

They had both met Todd Sexton about the same time. Even though it was Andrew's idea, Trevor went along with it. Todd didn't care either way, *just bring me my money, bitches!* It was the first, but definitely not the last time that Trevor had to resist the urge to smack the pock faced loser.

They would trade territory, making it more likely for them to maintain their anonymous existence. In their own towns, there would be too many questions and ultimately people they cared about would find out. They looked at themselves as traveling salesmen. Andrew would take a region that included Gladstone and Escanaba. Trevor would take Rapid Junction to Manistique. From an economic standpoint, it was a far better deal for Andrew. Therefore, he agreed to pay Trevor 20 percent of his keep. This made it a very agreeable for Trevor. As they got to know each other better they came up with their 'doomsday scenario.' Both had keys to where they kept their stash and money. If one were to get arrested, the other was to salvage what remained. The deal ended with them splitting any money that was recouped.

Trevor looked down at the money, which was mostly in twenties, fifties and hundreds. He thought about counting it right then and there, but realized it was time to go. He closed the wood door, kicked some dirt over the rusty ring, looked around to make sure everything was in place and then locked up. He ran to his car, rather than walk. Trevor was actually getting giddy at the thought of counting up the money. He had spent most of his, and only had a few grand in his secret stash. His girlfriend liked to go out to eat, especially after they had smoked much of his profits. The pit bull they owned wasn't cheap, and although he wasn't driving a sports car, he had managed to pay for his used Saturn with cash.

Trevor's girlfriend, Stacy, bounced her nine month old son on her hip as he counted the money. "Well? How much?" She couldn't contain her smile; this was an unexpected Christmas.

"Shut up," he said mildly. He had never been very good at math, but if his calculator was correct, Andrew had managed to save $21,820 in the past year and a half. *That boy has no hobbies.* Trevor showed his scrawny girl friend the total on the calculator. She jumped up and down like she had won the lottery, which in a way she had. She stopped suddenly and her face became overly serious.

"Let's keep it all."

"No, that'd be bull shit."

"Yeah, Andrew's a nice guy." She sulked for the rest of the day. $10,910 didn't sound nearly as good as the other total.

*   *   *

Andrew sat in the conference room; the same one he had been sequestered in. He looked around at the familiar faces of Houghton County's history of justice. *Hi, fellas.*

The lawyer standing in front of him was a diminutive man who did not appear to be the barracuda he presented himself to be in his commercials. *DUI, drug charges, not a problem. I know the law and prosecutors all over Michigan and Wisconsin fear me!* His stubby finger pointed toward the television watcher. He was not lying. Prosecutors did fear him; he did know the law and always made them work ten times harder to get a conviction. If you were up against Kevin Lewis, you had better not screw up.

"I'm not cheap, kid. You're parents are paying a lot for my services. I will not tolerate a liar or games, you got it?"

Andrew looked away from a serious looking man who had been the sheriff of Houghton County from 1922-1926 to Kevin Lewis.

"Yes." He thought about adding in sir, but he didn't want to come across as disingenuous.

"Start from the top then. How did you get involved with Sexton?"

Andrew told him of his trip to Michigan Tech a year and a half earlier in which Sexton had recruited him, how he had lied to his parents about working at Taco Bell, and how the Toad ran his operation. Lewis mostly listened and took down notes as Andrew rambled through his story.

" . . . so the plan was for me to take over his operation next year," Andrew explained to him. He noticed Lewis look up and begin tapping his pencil on his legal notepad. "What?"

"Did Sexton have a log of his sales?"

"Yes."

"And have you seen it?"

"Yes." Andrew nodded.

"Did he record people's actual names or did he use some kind of code?"

Andrew knew where he was going with the questioning. He didn't relish the idea of becoming a snitch, but would do anything in order to save his ass and have a future with Wendy. "Code." He smiled slightly, trying not to be too smug.

"Kid, this might just be your get out of jail free card."

Andrew listened as his lawyer explained the process of bail and the hefty price tag that came with it. He struggled to focus on the rest, his mind firmly on Wendy.

CHAPTER TWENTY EIGHT

Steven took a long look at his black Hummer and knew that the vehicle would be gone in short order. Andrew's bail had been set at $150,000. Steven and Melissa had to come up with fifteen grand themselves.

"Steven, let's go," Melissa barked

He turned toward his wife. She was standing next to her son's lawyer who was holding the door open for her. Steven hustled to where the two were waiting for him.

Inside, Andrew exchanged his orange garb for his clothes. A male deputy sheriff led him down a cold, sterile hall to the moment he both cherished and dreaded. He spent only parts of four days in jail, but it was enough to let him know those would be the only days he would ever spend behind bars. He still didn't know where he belonged, but knew it wasn't there. Wherever it was, it had to include Wendy.

Andrew, his mother and father, and his lawyer stood outside of the black Hummer that would soon be up for sale.

"Okay, folks, tomorrow we meet with Mandy Sherman, the prosecuting attorney. She's going to try to play hardball. She's going to act as if you are the scum of the earth and that any deal she brokers will be the kindest thing she could ever give another person. You can't react, you just need to let me do the talking and let my emotions speak for all of us. Can you do that?"

Andrew thought, *with pleasure*, but said, "Yes, I can do that."

He had no idea just how hard that would be.

* * *

Maggie lay in Conner's bed with his arms wrapped around her tiny frame. She skipped work and school for two straight days. Conner, who was on summer break but staying on campus to work a job painting dorms, also skipped work.

T. D. Croel

"Why would he lie to me?"

Conner leaned down and kissed the top of her head. "He just wants to protect you."

Maggie rolled over and leaned on her side, propped by her elbow. "Why wouldn't either one of them tell me they were together?"

Conner shrugged his shoulders.

*   *   *

Savannah set her lunch tray down and looked toward Wendy who only played with her green beans, turning the wretched cafeteria food over and over with her spork. Savannah decided not to press her friend for details; instead offering up friendship. "Listen, I don't know who you think you're kidding. I know you are in love with Andrew, and I know all of this shit has got to be killing you. So, when you're ready to talk, I'm here for you. Okay?"

Wendy looked over to her friend. "Okay." They ate the rest of the lunch in silence. Savannah wondered if she would ever be able to tell Wendy of her own ordeal.

*   *   *

After bailing out Andrew, Steven and family scrambled to make it to the district game being held in Stephenson, another small Yooper town. They arrived in the fifth inning. None of the teams in the district were very good, but Steven still felt nervous.

Steven raced up to the field as Melissa and Andrew walked slowly behind him. A lady sitting at a cardboard table set out by a sidewalk waved her arms for Steven to stop. She had a cash box in front of her. She already regretted volunteering for the thankless job of ticket taker.

"I'm a coach," Steven hollered as he ran by her.

Steven was panting by the time he reached Marie who was sitting in a lawn chair with her scorebook in her lap. He looked down at the visitor's side and saw no little diamonds filled in representing runs they had scored. "How many we got?" He didn't give her a chance to answer. He snatched the scorebook and turned it over. The other side looked just like the visitor's; no runs. "Are you kidding me? We beat this team nine to nothing last time."

Marie looked up and held out her arms. "I don't know what to tell you, Steven. No one is hitting."

Steven dropped the scorebook into her lap and walked into the dugout. Normally the girls would have cheered his arrival. This time, however, they were fearful of his reaction. "Ladies, ladies! What's going on?"

A few minutes later Melissa strolled up to where her best friend sat. "We need to talk, the four of us."

"I know. How about this Sunday?"

In the bottom of the seventh inning, Savannah hit a triple to the fence, and then scored on a wild pitch. She also pitched the fifth perfect game of her career. She couldn't help but smile when Steven ran out of the dugout and hugged her. The smile disappeared when she turned and saw Melissa. *She never comes to the games.* Savannah also noticed Andrew standing next to her and figured they must have all come directly from jail.

The teams shook hands and Savannah was congratulated on her gem of a pitching performance by nearly everyone. The other team went into the game believing they had no chance. The fact that they lost 1-0 in the bottom of the seventh made them feel good about their performance. Not one of them walked through the line with anything more than a smile. It was almost impossible to tell which team had actually won the game. Steven congratulated the other coach for giving his team such a battle. The little woman smiled, ear-to-ear.

Savannah skipped out on cleaning up the dugout and carrying any of the equipment to the bus. Instead she walked over to Andrew, who was standing alone.

"Hey, jailbird," Savannah said playfully.

"Nice hit, Babe Ruth."

She changed tones. "What the hell, Andrew? Wendy is freaking out right now."

"I bet," he said. His smile evaporated.

"You ready, Andrew?"

Savannah closed her eyes. The sound of Melissa still stopped her heart.

"Yeah," he responded. "See ya around."

"Bye."

Melissa continued to walk toward the parking lot. Without turning around she said, "Congratulations, Savannah."

"Thanks," Savannah answered in a barely audible tone.

Savannah had never liked Melissa, but since her affair began with Steven, her feelings about the woman changed from a mixture of fear and annoyance to one of fear and guilt. And the fear was ten times more powerful. *That woman will kill me when she finds out.*

*   *   *

Andrew asked his parents to sit outside while he spoke to the prosecuting attorney. He couldn't face the idea of them hearing his intimate drug dealing details. Lewis suggested that that was a good idea. During the ride over to the prosecutor's office Andrew had been alternately showered with compassion and love, and then scorn and anger. He took it all; he knew at the least he deserved the latter serving of parental love.

The prosecuting attorney, Mandy Sherman, came into the room with a scowl. She set her briefcase down, ran both hands against the back of her expensive black skirt that came from Saks in Chicago, and sat down across from Lewis and Andrew.

"Young man, I hope your lawyer didn't make you a bunch of promises that he can't keep. This is serious business." She slapped her hand down on the table to emphasize just how serious it was.

Andrew didn't blink.

"Ms. Sherman, I have not promised him anything." He leaned in to garner her attention; she was still staring at Andrew. Finally, she turned to meet his eyes. "What are you offering?"

"Your client cooperates with authorities, gives us all of the names, addresses, et cetera in Sexton's log. All charges are dropped against him, except for trafficking a drug house and possession."

Lewis didn't bat an eyelash. "We want all charges dropped."

"Not a snowball's chance." She leaned back and put her hands behind her head. She stared at Andrew. "We have surveillance of the kid for three months; we have him dead to rights. Do you really want your client serving seven years?"

Inside, Andrew's mind froze in fear on the number seven. He barely made it through four days; *seven fucking years?* He kept a steely resolve and met her stare. He could see the slightest grin forming on the corners of her lips. *She knows she has me.* Andrew finally looked away.

"Do you really want fifteen dealers walking around?"

Sherman returned her eyes to the man who had embarrassed her one too many times in a court room.

Sherman stood up, "I'll see you in court."

She met Andrew's eyes one last time and winked at him, before walking out.

Lewis looked to Andrew. "You alright?"

"Yes, and you were right, she is a bitch."

"You don't know the half of it. She thinks that you are going to beg me to make the deal."

Andrew interrupted. "Should I?"

"I can't answer that for you, so let me break everything down for you and then you can decide with your parents what you need to do."

Lewis explained to him that if push came to shove, he would clear him on the conspiracy charges; but probably not the other two. Therefore he would be right back at where the plea bargain would put him. The big difference would be that an unsympathetic judge would probably give him the stiffest penalties he could. If he saved everyone a lot of headaches, than the judge would most likely give him probation, some fines and nothing else.

"I'll take the deal."

CHAPTER TWENTY NINE

Marie sat on the edge of Wendy's bed with her hands clasped and her back to her daughter. Wendy sat against the wall with her arms wrapped around her knees. Marie had had plenty of 'womanly' talks with her daughter over the years and knew that one day she might have to discuss the loss of her daughter's virginity. She knew how uncomfortable it might be. However, the thought of having the discussion at this moment and about *this* boy had her on the brink of hysteria.

Marie continued to wring her hands before Wendy finally relieved the pressure. "No, Mom, we didn't have sex if that's what you want to know."

Marie hadn't realized she had been holding her breath. The air escaped her in a giant 'whoosh' and she put her hand to her heart. She turned to Wendy, who with squinted eyes; shook her head in disgust.

"Thank God." It was not meant to be said aloud.

"Thank God?" Wendy clenched the blanket under her body with both fists leaving hand marks. "Would it be so horrible if I had?"

Marie closed her eyes. She wanted to tell her daughter *yes, yes it would be horrible.* Instead she propped herself up and stood, turning to meet her daughter's intense stare. "Honey, you just don't understand." She turned and left the room.

* * *

Although, Marie and Paul had discussed the need to talk with Melissa and Steven about their children and their peculiar situation, they didn't actually discuss what their stance would be. Marie had assumed that Paul would agree that the children needed to know.

Paul stared at the beer that Steven had in his hand and it took everything he had not to ask him to go grab another. Melissa was the first one to speak up about the issue at hand, and not just idle chit chat.

"So, what are we going to do about Andrew and Wendy? Obviously, we can't let this go on."

"Obviously," Paul said in a tone that earned him the steely glare Melissa was known for.

"We have to come clean wit dese kids, eh?" Steven asked, looking around the table for a response. "Don't we?"

Marie spoke up. "Yes, as much as I don't want to, I don't see any other choice."

CHAPTER THIRTY

1981

Marie and Melissa began avoiding each other after Marie's meltdown following Andrew's birthday party. For Marie it became too difficult to see her best friend with a child. For Melissa it became too hard to enjoy her child knowing her friend's pain. When they were around each other they mostly fought. It was usually Melissa who provoked Marie.

Marie's pot boiled over after she made an innocent joke about Steven's intellect. Melissa and Marie often bantered about Steven's intelligence and Paul's sloppiness. Melissa freaked out on her and kicked her out of her house. Both knew it wasn't about the comment, but about an angst that wouldn't disappear for either.

A week passed before Marie stormed over to Melissa's house in the middle of their favorite soap opera. The pair had been watching the same show together for as long as they could remember. Now they were watching it separately.

Marie burst through, pushing the door harder than she expected. The knob smashed into the wall, putting a little hole in it. At that moment, she didn't care.

"I am so sick of your . . ." Marie yelled.

"It's my fault." Melissa sat at the kitchen table, the television was off. She only watched the stupid soap opera because her very best friend in the world did.

"What?" Confused, Marie quietly shut the door and walked into the kitchen and sat down across from Melissa.

Melissa grabbed on to Marie's hands and held them, a little tighter than she had expected to. "Everything," she responded. "I know what he did to you."

*   *   *

Winter, 1965

"Scoot over," he demanded as he reached down and touched her.

Melissa, used to his early morning visits, was long past being a sound sleeper. She stared first at his hand which rested on her left breast and then into his yellowish eyes. The light of the moon spilled onto his face. She could make out the ever increasing broken blood vessels on his nose.

"I can't." Melissa motioned behind her on the bed.

Marie snorted as if on command, confirming the reason her friend couldn't move over.

John Peterson opened his mouth, revealing teeth that matched the hue of his eyes. Twenty plus years of hard drinking and smoking were quickly deteriorating his body. His aroma authenticated this fact. He smelled like a corpse.

"I see."

"I have to go to the bathroom." Melissa jumped up.

"Hurry back," Peterson said eerily as he set his eyes on his next victim.

Melissa stood under the doorway. The light from the moon was now cast on her. She slowly backed out of the light, it was too intense.

She skipped the bathroom and walked downstairs where she settled herself on the flower printed couch that once belonged to a great-grandmother. Her step-father had only touched her and in return had made her touch him. Melissa, who went to a Catholic church every Sunday since she could remember, skipped over every prayer she had ever had to memorize and chose a more personal appeal to her God. In a kneeling position on the antique couch, she positioned herself toward a portrait of Jesus. Jesus looked at her with suspicious eyes.

"Please, God, don't let him hurt her—please, please, please . . ."

The number of pleases reached the thousands. The knuckles on her fingers began to ache as she pressed them together like a vice.

" . . . please, please, please."

Melissa's eyes darted open and her pleas momentarily ceased. She ignored the indicting Jesus and focused on the sounds of the second level. She heard her door close and then the creaking sound of the floor board. Next, the rasping sound of her mother's door being opened and then closed.

That was too quick. *He came to his senses and realized how much trouble he would get in.* Melissa let herself believe this as she fell asleep. The next morning when she saw her stripped bed stained with her friend's blood, she still held out hope that it was nothing more than a bad menstrual cycle. The following day on the bus, however, the void in her friend's eyes gave her the truth and in the process shattered her belief in God. Not in his existence, but in his character.

*   *   *

"No." Marie said, with her hands still firmly held by Melissa's.

The word came out no, but in her mind she was sure she had said, *yes. Yes, YOU had to know he was a monster; YOU left me! YOU allowed it to happen to me, and now look at me . . . I can't even have a baby. I have had to hide so* much from so many people!" Marie suddenly became aware that her thought process had become spoken words. Melissa let go of her hands.

Hearing she was responsible from the victim was so much more powerful than admitting it herself. Selfishly, Melissa became momentarily angry. *How dare you! I'm about to volunteer the greatest gift you could ever receive! How can you say this to me?* Melissa didn't say these things as they went through her mind; she simply recoiled.

Melissa, who had given the plan so much thought, came back to her senses and loosened her facial muscles. She forced a smile to her face and grasped on to Marie's hands again. She felt a little resistance, but held them even tighter. This was a battle she was not going to lose. "I'm going to have your baby."

"But, I don't even find you the least bit attractive." Marie was trying to be funny, but the tone just wasn't there.

"I'm serious. I have a child and I can always have more later."

Marie removed her hands from Melissa's and stood up. She shook her head, gently at first, then violently.

"No." She looked down. "I can't have you do that. How is that going to work, Melissa? Did you really think this over?" She mocked the situation and her friend as she held an imaginary baby in her arms. "Hello, baby, this is your aunt . . . oh, and also your mother." Melissa sat back and took in the tirade. It wasn't anything she hadn't thought of, but somehow hearing it from Marie's mouth made her see the situation in a whole new light. She crossed her arms and raised her eyebrows, suggesting to Marie that she 'go on.'

"Do you really think you could let go of this child? You'd be giving me a *baby* . . . not a fucking vacuum cleaner!"

"Well, I'm pregnant, so if you don't want it, I guess I will abort it."

Marie shook her head, turned and stormed off. She threw the door open and didn't bother to close it. The guys had just come back from the lumber yard and were setting two-by-fours down in the garage when Marie stomped across the yard, her little legs getting buried in the snow deposited from an early spring blizzard.

Paul and Steven looked at each other, laughed, and then reached into the bed of the pick-up and continued their job. Marie and Melissa, being so close for so many years, could at times act just like sisters. The guys, on the other hand, rarely spoke an ill word toward one another. They could get into arguments about hunting and fishing, but nothing ever serious. Both would walk away knowing they were right. Their greatest debate; *lures or minnows; which is better for catching walleye?*

CHAPTER THIRTY ONE

Both women spent the rest of the evening thinking about the 'offer.' Melissa was beginning to feel silly. *She's right, I am an idiot. And a baby isn't going to take away the fact that she was raped.* She decided that guilt in having done nothing to stop her friend from being hurt was maybe something she was supposed to carry with her for the rest of her life.

Despite being 14 months old, little Andrew still loved his mechanical swing. The wind-up machine was in need of a new cranking. Andrew let everyone know it. "MA! MA!"

Steven looked at the child with annoyance. Melissa ignored him. Her biggest challenge now was going to be telling Steven that she was pregnant again. They had agreed that one was enough.

Andrew continued howling. Melissa, who was sitting with her legs up to her chest in the recliner, was suddenly drawn back to reality. "You can't crank it for him? You like that sound?" She did not wait for an answer; she got up and cranked the swing. Andrew slowly stopped wailing.

Steven still refused to change a diaper or get up in the middle of the night with the baby; even when Melissa had the flu. To Melissa, it seemed that Steven would never accept fatherhood as a responsibility. How was he going to respond to a second crying child keeping him up, or distracting him while he watched some 'stupid' fishing show, or God forbid, bowling? Their relationship was strained enough as it was. She suddenly felt stupid. Getting pregnant with Andrew forced Steven's hand; but, *how was this going to help?*

*   *   *

A small yard away, Marie stood at the sink. She moved the wash cloth in a circular motion around the plate as she stared into space. She had been washing the same dish for nearly five minutes. Paul walked up behind Marie and put his hands around her. He took the plate from her hands, rinsed it and set it in the dish strainer.

"I think it's clean," he cackled. He swung her around and wiped his hands dry on her butt. Paul cackled again causing Marie to laugh with him. She put her arms around his shoulders and looked him in the eyes. "What were you and Mel talking about?" Paul was the only person who called Melissa by that name.

"Something pretty big," she responded. She leaned in and gave Paul a quick kiss on the lips. Her voice quivered, "We need to talk."

She led him into the living room and they sat facing each other. Paul never said a word, not one word. His eyes were kind when Marie needed them to be that way. He squeezed her hands in just the right way when Marie needed to feel his touch. Paul was never one to be the great communicator. However, he did have the intuition of knowing when it was time to say something and when it was time to keep his mouth shut and listen.

Marie told her story of John Peterson, sparing him none of the horrendous details. Things became so clear to him; he wanted to go back in time and murder the already deceased man. Marie explained that she had thought that she long ago had forgiven Melissa. Paul had a hard time understanding how she ever could. Marie's story would eventually lead her to the conversation that she had with Melissa and the reason for their fight. Paul could not contain his silence anymore, he tried to speak, but only nonsensical syllables came out.

Marie let him off the hook and asked him straightforward, "So, what do you think? Crazy, huh?"

He finally formed real words. "What do I think?" Paul took his hands back and put his right one through his thin hair. "What makes you think Steven would even go for it? I know he doesn't even know about it, yet. And you know damn well that Melissa aint having no abortion."

Marie also believed the same thing; but didn't acknowledge her husband as being right. She didn't plan on saying the words, but once she started it just seemed to make more and more sense to her. "I want a baby . . . . I want a baby, and she can give us one."

"You realize our friendship with them will be over?"

Marie knew he was right, but still said; "It doesn't have to be." She grabbed hold of his hands again. "We have all been through so much, we can get through this. Sure, it will be awkward, but . . ."

Paul cut her off, "But, nothing. If we all agree to do this, we also have to agree that this child will never know who its real parents are. One of us will have to leave, that's the only way for this to work. I know Steven wants to go back to the UP. He hasn't actually said so, but he mentioned that 'old man' Sheridan keeps asking him when he is going to come back and become his top guy again. He wouldn't have told me that if he wasn't thinking about it."

"What about your business? You guys have put in so much work already."

Paul shrugged his shoulders, "It's not the most important thing . . . ." His voice trailed off.

Marie knew what the subtext was. *The most important thing is that WE have our baby.* She stood up and began pacing. "Yeah? Is this a yes?"

"Yes, eh?" Paul raised his left eyebrow. Marie squeezed her husband tight. She kissed him all over his face until her lips met his. She kept them there and gently eased her embrace.

Steven stormed out of the bathroom like a bull after red. "What is this, eh? What is this?" He held an early pregnancy test in his large mitt.

Melissa had already 'killed the rabbit' when she got the official news from her doctor earlier that week, but decided that maybe this was the easiest way to tell him. She set it right next to the toilet paper roll.

Melissa set the book she was reading to Andrew down on the coffee table. She smiled when she heard his normally low baritone voice become shrill and high pitched. He always got that way when he was excited.

He stood in front of Melissa waving the pee stick in her face. "What is this, eh?"

"What the hell do you think it is?"Andrew pointed to the book, wanting his mother to continue. "Not now, Andrew."

The child looked up at his father; they shared the same dopey expression. Little Andrew just drooled a little more.

"Looks like someone is about to get stinky." She held him up to Steven. "Care to change him?"

"This is great! Just fucking great!" He ignored her question and got back to the topic at hand. "How the hell did this happen?"

Melissa started to open her mouth; but was quickly rebuffed by Steven. "And don't give me some smart ass answer, either."

"Does it really matter? Either way, I know how you feel about children. I will take care of things; you don't have to worry about nothing." She put Andrew on his back and pulled down his pants.

"Mama, I poop."

"I know, sweetie."

"Wus that mean? I don't hafta worry about nothing."

"It means just that, do I really have to spell it out?" She pulled back the plastic tape holding together Andrew's diaper and admired his handy work. "Could you grab me some wipes?"

"Fine, no more babies." He pointed at Andrew. "That lil shit monster is enough." He handed her the baby wipes and stormed off to bed.

*   *   *

The next day when the men had gone off to work, Marie walked next door. She carried with her Andrew's little Detroit Tiger cap that Melissa had left behind on a previous visit. It was the perfect excuse to stop by. Melissa saw her walking up the little driveway. She opened the door just as Marie was about to knock.

Melissa didn't know exactly what the meaning behind the visit was, so she gave off a neutral vibe. "Come in." It came casually and without feeling. "Want some coffee?"

Marie followed her into the kitchen. "Sure."

Melissa poured them both a cup. Both had always drank their coffee black. She set a mug in front of Marie who was now sitting at the table. The mug had a picture of Marie and Melissa on it. They had had them made at one of those mall printing places that put pictures on everything. Each had their own mug that showed the two dressed up in red, white and blue in honor of Independence Day from the previous summer.

Marie held up the little hat with the old English D on it as she sipped from her coffee; then set it down on the table. Melissa nodded, realizing the reason for the visit. She assumed this was Marie's way of sweeping everything under the rug and moving on. There would be no rehashing of the previous night's conversation; no apologies, just moving on. *Oh, Marie, I wish I could forget things as easily as you.*

"How do we do this?"

Melissa who was about to say thank you for bringing the hat back, realized her mouth was still agape and quickly shut it. She thought about asking 'how do we do what?' but decided that it was pretty stupid to act coy.

"We go to a lawyer and he draws up the adoption papers. It will cost a few hundred dollars. I go through nine months of being fat again, ten . . . twenty hours of hellacious labor, and hocus pocus, you have a baby!"

Marie did not laugh at her friend's attempt at humor. "If we do this, no one can know, I mean no one."

"So, I become a hermit in this house, is that what you are saying? Cut off from the rest of the world?"

"Yes, something like that. No one in your family can find out. You go as long as you can, telling people you're just putting on a little weight, then when you can't hide it any longer, you go into hiding."

Melissa's face went from smiling, to blank and then to a bewildering anger. "Excuse me, are you seriously going to tell me what I can and cannot do?"

"Melissa, think about it. Do you really want to explain this situation to *anyone* . . . ever?"

Melissa's face softened. "No."

"Melissa, if you don't want to do this, you don't have to. I won't think anything about it. I couldn't do this for you. The fact that you would even offer it is pretty amazing to me."

"I owe you . . ."

"Nothing," Marie finished. "You owe me nothing. I forgive you."

Melissa noticed the look in Marie's eyes change with the last comment. They had the faraway gaze to them that she remembered from her ghost walk on the bus. She knew all was not forgiven, but hoped her act of sacrifice would at least make past demons forgotten.

"So, do you think Steven will really go for this?" The life was back in Marie's eyes.

Melissa snorted at the comment. "Yeah, I think he will go for it. I told him I was preg-o last night; he didn't take it so well. Do you think it would be best if we moved away?"

She looked across the table at her friend. Andrew's babbling came through a baby monitor plugged into an outlet in the living room.

"I better go get the monkey."

She knew what the answer was from the look in her friend's eyes.

CHAPTER THIRTY TWO

Geoff Ogilvie rustled the papers on his oak desk, searching frantically for the legal documents he had prepared for the four people sitting in his office. "Kelllllly!" he hollered. Kelly, his older and very experienced secretary, stood to his left with the papers he needed.

"Right here, Mr. Ogilvie."

Ogilvie turned to his right, then quickly to his left. In his secretary's hands were the papers he was looking for. Her fingers were tinged with yellow.

Melissa looked on more nervously than anyone else. It wasn't the absurdity of the lawyer in front of her. His desk had papers scattered a mile high; he had a coffee stain on his shirt and pens behind both ears. It was the decision she was making. *How could a woman give up her own child?*

She had told herself she had only wanted one child all along, but she knew it was a lie. Melissa had been scared to death to have Andrew. The truth was, she got pregnant to trap Steven. She never felt the maternal instincts that other women talked about. But she had no doubt that she loved her child and that she was a damn good mother. Andrew was never going to go without a meal, miss a practice, or get bad grades. Her parenting skills were working just fine for Andrew and they would work just as well with any other child—but, what about the one she was carrying; the one that belonged to her friend. Melissa erased the thought and became increasingly irritated by the needle-nosed attorney in front of her. *What is wrong with this guy?*

"Thank you, Mrs. Conger." He took the papers and set them in front of him. He separated them by copies and let out a huge sigh. "Well, Mr. and Mrs. Fonduluc . . . Mr. and Mrs. La Claire, I have to tell you, this is not your run of the mill adoption situation. Normally, the birth mother or parents do not know the adoptive parents . . . or there is artificial insemination involved . . ."

Melissa tuned him out, *give me a sign, God; just give me a sign . . . or damn it, give me the strength to actually go through with this.*

"I have to remind you," he was looking at Steven and Melissa. "I represent the La Claires. I would strongly urge you to get your own lawyer."

Melissa opened her mouth to say that was a good idea, but she quickly snapped it shut when her husband blurted out, "That won't be necessary, everything is on the up and up." He turned to his buddy, Paul, and smiled. Paul didn't smile back, he turned toward Melissa.

The lawyer continued, "As I told you previously, Melissa can back out at any time . . ."

Steven jumped in, "Oh, she wouldn't do that. Her word is solid."

"Of course she wouldn't!" Marie nearly screamed as she jumped out of her seat. Everyone's eyes, except for the lawyer's, turned to her. She quickly sat back down, her hands clenching the handles on the old wooden chairs that matched the desk.

The lawyer casually moved on. " . . . up to the birth of the child. After that, she could change her mind, but then the justice system would have to get involved. But, since her word is solid as this desk . . ." He patted the sturdy oak desk that had originally belonged to his grandfather. " . . . then I guess we have nothing to worry about."

Ogilvie turned the papers around, showed each couple where the lines were to sign or initial.

Melissa somehow managed to control her nerves and steadied her hand as she signed and initialed every spot as instructed. *You can always change your mind; you can always change your mind.* Steven signed in the wrong spot twice, and scratched them out before he was finally done. Kelly came in with her white out and sighed deeply as she brushed the white drying liquid across Steven's mistakes. Melissa could tell how annoyed she was. *Welcome to my world!*

CHAPTER THIRTY THREE

For weeks Melissa and Marie did not speak of the adoption; they talked about how frustrating their husbands could be; about which doctor on General Hospital was more sleazy, about what sale was going on at their favorite grocery store; everything but about the baby. Marie knew every move that Melissa had made since the deal was struck. She hardly left the house and she doubted that she would have told her younger brothers. Since her mother had passed away the year before and her father was long out of the picture, Marie didn't know who she would tell if she had wanted to. Marie also knew that Melissa hadn't gone to see a doctor, which couldn't be a good thing. *That's my baby you got in there, lady!*

The 'baby doesn't exist game' went on for another two weeks before Marie had finally had enough. She decided that since Melissa hadn't taken care of certain matters, she would. She called an obstetrician/gynecologist and set up an appointment. Marie let her fingers do the walking and turned to the Yellow Pages. She found the first listing and dialed.

"Dr. Kendrick's office, how may I help you?"

"Hi, my name is Melissa Fonduluc," Marie lied. "I'm in need of a good OB/GYN," she said truthfully.

"Time to go where?" Melissa said as she finished changing Andrew's diaper. He was now eighteen months old.

Marie sighed and gently tapped her foot against the floor. "I'm not trying to tell you how to do this, and I know it must be hard . . . but, you have to go see a doctor. It's been over twenty weeks."

Melissa didn't look up; she tucked a tuft of hair behind her ear and smiled at Andrew. She put her finger on his nose and pulled it back as he tried to grab for it. The game went on a few more times, before

Melissa grabbed her little boy and brought him to her hip as she stood up. "Let's go."

Marie closed her eyes. She hadn't realized it, but she had squeezed her keys so hard they formed an indention in her hand. She rubbed her palm and sighed deeply. *She's not going to make this easy at all.*

*   *   *

They walked into Dr. Kendrick's office and Marie headed to the receptionist's window when she remembered that she wasn't actually going to be the one getting examined. It was easy to fool someone over the phone that you are pregnant. It might be a tad more difficult in person. She looked back at Melissa who was bouncing Andrew on her leg and decided she could at least sign her in.

After a short wait, Melissa's name was called. Marie looked up at her. "C'mon," she finally directed.

I'm not going to like this at all, but I'm not going to say a word either, Marie thought to herself as she walked to the examination room. She took hold of Andrew as she followed Melissa, who had the walk of a pregnant woman, but definitely not the glow. Melissa was weighed, asked about allergies and an assortment of other questions before being led to an examining room. She hopped up on the long padded table. A nurse came in and took her blood pressure and then checked her heart rate. The woman was humorless and made no effort at small talk. Melissa didn't mind at all. Marie sat in the chair and read a book to Andrew.

Dr. Kendrick walked in; he was in his mid-forties, and had the slightest hint of grey in his hair and in his goatee. Marie thought the goatee made him look alluring and mysterious, like some mountain climber trekking his way through the Himalayas. His piercing blue eyes and flawless complexion made him very attractive. Melissa momentarily forgot about her 'freeze out' of her friend and Marie forgot about her anxiety. They exchanged the look that all women share with their best friend when they are intrigued by the presence of a good looking man. Melissa mouthed, *damn!* Marie nodded in agreement. Dr. Kendrick smiled coyly, they had been caught.

He offered out his hand. "Hi, Doctor Kendrick."

"Melissa Fonduluc," she said as she took the doctor's soft hand in hers.

He smiled and turned to Marie.

"Marie, best friend," she called off as if stating her rank in the military to a superior.

"Nice to meet you both." He turned back to Melissa. Marie gave her friend another look and shot her a thumbs up. "You realize that you are in for a lecture?" He raised his eyebrow.

"Yes, doctor."

After giving Melissa a stern talking to, the handsome doctor examined her belly with his hand. He pushed and prodded, making Melissa grimace with each touch. He asked her many of the same questions she had already been asked.

"Um, I think I've been asked these questions already."

Marie knew how irritated her friend was and had to give her credit for at least trying to hide her irritation.

"You'd be surprised how honest people become when they're talking to the doctor, instead of a nurse's assistant," he said with a smile.

He placed his stethoscope up to her belly and Marie noticed that his facial expression had changed. She inched forward as Andrew began to squirm for the first time since their visit.

He took the instrument off of his ears and placed them on Melissa's. She looked at him oddly. He placed the black diaphragm piece onto her heart. "Hear that?"

"Yep."

"That's your heart."

He moved the diaphragm down to her belly and moved it around. "Do you hear a heartbeat?"

"Yeah?" It came out more as a question. "It sounds like it has an echo."

"Well, not quite an echo."

Marie prayed, *please, God, don't let anything be wrong with my child.* She knew this was a silly thought. *What kind of sick doctor would make you listen to something wrong with your child and then be smiling about it? It would be like a doctor taking your hand and placing it on a tumor. And that, my friend, is the actual lump that is going to kill you!* She erased all unnecessary thoughts and simply waited it out.

"What is it, then?" Marie asked. She looked up and saw that Melissa felt she should be the one that asked that question. "Sorry."

The doctor turned quickly and shot Marie a smile, before turning back to Melissa and delivering the news that would forever change everyone's life. "That is two heartbeats. You are having twins."

CHAPTER THIRTY FOUR

The nurse's technician explained to Melissa that the twin's growth rate was fine, that their skull's circumference was within normal measurements and that their heart rates were okay. Nothing else on the imaging suggested there was anything wrong.

She asked the ultrasound technician a million questions, including; "Can you tell if they are identical or fraternal?"

"Well, if they were sharing one sack we would definitely know that they were identical, but they aren't. This is actually a good thing, because a single sac delivery of twins is very dangerous. However, since they each have their own sac, it doesn't mean that they aren't identical. It could be either. You're just going to have to wait and see."

Melissa finally asked her last question; "So, there isn't anything wrong with *either* child?"

"Not that we can see," the man with the balding head answered. "These machines are getting better, but they don't catch everything; so keep going to your doctor for regular check-ups. You will have another ultrasound in a month, we should know even more then." He put his hand on hers, normally something that would make her skin crawl. On this occasion, she actually welcomed any form of assurance she could get. "Everything is going to be just fine."

Marie was furious when she found out that Melissa had gone to the ultrasound without her. She kept it in, however, and saved it for Paul.

"I can't believe she would do that!" She paced around their little living room. "I know she's up to something. She's going to change her mind, I know it."

Paul, sitting on the couch, watched his wife manically move about the room. He tried to calm her. "Honey, you don't know it. She probably just didn't want you making her nervous, that's all. It can't be easy on her."

"Don't!"

Paul threw his hands in the air in frustration.

"What about what we are going through? Huh? You think this is easy?" Exhausted, she plopped into a recliner. The old chair, swayed back and forth until finally settling in place. Marie sat sprawled out and waited for her poor husband's response.

"No, this isn't easy on anyone." He walked the three steps across the room and knelt down on his right knee and took her hands in his. "She said they're both healthy, right?"

Marie nodded.

"There you go."

Melissa decided that she was not going to go through the next step twice; she would tell the three other people involved in the soap opera at one time. She invited Paul and Marie over for a cook out and a game of euchre afterward. Paul and Steven stood over the grill and seared their steaks to perfection. Steven was pretty much useless for anything else around the house, but the man could grill. The guys drank beer and talked about a horrendous week at work. The women talked constantly, but said absolutely nothing of any significance.

Melissa finally brought out a deck of cards. It was a beautiful, warm July evening. They sat in the Fonduluc's backyard at a picnic table made of ash by Steven and Paul. The La Claires had an identical table in their backyard. She sorted through the cards, taking out all of the two's through eights; except for the fives, they would be used for scoring. Euchre was their favorite card game; the foursome had spent a thousand evenings playing the game. Steven was terrible at it, but Melissa was the best of the four, and made up for her husband's idiotic play most of the time. They grew up on euchre, were introduced to the game by their parents, and would eventually pass it on to their own children as well. Euchre, hunting, fishing and pasties were Yooper ways of life.

Melissa dealt out the cards one at a time until a jack of spades was set in front of Marie. "Your deal."

"Is it?"

Steven and Paul immediately halted their conversation. All eyes were on Melissa as she answered the cryptic two word question.

Melissa knew when she was being called out by her friend. She refused to play the game of *What do you mean by that?* It would be insulting to Marie and just a waste of all of their time. She had set up the cookout for one reason; and it was time to get back to that purpose. She said it bluntly, without emotion and with a certain sternness that only Steven was used to.

"I'm keeping one of the babies."

Paul and Marie said nothing; they just fixed their stare on Melissa. The couple was powerless to do anything about it, and simply waited for the rest of the rules, before unleashing their many questions.

Steven, on the other hand, was simply shocked. "What?"

She ignored her husband and fixed her eyes on both Paul and Marie, alternating between the two. "I want another child, and I might not ever get the chance again; especially with him." She quickly glanced over to Steven, before moving her eyes back to Paul and Marie. "You will get the first child . . . your daughter."

Paul and Marie turned their eyes to each other; hearing the words 'your daughter' momentarily paralyzed them.

"The second child will be our daughter." Melissa held out her hands and took Steven's in hers. "Our daughter," she repeated. Those two words had almost the same power on him.

"Our daughter." He smiled. "My little girl."

Marie and Paul had been holding hands without even realizing it.

Marie finally snapped back to reality. "They're twins, how can you . . . we separate them like that."

"We're going back to the UP. You guys are staying here. After the children are born, we no longer know each other."

The foursome sat in silence. Euchre would not be played that night.

CHAPTER THIRTY FIVE

"I just know she's going to change her mind. How could she not?" Marie was having another periodic breakdown. The anxiety for both Paul and Marie augmented exponentially with each day.

Paul would try to be rational and give a logical reason as to why Melissa wouldn't change her mind. However, each time his answer came out shallow and without much merit. He couldn't understand how Melissa would be able to deliver two tiny little creatures to the world and then hand the first one off to someone else. Paul was a traditional, old fashioned, narrow minded man from the Upper Peninsula of Michigan and he could figure out the insanity of the situation.

The worst months of the pregnancy ended with the humidity and heat of a very warm Michigan summer. As the temperatures began to cool with the coming of autumn, the La Claires and the Fondulucs saw less and less of each other. Paul took on a young man to replace Steven in their business venture. Once Steven accepted, and more importantly, embraced the fact that he would be going home soon; he checked out from everything but putting in his daily work shift. Even at work he was next to worthless. He showed up late and made any excuse to get out early. On a positive, he began to change at home. He started to play with little Andrew and occasionally he even changed a diaper; but for a man with large hands it was a difficult chore. His enormous mitts were not nimble at all. Melissa was just excited to see his newfound appreciation for being a family man and melted a little inside every time she saw Andrew light up when his father came home.

Once Melissa found out she was having twins, and more importantly keeping one of them, it no longer made sense to live a life of exclusion. She told everyone she knew that she was going to be a mother again and that it was going to be a little girl.

Marie, who had been the one to insist upon her going to see a doctor in the first place, no longer went to Melissa's check-ups. At first she made excuses of having other things to do; eventually Melissa just stopped telling her.

Melissa turned 30 in October and decided that she was deserving of her very own birthday party. Her best friend wasn't going to throw her one, so she made sure that Steven got the credit; even though he made no calls, bought no party favors, but was able to stay out of the way as ordered. Melissa invited every person she had met in the year and a half of living in the Lower Peninsula. Her party was a rousing success. It went into the wee hours of the morning, but two attendees were noticeably absent. Paul and Marie; at her insistence, had a wedding to go to. This was not a complete lie, but under ordinary circumstances Marie always would have chosen her best friend's one and only 30th birthday over the wedding of a second cousin she had only met once.

*   *   *

"Steven . . . . Steven . . . ." Melissa tapped her husband on the shoulder. This continued for several more seconds. Each call of *Steven* got a little louder and the tapping transformed to jabbing. "Steven! I'm having contractions!"

Steven, who had been a sleep for a few hours, opened one eye and smacked his lips as he tried to take in what his wife was telling him. "That's nice, go back to bed. They go away."

He rolled over. Melissa grabbed her own pre-packed travel bag and set it in the backseat. She grabbed little Andrew out of his crib and wrapped him in a heavy blanket then walked him next door, careful to cover his face in the chilly air, and rapped her knuckles on the door. A few moments later Marie stood in front of her. She did not act surprised in the least that someone was knocking on her door at three in the morning.

Without saying a word, Melissa handed over her first born, who was still sound asleep. Marie took him and smiled. Melissa knew it was sincere and that the deep freeze between the two was temporarily over.

"Wish me . . . wish us luck," Melissa said, returning the smile.

Nearly seven and a half months of incredible unease and angst came out of Marie in a flood of tears.

"I'm so sorry. I've been such a bitch. I just want this baby so bad." She looked down at Melissa's stomach, while still holding Andrew.

Melissa took her hand.

"I know. Trust me, we both are going to be mommies of beautiful little girls. I couldn't take that away from you." Marie took her hand back to wipe her tears away. "You believe me, right?"

Marie nodded her head and tried to bring back her smile.

Melissa felt another contraction and reflexively clutched her midsection. "Woooh."

"How far apart are you?"

"Five minutes," Melissa lied.

She was actually closer to ten, but wanted to get to the hospital as fast as she could. Somehow, she believed that if she was at the hospital, things would naturally happen faster.

"Go, go!" Marie pushed her out the door as Andrew began to fuss.

"I love you," Marie said and meant with all her heart.

She realized that not only was she hours away from being a mom, but that she was also about to lose her best friend to the most incredible sacrifice she could imagine.

"I love you, too," Melissa responded as she hustled across the dew covered, but worn out path between the two houses.

She walked into the bedroom and wasn't surprised to find Steven snoring away. In her hand was a glass of cold water. Melissa contemplated whether or not to dump it on him; then decided that she most certainly would. She figured the game of 'wake up, Steven' could go on forever. She knew it would end with her getting pissed and she didn't want to end up feeling that way on what would be the most important day of her life. If *he* got pissed, on the other hand; oh well.

As if in slow motion, she lifted the glass high over his head. Steven's wife slowly cocked her right wrist and the first trickle rolled over the lip of the glass. It landed on Steven's cheek. He instinctively wiped it away; then a bigger drop landed on his eyelash. Before he had the chance to wipe any more water away, the whole glass of water came pouring down over his head. Steven bolted upright in an instant and had to catch his breath. The coldness of the water sent him into momentary shock. He quickly regained his senses.

"What the fuck, eh!"

"It's time to go," Melissa said in the calmest voice she could muster.

Steven looked around, took in the scene and everything began to click.

"Right, right." He jumped up; a little too fast and got light headed. He fell back to the bed.

"You're clothes are right there."

She pointed next to him. Melissa took in the sight of his nakedness and admired his manlyhood. *That magnificent tool of yours is what started all of this.* It was also what triggered her contractions; they had made love earlier that night.

Steven grabbed his underwear and pulled them up over his legs to the beginning of his torso. He did the same with his pants and threw a plaid shirt on without buttoning it.

"Time to go, babe!"

He grabbed her face and held it with both hands. He gave her a kiss on the lips. Melissa didn't mind his foul breath at all, but did suggest that he give them a quick brushing before they left. She might not mind now, but who knew how long she would have to endure it during labor.

They arrived at St. Joe's Hospital in Flint and Steven pulled up to the ER circle and put his car in park.

"Steven, they don't have valet service."

"I was going to drop you off, then park."

"Just park over there," she said, pointing to the ER parking lot.

Melissa assured him that she could walk the distance just fine. She didn't want to be without Steven for any amount of time. He held her hand as they walked through the doors of the ER. There were people with cuts, nasty cases of the flu and various other ailments. There seemed to be an unusual amount of ER customers to Melissa, even for a Saturday night in a tough town.

She was asked the normal questions and had her heartbeat and blood pressure checked before being directed to have a seat in the waiting room. It was only five minutes, but it seemed like an eternity that they sat in the 'room of gloom', as Steven coined it. She felt like everyone was staring at her. Being an ER; everyone was staring at everyone else. People naturally wanted to know what was going on with the other person. In Melissa's case it was easy to see what was going on and how it happened. She looked over at an African American man in his forties who was holding a blood soaked cloth to his forehead. Next to him was a woman of the same race, but three times his size. Melissa could only assume she was the reason for the man's visit to the ER. She looked like she hated the world, almost as much as she hated the man next to her. The reality was that the man had come home drunk, hit his head on the sharp edge of a cabinet and began gushing blood all over his sister's white carpet. If Melissa had known this story, she could have sympathized with the woman's plight.

"Melissa Flonduck!" A voice called out. No one ever got her name right.

Melissa patted Steven on his knee to get him up. He was in a daze. *This is going to be a long night if he's going to be this loopy,* she thought to herself. He got up like an obedient puppy and followed her as she followed the triage nurse. An overly bubbly woman took their insurance information.

"It's going to be just the absolute best experience ever!" Melissa looked at her petite frame and knew that she had not experienced child birth yet, but smiled anyway.

Melissa was given a room to herself to start. They sat there for hours as Steven drifted in and out of alertness. Nurses came in and checked her vitals, asked how she was doing and timed her contractions. Her water still had not broken, but her contractions were now seven minutes apart. She asked if her OB/GYN had been called; he had not she was informed. They would wait until the contractions were closer and her water had broken. She still had a while to go.

*   *   *

Marie did not sleep at all. She lay on her bed with Andrew cradled under her bosom. She admired his beauty and began to hate herself for having any doubts about Melissa and for having had brief, but nonetheless, hateful thoughts about the little baby boy who was breathing heavily next to her. With his fine blonde hair and rosy little cheeks; how could she ever have had any ill feelings about something so precious? She gave him a kiss on his cheek. She began to cry. One little tear at a time traveled down her cheek and splashed on Andrew's face. They were the kind of tears shaped like rain drops; they were heavy and salty. Each one seemed to have its own meaning. *This is one is for being hateful. This one is for doubting my best friend. This one, for the little girl I used to be, the one who was brutalized by an evil human being.* The meaning of each tear began to change as Marie decided it was time to let go of so much pain. *This one is for the little girl that will be the light of my life.*

This one is for my husband; no matter how stubborn and unemotional he may be, he has always been there. This one is for how great my life might be . . . will be. The tears stopped. She looked down at Andrew, who was now awake. He giggled; causing Marie to do the same. He was covered with her sticky wet tears. They coated his eyes, and the saltiness of them was the only thing left over from what had splashed on his cheeks. She couldn't help herself; this was going to be the greatest day of her life. She leaned down and kissed him smack on the lips. "Oh, you beautiful, beautiful boy!" He giggled again; Marie joined him.

Four hours after she had left, Marie pictured Melissa all sweaty with her legs spread wide as she breathed heavily. She couldn't picture her friend screaming, like she knew most women would. It just wasn't like Melissa to be that way. Paul walked into the bedroom with just a towel on.

"You're going to call me as soon as you find anything out, right?"

"Yes, dear," Marie responded, but never took her eyes off the blue eyed child that she was currently playing patty cake with.

*   *   *

Melissa sat in her assigned bed frustrated that her water still had not broke; aggravated that Steven was now back asleep and snoring. Her irritation reached a peak a few minutes later when another woman was wheeled into *her* room. The woman smiled at her; Melissa gave her the dirtiest look she could manage. The woman recoiled; it was her first baby. *Wow, am I going to be this big of a bitch!* She looked back at Steven; *good luck, buddy.*

*   *   *

Marie, who had fed Andrew twice, watched countless *Barney* videos with him and played patty cake until she thought her hands would fall off, nearly snapped at 3:30. It had been twelve hours since they had left for the hospital. No matter how many times she tried to be rational, her mind raced to a vision of Steven and Melissa running out of the hospital; each with a baby under an arm. She knew as she looked at little Andrew, that it was ludicrous. Still, *why haven't you called Steven! I know she's had the baby, I know you guys are plotting!*

She couldn't help herself, she began to sob.

Andrew waddled over to her and held out his hands. "Mama?"

Marie held out her arms and took little Andrew in them. The sweet boy was trying to make her feel better. Paul walked in a few minutes later; Marie wiped the last of her tears away. He set his tool belt aside and walked over to where Marie and Andrew were and plopped down on the floor next to them. He put an arm around his wife and rubbed her back.

"Our little girl is coming, hang in there."

Marie feigned a smile for her husband. She had no choice but to hang in there.

*   *   *

"Mrs. Fonduluc," the doctor on duty began, "I think we can probably send you home. Your contractions are still pretty far apart and your water still hasn't broken. You probably were having false contractions."

Melissa wanted to protest, but the sight of Steven cackling away, watching cartoons was enough for her to want to be home too.

"I'll get your discharge ready. We'll see you back here in no time." The doctor left to check on a woman in the next room.

"Oh, shit!"

Steven clicked the remote control. He changed the channel to a different cartoon. That one had lost his interest.

"What is it?"

"My water, oooooooohhhhhhh," she said before clutching her belly again. "Get the doctor."

Steven jumped up as directed and found the doctor. He ran back in a few moments later. He looked down at his wife's groin area. His facial expression suggested to Melissa that he expected her to be holding a delivered baby.

The doctor casually strolled up to Melissa and lifted her gown.

"Well, you definitely are in labor, Melissa."

Melissa sighed in relief when she saw the handsome Dr. Kendrick walk into her room two hours later. He casually put on a pair of latex gloves and inserted a finger into Melissa's vagina. She scrunched her face; a reflex for anytime a man other than her husband had to insert anything in that part of her body.

"Five centimeters dilated and thirty percent effaced. We're getting there."

We? Melissa thought. The doctor was losing his attractiveness to her.

"Just breathe, der, honey," Steven chimed in. Melissa was not currently having a contraction. She did not say what she wanted to; she simply smiled. Steven had not attended child birth classes the first time around and she had to deliver Andrew without anyone in the room with her. She decided she would be nice for as long as possible.

Another two hours passed and her situation and attitude changed. "How . . . ." Pant, pant, pant. " . . . long?" Melissa looked at the doctor who she now found completely repulsive. She grunted as she went through another harsh labor pain.

He threw his rubber gloves in the trash bin. Steven made a disgusted face as he saw the end of the glove covered with yellow and red stains.

"Could be forty-five minutes, could be four to five hours." He pointed to her exposed area. "They'll let us know when they're ready." He walked out and slapped a hand on Steven's shoulder. "Twin girls, dad. Double the trouble." He smiled and left.

The doctor didn't know of the arrangements made by the Fondulucs and the La Claires.

Forty-five minutes did turn into five hours. By this time Melissa had been given an epidural; something she had refused with her first child. She lasted as long as she could, before giving into the pain. She felt a weird sensation as the nurse poked her with the long needle. Within moments she was the happiest person in the world. The pain had subdued to a dull throb which she could easily tolerate. She released her titan grip on Steven's hand. As she brushed her sweaty hair back off her forehead, Steven rubbed his hand, trying to get some of the feeling and color back.

"Sorry, babe," she said smiling.

Steven looked to the nurse and asked, "Can you score that stuff on the streets? She never says she's sorry."

The nurse smiled politely before exiting.

*   *   *

Paul and Marie sat in silence as they ate a meal that lacked all flavor. Andrew was on their bed, out for the night. He had been a good boy all day, but over the past couple of hours he began to want his mom—he'd never been away from her for that long. As hard as Marie tried to console him, he still cried himself to sleep.

"I'm calling the hospital," she said without emotion.

Paul did not object. Any news had to be good news. Marie called the hospital and told the receptionist that she was Melissa's sister from out of town.

The lady called up to the maternity ward before returning to the phone she had just answered. "Ma'am, your sister has not delivered her baby, yet."

"Okay, thanks." Marie hung up the phone and looked to Paul. "Not yet."

At least they haven't run off, she thought.

*   *   *

Doctor Kendrick came in the hospital room for the last time. He checked the EFM, saw everything was normal with the twin's heart rates and then donned his gloves again.

Dr. Kendrick raised his eyebrows to Melissa. "This could be it."

Damn well better be. He inserted his fingers, took a look around and then smiled first at Melissa and then at Steven.

"Let's have a baby."

He pulled off his gloves and tossed them into the garbage bin. Steven didn't look this time. His eyes were firmly on Melissa. Neither could hide their excitement or relief.

The doctor said a few words to the nurse and then hustled away.

A nurse came in a few moments later and tossed Steven a pair of blue scrubs. "Put these on," she ordered.

Two orderlies wheeled Melissa's hospital bed away.

"Hurry up, Steven!"

Melissa was the second woman in the past minute to boss him around. He walked into the bathroom and began to take down his pants. He stopped suddenly, not knowing if he was supposed to put on the scrubs over his skin or over his pants. He didn't want to be yelled at, or worse embarrassed. He walked out and found an orderly cleaning up.

"Hey, doc, do I put these on over my pants or over my skivvies, eh?"

"They go over your pants, man." The hospital employee did not correct the Yooper on the incorrect title.

"Thanks, eh." Steven walked back into the bathroom and put the pants and shirt on. He stopped again, confused. *Why are there three head caps?* He stared at the three pieces of material with elastic banding.

Doctor Orderly looked up from his cart and shook his head.

"Brother, the two in your left hand are for your feet." He shook his head as he pushed the supply cart out of the room.

"Hey, danks!" Steven hollered after him. He put them on his feet and walked to the nursing station just outside his room. "Hi, uh . . . where do I go?"

A nurse smiled at the giant man in front of her.

"Follow me, dad."

She led him to the delivery room where he found his wife in what seemed to be the worst agony a person could suffer. He thought quickly about taking the rest of the mission off. *I should go wait out there! This ain't no place for a man.*

His thoughts were short lived as Melissa caught him out of the corner of her eye. "Get your ass in here! Where the hell have you been?" It was followed by a blood curdling, guttural scream.

"Let's relax, now." The doctor looked at the nurse and raised an eyebrow. Melissa noticed, but did not say anything. *Fuck you both. Want to trade spots?*

Melissa gripped Steven's hands and followed the directions of the nurse and Dr. Kendrick. She pushed when they said push, and breathed as directed, too. Within twenty minutes of Steven's arrival she heard the words she had hoped to hear hours earlier.

"Here she comes!"

The handsome doctor began to maneuver the small being as her head slowly oozed through Melissa's vaginal opening. He twisted the head slightly and then turned the shoulders; once the first shoulder came through, the rest of her body came out easily. The doctor held the little body out in front of him. Within seconds the child announced its birth to the world with a shrieking cry. Her little face was contorted, red and slimy . . . but she was beautiful. The doctor held the small child out toward Steven.

"Dad, you want to cut the cord?"

Steven couldn't edit his response. "Oh, hell no!" The doctor and nurses both laughed. Melissa was not amused. For the first time since she started her actual delivery, her mind was on nothing but how she could give this child away.

"Alright, I guess I will earn my money." The doctor skillfully cut the cord; then attached the clamp to the baby's cutoff umbilical cord. "Mom, are you ready to see your baby?"

Melissa froze. *It's not my baby.*

"Mom?" Dr. Kendrick was holding the baby in front of her. She stared over the baby's shoulder and her vision was of her best friend, Marie. The image quickly changed from the 30-year-old version of Marie to the 13-year-old edition. Behind her she saw her vile stepfather. She could smell his scent; cheap aftershave and foul alcoholic breath. Melissa cried; it was a slow grinding sob. She put her hands up to her face. She thought if she closed her eyes she could eliminate the image, but it was still there. The doctor looked at the nurse who shrugged her shoulders.

Melissa's mental anguish was quickly taken over by the physical pain of another contraction. The doctor handed the baby off to a nurse. The nurse assessed the child and recorded her Apgar scores on a chart. The child scored a perfect 10. The baby, naked to the world, was set on a table and measured and weighed. She came into the world at 5 pounds, 8 ounces and measured 18 inches long.

The delivery of Margret Anne Fonduluc came nine minutes after her sister's at 12:03 a.m. on November 14, 1981. The twins would not share the same birthday, or anything else for the next eight years. Maggie's face was turned down as Dr. Kendrick began the same maneuvers with her as he had with her sister a few minutes earlier. Melissa could feel the baby being twisted in her vaginal opening.

"Nurse."

The African American nurse came over to Dr. Kendrick's side. "Unilateral complete," he said in a very clinical tone.

Melissa's maternal instincts and insecurities kicked in. A doctor didn't just call over the nurse and then say something like 'unilateral complete' and it not mean anything. The doctor nodded and continued the delivery. Like her sister before her, once Maggie got one shoulder through, the rest came easily. Maggie screamed her arrival to the world shortly after coming out. Dr. Kendrick was not smiling as he had been for the first delivery; this did not escape Melissa. Her concern peaked when he clamped Maggie's umbilical cord and then handed off the baby to the nurse without even offering the chance to see her. Had it not been for his expression and the extremely brief conversation between her doctor and nurse, she would have just assumed that he was not aware that only the second child belonged to her.

"What's wrong?" She meant for it to come out as calmly as possible, but it came out louder and more panicky than she wanted. Dr. Kendrick turned to his patient. "Melissa, your second child has a cleft lip and palate. Do you know what that is?"

Melissa couldn't believe what she was hearing. She had an uncle who was a 'hair lip,' she knew exactly what her baby had.

"I want to see her!" Melissa did not try to control her response this time.

The nurse finished her Apgar test; Maggie scored a six. Dr. Kendrick nodded for her to bring the baby over. The baby was wrapped in a blanket and handed to Melissa.

Steven could not contain his response; he gasped. The child had a huge hole where her top lip should have been. It extended up to her right nostril, which appeared to be caved in. Melissa now understood what the term unilateral complete meant. The gap extended in one direction, completely up to the nose. *Unilateral complete.*

Melissa tried to hold back her shock. She tried to look at the little blue eyes staring back at her; to contain her raw emotions. She tried to show the baby only love; but she couldn't. She saw a lifetime of being made fun of, a childhood of surgeries, a beautiful face marred by God's hand. She wept again and handed the baby off to the nurse. Maggie's eyes did not leave her mother's face. She seemed to crane her neck back as she was being swept away.

Melissa's body pushed out the placenta, she didn't notice. She felt none of it; her mind blocking out any physical pain with the mental torment that currently occupied her thoughts. *This is not how it's supposed to be, damn it.* Steven put a hand on his wife's shoulder, she pushed it away. Melissa continued to weep; her right forearm covering her face.

"Mr. and Mrs. Fonduluc, I'm sorry that your little girl has this medical issue; but trust me, she will get through everything just fine. She's a beautiful little girl; you have two beautiful little girls. Both of them are going to need you. Mrs. Fonduluc, do you understand?" the doctor asked.

Melissa did not remove her arm, but nodded. She just wanted to be left alone.

CHAPTER THIRTY SIX

An hour later, Melissa was in a different room. She lay on her side and stared out a window. Steven was pacing behind her.

"You want me to call Paul and Marie?"

She didn't turn around, she only shook her head.

Melissa contemplated every scenario. *I can keep both; everyone is aware that I can do that. It's still my choice!* She saw the image of her best friend; her step-father behind her kissing the girl's neck.

"Go away," she said with no emotion.

Steven assumed she was talking to him and slipped away to find some food.

* * *

"Why haven't they called?" Marie looked at Paul for an answer, but knew she wouldn't get one; at least not a satisfactory one.

He didn't try to make something up; he just raised his shoulders in joint conjecture. Marie had called the hospital every hour. The last time she called, at 1:00; she had been given the news by a different receptionist that Mrs. Fonduluc had delivered two little girls; mother and daughters were doing fine.

* * *

I can tell Marie that the 'hair lip' was the first baby. Melissa immediately felt guilty for thinking of the little baby in those terms. A nurse wheeled in the babies who were lying side by side. They were holding hands.

"Are you ready to hold your little girls?"

Melissa sat up. *I'll never be ready.*

"Yes." Her voice was very raspy, having been dry for so long. She grabbed a cup of her water and took a sip. "Yes," she repeated more audibly.

The nurse handed her her firstborn. Melissa cradled the baby in her left arm. The tiny pink faced child immediately began to squirm and cry. The nurse then carefully handed over Maggie. Melissa cradled the other little baby in her right arm. She looked down at both babies. Maggie looked up at her and seemed to be smiling. The rational part of Melissa knew that it was simply the malformation of her mouth that made her appear to be smiling; but something inside her told her the baby was communicating with her. Maggie blinked and turned her neck, taking in the view of the woman who she would call 'mom' for the rest of her life. The other child was now screaming. Melissa tried to quiet her, but couldn't take her eyes off of Maggie.

"They're both so beautiful." The nurse stood by her side. "Do you have names, yet?"

Melissa looked up and shook her head.

"Are these your first," the nurse asked, a friendly smile on her face.

"No," Melissa responded, "I have a little boy who is sixteen months.

"Nice. I have a little boy too. He's seven. You want to see a picture?"

"Sure," Melissa responded with her eyebrows arched.

She thought it was a little strange that her nurse wanted to show her a picture, and even more strange that she had a picture ready in her pocket. The nurse handed over the photo. Melissa immediately understood the purpose for sharing the picture. A scar above the boy's lip extended to his nose. The boy's smile was a mile wide, however. He appeared to Melissa to be the happiest boy alive. Despite the scar, the boy was very cute.

"He's a doll."

"Thanks," the nurse replied. She put a hand on Melissa's arm. "It's going to be alright, you know."

"I know." And Melissa did know. She was grateful to the nurse for giving her perspective.

Steven walked in at that moment, pulling apart the metallic foil of a potato chip bag with his hand and mouth. In his other hand he was holding a can of pop and a candy bar.

"Welcome to the party, pops!" the nurse exclaimed.

She reached down for the first child and picked her up. She received a look from Melissa that this was okay. She held out the baby to Steven. He set the chips, pop and candy bar on the tray that held the food that Melissa couldn't eat. He took the squirmy, crying baby into his arms. She was so tiny compared to his big paws.

"Hi, der, little girl." He poked a finger onto her button nose. She stopped crying.

"I'll be back in a few minutes," the nurse told the couple before leaving.

Steven followed the nurse out with his eyes. He walked around his wife's bed and peered around the curtain, before turning back to Melissa.

"Which one we keeping?"

"This one," Melissa answered without taking her eyes off of the little girl who had already stolen her heart.

Had she not been having the same thoughts only a little while earlier, she may have scolded her husband for even suggesting such a notion.

"You sure?"

"Yes." This time she turned to her husband. The answer came out as sternly as a mother telling a child for the second time she is 'sure' that he can't stay up any longer. "That one . . . ," she motioned to the baby Steven was holding. " . . . doesn't belong to us." Her voice cracked before she could finish.

They were the most painful words she had ever spoken in her life. She wasn't totally convinced that she meant them. However, she forced herself to accept and believe the words.

"Should I call Marie and Paul, now?" Steven asked.

"No, they can wait."

She knew it was cruel and that Marie and Paul must be going through hell, but she decided that she was going to have a proper goodbye with the little girl who would not be spending the rest of her life calling her 'mom.' She didn't want Marie or Paul anywhere around. She deserved at least one day with the little girl. They would have her for the rest of their lives. They could survive another few hours of torture.

*   *   *

Marie and Paul tried to sleep. Little Andrew, a constant reminder of the child they were so close to being able to call their own, lay between them. Marie and Paul took turns looking over at the digital clock; they went to bed at 2:30. At 5:30 Marie jumped up out of bed.

"I can't take it anymore, let's go."

Paul didn't argue; he hopped up and got dressed. Marie picked up Andrew, who slowly woke up. She took him in the living room and changed him; afterward handing him off to Paul while she went and got changed. A few minutes later they were out the door and on their way to the hospital.

They arrived and were informed that they would not be able to visit until 8:30. They said fine and parked themselves in the waiting room. They took turns keeping Andrew amused. The child wandered around in a circle, holding onto his baggie of Cheerios.

*   *   *

Melissa woke up around eight; she had slept for six good hours. Steven; lying on the uncomfortable chair, did not. The babies were in the nursery. Both children were considered healthy, despite Maggie's facial condition. Melissa pushed the button requesting a nurse. Within seconds, a pudgy nurse with a nasty disposition strolled in. She didn't say a thing, just arched her eyebrows. *Yeah?*

"I would like to see my baby."

"Both of them?" the woman asked, seemingly put off by the question.

"Just my firstborn for now, thanks." Melissa tried to force a smile; then decided that she didn't need to. She didn't care about trying to appease the bitch nurse.

A few minutes later, the nurse brought in the child. She had a pink cap on her head and was wrapped tightly in a blanket. The nurse handed her over to Melissa who repositioned herself in her propped up bed.

"Anything else?"

"No."

"Okay," the nurse replied. She set down a baby bottle on the tray next to Melissa. "When she wakes up she'll be hungry."

"Thanks."

Melissa watched the nurse waddle out; then turned her attention to the little creature in her arms. She had a thumb to her mouth as she suckled on the very edge of it. Her eyes were squeezed shut.

"Hi, baby."

A single tear seeped from Melissa's left eye and made its way down her cheek before finding a resting spot just above her lip. As she spoke, a stream of tears followed.

"I need you to know something . . . I love you very much, but I made my best friend a promise. You see, she can't have babies, and she wants one so, so bad.

The child's eyes fluttered open. She tried to take in the voice and face above her. Unlike her earlier visit, she was not restless; she looked up at the birth mother and appeared to be listening intently. A teardrop descended from Melissa's chin and hurdled through the air splash landing on her little nose. The baby blinked, but continued to listen to her mother.

"So, I decided that I would give her a baby. I didn't know you were going to have a sister . . . I know you two would have been . . .

Melissa couldn't control her sobbing. Steven was now awake. He sat upright, but did not say a word. He watched his wife say goodbye to a child that he had fathered but would never be able to call his own.

" . . . close. And I'm sorry that I'm taking her away from you.

The child blinked up at Melissa as another tear drop splashed, this time on her forehead. Melissa wiped the salty wetness away with her sleeve.

" . . . but she needs me . . . you . . . you don't. Marie will be your mother and Paul will be your father.

As if on cue, the child began to cry. It was not the scream it was earlier, but it was harsher to Melissa's ears.

"Baby, please . . . you will have a great life . . . I promise you."

Melissa couldn't take it anymore; she and her baby cried together. Steven got up and took the little girl from his wife's arms. Melissa did not protest; her eyes were shut tight. The emptiness in her heart began that moment and never went away. A fire of anger and guilt began to burn in her core; sitting right next to the emptiness.

Steven took the baby to the nurse with the poor attitude and handed her off without saying a word. He walked back to his wife's room and knelt down by her side, taking her hand in his.

"I love you."

"I love you, too." Melissa buried her head in his arm and continued to sob.

After the moment had passed and Melissa realized she was out of tears, she looked over to her husband.

"You can call Marie now."

Steven dutifully walked out and found a pay phone. He dialed his best friend's number and waited for a quick and anxious 'hello!' but it didn't come. Instead, he got nothing but one ring after another. After twenty rings, he hung up. *That's strange.* He walked back to the room with his arms crossed.

"No one is answering."

"They're here, Paul. Find the waiting room, get Andrew and tell them to go home. They will get their baby when I've been discharged tomorrow."

The serious, emotionless Melissa was back; and she was ordering him around like a foot soldier.

Steven did as directed. He found the waiting room and there sat Marie and Paul. They looked more tired than even he felt.

"Come here, big boy."

Andrew, who was sitting on a chair across from Paul and Marie, turned to the familiar voice of his father. He waddled over to Steven who scooped him up and hugged him.

"Dadda!"

Marie and Paul turned their attention to Steven as well, waiting for any kind of indication as to what was going on.

"Melissa says to go home." He grabbed Andrew's baby bag and turned to head back.

"That's it!" Marie screamed. The other people in the room stared at her. "What about my baby?"

Steven did not turn around.

"Your baby will be delivered tomorrow, after Melissa is discharged." He turned the corner and was no longer seen.

People in the waiting room turned to each other to try and decipher what they had just heard.

CHAPTER THIRTY SEVEN

Later that day, Melissa's favorite nurse came back. She showed more pictures of her son and explained to both Steven and Melissa what they could expect in terms of Maggie's procedures, operations and the like. She was extremely comforting. Her son was also a unilateral complete. It was one thing when the doctor explained these things to them; but when someone who had actually been through a similar situation told them, they believed every word she said. She knew firsthand every fear that they had and did her best to ease their worries. The nurse showed Melissa how to use the specialized nipple allowing Maggie to properly suckle the rubber end of her bottles.

Andrew had been good all day, but was finally getting to the point of being too much for either Steven or Melissa to handle.

"Steven, you need to take the little guy home. Get some rest yourself, okay. I should be discharged early tomorrow morning. Why don't you come back here around seven?"

"You sure?"

"Yes," she answered.

She curled a finger at him, motioning for him to lean down. He did as directed. Melissa planted a kiss on his cheek and hugged him. He slowly returned the embrace.

"Thanks for being here, you've been terrific. I couldn't get through this without you."

Steven beamed. "You're welcome."

The next day Melissa made the longest walk of her life. She crossed the beaten path that existed between her yard and Marie's holding the little child in her arms. There was no need to knock. As soon as she got within twenty feet of the house, the door was wide open. Marie crossed her arms, then put them to her side, then her hips . . . finally she just clasped her hands together as Melissa walked up the steps.

Melissa did not initially have the will to hand over the bundled child, so she chose to speak first.

"I can never speak to you again, see you again, or know anything about this child."

She slowly held the child forward. The baby was asleep; she was wearing a little white coat with the hood in the shape of a lamb's head; little ears and all. Marie took the child in her arms and nearly fainted. Neither Paul nor Steven were anywhere in sight. It was not their cross to bear.

"I can't tell you how grateful I am," Marie began.

Melissa put up a hand. She had run out of tears, but had to stop her friend. She didn't want to hear her appreciation or undying gratitude. At that moment Marie was nothing more than the woman who was stealing her baby.

"Don't." Marie stopped and stared at her one time friend. "We're even."

CHAPTER THIRTY EIGHT

Andrew wasn't allowed to attend graduation or even come back to the high school to pick up his belongings. Melissa thought about calling Kevin Lewis, but Mr. Spivey wore her down. She wasn't in the mood to fight the man; she was ashamed enough of what her son had been doing the past year and a half. She was more ashamed that she had no clue. The woman once would have come unglued on any teacher or administrator who inferred that her children were less than honorable, intelligent or hardworking. She sighed as she cleaned out his locker. *Where has the time gone?* She felt like a woman almost half way to a hundred. Melissa looked around at all the teenage girls with their unwrinkled faces and perfect little bodies. She hated them all; especially the tall, athletic one who wore too much makeup who just happened to walk by.

* * *

Trevor was paid a visit by the state police, as had every person logged in Andrew's confiscated cell phone. Since his call from Wendy he knew to lay low and also to get rid of anything that might incriminate him. All of his stash and money was safely deposited in his hiding place; a place only one other person knew about, Andrew. He acted aloof to O'Reilly's questions and even taunted Mackey. Mackey had once picked him up at a party and issued him a minor in possession (MIP). That didn't bother him; he could respect anyone who was just doing their job. It was the way the guy manhandled him, and even worse talked to him; like he was less than a cockroach. That kind of shit pissed him off.

"Have I ever purchased marijuana from an Andrew Fonduluc?" He scratched his chin. "I don't even know any Andrews and I certain wouldn't buy drugs, officers."

The sarcasm eluded neither State trooper.

"Asshole, why does your name come up in his cell phone?" Mackey asked, inadvertently spitting on Trevor.

Trevor wiped the dot of spit off his cheek and leaned into Mackey as if ready to reveal a secret. Mackey backed off a bit. "Well, Trooper Mackey," he began, knowing full well that it was Sergeant Mackey. "I have long suspected that my girlfriend has been cheating on me." He said it softly enough that Stacy, who was sitting on the couch playing with their child, Trevor Jr; could not hear. "Maybe this is the guy; look at the big-melon on that kid. He can't be mine." Trevor looked over at his girlfriend and the child he would die for. "Bitch, you been cheating me?"

Stacy knew he was playing, but was still embarrassed by him. "Shut up, asshole;" she responded with little emotion. "Daddy's being a dumbass," she said to the cooing child.

Mackey's face reddened as Trevor's smile widened. O'Reilly stepped in between the two.

"Let's go." He patted Mackey on the back, before turning to Trevor. "Be careful, young man."

"Always," Trevor smiled with his arms outstretched. As soon as the police were gone, his smiled evaporated.

"I've got to talk to Andrew," he said to himself, but his much smarter girlfriend heard it too.

"That might not be a good idea, right now."

I know. Thoughts of running off with the twenty grand occupied his mind more and more. *I can go to some tech school, become a truck driver or something; learn how work with computers. Anything is better than this shit.* He walked into the bathroom and got out a pink bottle of medicine. He was being rescued by Pepto-Bismol on a regular basis.

* * *

One by one, the names on Sexton's coded list were coming to life. They were fathers; single guys, a young woman, and even a 50-year-old former cancer patient who had gone from using it for medicinal purposes to becoming a dealer. They were lots of people with various backgrounds from as far west as Eau Claire, Wisconsin and as far east as Sault St. Marie. Sexton's empire stretched across two states, covered practically the entire Upper Peninsula and reached into a foreign country. The Wisconsin State Police and the Royal Canadian Mounties were welcomed to the fold. Andrew had only met some of the people, but he knew every name and every address.

He gave them every name, but one. Trevor still had his money, and although they weren't exactly friends, a pact was made.

"So, it's like that?" Mackey seethed.

"Like what?" Andrew responded.

"Fuck this bull shit!" Mackey stormed off.

Andrew watched him go and then turned his attentions back to O'Reilly.

"Alright."

"Alright?" Andrew wasn't sure what that meant. *Is he going to let me off this easy?*

"Yep. I know who number fifteen is and we will catch him. So, obviously you must have some reason for protecting Trevor Spicer."

Andrew knew his facial expression confirmed it for the State trooper. The man stood up and held his hand out. Andrew sighed before taking it. O'Reilly held it firm, and much longer than Andrew thought was necessary. "Kid, don't mess up this opportunity to turn your life around. Trust me; you won't get off so lucky next time. When are you going to be sentenced?"

"Beginning of August," Andrew responded. O'Reilly nodded his head and finally let go of his hand. Andrew would never see either Statie again.

∗   ∗   ∗

Melissa lay on her back. Her breasts, once full and firm, had lost their shape long ago. The flesh, no longer defying gravity like those of a teenager, settled in on her sternum like a beanbag chair with a fat kid in it.

Steven stood at the foot of the bed and zipped his jeans up. "I've got to go."

"What? Where?" Melissa sat up. Suddenly conscious of her aging condition, she pulled the sheet up over her breasts.

"We're having a coach's meeting to discuss the teams we will most likely be playing at State."

Melissa didn't protest. She was envious that he had something to take his mind off of their son's dilemma.

Steven pulled his ridiculously large black Hummer into the parking lot of the Robin's Inn. He drove around to the back and saw what he had hoped to see. He pulled around the back of the lot and almost clipped a green dumpster. He backed his vehicle up and pulled out of the local bar and drove off to his real destination.

"What are you doing here?"

Steven stood on Savannah's front porch and stared at his lover. "I miss you so much."

"Steven, are you insane?" Savannah hissed in a whisper. Her tone softened "I miss you, too."

Steven leaned in and tried to grab her. She pushed him away and mouthed the word *no*.

"Honey, who's at the door?"

Steven took a quick step back, almost falling off the fading stained wood porch in dire need of a husband's refurbishing touch. He looked to the driveway for confirmation that Sharrie's vehicle was not there and back at the Inn like he had seen.

"Just coach, Mom."

Savannah sighed as she heard the creaking of wood as her mother traipsed down the stairwell.

"Well, invite him in."

Behind his mistress, stood her mother. A ménage a trois fantasy was the furthest thing from his mind. He thanked God for his close escape.

"Oh, that's okay. Was just telling the kid to get some sleep for our long trip tomorrow."

"Hey, you think you could give me a ride up to the bar?"

Savannah turned sharply to her mother and barked, "You can't walk? It's like three hundred yards."

"I can walk, thank you very much. But, why should I?"

"Sure," Steven said hollowly, not taking his eyes off of Savannah.

Sharrie grabbed a jacket and pushed her way past her daughter.

Steven declined Sharrie's offer to come in for a beer on the house. He was not going to get what he wanted that night, so he headed back toward home. Steven looked in the rearview mirror and saw the grey in his beard and the brownish hue under his eyes. He looked every bit of a man nearing fifty.

Depressed, he gripped the steering wheel as hard as he could and gritted his teeth. He slammed on the breaks of his three ton vehicle. It came to a screeching halt, spraying gravel as it came into contact with the shoulder of the road. With his vehicle half on the road and half on the shoulder; he set his head down on the steering wheel, blaring the horn in the process. After a few moments he jerked his head back, hearing the light tapping of a weak sounding horn. He looked in his rear view mirror—a Ford Festiva.

Steven pounded on his horn. The Festiva driver pounded right back. It was like a calico cat roaring back at a lion. The smaller feline won. Steven pulled his vehicle all the way off the road. To his left he eyed the Rapid Junction Tavern. He pulled in. The Festiva passed and gave him one last piece of mind.

Fuck you, I'd crush you like a monster truck.

It was nine p.m. on a Wednesday and the *other* bar in town only had two customers. Steven walked through the door and sat in a high back bar stool with a ripped vinyl seat.

"Hey, coach!"

Steven smiled. He hadn't realized that Meghan Johnson, Carly's sister, bartended. It didn't seem like she was old enough. The buxom girl with raven hair played short stop for him two years earlier.

"Hi ya, Meggie."

Two hours, four beers and three shots passed. The other two customers long gone, Steven was alone with his former player. Both had exchanged innocent flirtation up to that point.

Meghan traded sides of the bar and sat next to Steven.

"Coach, you ever smoke pot?"

She took a sip of a beer, although she was still a year away from being legally old enough to drink.

"Back in the day, sure."

"You want to bring back the day?" Meghan raised her eyebrows in unison.

"You betcha."

Meghan jumped from her bar stool. "Okay, help me clean up, would ya?"

"Sure."

Meghan ran around the place trying to clean up. She moved a wet cloth over the bar, smearing crud into the bar, more than actually cleaning anything up. Steven watched more than helped, not knowing what to do.

Meghan grabbed a bucket and filled it with ice. "Hey, grab that tray of fruit, would ya?"

Steven grabbed it and followed her to the kitchen. She opened the lid of the ice machine and leaned over and tossed the ice from the bucket in with the rest of the ice.

Steven looked at her from behind. Her ass was round and hard; her jeans framing it perfectly. He set the tray of fruit down and stepped over to the twenty-year old girl.

She turned around just in time to meet Steven's lips against hers. Not expecting it, her eyes bulged and she tried to push him off. He grabbed her by the ass and pressed his lips harder against hers. She turned her head and pushed at him harder and with anger.

"What the fuck, coach?"

Humiliated, Steven swung his hand at the tray of fruit, sending lime, lemon and orange slices everywhere.

CHAPTER THIRTY NINE

"You sure no one followed you here?" Trevor asked; his eyes a steely flint. Andrew knew he had been living in fear and paranoia for the past two weeks. He also knew that both Mackey and O'Reilly were on vacation for a week; something he coyly got them to divulge as he feigned interest in their personal lives. He doubted that they would bother to send someone undercover to spy on him.

"No one followed me. Do you have the money?"

"You really think it's a good idea?" Trevor asked.

"Yeah, I do."

"Alright."

Andrew followed Trevor over to his mother's house. The woman, watching a soap opera, did not budge or acknowledge Andrew or her son as they entered and Trevor offered no introductions.

"Fucking, cheating whore!" the woman screamed at the actress playing a fucking, cheating whore on television.

Andrew stopped and turned around. He knew of the woman's Tourettes, a disease that left a lifetime of mental scars for Trevor and of her impending schizophrenia.

"Come on," Trevor ordered.

Andrew followed him to the end of the hall. Trevor pulled down a string that dangled from the ceiling. A panel came down. Trevor unfolded the attached ladder and slowly climbed up. Andrew stood in the hallway; watching Trevor above him, but listening to the crazy woman in the other room. Any other time he might have resisted the urge to laugh. But getting his money was his only priority.

"Asssssssssssssss hole!"

Trevor came down with a familiar bag. He handed it to Andrew, but didn't immediately let go. "Here you are."

"Did you take out your half?"

"Yes." Trevor gulped. His eyes were intense. "If you fuck me over, I will end your life."

"I won't," Andrew responded as Trevor finally released the attaché case. He didn't bother to tell him that they already knew.

CHAPTER FORTY

"No!" Paul bellowed.

In the living room, Paul stood up from his chair and walked away from his wife. He knew that if he wanted to win the war, he was probably going to have to give in on this battle. Paul understood that it was impossible to control his daughter's every move. He knew she had to be let out of the house. However, he still didn't trust her. He figured she'd run to find Andrew the first chance she got. He also considered the fact that they might run off together. How would he ever be able to explain things to her then? The stubborn side of him did not want to give in, but the rational, cunning side of him turned on the light switch. He walked back from his bedroom to the living room.

"Alright, she can go," he began. "But only if Andrew doesn't."

"Okay, I think that's fair." Marie responded. "Andrew never goes to the games."

Stoic, Paul stood and received a kiss on the cheek from his wife.

*　　*　　*

The team headed downstate the day after Steven's humiliation at the Rapid Junction Tavern. The semi-finals and championship games were being held in Battle Creek, a seven hour drive. Steven had Dr. Dedrick drive. He was also sharing a room at their hotel with the ER doctor. There was no chance of giving in to his urges to find an alone place for he and Savannah. Nearly half the town would be coming down for the game that Friday. They included people like the drug store pharmacist, Thomas Feister.

The rabid following also included most of the Rapid Junction teaching staff and administration, including Mrs. Huttle and Mr. Spivey.

Paul insisted that they did not have enough money to pay for a motel for two nights, so Wendy and Marie headed out at 4:30 in the morning. Paul, staying true to his word, was not going to cross the bridge. He kissed his wife goodbye and closed the car door. It was still dark out that early in the morning. Wendy ran out of the house with a blanket; even in the middle of June, the morning air was chilly.

"Hey," Paul said softly. Wendy froze in her tracks before she got to the car. Paul walked over to her. "I still love you, ya know?" He held out his arms and put them around Wendy, who was draped in the blanket. He could forgive her for not hugging back, since her arms were trapped. But, the recoil he felt from her body hurt to the core.

"I know," she muttered back coldly.

That hurt even more. He stepped away and watched his daughter get in the car. Wendy felt bad, but she was caught off guard and didn't know how to turn off her emotional force field. He came near and it went up. Half a mile down the road, she almost made her mom turn back. The feeling passed and she only said, "Never mind," after her mother asked what she had said.

Paul would have been gone anyway, as soon as their car was out of sight; he was busy hooking up the battered boat to his equally battered truck.

The Rockets got to Bailey Park at noon. They had a team brunch beforehand. Savannah couldn't contain her nerves. She hadn't eaten a thing at the Denny's and wouldn't look at or answer Steven.

"What's the matter, girly?"

She kept pacing and ignoring him.

Their game was scheduled after a Division 1 contest. Savannah's nerves settled as she marveled at the talent that she witnessed on the field between the two teams that came from schools that had five times more students than Rapid Junction had citizens. She wondered if she could compete with the heavyweights. Savannah decided she could and quickly regained her swagger. *I've come too damn far to go home now.*

She watched her opponents for the day get off their bus. An evil smile swept across her face. She was going to get her chance at revenge against the team that had knocked them out in the quarterfinals the year before. Savannah was going to get another shot at the pitcher who outshone her the year before. The Rockets were facing the defending Michigan state champions. The one thing the two schools had in common was a very small student body; after that they could not have been more different. Rapid Junction was a tiny little UP town that struggled to find its own identity in a sea of similar small Yooper towns. Birmingham St. Josephs, on the other hand, was a school where doctors and General Motors execs sent their spoiled kids to get an education and win state championships.

Savannah looked down at her uniform. It was decent, and even fairly new. Steven had gotten the boosters to buy new uniforms when the girls were freshmen. Up to that point the Rapid Junction softball team had not received new uniforms in over ten years. Compared to the major league looking threads of the St. Joe Blackhawks; however, they seemed shabby. They filed by Savannah as she stared each one in the eye. Normally a team who knew who Savannah was would avoid eye contact. She was an intimidating figure. Each girl returned the stare; no one flinched or looked away.

Savannah heard one of them mutter to another, "melt down!"

In a close playoff game the previous year against the Black Hawks, Savannah lost her cool and composure and cost her team the game and a possible state championship. *Keep talking.*

Wendy entered the dugout and was mobbed by her teammates. The teammate she was most interested in, however, sat alone at the end of the bench in deep thought.

"Hey coach, can I sit in the dugout with you guys?"

Steven jumped to his feet, gave her a bear hug and lifted her off the ground. The giant man finally put her down, then, gave her bad news.

"I would sweetheart, but the rules say that nobody but those in uniform can be on the bench."

"That's alright, I will sit with my mom."

"Wait a second." Steven walked back to the ball bag and pulled out Wendy's jersey and tossed it to her. "Here you go. You can be my assistant coach, eh?"

Wendy smiled and put the jersey on over her t-shirt. She had been so preoccupied with thinking about Andrew and all of his troubles, her own battle with her father, general self pity and the like, that she had completely forgotten how much playing softball meant to her. She sat down next to Savannah, who still hadn't acknowledged her.

"Nice to see you, too."

"We've got to win this." Savannah turned to Wendy. "I want this *almost* as much as anything I've ever wanted in my life."

Savannah turned and her eyes became fixated on Steven who was talking with the umpire. Wendy noticed and suddenly *knew*; she couldn't believe that she hadn't seen it before, but at that moment, she knew. She didn't want to know it, tried to erase the thought from her mind; but it was etched. *It's just a crush, nothing else,* she finally convinced herself. Wendy decided to refocus Savannah; she licked her finger and stuck it in her ear.

"Wet Willy!" Wendy's smile was a mile wide.

Savannah jumped up and scrubbed her ear with her index finger. "Godddddd, I hate when you do that!"

Steven came back to the dugout. "Alright girls, let's do it."

Savannah stormed off, but turned back when she reached the first baseline. "Paybacks are a bitch!" A rare smile on her face.

She took her first practice pitch, arched her neck and rubbed her ear against her shoulder eliminating the remaining spittle. Hennie tossed the ball back to Savannah, she snagged it out of the air like a fly and looked over at Wendy and shook her head, still smiling.

Wendy smiled back like a kid posing with a cheesy grin for a fifth grade school picture. After Savannah turned back to deliver her next practice pitch, Wendy's mind went back to the topic that demanded its attention. She looked at Steven and prayed she was right about it being only a crush; but she knew she wasn't. His eyes were firmly on his star pitcher. Wendy recognized the look; it was exactly how Andrew looked at her. Wendy did her best to erase the depression that set in.

"Coming down!" Hennie hollered.

She caught the last practice pitch and fired a strike to second base. The freshman, Allie Dedrick, caught the ball, made a fake tag and tossed the ball backward out of her glove to the short stop who caught it with her bare hand and fired over to the first baseman who then tossed the ball to the third baseman. The third baseman dropped the ball in Savannah's glove. The other infielders sprinted to Savannah and held their gloves upward toward each other.

"Three up!" Savannah screamed.

"Three down!" Her infielders roared back.

"Tough D!" Savannah screamed again.

"No E!" Her outfielders shouted; then sprinted to their positions.

The game cruised by with neither team scoring in the first six innings. In the bottom of the sixth, however, things came unglued; but this time it was the Blackhawks who couldn't get it together. The first two batters for the Rockets struck out without even making contact. Savannah came to the plate. She swung at the first pitch and hit a high fly to the first baseman. She threw down her bat and sprinted toward first base. Savannah had no intention of distracting the first baseman; but was happy, nonetheless, when the girl took her eye off the ball just long enough to see her scowl. The ball glanced off her glove and rolled toward the fence in front of her dugout. Savannah clapped her hands, excited about the girl's misfortune as she stood on first base. The first baseman protested to the umpire.

"There is nothing wrong with running out a pop out."

"Did you see her face?" The girl asked incredulously.

The umpire laughed. The catcher and pitcher stood with their hands on their hips as the ball sat near the fence. Halfway through the argument and confusion, Savannah alertly took off for second base. The pitcher screamed for the catcher to throw the ball. The catcher, caught off guard, tried to throw without having a good grip. The yellow Wilson ball went straight up in the air and landed halfway between the pitcher and the first baseman who continued arguing her case. Savannah took off for third base. People cheered, cursed and were genuinely excited. The Blackhawk first baseman finally got her act together and picked up the ball. She threw a strike to third base, but a fraction of an inch too late. Savannah slid under the tag. She looked up at the umpire who emphatically crossed both arms in a manic motion and hollered, "Safe!"

Savannah jumped up and madly clapped her hands, dust flying everywhere. The third baseman, the one who had earlier muttered 'melt down,' bit her lip and slammed the ball hard into her glove. The umpire signaled time out. The other coach ran out to the field and found the home plate umpire. The other umpire joined his peer.

"What's going on here?"

"Your girl dropped a ball in fair territory, the other player ran around the bases. Never had a dead ball, Coach," the home plate ump explained.

The coach then looked at the first base umpire. "Why didn't you signal fair ball, then; instead of carrying on a conversation with my first baseman?"

"Not my call coach, the ball didn't pass the bag. It's Joe's call." The ump pointed back to the home plate umpire.

"And I did this the whole time the play was going on." His arm pointed to the left, the signal for a fair ball.

The coach shook his head and asked for time. He walked out to the mound as the umpires discussed what had happened. The entire team converged to the mound, including the outfielders. Dr. Dedrick congratulated Savannah as her team cheered her on from the dugout.

"Okay, guys, we need to shake it off right now," the coach began. He looked at his pitcher. "You've got to go after this girl and get her out. No damage yet, guys." He looked into the eyes of his players, he saw damage. "You okay?" He asked his pitcher, who looked the least okay of everyone.

"I hate that bitch," she said, looking over at third base.

Savannah held out her hands and clapped them again, just for her. *Melt down,* Savannah thought to herself.

"Just focus on the next hitter." He held out his hand, his players put in either a hand or a glove. "One, two, three!"

"Blackhawks!"

Savannah looked to the bench; she caught Steven's eye. He nodded his head. She nodded back. It was a gutsy move, but no one was hitting the other team's star pitcher.

The pitcher delivered the next pitch with a little more ferocity. Savannah led off just as the pitch left her hand. Trina Stevens, the Rocket's short stop, swung at the pitch and missed. Savannah was about ten feet off the base. The catcher did not look at her and tossed the ball back to the pitcher, who then turned her back to the plate just as she caught it. A bad habit she had had for a long time; one that both Steven and Savannah remembered from the year before. As soon as the ball was about to reach her glove, Savannah took off.

The third baseman screamed, "She's going!"

Savannah barreled toward the plate. Trina jumped out of the way.

Savannah turned toward the pitcher for a split second. In that time she saw the girl, on her heels, throw the ball. The catcher jumped up to catch it just as Savannah slid safely beneath her. When she came down, however, her cleat landed directly on Savannah's pitching hand. The Rockets and their fans cheered louder and more raucously than they ever had before. Savannah winced in agony and clutched her right hand. She looked down at her middle finger; it had cleat marks on it and a little blood from their indention. *Shit.*

Savannah jumped up and jogged to her dugout. She held her hand, but tried to hide the pain with a stoic face. Steven raced toward her, pushing players out of his way.

His voice was filled with panic.

"What happened?"

"I'm fine," she pushed her way around him and sat down next to Wendy as everyone congratulated her. They held out their hands for high fives, but she ignored them. They patted her on the shoulder instead.

Savannah felt Wendy's elbow in her ribs. "Let me see it." Savannah glanced over to Steven to see if he was looking, he wasn't. She took her hand out from under her glove and showed Wendy. "Oh, man." The finger was swollen to nearly twice its size and was changing color.

Savannah heard strike three and stood up; she turned to her bag which was on a hook behind her. She unzipped it and pulled out her sunglasses. The weather didn't call for them; it had been grey and cloudy all day. She sprinted to the pitching circle and grabbed the ball.

"Hennie, come here," Savannah ordered.

"You exthited, or what?" Hennie lisped.

"Yeah, Hennie, I'm geeked. Tell the ump I don't want any practice pitches."

"Okay?" Hennie responded, her eyebrows arched. She ran back to the plate and accidentally spit on the umpire. "We're good." She put on her mask and yelled, "Batter up!"

The umpire laughed and shook his head before making it official himself, "Batter up!"

The other team looked confused, but the girl in the on deck circle swung her bat one more time and approached the plate. Savannah's own players were confused as well, but threw their practice balls in. Steven walked over to Wendy and sat down next to her.

"Look at her. She's so cool she's wearing sunglasses, now." The voice belonged to the opposing pitcher.

Savannah had no idea how it was going to all work out, but knew she wasn't giving up the ball to anyone. She was going to finish the game no matter how much it might hurt. She rocked back, then came forward as she turned her hips and released the ball. The true pain didn't come until the ball rolled off her damaged middle finger with all the pressure that is needed to deliver a fast ball. The ball sailed toward the plate, but noticeably slower than her usual 60+ mph fastball.

The umpire hollered, "STRIIIIIIIIIIIIIIIIKE one," he pointed his right finger toward the visitors bench.

The girl at the plate looked confused. Savannah had three pitches in her arsenal: a devastating fastball that sailed away from lefthanders and into the hands of a right hander and a riser that seemed to start off at the belt buckle and end at a batter's eyes. Her best pitch, however, was a change-up, a pitch that seemed to be coming out of her hand like a fastball, but suddenly put on the breaks. The ball would drop as it reached the plate. Batter after batter would end up looking foolish as they finished their swing, sometimes before the ball even crossed the plate. Steven called it the Bugs Bunny slow ball. *Strike one, strike two, strike three . . . you're out,* he would cackle.

Steven, Wendy, Dr. Dedrick, the other assistant coach and two lone bench players cheered from the dugout. "Come on! Thatta girl. Two more just like that," they bellowed.

The entire bench and coaching staff for the other team stood in their dugout, grabbing on to the fence and rattling it. They wore their visors upside down, trying to bring their team luck with the time honored 'rally caps.' Fans for both teams, as well as hundreds of other fans of the sport, stood on their feet and rooted for one team or the other, or were there to simply watch a great game.

Savannah caught the ball back from Hennie, who pumped a fist. The first tear sprung from Savannah's eyes. She grimaced, but didn't make a sound.

The tension in the batter's face disappeared. Savannah knew the girl gained a new sense of confidence.

Savannah threw her the same pitch. The girl didn't miss; she swung with everything she had and sent the ball deep. Savannah momentarily forgot about the pain in her finger and jolted her body toward left center field.

"Come on, Alice!" she muttered.

Alice Hayward, a freshman centerfielder, who after Savannah was the school's best female athlete; drop stepped to her right and sprinted toward the high sailing ball. She was a true athlete, and although she didn't get much action in the outfield with Savannah pitching, she was always ready. She ran under the ball and at the last second stretched her glove out. Savannah sighed as the ball found its place safely in her glove. Alice bounced off the fence and turned back to the field to show the umpires she still had the ball.

The crowd either cheered wildly, or let out a collective 'aw.' The ball came back into Savannah, who despite everything that was going on, refused to show any emotion.

Hennie held out one finger between her legs and then patted her right thigh; a fastball on the inside corner. Savannah shook her head. Hennie moved over to the other side of the plate and signaled again for a fastball and patted her other thigh. Savannah shook her head again. Hennie put out two fingers for a rise ball.

Frustrated, she closed her eyes behind her sunglasses, then hollered, "Time out!" The umpire gave her time and Hennie ran out to her. "Listen, don't worry about any signs," Savannah began. "I'm throwing all curves."

"You throw a curve?" Hennie asked bewildered, her hands on her hips.

"I do now," Savannah said. "Just set up inside or outside."

"Okie, dokie." Hennie pulled her mask down and sprinted back to her position behind the plate.

Savannah learned a curve ball at a pitching camp she attended after her freshman year. She didn't feel it was nearly as good as her other pitches, and so she only tried it occasionally her sophomore year, and not at all as a junior. The grip for the curveball she learned, however, put more pressure on her index finger rather than her middle finger.

"Everything okay?" Steven hollered.

She ignored him. She threw the next pitch, and although it didn't break much, it was effective enough to throw off the batter. The ball caught the end of her bat and dribbled toward the mound. Savannah pounced on it and threw a bullet to first base. The throw beat the speedy runner by half a step.

"Out!" the ump bellowed.

"Come on, Savannah! One more, girl!" *Wendy.*

Steven, she knew, was pacing.

Savannah got the ball back and circled the pitching plate once. She had never felt so much pain in her life. The tears streamed down her face in full force. She wasn't sure if anyone noticed and really didn't care. She looked up and saw her counterpart in the batter's box. *So, it comes down to you and me. Perfect.*

Hennie set up outside; but not used to the pitch the ball escaped Savannah's hand and stayed on the inner half of the plate, the other pitcher turned her hips with extreme might, but a tad bit too early. The ball took off like a rocket, and had plenty of distance to be a homerun. Savannah did not turn to watch the ball; she knew it was way foul. As if at a Fourth of July fireworks display, the crowd let out a chorus of 'ooohhhhhhs and ahhhhhhs.'

Savannah slapped at the ball as it came back to her from Hennie, upset with herself for throwing such a bad pitch. The ball ended up being smacked to the ground rather than landing in the webbing of her glove. She picked it back up and looked to the batter. The girl smiled; *I've got you, and you know it.* Savannah's next pitch was much better, but shouldn't have been swung at. The ball tailed down and away from the batter. The girl swung anyway, corkscrewing herself in the process. Savannah knew the feeling of wanting something so bad. The girl swung her bat toward the ground like she was chopping wood. Dust and dirt flew everywhere. *Who's got who?*

The girl was given a quick warning before setting up in the batter's box. Savannah took her eyes off of the batter and took in the crowd. The tension was thick; the collective heart of the crowd raced along with Savannah's.

Savannah stepped off the pitching plate and called time out. Hennie raced out to her pitcher. Steven raced out of the dugout. He got about two feet.

"This doesn't concern you," Savannah barked.

He stopped in his tracks and headed back to the dugout. Many in the crowd laughed; especially after Steven threw his arms up in the air comically. *Clown.*

"Wus up?" Hennie asked with her hand on her hips.

"Fast ball," Savannah replied.

"Okie, dokie." Hennie began to return to the dugout, then turned back. "Where?"

"Doesn't matter."

And it didn't. Savannah knew this was going to be her last pitch; of the game, the season, and most likely her career. For one pitch, she was going with her fast ball. Damn the pain. Savannah did not see the girl grit her teeth or sway her hips in rhythm as she got ready for the pitch. She did not see the girl at all. Nor did she see the umpire or Hennie.

She saw her mother on a barstool, her father surrounded by his new family and Steven . . . flanked by his wife, Melissa. She saw herself nine months pregnant.

Savannah closed her eyes then rocked back in her windup. She raised her arms high and turned her hips with all the energy she could muster. Her arm came slinging downward, and she let the ball come out of her hand with all the might she had. The ball rolled off her middle finger as she snapped her wrist. The pressure she put on the ball with her middle finger caused it to become momentarily numb. The physical pain surfaced after all the energy was transferred from the ball back to her damaged tendons. Before the ball even got halfway to home she let out a blood curdling cry. The batter didn't stand a chance. Even if she did expect a fastball, she wasn't going to catch up to this one. She swung with all her might, but way too late.

"Strike three!" the umpire exclaimed.

Savannah slumped to the ground and sobbed. Every emotion she had bottled up for the past few months came rushing out. She no longer felt her mangled finger. She felt the mental torture of not being able to be with the person she loved; the pain of knowing that she had a living thing inside of her, a creature that would need her. In her pain, she said goodbye to the little girl who had once stood up for her best friend to a Troll from the other side of the bridge.

As if trapped in a bottle, she took in the scene around her. Her teammates jumped into each other's arms in excitement. Some stood around her and clapped her on the back. She couldn't hear them or feel them, however.

"I know, girl . . . I know." Savannah's trance was finally broken. She buried her head in Wendy's arms.

After a few minutes the celebration diminished. Savannah looked up and found Steven standing alone by the fence. He was a million miles away from her. As much as she appreciated Wendy at that moment, she wanted it to be his arms around her.

*   *   *

Steven traveled along with Savannah and her mother to the ER after the game. As he feared her finger had extensive ligament damage.

"Will she be able to pitch tomorrow?" Steven asked.

The doctor raised his eyebrows. "No coach, not tomorrow." He patted Steven on the shoulder and chuckled as he walked away.

"I'm still playing, tomorrow, coach."

"You heard the doc," Steven responded with his arms on his hips.

"He said I couldn't pitch, not play. "DII me, I can still hit."

"Fine, but who's going to pitch?"

Only one person other than Savannah had pitched all year, and that was Hennie. She hit three straight batters during a rout. Savannah was sent back in to spare the backs of the opposing team.

"Alice."

"Alice?" Steven seemed to consider it more than question it.

"Yeah, she used to be a really good pitcher in youth ball. She'll be alright."

"Gotta be better than Hennie," Steven replied in all seriousness.

Savannah laughed aloud. Steven joined her in laughter and put his arm around her. Savannah put her arms around Steven, making it a hug. He put his other arm around her and took in the smell of her. It brought back memories and his dick stiffened.

He caught Sharrie out of the corner of his eye. His first instinct was to immediately step away from Savannah. She only smiled at him. He was safe; it was not the glare of a woman who wanted his head on a stick for sleeping with her sixteen-year-old. It was the smile of a satisfied parent who appreciated his role in her daughter's life. She even mouthed the words, *thank you.*

He squeezed Savannah and shook her side to side. It was an 'oh, you!' hug; the kind of hug buddies give each other. All the while his growing penis poked into Savannah's side.

Sharrie's expression changed. Steven had seen the look on many women in his lifetime. It was the look of lust. She pulled her hair back and put a hand to her chest. Her eyes did not leave his. The thoughts of a mother/daughter ménage a trios came back to Steven. *I'm a dirty, dirty boy.*

Savannah walked into the lobby of the hotel. Many on the team jumped up from the lobby couches to get the word they dreaded. Savannah didn't need to say anything; the metal splint on the middle finger of her amazing pitching arm said it all. With a yellow softball in her good hand, she walked by everyone and found Alice Heyward. The stocky freshman with a bad case of acne and no sense of girliness about her held out her hand and Savannah placed the ball in it.

"It's all you, freshman."

The girl forced a smile, showing off her crooked teeth. Savannah spent the rest of the day playing pitching coach. In two hours, she taught the girl everything she knew about pitching. She worked on her grip, her release point and her windmill windup. The girl was a natural and would be fine. The good news was that they would be playing a team that barely finished the regular season with a winning record. The small school from the southwest corner of the state had caught lightning in a bottle during the tournament. Their pitcher was only average, but they managed to hit just enough, field just enough, and get extremely lucky along the way to end up in the championship game. In the quarterfinal, they faced the team that Savannah was sure they would play in the championship game. The team's star pitcher, however, was caught drinking and was forced to sit out. Savannah had considered the team lucky. However, in the semifinal they played a very good team with their best pitcher available, and had spanked them 7-2. Savannah knew that if she were pitching, the game would be over before it began; no one had scored more than two runs on her all year and that included some very good larger schools. However, she wasn't pitching and knew that the Rockets shouldn't take anyone lightly.

*   *   *

"Take a walk, Hennie," Wendy demanded.

"Okay," Hennie said, smiling before she left as ordered. Right before she closed the door she turned around to ask, "For how long?"

"I'll come get you. Go wait in the lobby."

"Okie, dokie."

"Love that kid," Wendy said as she plopped down on the bed next to Savannah who was watching Sports Center on TV.

"I don't want to talk," she told Wendy before turning up the volume.

Wendy sighed. "You have to tell someone, you know."

"Well, you seem to know, so consider yourself told." Savannah turned up the volume more.

"Okay, let's start over. What are you going to do about this?" Savannah turned up the volume even louder. Wendy raised her voice to be heard. "I can play this game," she said in a normal voice. "YOU HAVE TO END IT, SAVANNAH," she screamed into her ear.

Savannah threw the remote across the room; the batteries flew out the back. "I don't have to do anything, you don't understand."

She pushed herself up with her good hand and walked toward the door; the ESPN sports anchor's voice blared in the background. Wendy watched as her friend stormed off. She wondered if she should tell her mother. Wendy had hoped, even prayed, that her 'gut feeling' about Savannah and Steven was untrue. If this came out it was going to destroy Maggie and ruin a marriage. *And God, what about Andrew?* She knew that Andrew never had the respect for his father that a person should have, but there was no doubt that he loved the man. She wondered how it would affect him. Since her phone had been confiscated, she had all but given up hope that she would talk to him anytime soon. She stared at the hotel phone and picked it up.

"If she answers I will hang up real quick," she said to herself as she dialed the number.

Wendy pulled out her *for emergencies only* credit card after a prompting from the operator. She prayed that her parent's didn't look at their bill. She also prayed the right person answered. It rang three times before the voice she prayed for answered.

"Hello."

"I love you so much." She couldn't control the words anymore than a poorly constructed dam can hold back water during a flood.

"I love you, too."

Wendy slumped to the floor. She didn't feel the knobs of the dresser scrape across her back on the way down. "I'm so sorry for everything that happened." The flashflood of words kept coming. "I wanted that night to be so special, and it was. I was going to . . ."

"Slow down," Andrew interrupted. He chuckled then began, "My mom is in the basement doing laundry so I don't have much time to talk." He took a deep breath as did Wendy. "I want you to run off with me. I know this is crazy, but . . ."

Wendy heard Melissa's voice.

"Yes." Wendy said it again, "Yes." Then she heard click. *Please have heard me.*

*   *   *

Hennie fell asleep at eight p.m. and immediately began to snore. Savannah, exhausted, fell asleep shortly after her roommate for the weekend did.

Savannah's alarm, set on low, went off at 1:00 a.m. Hennie stirred as the alarm buzzed. "Ten more minutes, Mom," she called out.

Savannah bolted upright. No one really expected any of the girls to do something as stupid as get drunk, smoke or sneak out for a late night romp with their coach, so security was nonexistent.

Savannah's biggest challenge was how to get Steven without waking up Dr. Dedrick or worse, making him suspicious. If Dr. Dedrick answered the door, *My finger is killing me, I think I might need to go back to the ER; can you get Coach?* If Steven answered the door she would waggle a finger at her lover seductively; he would follow her to the elevator where they would climb up to the roof and make love and figure out how they were going to be together forever. She would tell him that she was pregnant and he would hold her and tell her it was alright. Savannah begged herself to believe that this was how it was all going to play out. But that little evil part of her mind, the part that 'tells you the truth when you least want it to,' took over. *Stupid, stupid little girl,* the monster in her mind told her over and over again as she walked down the hall.

She took the stairs up one floor and stood in front of the Holiday Inn room. She closed her eyes and told the monster to shut up. Her brain complied; it was smart enough to know that the heart was in control. *Fuck you, then; stupid little girl. See what happens.*

She closed her eyes, sighed heavily and then lightly rapped her knuckles on the door. Nothing. She waited a few more seconds, then rapped again a little harder. She heard moving in the room and held her breath. *C'mon, Steven, c'mon!*

Dr. Dedrick, who had given up all of his vacation time to help coach the team, answered the door. The man squinted through the light that entered the room from the hall.

"Savannah? What's wrong, hon?"

"Hi, coach; is Steven here? I think I might need to go back to the hospital, my finger is killing me."

"When was the last time you took a Tylenol 3?"

"Two hours ago."

"Not working, huh?" He scratched his head. "Steven."

The doctor came back to the door a few seconds later. "He must have stepped out for a while; he probably can't sleep with all the excitement. Do you want me to take you?"

"No, that's alright. I'll go get my mom," she said. Her voice hid her dismay and shock at the revelation, her eyes did not. Without his glasses on, Dr. Dedrick didn't notice.

"You might just want to give it a couple more hours; it's really not a good idea to try to take anything stronger unless it's really necessary."

"Yeah, I'm probably just being a baby."

"If there's one thing you're not, it's a baby."

Savannah turned and walked away. *Where are you, Steven?* It was possible that he had driven around Battle Creek and had found himself a barstool to cozy up to. She realized her rendezvous was not going to happen. Disappointed and unable to keep her emotions under control, she decided that the time had come to confess all her deepest, darkest secrets. She went to the fifth floor to see Wendy. She would take *her* to the roof top and figure things out. *Now, you're talking some sense.* Savannah wished that Maggie was there, too. But Maggie wasn't coming until morning; she had promised she wouldn't miss the championship game, but she wanted Conner to be there too and he had to work Friday.

The elevator stopped on the fifth floor. Savannah didn't realize that she was crying. The door opened and she nearly lost her mind. There standing just around the corner from the elevator, which was right next to Wendy and Marie's room, was Steven. *What are you doing on the fifth floor, Steven?* Steven leaned next to the wall. She could tell he was drunk and she could tell he was talking to someone. He put up a finger to his mouth to shush the person. Savannah knew exactly who the other voice belonged to. Steven, drunk off his ass, slid down the wall. He almost fell to the floor, but was caught when an arm reached out for him. He grabbed hold of the arm. Being much heavier than the woman, his weight pulled them both to the floor. Sharrie Sanders landed on top of Steven and they giggled uncontrollably. They both shushed each other, which made them laugh even harder. The elevator door closed.

Savannah slumped to the floor. *Told you so.* Her mind mocked her. She took it out on her face. She slapped her cheeks; first her left side, then her right side. This was not enough to shut the 'truth' down. Her mind taunted her; *oh, ouch . . . stupid!* She balled up her hand and wailed on her face. *Hey dumbass, you're hurting your face, not me . . . now go up to your room and let's figure out what we're going to do.* Her mind began to empathize with her heart. *Come on old friend, we can figure this out together.*

CHAPTER FORTY ONE

Savannah wiped the tears away as the door of the elevator opened. She walked to her room and planned out her next steps. She lay on her bed, trying to ignore Hennie's snoring and sleep talking. It didn't take her long to figure out her plan. Her scorned heart compromised with her brain. First, win the state championship the next day. This was for her alone; not for Steven. She knew this would be her last day to truly enjoy being young. Second, Steven must die. To get back at her mother, she would then take her own life. Her father could rot in hell with the knowledge that his desertion led her into the arms of a man his age. She got up out of bed and found some stationery. She sat for over an hour tapping the pen on the pad of paper; not knowing what she should write. Once she began, she found it awkward with the splint on. She took it off and threw it across the room. She found her bottle of Tylenol 3 and took two more pills; she skipped the water. Savannah ignored the throbbing pain as she finally began writing what turned out to be her suicide letter. *To everyone concerned: I refuse to apologize for my actions. However, to my dearest friends, Maggie and Wendy; I only wish I could have been a better friend to you both ...*

She went through an entire stationery pad and told the whole sorted story of her affair with Steven, her pregnancy, her hatred for her mother and father, and why she felt she needed to kill Steven. She finally fell asleep clutching *her plan* in her good hand.

The next morning came fast for Savannah. She woke up to find Hennie well rested, doing jumping jacks. "Hey, Vannah! You exthited or what?" Savannah saw the spittle fly out of her catcher's mouth.

"Yes, I am! Hennie, my dear!"

Anyone who knew Savannah would have assumed she was mocking the girl; but Savannah was truly rejuvenated and didn't mind being silly with her pudgy teammate. She hopped up and did jumping jacks right alongside Hennie.

T. D. Croel

"Hey, what happened to your face? I thought you hurt your hand."

Savannah turned to the mirror and looked at her face. She had a scratch on her nose, and bruising on her left cheek and above her right eye. "Well, holy shit, how did that happen?"

Hennie stopped her jumping jacks and held her hands to her face. "Oh, shoot."

"What?"

"I sleepwalk a lot, and sometimes . . . well, my mom says I can do some crazy things . . . do you think I might have done that to you? I had some crazy dreams last night."

"I don't know, maybe," Savannah responded with a serious expression on her face. She walked up to Hennie who took a step back. Savannah kissed her on the forehead.

"But, I forgive you. We have a championship to win!"

*   *   *

Wendy and Marie met Savannah and her mother for breakfast in the hotel restaurant.

"Gee, Mom, you don't look like you slept too well," Savannah said, only slightly hiding her mocking tone. *How was he, Mom? Pretty fucking awesome, wasn't he? Whore!*

Sharrie rubbed her temples. "I hate these hotel beds. They're just so uncomfortable."

Marie agreed that the beds were not nearly as comfortable as they looked and began a conversation with her. As they talked, Wendy began her own conversation with Savannah.

"You think we will win today?"

Savannah kept her glare on Sharrie; picturing her face when she found her body. A sinister smile crept its way on to her face. She finally turned to Wendy and couldn't hide her smile. "Huh? Oh, hell yeah, that team is going down. I just wish you could play."

"Me too." Wendy put a hand to the side of her face and placed her fork into her eggs and sighed. No one noticed the bruising on Savannah's face; her application of makeup hid her self-imposed injuries fairly well.

*   *   *

Andrew stood in the kitchen with his head against the wall and his right hand on the phone. He closed his eyes and sighed as he listened to the annoying chime. He picked it up on the eighth ring and slowly put the receiver up to his ear, praying it was Wendy. "Hello?"

"Andrew," the voice on the other end began. "It's Uncle Paul. What are you doing right now?"

Now that's a loaded question if I ever heard one. His every thought involved the man's daughter. "Nothing, just got up, why?"

"I thought you and I could go fishing, we haven't done that in a few years."

Andrew closed his eyes. He knew what his answer was expected to be; what it was going to be. He had no choice, there would be no excuses to be made; the man was ordering him to go fishing with the intentions of demanding that he stay away from his daughter.

"Yeah, that sounds like fun. I haven't been fishing in so long," Andrew answered with zero emotion.

Andrew hung up and drew a breath of confidence. *This is a good thing; I'm going to tell the man how I truly feel about his daughter. If he can't respect that, then he isn't the man I thought he was.*

*   *   *

Being the designated hitter, Savannah could do nothing but watch her freshman protégé struggle throughout the entire game. It wasn't the girl's stuff that worried her, it was her confidence. After three innings she had given up three runs. And it was fortunate that was all they had. The Marauders of Caston did not have many hits, but were helped by four walks and two Rocket errors. Savannah was beside herself, but showed little emotion as she stewed on her part of the bench next to Wendy. Neither said a word. Savannah refused to look at Steven who stood with a foot atop an upside down paint bucket. He spat one sunflower seed after another to the dirt outside of their dugout. Savannah could not see it, but she could hear it. It was a stupid little habit that never bothered her before, but now it made her skin crawl.

Fortunately for Savannah and her teammates they had scored three runs themselves due to the fact that the other team's pitcher threw just how they expected. She threw pretty hard—mid-fifties. However she had no movement on her pitches and the Rockets, playing a tough schedule, were used to facing hard throwers.

In the bottom of the fourth inning Savannah came to the plate with the game still tied 3-3. She laced a ball down the left field foul line. She sprinted around first toward second base. The girl in left field slipped as she tried to pick up the ball. She stood up and fired the ball back toward the infield. Savannah rounded second and eyed Dr. Dedrick who was holding up both hands and telling her to stand up. Savannah bolted right past her third base coach. His eyes were bugged out.

"No!"

The third basemen caught the ball as Savannah was halfway around the bag. She fired a perfect strike to the plate. Savannah did not bother to slide, instead she ran into the catcher. The girl held on to the ball, but ended up on her butt. She immediately held up the ball to show the umpire who had already called her out. The umpire walked over to Savannah who was walking toward the dugout, holding her hands clenched so tight that her finger nails dug into her palms. She stared at Steven who was beside himself. Savannah did not hear a word the umpire said to her.

"You have to slide young lady, next time you're out of the game." When Savannah didn't respond, he asked again with the tone of a parent angry over being ignored. "Did you hear me, young lady?"

"Yes!" she said louder and with attitude.

She put a shoulder into Steven to get by him. Steven, who was holding both arms up in the 'why' stance, fell backward into Alice. The other coach came out to argue that she should be kicked out. The umpire calmly explained to the man that he wasn't about to kick out a player in a game this important unless it absolutely merited it. The coach accepted the umpire's decision and sat back down.

Savannah threw herself down next to Wendy, who knew better than to say anything, and then slammed her helmet onto the dugout floor.

"You need to cool it, girly!" Steven said, responding to her temper tantrum. Savannah coolly turned toward the man who had stolen everything from her and smiled. It was sinister and full of contempt. *I know, Steven. I know!* He immediately turned to the batter.

"Come on, Trina; let's get something started."

At the top of the seventh inning the score was tied five to five. Again Alice had walked the bases loaded, this time with no one out.

She managed to strike out the next two batters and it looked as if the Rockets would only need to score one in the bottom of the seventh inning when the next batter had an 0-2 count on her. Hennie set up inside and flashed two fingers and patted her left thigh. Alice let go of the pitch and it slipped just slightly out of her hand. The ball rose, but kept going inside toward the batter. The girl could not escape the incoming missile. As she turned toward the umpire and Hennie, the ball caught her square in the back. She felt nothing and began clapping in excitement as she ran down to first base. The stitch marks and bruising she would have to endure were well worth the RBI that gave her team the lead in the final inning.

Hennie called time out and walked out to the mound. "Hey, ith okay," she handed her the ball and patted her on the shoulder. "Jus thro stwikes, okie dokie?"

Alice, not one to respond with okie dokie, nodded her head. She was shaken, however; she didn't want to hit another batter. She shook off Hennie's signal for a rise ball and settled for a fastball. Nervous, she under threw the pitch. The ball bounced in front of the plate and then ricocheted off Hennie's chest protector. A second runner came into score. Steven walked out to the mound with his head down.

"We just need one more batter. You have to bear down here, okay?"

Alice nodded.

"Step up, freshman! Trust your stuff. Come on, now!" Savanna clapped her hands and sat back down next to Wendy, who had both hands on her face.

"It's over," she sighed.

"Bull shit. It's over when I say it's over."

Alice sighed, took the sign from Hennie and began her windup for another rise ball. She launched the ball right down the middle, where the batter could not catch up to it. Alice followed it quickly with two more identical pitches.

The team walked slowly off the field. In the beginning of the season, Steven used to time them. If any girl took longer than eight seconds to get off the field; including the furthest outfielders, the team would have to run circuits after the game. The girls always sprinted off the field—but not this time.

Steven waved his hands in the air manically, motioning for the girls to join him. "What is this? Walking off the field? This isn't over. We just need two runs to go to extra innings and three to win. You think this girl is good, eh?" He looked around, no one said a word. "Well?"

Savannah stood a few feet away from the circle with arms folded.

"Okay, hands in," Steven ordered. "Win, on three." All of the girls put their hands in. Savannah, still standing a few feet back, only thrust hers in that direction. No one said a word to her, even Steven. "One, two, three!"

"Win!"

Fuck you.

* * *

Andrew and Paul were three hours into their fishing venture. The salmon were biting hard and they were enjoying their successful angling. Paul did most of the talking, mostly about fishing and stories from childhood. After three hours Andrew began to relax, believing that maybe Uncle Paul actually did just want to fish. As he began to let his guard down, Paul threw the first fastball his way. "You really like Wendy, don't you?"

Andrew felt a quick jolt to his heart and his breathing got heavy. *Maybe Paul called me out here to give me his blessing.* "Yes, but it's more than that." He desperately tried to slow down the pace in which his heart beat.

Paul cast his line out and slowly turned the reel. "You realize it has to end, don't you?"

Andrew's initial hopes came crashing down. He thought carefully about what his next words were going to be. His heart now ached. Finally he answered. "No, it doesn't have to end . . ." His mind began to say 'uncle,' but that would only confirm the idea that the two families were somehow connected by more than friendship. " . . . Paul." Andrew reeled his line in and set his pole on the floor of the boat. "It's not like we're really family, there is no blood involved."

"She's your sister, Andrew, not your girlfriend." Paul's back was to Andrew. He slowly reeled in his line before turning to Andrew. He set his pole down and crossed his arms.

Andrew shook his head trying to grasp the meaning of what he was hearing, hoping he meant that she was 'like' his sister. "What are you talking about?" he finally spit out.

"Wendy is your sister. She's Maggie's twin."

Lightheaded, Andrew stumbled to a seated position and nearly fell overboard. He shook his head repeatedly, saying, "No, no, no . . ." Finally he looked up at Paul. "How?"

Paul sat down across from him and began to tell him the entire dreadful odyssey. He began with the rape of his wife at the hand of Melissa's stepfather. Halfway through the story Andrew turned and deposited his stomach into Lake Michigan.

*   *   *

The Rockets got out of their funk quickly as Wendy became cheerleader. She marched up and down the dugout mandating that each player get up off the bench and cheer next to the dugout fence. She also instructed them to put on their rally caps. Each girl dutifully turned their visors upside down and put them on their head.

Marie could not control her pencil; she kept doodling without even knowing it. There were pictures of kitty cat faces, stars and moons, and various drawings of unknown creatures; each in pairs. Not really being the official book; that was being taken care of by the MHSAA, she allowed herself to neglect her scoring duties. The stress and pressure of the game was getting to everyone involved on both sides.

Maggie, who had arrived only a few innings earlier, hollered out to her classmates. "Come on, Rockets! Let's do this thing!"

Conner looked on; he knew what kind of fan she could be. Normally shy and reserved, he cupped his hands around his mouth and chanted. "Let's go Rockets! Let's go!"

After repeating it a few times, he had the entire Rapid Junction cheering section chanting with him. The Yooper following drowned out the opponent's cheers within minutes. Maggie put an arm around her future husband and squeezed him gratefully.

"Let's go Rockets! Let's go!" Maggie responded in unison with the crowd.

Dr. Dedrick's honor roll daughter led off the inning. She was the eighth batter in the lineup. The first pitch she faced she lined up the middle; the pitcher had to duck to get out of the way. The Rockets in the dugout cheered wildly, their fans followed suit, and Conner kept his chant going.

Allie Dedrick raced to second on a wild pitch. With the count one ball and two strikes, the next batter, Kara, hit a dribbler off the end of her bat. The ball rolled halfway between the pitcher and catcher. Both were slow to move. Kara sped down to first base as Allie moved on to third. The pitcher picked up the ball and sighed.

With runners on first and third base, Alice came up to bat. Having taken Wendy's spot as the leadoff hitter, she too was taught to slap hit. The third baseman was playing in as was the short stop.

"Hey, don't worry about that runner at third. Let's get an out at first or second here," the Marauder's coach directed to his team.

Alice looked at the first pitch, wanting to time it. On the next pitch, Alice reached out and slapped at the ball. She hit a perfect high bouncer that eluded the third baseman. Allie scored easily. The shortstop backhanded the ball; she had no chance at a force out at second base. Instead she made a frantic attempt at trying to get Alice out. The ball went to the left of the first baseman and down the fence line. Kara moved on to third base and was waved in by Coach Dedrick. Alice ran all the way to third. The Rocket's fans exploded in approval. Steven was beside himself. Along with the girls he began pounding on the fence. Now the game was tied, there was no one out, and the winning run was on third base.

Conner began his cheer again. "Let's go Rockets! Let's Go!"

No one heard or saw the home plate umpire signal out and point toward home plate. "Out! Out! The batter is out. She stepped on the plate."

The umpire pointed to the bench for both runners to go back to their bases. No one seemed to be paying attention to him, except for the other team's coach. Realizing what was going on he raced up and down the bench telling his dejected girls the good news. Finally, the umpire got Steven's attention. "Coach, your batter is out. The other two runners need to go back to their bases."

"What?" Steven could not believe what he was hearing. "Why?

"She stepped on home plate."

Steven exploded. "Oh, bull shit!"

"Coach, control yourself or I will kick you out."

The umpire turned his back and headed back to home plate. He was rewarded with the responsibility of umpiring behind the plate for the championship game for a reason. He was a twenty year veteran of high school softball umpiring and knew when to kick a coach out and when to walk away. Steven had no choice but to tell his confused players to go back to their bases.

Alice was informed by the third base umpire that she was out. She bit her tongue, knowing that it was the right call. *This just keeps getting better*, she thought to herself sarcastically. Allie and Kara ran past her as she approached the dugout. Steven waited for her and took her gently by the shoulders when she approached.

"Did you step on home plate?"

"Yes." She wanted desperately to run right past him and sprint straight out of the park. She felt that the whole world was staring at her in judgment.

Steven began to lecture her. "How many times have we talked about . . ." He stopped, realizing that that was not the time for a teaching moment. "It was a nice hit." He patted her on the back. Alice sat down and stayed on the bench until the game was over.

Instead of being tied with a runner on third base and no one out, the Rockets were still down by two with one out. Charlotte Newsome, the right fielder, struck out on three straight pitches. The mood of the two dugouts shifted like a mighty wind on Lake Superior during a storm. It was now the Marauders who were hooting and hollering in their dugouts. For the first time it was their fans who were shouting louder than the Rocket fans.

"Let's go Marauders! Let's Go!"

Hennie waddled up to the plate. She had had to go to the bathroom since the third inning, but she feared being stuck in there while she was supposed to be out behind home plate. So, she had held it. She was so distracted by her bulging bladder; in fact, the first pitch sailed right by her and hit the catcher's mitt with a thud.

"Strike," she said in unison with the umpire. Hennie was always a favorite with umpires because of her enthusiasm and perceived witty banter with the umpires. She did the same thing with the next pitch, only she was paying attention this time, and the ball came in high. She tracked it all the way to the catcher's mitt and with the umpire said, "Ball!"

Savannah stood on deck. She didn't take any practice swings. She just stood and watched what was unfolding. The third pitch came in low for ball two. The umpire had given Hennie a dirty look after she made the last call a joint effort. Not wanting to annoy him, she kept silent. The fourth pitch was also low for ball three. The mood of the Rockets and their faithful fans began to pick up again. Steven gave the take sign to Dr. Dedrick who relayed it to Hennie who looked on with exuberance. She nodded her head. The third base coach could hear her say 'okie dokie' in his mind. Hennie pushed out the bat in front of her like she was going to bunt. The ball came straight down the middle and Hennie quickly pulled her bat back.

"Strike!" shouted the ump.

"That was a good pitch. I wish I coulda hit it," Hennie said, turning toward other team's catcher.

The other girl wanted to tell her to shut up, but didn't. She just wanted her pitcher to throw one more strike and end the game. Similar to Alice, the stress was getting to her. She just wanted it to be over.

The next pitch came in on the outside corner. It was too close for Hennie to take. She stuck her bat out and fouled the ball off toward first base. Both sides sighed; the Rockets in relief; the Marauders in anguish. Amazingly, Hennie would foul off five more pitches. Each time the crowd sighed. Both team's fans had stopped chanting. The pressure was felt by everyone and the game became eerily silent.

On the twelfth pitch of the at bat, the ball came across the plate just under Hennie's underarms. Normally she crowded the plate, so it wasn't automatic that this was a ball. She immediately turned to the umpire, who slowly signaled ball four. "Oh, thank God!" She held out both hands toward the umpire as if he were her golden idol. "Thank you, thank you!"

The umpire would question that call the rest of his career. His initial instinct, the one umpires are taught to follow, was to say strike. However, his fondness for the lisping catcher and the excitement of the game got the best of him. Hennie ran down to first base awkwardly, like a toddler doing the pee-pee dance.

"Courtesy runner, blue!" Steven hollered.

At that moment, Hennie breathed a huge sigh of relief. Thank God I'm a catcher, she thought. As the courtesy runner ran out to first base and clapped hands with Hennie, she smiled at the irony. Normally it was a rule designed to speed up the game so that she could put her equipment on. Today, however, it benefitted a girl who was about to piss all over herself. Hennie ran straight past her coach and teammates and headed for the nearest port-a-potty.

The bases were now loaded and the Marauders were still up by two. Up to the plate sauntered Savannah. She tugged on the batting glove that covered her left hand. She raised her bat in the air and waggled it.

"Timeout!"

The home plate umpire signaled time.

The opposing coach waved his hands for the entire team to meet him in the center of the diamond.

Savannah stepped out of the batter's box and looked at the gathering in front of her.

While the other coach was talking, Steven slowly made his way to Savannah. She took a few practice swings, whipping the bat across her body with the end of the barrel slamming into her back. Steven stood in front of her and winced.

Savannah turned away from Steven as he approached. She scanned the crowd and saw Maggie and Conner. A slight smile pursed her lips as Maggie waved to her. She searched all around and saw many familiar faces, but just as many unfamiliar ones. The one face she strained to find was nowhere in sight. Her father, who had promised her that he would be at the championship games—as long as his new wife didn't go in labor—was nowhere to be seen. At that moment, his young wife was delivering their second child and his first son. The furthest thought from his mind was what he was missing halfway across the state.

Steven finally spoke. "They're not going to give you anything good to hit. They would rather walk in a run then let you beat them. You nervous?"

Savannah kept her back to him. "Go sit down, Steven."

"Everyting is going to be okay, ju know?" It always came out as Juneau, the capital of Alaska.

"Did ju know I saw you with my mother last night?" Savannah asked, mocking him with her own Juneau. She finally turned around and stared directly at him. It was his turn to look away.

"Batter up!" The umpire bellowed after he had chased the other coach back to his dugout and the players back to their positions.

"Nothing happened," he said unconvincingly as he jogged back to the dugout.

Savannah watched her former lover jog back to the dugout. She shook her head. The giant man was a child. She almost felt sorry for him—almost.

She blew out a deep breath and stepped into the batter's box. The first pitch came in well outside, just as Savannah knew it would. Steven was right, the other team was not going to throw anything close to her, hoping she would self implode like she did earlier in the game when she tried to stretch the triple into a homerun. Savannah swung at the pitch any way, putting no effort in it and not coming close to making contact with the ball.

"Strike!" The umpire said, almost asking it, rather than stating it.

A gasp shot through both crowds like wildfire. Savannah could hear people asking what she was doing. She stepped out of the batter's box and looked at Steven in the dugout. Although there were a dozen girls surrounding him, he stood alone. He made no attempt to stop her. He stood silently with his arms crossed. *Stupid asshole!*

She looked to Wendy. Her arms were outstretched. Savannah didn't expect her to understand her motives. No one could.

Savannah stepped back into the batter's box. The next pitch was even further outside. Savannah's swing was even weaker and more uncommitted to touching anything but air. The umpire, still confused, bellowed, "Strike two!"

The pitcher smiled and shook her head. Savannah stared at her blankly. The girl tossed the ball into the air and let it land in her glove. *Silly girl.*

The Rocket faithful groaned, and whispered to each other. Many murmured that she had finally had it with her overbearing coach and this was her way of teaching him a lesson. Others simply thought that she had lost it and couldn't handle the pressure. The catcher set up even further outside; the pitcher did not miss her target. This time, however, Savannah began to meekly swing at the pitch but stopped at the last second. This brought even more groans and more private discussions among the fans. Steven stood silently in the dugout, arms still crossed.

Savannah stepped out of the box again and glanced over to Maggie. Conner had his arms around her. Maggie had never looked at her with hatred before. It was more than Savannah could take; she quickly looked away and stepped back into the box.

The pitcher took the throw back from the catcher and looked at Savannah quizzically. The next pitch came in a little closer to the plate. Again, Savannah acted like she was going to swing then stopped. This time she smiled back at the pitcher. The umpire barked, "Ball two!" He put up two fingers on both hands and showed them to each team. "Two and two."

Again the murmurs came. The pitcher, as ordered, threw the next pitch outside as well. This time, Savannah did not move the bat from her shoulder. "Full count," the umpire ordered.

The pitcher snagged the ball back from the catcher. Savannah turned her attention to the opposing coach. She could see the wheels turning in his head. This wasn't softball, it was chess. She nodded her head to him. She turned back toward the pitcher.

"Time out!" The coach was too late.

The pitcher stepped back and began her delivery. The determination on her face let Savannah know what was coming. As the girl came toward home plate in her windmill windup, Savannah sprung into her stance and held the bat firmly above her head. *Checkmate.*

"*No!*" the coach screamed.

As the ball came straight toward home plate, Savannah twisted her hips and with her body fully turned and facing the pitcher she brought the barrel of the bat toward the ball. Swinging as hard as she could, she connected perfectly with the ball on the sweetest part of the barrel of the bat. The ball left her bat twice as fast as it was delivered. It sailed toward the left fielder for the Marauders.

Savannah stood at home plate and watched it the entire way. The leftfielder raced to the fence; the ball sail over her head. The fences were only 205 feet away; the ball landed fifty feet past the mark and on to another field, almost taking out a right fielder. Allie, on third base, clapped her hands and jogged toward home plate. The other runners began moving as well. Savannah finally began her home run trot as the Rocket fans went wild.

"Thatta girl!" Coach Dedrick told her as he clapped her on the back after she touched third base.

She never smiled once as she rounded the bases and touched home plate. Her teammates mobbed her, but Steven stood alone in the dugout; the loneliest man in the world.

Hennie ran out of the bathroom toward the field. "Did we win? Did we win?"

*   *   *

Paul placed his hand on Andrew's back after finishing the story. Andrew was still positioned over the edge of the boat. Although he was done vomiting, the sickness he felt inside was going nowhere.

"Don't touch me," Andrew managed to get out between bouts of dry heaves. He turned and finally sat down on the faded sky blue upholstery covered seat. He held his forehead and pushed his sandy brown hair back. "What now?"

Paul sat back in the chair opposite of Andrew. "That's up to you." Andrew looked up. "Is it?"

His glare was menacing, apparently inherited from his mother. He didn't feel there would ever be anything within his control again. He couldn't control his feelings for the girl he felt nothing but a passionate love for, who all of sudden had become his flesh and blood sister. He thought of his other sister, and the urge to vomit came back. He stood up and pounded on his chest. "What am I supposed to do with this?"

"Your love for Wendy doesn't have to go away, Andrew. It just needs to turn to the love you feel for Maggie."

Andrew paced the small walking area of the boat. "Oh, that easy, huh?" The rage continued to brew inside of him; he didn't care what Paul might say or do to him at that moment. He felt completely entitled to his emotions. "Why couldn't you guys just tell us? How hard would it have been if you sat us down when we were eight, ten, twelve, fourteen . . ."

"We should have, but we didn't." Paul stood up and faced the much taller boy in front of him. "I'm not going to tell Wendy."

Andrew shook his head in disgust. "You're just going to continue to keep this from her? And what do you expect me to do?" Andrew began a sarcastic rant. "Oh, I'm sorry Wendy, I changed my mind. You're a nice kid; but, well you're more like a sister to me . . . . Hah!"

Exhausted from the news and the tirade, he sat down again. Paul stayed standing. "If you choose to tell her, then that's your business. But, look what this has done to you. Do you really want Wendy and Maggie to go through this, too?"

Andrew looked up again. "How fucking unfair is this?" *So fucking unfair.*

CHAPTER FORTY TWO

"Hey, guys!"Maggie exclaimed.

She sat down at a table in the Robin's Inn next to Wendy who was holding her hands together and had the look of a parent about to deliver the news that that the family dog just got hit by a car. Savannah, with arms crossed, had the look of the driver who ran over the dog. Maggie's expression changed to that of the child about to be delivered the devastating news. "What's going on?" Wendy and Savannah looked at each other one last time, before Wendy turned to Maggie and began. "Maggie, you need to see your mother."

Maggie leaned back in her chair and shook her head as her tongue went to the scar on her upper lip. Conner, like the seasons, seemed to suggest the same thing every three months. Melissa found her address each time her daughter moved and wrote letter after letter. Maggie read the first letter; then never opened another. She would look at the return address and throw it in the garbage. Early on, Conner picked them out of the trash can and read them. He would tell Maggie what was written whether she wanted to hear it or not. After a year of hearing Conner paraphrase her mother's letters, she finally learned to rip the letters to shreds.

"Is this what I'm here for?" Maggie held out her hands. "If it is, I'm going to leave. She killed my father and drove my brother away. I can't . . ." Maggie thought about what she really wanted to say. "I don't want to forgive her. I don't want to sit down with her and act like all is well, because it's not."

Tears began to well in Wendy's eyes. "She didn't kill your father, Maggie."

* * *

The Monday after the Rapid Junction Rockets softball team won the Division IV Michigan state championship in softball, Rapid Junction celebrated with a parade through the small town. Savannah was hailed as a hero and her legend began to form. Younger girls tossed their soccer and basketballs in the closet and begged their parents for gloves and bats. Savannah managed to cover her bruises and scratches and looked like royalty as she sat on top of a convertible Corvette and saluted the crowd. She waved to the little girls and reached out to touch their giddy hands. Wendy, who was no longer an official member of the team, was allowed to sit in the front seat next to the driver. She turned and looked up at Savannah who was in full glory. "Celebrity!"

Savannah thought about flipping her off, but with hundreds of spectators lining the street she realized that no matter how subtle she may have thought she was being, someone would notice. This would not be very ladylike and definitely not worthy of her newfound role model status.

After making it back to Rapid Junction late Saturday, she hadn't stopped thinking about how she was going to execute her 'plan.' For the moment she had forgotten about everything but enjoying the attention and adulation she was receiving. For those brief moments she felt like a carefree, un-pregnant, 16-year-old kid again. It felt great.

After the brief parade down US 2 that began at the Robin's Inn and ended at the school, a ceremony was held in the gymnasium where the girls were awarded their medals again, but this time for the entire community to see. Principal Spivey and Assistant Principal Huttle gave quick speeches commending the girls and their coaches. Savannah was sure that she heard a pause when Mr. Spivey mentioned Steven's name. She remembered the looks he gave both her and Steven. Originally, she thought that he was just another nosey jerk, but now she began to see him as a man who might actually care about his students.

Savannah shook her head when Steven spoke. He sounded like such an idiot to her. She wondered what she had ever seen in him. He was nothing but a little boy in a large man's body who cared about no one but himself. She gave the quickest speech of all. Savannah strolled up to the podium and simply said, "It's been such a long season. Thanks." She sat down and the superintendent thanked everyone for coming and the day's festivities were over.

When she got home that day she took a long nap. She dreamt of being a little girl sitting on her father's lap as they watched football. Later in life she would watch *Remember the Titans* and think, *that girl used to be me.* Her father would let her tackle him over and over again in the backyard, each time critiquing her performance. *Let me tackle you just one more time, pleeeeeeeease?* He always relented. Then one day he was gone, because he and her mother hated each other. He hated Sharrie so much that he chose to leave them both and start a brand new life.

Savannah woke up and looked around, half expecting her father to be sitting beside her bed, but he was nowhere in sight. She yawned and contemplated whether he should be added to her list. She threw herself back on her bed; the nap gave her more than much needed rest. Along with the parade and ceremony it gave her the clarity she needed to overcome her temporary streak toward insanity. She realized that she wasn't going to be killing anyone, including herself. She sank into a deep depression. *What now?*

As much as it pained her and as much as it went against her principles, she realized that she wanted an abortion. It was the only way that everything could go away and her life could go back to normal. Sure it would let Steven off the hook, but so what. She was getting off the hook, too. It wasn't all his fault and she knew it; she had seduced him. Life could be good again. She needed to erase all traces of Steven and her personal renaissance could begin.

She walked out of her bedroom and called out for her mother. She checked the clock and realized her mother was already at work. Savannah picked up the phone and dialed. She didn't care who answered.

"Fondulucs, this is Steven." Steven reached into the refrigerator, grabbing his sixth beer of the day.

"We need to talk, Steven."

"Have you told anyone?"

"No, Steven." She heard the breath escape from his mouth on the other end of the phone. Always thinking of himself. "But, we still need to talk."

"Okay, I will be right over."

Savannah sat on the couch as Steven pushed the door open. She was still in her normal sleeping attire, a football jersey, one from when her father was the coach. Although she was wearing shorts under the long jersey, it appeared that was the only thing she was wearing. She was not, however, wearing a bra. Steven had that look in his eyes. Savannah had not intended to look sexy and felt anything but. She wasn't wearing any makeup, her hair was a mess and she was in a football jersey. Savannah had no idea of just what might turn a man on.

"Hey, girly."

His eyes became transfixed on her breasts. Savannah crossed her arms and registered mild disgust. Realizing that she wasn't wearing a bra, she decided to let his wandering eyes slide.

"Will you sit down?" she requested.

Steven walked through the kitchen and into the living room where Savannah sat on the couch. He sat down next to her, but with room for a person to sit between them.

"So, let's talk, eh?"

"Steven it's over and I'm sorry I've been acting the way I have." She waited for his response. She wasn't sure if he would react like a rejected lover or with incredible relief. She saw neither in his eyes. She saw the tenderness that had caused her to fall in love with him.

"You don't need to go apologizing; I'm the one who should be sorry."

Savannah looked at the large hand that was being held out to her. She took it. "I know you slept with my mother, but I forgive you," she lied. For that she would never be able to forgive him. A part of her didn't want to forgive her mother either; but she knew that the woman had no idea of her true feelings for Steven. He rubbed his jaw. She could tell he wanted to speak, but he remained quiet. "But, Steven, there is one thing you need to know."

Steven stopped grinding his jaw and fixed his eyes on hers. "Yeah?"

"I'm pregnant."

The words shot through the air like a bullet whizzing at its victim. There was no way to dodge the speed or avoid the colossal damage that such words can cause. These were the words she feared saying. She considered not telling him, but felt he needed to know what his actions had caused. He needed to feel some of the anguish and fear that she had been feeling.

"What?" It came out as a whisper. He pulled his hand back and stroked his beard.

"I'm pregnant," Savannah repeated.

Steven put his hands on his head and shook.

Mother fucker! You're trying to console yourself and not me?

"What are you going to do?" He whimpered.

She lied. "I don't know."

Steven snapped. "What do you mean you don't know!" he barked as he removed his hands from his head and grabbed hold of Savannah and shook her with one mighty jolt.

Her head snapped back and her neck immediately ached. She tried to pry Steven's hands off of her; but he was simply too strong. His grip intensified and it seemed she could feel his fingers tightening around the bones inside her arm.

"*What* do you mean, Savannah?"

There was a rage in his eyes that she had never seen before, one that she didn't think he was capable of. Steven finally released his grip just enough that Savannah was able to pry one hand off. Steven let go of the other arm on his own. She stood up and pointed a finger at him. "Don't you *ever* touch me again, do you *understand*?" She shook uncontrollably.

The tender eyes were back. "I'm so sorry. Please, forgive me." He walked slowly toward her; her finger still poking through the air in his direction. He took her outstretched hand and put it to her side. He put his arms around her. "Please, I'm sorry," he whispered in her ear.

Tears and snot ran from Savannah's openings and onto Steven's shirt. She couldn't stop the sobbing; her arms were still by her side. He gently rocked her and told her that he was sorry and that everything would be alright. Finally she relented, and put her arms around him and joined in the embrace. "What are we going to do?"

The naïve little girl was back. Her childish infatuation for a man who was nothing more than an adulterer, and technically a pedophile, came back. Her longing to replace the love of her father with that of a man his age came racing back. She felt that she needed Steven all over again. As close as she had come to finally getting rid of him, her true path toward maturity came to a standstill. She responded with what she truly felt at that moment. "I want to keep it, Steven," she sobbed. "This is *our* baby!"

Savannah could feel the tension that raced into his body, but ignored it and focused instead on what he said. "Okay, baby, okay."

He moved back from her and kissed her on the forehead. As she wiped the tears from her eyes, he pulled his right arm back with his hand balled in a fist and he slammed it with all his might into her stomach. She never knew what hit her. The air escaped Savannah with a mad rush as she fell to the floor. She was so unprepared for the attack she fell backward without being able to throw her arms out to soften the landing. Her bottom hit the wood floor with a thud and gravity took over as her head slammed backward and connected with the television screen. Her brain told her to grab the back of her head, which was beginning to bleed mildly; but it was her stomach that hurt the most. As she began hyperventilating trying to catch the breath that had been knocked out of her entire body, Steven came in for his next attack. He kicked her hard in her stomach.

"Aghhhhhhhhhhhhh!" she cried.

Her mind desperately tried to figure out what was going on. It wanted to get her mouth to work so that she could beg him to stop. But her brain was trying to convince her body that it was going to be alright and relax while it worked on getting the lungs working again. She lay on her side, gasping and crying.

Steven leaned over her as she lay on her side, still trying to figure out how to get her breathing under control and to make sense of what was happening to her. He held out his fist above her face. Savannah could make it out in the corner of her eye. A part of her wanted him to just pound her into oblivion and end it all, but her reflexes took over and she closed her eyes tight readying herself for the blow she knew was about to come.

"You stupid little bitch! Tell anyone about this and next time I will kill you."

He brought his fist down and stopped it right before her temple. With closed eyes she could not see it, but she could feel its presence. When it stopped, she opened her left eye and peered up toward the towering man. Everything about him had turned to pure evil. She wanted to hate him more than anything at that moment, but instead her hatred was placed firmly on herself. She closed her eyes and slowly began to regain her breath. When she finally opened her eyes, he was gone.

*   *   *

Maggie shook her head angrily as Wendy paused, allowing the information to sink in. She pointed an accusing finger at Savannah. "She's a lying whore."

Savannah, who had to endure not only the actual event, but the retelling of it; stood up and looked at the girl who she had spent a lifetime sticking up for and protecting and could only gasp. She finally relaxed enough to get out, "Maggie, this is the truth." She sat back down. "I didn't want any of this to happen; and trust me, I take full responsibility for my part. But what he did was nothing short of complete and total brutality."

Tears streamed down Maggie's face. "I just don't understand, how could I not know what was going on?" Her nasally voice created a whistling effect for some of the words.

She felt Wendy's hand on hers and heard Savannah sigh. "I know this is tough, but you need to know what really happened," Wendy said.

"But did he really deserve to die?" Maggie wanted to take back the question as soon as it left her mouth. *Of course he deserved to die; what if this had happened to my child. I would kill the man.* She looked to Savannah, believing she was looking at her father's true killer. *But, why would my mom take the fall?*

*   *   *

Steven plopped himself down in his comfortable leather recliner. He pulled the handle on the chair back and the leg rest kicked up. The jolt caused a little bit of his beer to pop out over the lid. He licked the beer off his hand and flipped on the television. He chuckled as Joey appeared on his screen with a turkey on his head.

"Fookin, Joey!"

He almost spit out his beer as he watched the rerun of his favorite show and character. His son stood in the kitchen and looked at his father.

"I'll miss you, pops," he said in a whisper as he looked at his father take another chug of his beer before nearly spitting it out again. With his backpack and guitar strapped over his shoulders and a large duffle bag in his hands, he quietly walked away.

*   *   *

"Mom, Savannah's having some problems, can I go over there and see what she needs." She had no idea of exactly how severe her problems were.

Marie, arms akimbo, looked to the floor then back up at her daughter. She held up one finger. "One hour, Wendy. Okay? If your father comes home and finds you gone he's going to go ape shit. And frankly, I don't want to deal with it."

"Thanks, Mom. One hour."

Wendy held up one finger then blew a kiss to her mother. Marie snatched the kiss out of the air; but not with the exaggerated glee she did when both she and Wendy seemed so much younger and free of family strife. She put the kiss on her cheek and smiled.

"Well?" Wendy said with eyebrows raised.

Marie shook her head and blew a kiss back; she couldn't help but smile. The young woman standing across from her had given her so much to be thankful for over the years. Wendy, keeping with her mother-daughter tradition, tracked the side winding kiss that seemed to be knuckling its way across the air, zigging and zagging the entire way. Her eyes darted in all directions until she finally reached out and snagged the imaginary symbol of her mother's love and planted it firmly on her lips.

"I love you, Mom."

When Wendy was first beginning to speak and first used the word 'mom,' Marie's heart seemed to melt. She would make Wendy say it over and over again, never getting sick of the sound of that word. Over time, the novelty of the word wore off. Marie slid into an acceptance of her role as mother and heard the word as any other mother did. Sometimes she wanted to cover her ears at the 'whininess of 'mooooooommmmmmmmm' when Wendy was not getting her way. Other times it just seemed like a broken record. "Mom, where's my shoes. Mom, I need two dollars for lunch. Mom, are you listening to me? Mom, Mom, Mom . . ."

But occasionally, the freshness of hearing those words would come back for Marie. This was one of those moments. She wiped a tear away from her cheek and repeated the word. "Mom." Marie giggled lightly, feeling the burden of the recent days flittering away for the moment.

Wendy sat on the couch and shook her head as Savannah recounted the horror she had just faced. Wendy gasped and put her hand to her mouth when Savannah confessed her pregnancy.

"We've got to get you to the hospital!" Wendy exclaimed.

"No," Savannah replied calmly. "I'll be alright."

"Then the police," Wendy said in a stern voice that suggested she would not accept another alternative. She reached for the phone. Wendy was actually going to call her mother first, but had the phone put back down on the receiver by Savannah.

"I need a ride."

"You're not actually thinking about going over there, are you?"

"I'm going to tell his wife everything. She deserves to know what kind of person he really is." Savannah was unusually calm; there wasn't an edge in her voice that normally was there even when things were perfectly fine. Something didn't seem quite right about her, but Wendy chalked it up to a mild case of shock.

Wendy shook her head. "I don't think that's a good idea."

"You don't think she should know?" Savannah asked, her voice still lacking of all emotion and expression.

"Oh, she deserves to know, but maybe right now isn't the best time." Wendy pondered the situation. "Let me tell my mother, or you should tell your mother." Wendy liked that idea even more.

Savannah licked her lips and finally showed a trace of emotion as she laughed. "Fuck that woman." She looked at Wendy, who wished her friend's expression would go back to the zombielike resemblance rather than the manic one that was plastered over her face. "You think I was the only one he fucked?"

"Oh, Jesus Christ," Wendy said as she closed her eyes. She immediately went back to the breakfast she shared with the woman just two days earlier. She figured out why Savannah was acting so strange toward her mother.

"You can either come with me or not, but I'm going over there."

"Okay, okay. Let's go."

"I've got to go change real quick."

Savannah gingerly walked up the stairs to her bedroom and closed the door. She pulled off her shirt and examined her midsection. There was a red mark in the shape of Steven's boot on the right side of her stomach. Beneath it, the fetus inside of her which was a little more than eleven weeks old, lie still. The blow from the kick severely damaged its developing brain. Unaware of the lifeless body inside her, Savannah went to the bathroom that adjoined her room and ran cold water over a wash cloth. She dabbed it to the back of her head, cringing at the stinging sensation. She examined the slightly dark color on the cloth and realized that the bleeding was insignificant, even if the headache she had was not. She looked at her face in the mirror. Savannah felt like a woman four times her age. She limped to her dresser and grabbed a pair of shorts and put a bra on, then a t-shirt. She reached all the way to the back of the drawer and pulled out a shiny black object. Savannah examined the 'glow' of the item and admired the power that she felt from the mere presence of it in her hand.

"Stupid ass," Savannah said to the shiny black .45 millimeter pistol. She looked around and found her purse, placed it inside and walked out to join Wendy. "Ready?"

"Hell, no."

Wendy's other motivation for going over to Steven's was to see Andrew. Even under the circumstances, she would do next to anything just to be within a few feet of him. They pulled up into the driveway. Wendy looked around, but only saw Steven's vehicle. Maggie, not surprisingly, was gone, as were Andrew and Melissa. They walked through the empty garage that showed off shiny tools. Not unlike the revolver, they were also for show. The screen door was open and they could hear the television.

"Savannah, no one is here but Steven. Let's go."

"That's okay, we can wait."

"Savannah!" Wendy said, trying to keep her voice down. "Don't you think he's a little dangerous?"

"Not as dangerous as I am," Savannah said, then reached into her purse and pulled out the gun. She pushed Wendy out of the way and stormed through the door. She walked through the kitchen and into the living room. There he was, drool on his chin, sleeping in his favorite recliner.

Wendy, who had to brace herself against a riding lawn mower after being pushed, ran after her friend. "Savannah, no!" she screamed.

A car pulled up the driveway.

As she got to the living room, Wendy saw Steven wake up. Savannah had the revolver pointed in his direction.

"Whoa, now. Whatcha doing there, girly?"

Wendy walked to her side slowly and carefully. The gun wavered back and forth in Savannah's hands. The gun, fairly heavy to begin with, was carrying the extra weight of 'doubt.' Wendy wanted to reach over and grab the thing, but was afraid that any sudden movement might cause the gun to go off.

Steven smiled; mocking the girl he had just finished abusing. His look was sinister and to Wendy, it looked like he had lost his grip on humanity. The man, who had only been flawed before, was now a complete monster. This was a man who no longer cared about what happened; who found out, or what impact it might have on people. This was a man who had nothing to lose.

He stood up and spoke. "Put the gun down, missy."

"Fuck you," Savannah responded in a weak and unconvincing voice that didn't seem to belong to her, one that Wendy didn't recognize.

"Fuck me?" He cackled. Normally his laughter was goofy and contagious. But now, it echoed like the snort of an evil pig.

Wendy stared on, wondering how she was going to make sure that this didn't end as gravely as she feared.

"You want to go another round, little girl? I'll give you what you want." Steven began to pull down his zipper. Wendy gasped. Savannah cried. She dropped The .47 Magnum and put her hands to her eyes and shook. "Oh, God, oh God, oh God . . ."

Steven and Wendy had the same idea at the exact same moment. *Get that fucking gun before something bad happens.*

Wendy dove past Savannah's feet and came up with the gun a split second before the drunken and older man could get it. In his condition and at his age, he no longer had the necessary reflexes to outmaneuver a younger, more athletic teenage girl. He fell back against the outstretched leg rest of the recliner. Wendy stood up with the gun held in both hands. Her initial plan was to get rid of the gun as soon as she could. However, the gun's power put her under a spell, as it had Savannah moments earlier. She held the gun steady with both hands and pointed it directly at Steven's forehead. She inched closer to him. He did not move, his eyes were transfixed on the barrel of his own gun. Then he removed his eyes from the revolver and looked up at Wendy and dared to smile.

"Tell her you're sorry," Wendy spat out. There was venom in her that she didn't know existed. Steven pushed the gun away, only for Wendy to push it back in its place and jab him in his forehead.

"I'm sorry, I'm sorry," he said as he pressed his palms to the ground and pushed himself up so that he was sitting on the end of the leg rest.

He scooted himself back just in the nick of time; his weight almost made the chair come crashing down on top of him. The chair rocked back and forth. He reached for the warm beer that was sitting on the end table next to him. He took a sip, then laughed; spitting the beer out; some of it landing on Savannah's face. He pointed his finger at Savannah who wiped spat out beer from her cheek.

"I'm sorry," he began again, "But, did you really expect that you were anything more than another little whore to me?" He waggled his finger at Savannah. Those were the last words he spoke.

The gun shot, incredibly loud and unmistakable, filled the air with a willowy white mist. The aroma reminded Wendy of the aftermath of a fireworks display. The two sixteen-year-olds looked at the body in front of them. The man lay on his black leather recliner with his hand out and his mouth agape, like he was desperate to call out final words before his impending death.

"Oh, my God," Savannah said. "He's really dead." Her voice sounded surprisingly calm, as though she expected everything to unfold the way it had. The pistol fell to the floor.

Wendy shook uncontrollably; then jumped when a set of arms held her by the shoulders "Go!"

Wendy stumbled to the kitchen, took a look back at Steven and threw up in the sink. Savannah continued to stare at her former lover. She was in shock. "GO!" Melissa ordered again.

She turned around and looked at Melissa like a confused puppy; incapable of tendering any realistic response. In a trance, Savannah responded, "I'm sorry."

"GOOOOOOOOOOOO!" Melissa screamed, then shoved her backwards.

Numb, Savannah walked toward the kitchen. "Come on, it's time to go," Savannah informed Wendy, robotically.

The two shell shocked friends walked solemnly out to Wendy's car. Wendy jumped at the sound of three additional shots that echoed from the house to the driveway. A zombie, Savannah didn't notice.

The first shot hit Steven square in the forehead. The second shot pierced his already stopped heart; and the last hit him square in the groin. He was dead and felt nothing; Melissa felt empty revenge.

*　　*　　*

Maggie sat with a blank expression on her face for what seemed an eternity. After the point in the retelling where her father had kicked the pregnant Savannah, Maggie had simply shut down. There were no more grimaces in reaction to the shocking revelations, no more angry shakes of her head to maintain her denial of what had happened, and no more *my Gods*.

"Mags? Are you alright?" Wendy asked.

"I have to go," Maggie said with the expression of an injured person in shock.

Maggie stood up. She stumbled toward the door, catching herself on a table. Her eyes were glazed over and she looked like a person walking away from a horrific accident; unaware that their arm was hanging by a thread. Wendy was joined by Savannah as each took a side of Maggie and tried to bring her back to reality.

"Maggie, what are you thinking?" Savannah asked.

Wendy had her eyes fixed on her friend as they each held an arm. Savannah rubbed her arm; something she used to do when Maggie would have one of her rare meltdowns. She would just rub her arm and soothe away her pain.

"I think I see a ghost." She broke away from the two and moved toward the spirit.

Wendy looked toward the door. Standing there; bearded, hair in a pony tail, and physically filled out, stood their ghost—Andrew. Wendy clasped both hands to her face. Savannah's jaw dropped and she put her hands akimbo. Maggie walked up to her brother and put her hands up to his face. "Is it really you?"

"Yes, Maggie, it's really me." There was an accent to his voice that no one seemed to notice.

Maggie broke from her trance and sobbed. She put both of her arms around him and hung on as if for dear life. Andrew picked his pint-sized sister up off the ground and held her close. His eyes, on the other hand, never left Wendy. Standing behind Andrew, temporarily ignored, was Paul.

Wendy's mind raced a million miles an hour; there were so many things she wanted to say. She knew that Maggie deserved first dibs at displaying her feelings, but if she didn't get a chance soon, she was going to burst. She never talked to Maggie about her love for Andrew; it just never seemed as important as what Maggie had lost; so when they did talk, she left it out.

Maggie finally let go and her feet slid back to the floor. She wiped her eyes and looked up at him. "You realize you can't just show up twelve years later and expect me to take you off the hook."

Andrew smiled at her. "I know. I hear I have a couple of nephews."

"Yes, you do."

Maggie went back to her chair and retrieved her purse. She opened her wallet and pulled out a plastic sleeve that held a dozen of the most recent family photos. She handed them to Andrew.

He pulled them out and was mesmerized by each one. "They're so beautiful, Maggie."

This time the accent came through thicker. "Where the hell have you been, by the way? Your accent sounds like . . . . Swedish?" she guessed.

"Beriktiga." *Correct.*

"God, you need to sit down and tell me . . ." She looked around at Wendy and Savannah behind her. " . . . us, everything."

"I will Maggie, I will. But first we need to talk to you and Wendy about something that involves our parents."

It was the pronoun he used, more than anything else that made Wendy's mind race to full attention. *We?* He obviously was referring to her father as the other component of the 'we.' She had assumed that Andrew had stopped by the motel first and that her father was nothing more than a deliveryman. Now, *he* was a part of a *we*, that needed to tell Maggie and her something important about their parents.

"Do you want me to leave?" Savannah asked.

Andrew and Paul looked at each other before Paul spoke. "No, you can stay. You've been affected by this madness as much as anyone else."

The three Yooper women felt an instant anxiety; *what is going on?* While Wendy was telling one story to Maggie; ironically, Paul was telling another to Andrew.

*   *   *

Andrew didn't find out about his father's death or his mother's incarceration for nearly a year. After leaving his father in the living room watching *Friends*, cackling and spilling beer, he drove his truck to Milwaukee where he then took a flight to New York City, and then to Sweden. He had had a passport already; having gone on a class trip to Spain the previous summer. As he walked through each gate he was positive that sirens would go off, attack dogs would be released, and guns would be pointed at him. Nothing happened, he simply walked through, and he was on one flight and then another and his new life began.

He had written two letters before leaving. One of them was given to Trevor to deliver to Maggie. The other he planned to deliver himself. In his letter to Maggie he told her that he loved her but he had to get away from everything that was wrong with their parents. He would be back someday and if she ever needed him for anything she could contact the man that delivered the letter to her. He never expected that it would be twelve years before he would see her again.

The letter never got to Maggie. It was thrown out by Trevor's girlfriend. It lay in a pile of junk mail. Trevor was livid when he found out what she had done, but was helpless to do anything about it. He had no idea where Andrew had gone off to, but assumed it was far away. All he could do was wait for Andrew to call him with his new contact number.

Andrew made that call a few weeks after settling in Stockholm.

"Hello."

"Hey, let me talk to Trevor," Andrew said an ocean away.

"He's not here," Stacy informed him. There was a distance in her voice.

"Can you tell him to . . ."

She cut him off; the distance in her voice gone. "*He's* not here!"

"Oh, shit, they . . ."

She cut him off for the second time. " . . . killed him."

I was going to say nabbed him. Andrew held the phone until he heard a dial tone. He dialed again; the phone rang and rang.

On the sixth ring he heard, "Hi, this is the Fondulucs." His mother.

"And we're not here right now!" Maggie and his voice—when they were so much younger.

"So, leave a message, eh?" His father.

He felt incredibly lonely. He thought about leaving a message, but didn't. Not that it would have mattered. He would spend the next year feeling guilty about Maggie. It was nothing compared to the guilt he would feel a year later when he made another call.

"Inspector O'Reilly."

"Congratulations on your promotion."

"Now if they would just ship me out of this backwoods district. How are you, Andrew Fonduluc?"

"I'm good. I need you to do me a favor."

"Andrew you know you have a warrant out for your arrest."

"Are you going to come get me? It might take you a while to get here."

"What's the favor, Andrew?"

"I have been trying to contact my family for the past year, but it says my parent's phone is out of order."

"Jesus, kid; you don't know."

O'Reilly filled him on what had happened and promised that he would give his number to Maggie. He never heard from his sister. He rightfully assumed that she was beyond angry at him for his desertion. While he was starting anew; she was left to suffer through the fallout of their mother's incarceration and father's murder.

Andrew's second letter sat over the blue edge of the mail slot for what seemed like an eternity. Andrew finally released it from his grip and heard the envelope slide down into a pile of other letters. He wondered if any of the others contained words nearly as powerful as his.

He had tried to deliver the letter in person, but could not force himself to be in Wendy's presence. He drove right by the motel, slammed on the breaks and reversed his direction heading to Milwaukee.

He lived up to his word and did not give all the details of why he left, but he did finish with *our parents have done nothing but lie to us. You deserve to know the truth and should demand it. Once again, I am sorry and I will always love you; but we just can't be together like we want. Start a new life like me; get away from the lies before they destroy you. Love, Andrew.*

Wendy flipped the letter over, looking for more words. The envelope had no return address. *He's never coming back. What happened to taking me with you? Demand the truth? What the hell is the truth?*

Part of her was simply relieved to get any information from him at all; it mildly eased the pain of reading its contents. After composing herself, she walked out to the bait shop where she heard her father trying to talk some out of town slacker into buying a $100 dollar rod and pole that he would probably never use again after that weekend. The man declined and took his earthworms and left.

"Hey, you."

"Hi, Dad," she said calmly. "What is it that you aren't telling me?"

Paul looked down and saw the letter in her hand.

"What do you mean?"

"Don't!" It came out quick and sharp and to the point. "Don't do that; just tell me what I don't know."

He reached for a broom and began cleaning a mess on the floor. "What's that in your hand?" he asked.

"A letter from Andrew telling me I should demand the truth."

Paul stopped his sweeping and pointed a finger at Wendy. "That boy is trouble; nothing more than a drug dealer."

Wendy ignored the drug reference. "What's the truth, Dad? What is it that you aren't telling me?"

The veins on Paul's head began to expand. "The truth? The truth is that Andrew is nothing more than a louse like his father. Where is he? Huh?" Wendy wanted to know the answer to that more than anything in the world. If she knew she wouldn't be there at that moment having this conversation with her father. Wendy did not respond. She closed her eyes; squeezing them shut, the tears came through anyway.

"I just want to know the truth," she finally said after reopening her eyes.

"I don't even know what that is supposed to mean."

"Fine, I will ask Mom." She rushed through the house and to her parent's room where her mother was folding clothes.

"Mom?"

"Yeah, honey," Marie responded without turning around.

"Why won't Dad tell me the truth?"

Paul stood behind Wendy. Marie moved her eyes from her husband to Wendy's. "What are you talking about?"

"You, too?"

Marie walked up to her daughter and put her hands on her shoulder. "The truth is . . . we love you so much that we will protect you from anything, including the truth."

Wendy closed her eyes again. The rage inside of her was overwhelmed by the hopelessness and she resisted striking out. She turned around and pushed her way by her father. "Fine."

* * *

Melissa was being held at Delta County Correctional Facility while she awaited trial. She was allowed visitation one day a week; Maggie visited her the first week demanding to know what happened. Melissa tried to give her a truth that she could accept, and hopefully receive a certain level of compassion. She knew that it would take time for Maggie to forgive her and begin to understand the type of person her father really was. Melissa had no idea that it would take a dozen years and the complete truth.

"Honey, your father is not a good person," Melissa said into the phone.

That was as far as she got. Maggie pounded on the window that separated the visitors from the inmates. Conner, standing behind her, put his arm on her shoulder. "You're not a good person! You know Andrew ran off? Huh? What did you do to him? Did you kill him, too?"

The other visitors and prisoners became much more interested in the drama that was unfolding in front of them. They halted their conversations; this was just too good to miss. For the three other women who were being held, the news of the murderous wife had already become the gossip of the jail.

A sheriff, clad in his brown uniform with gun in holster, grabbed Maggie by the arm and led her out. "I'll take her, ease up a bit," Conner told the sheriff who released her arm.

"She will not be allowed back." He pointed a finger at her.

"I don't want to come back here!"

Paul and Marie watched Maggie storm out of the waiting room, Conner in tow. They walked through the doors for their turn. "Melissa, what the hell is going on?"

Melissa sat across from Paul and Marie, separated by a thick glass window. Twenty minutes went fast and she didn't even get to the part that detailed who actually fired the gun first. She was led away; this time it was Marie who was shouting through the glass. "Melissa, write me what happened!"

The same sheriff who had grabbed Maggie by the arm began walking toward Paul and Marie, but backed off when they began to move out of the room with the other visitors.

*   *   *

A letter arrived later that week. Marie ripped it open so fast that she accidentally ripped the letter in half. She ran to a drawer and grabbed some tape. She half-assed put the pages back together, but managed to match the broken words up enough that she could easily make sense of what was written.

When she got to the part that explained that Wendy had picked up the gun; her heart nearly stopped beating. She clutched her left breast and hollered out to the bait shop. "Paul!"

Paul, who was in the bait shop, ran through the doors to the kitchen.

He began reading on the first page, but Marie made him skip it and flipped to the other side and pointed at the words. *Wendy picked up the gun; I don't know why I didn't race in at that moment and stop what was happening, but I was frozen with anger, with fear. At that moment I wanted to take that gun and shoot myself. I wish I would have. Wendy pointed the gun at Steven and ordered him to apologize to Savannah for everything. That's when I came to my senses and walked in. Steven said the most horrible things to Savannah. Apparently in addition to having an affair with her, he also knocked her up. I think that he may have hurt her . . . I know he did. God, how was I so blind to the evil inside that man? Wendy shot Steven in the stomach; I just told her and Savannah to go . . . to run. I called 911 and confessed when the police got to the house . . .*

Paul sat down and wiped the sweat from his brow. He looked over to Marie who couldn't stop shaking. "We've got to find Wendy, now."

Wendy had been missing for two days.

*   *   *

Two days after the death of Steven, his unborn child came out of Savannah's body with excruciating pain to the mother. Sharrie, tending to her bar—which amounted to chain smoking as she sat on a bar stool, flirting with the newest guy to enter the establishment, and drinking herself into oblivion—was not around when Savannah called 911. She tried to call Wendy first, but Paul, who answered the phone, told her that she was sleeping. He didn't recognize the panic in her voice and hung up before Savannah could tell him to wake her.

A patron of the Robin's Inn drove Sharrie to the hospital later. Dr. Dedrick, as it turned out, was the emergency doctor on duty that night and informed her that her daughter had miscarried and would be alright. The drunk mother walked up to the bed her daughter was sleeping in.

"Hey, slut! Wake up!"

She stumbled and almost fell. Dr. Dedrick caught her before she reached the ground. "If this is how you're going to act, you will have to leave."

"Sorry," Sharrie told the doctor. "Sorry, baby," she lied to her daughter.

Savannah looked up with empty eyes. She was drained of all emotion, and the medication helped in dulling her senses. She was, however, well aware of what she *should* be feeling.

Dr. Dedrick hesitated before he turned and walked out. Sharrie's eyes followed him before turning to Savannah. "Pregnant?"

Savannah mocked her mother. "Do you want to know who the father is?"

"Who is it?"

"The dead guy, Mom. You know, the guy you fucked in Battle Creek." Her eyes, glazed over, had just enough venom in them to penetrate her mother.

She put her hand to her mouth and gasped. "Were you the one . . ." She didn't finish.

"No," Savannah began, "I just wished I had."

*   *   *

The table of confession went from a party of three to a party of five. Paul took a deep breath and looked at his daughter.

       T. D. Croel

"Wendy, your mother was unable to conceive . . ." he began.

Wendy expected to hear a story about how she was a miracle baby. The name John Peterson came up and Maggie sat upward.

"My mother's step-father!" She gasped when she heard the description of what had happened to a young Marie, and must have happened to her mother multiple times.

Wendy felt a pain so sharp she thought she would stop breathing. She didn't have a point of reference like Maggie, but knowing her mother experienced such pain and not being able to tell her how sorry she was, was excruciating. She thought it was hard being the bearer of such bad news; it was so much harder to hear it. Wendy's mind raced. She blanked out as her father continued to hash out the story. The story of her own life fast forwarded. With the new information from her father, everything came together. She stopped her father. "Melissa is my mother . . . my birth mother, isn't she?"

"Yes." Paul swallowed hard.

Wendy became light headed and put her hand on the table to keep from falling backward. Savannah put one hand on hers and another on her shoulder.

"Honey, are you okay?" Savannah asked tenderly.

"No." The glazed look disappeared and she stared straight at her father. "And *he* is my birth father."

"Yes."

"You're my sister," Maggie said softly to Wendy as she put an arm around her. "My twin sister."

When they had first met 'as friends' they had talked about how cool it was that they were born one day apart, not realizing they were born in the same hospital, from the same mother, only minutes apart.

Wendy was still trying to grasp everything. She didn't know what she should feel—anger. resentment, joy, abandonment. The news was so much to deal with that she simply got up and walked away.

Wendy stood by her rented car; her butt against the hood as she leaned over with her hands on her knees. She felt like she was going to puke. Andrew suppressed an ironic chuckle; knowing the feeling only too well. He sat next to her on the hood of the car. He waited for her to come around. Wendy finally sat up and looked at Andrew.

"Well, I finally know the truth."

He smiled. "Kind of makes you feel like a character out of a V.C. Andrews book, doesn't it?"

"Little bit," she laughed. Her expression changed quickly. "You've had to deal with this knowledge for so long. What's going through your mind right now?"

Andrew thought about the question for a while before beginning to speak.

"I'm not going to lie to you and tell you that it was easy. I loved you the same way you loved me, and it didn't go away because I found out you were my sister. I've never been able to get truly close to anyone in my life because I was always hanging on to these feelings I had for a love I could never follow. It was so unfair; I denied myself the ability to love someone besides you. But, now I realize that I have to give my heart to someone else."

Wendy understood exactly what he was talking about. She had avoided love at all costs and found ways to avoid true commitment. She immediately thought about Ben and a sense of relief came over her.

"I met your boyfriend, by the way. He seems like a good guy."

"He is."

"Well, I don't know if he's the one. But, you owe it to yourself to find out. I love you, Wendy and I want the best for you. You and Maggie."

Wendy smiled. The truth had finally set her free. The emotion that she was searching for finally came to her—relief. Pure, sweet relief. She no longer had to wonder what happened to the love of her life; she no longer had to resent the people who had robbed her of that love, and most importantly she finally knew the truth. She had a lot to deal with, and knew that it wouldn't always be easy, but having Andrew back in her life as her brother was so much better than his absence.

CHAPTER FORTY THREE

Wendy said goodbye to Ben as he got in his damaged rental car.

"I feel like yesterday was the first day of my life," he said from a seated position.

Wendy had to smile at the irony of that statement. She hadn't told him of her ordeal yet. "You're going to give me everything I've ever wanted in life, aren't you?"

"Jesus, talk about pressure." His perfect smile radiated up toward the Channel 11 'Weather Specialist.'

Wendy leaned through the window and grabbed hold of her co-worker's hair, messing it up as she kissed his soft lips. He did not complain or bother to fix it the entire trip to Green Bay.

"I love you, Lady."

"I love you, too." She loved the sound of those words.

*   *   *

"I may have two mothers, but I only have one father."

Paul wept. Of all his fears about revealing the truth, the biggest was being erased by the role of blood over love. Wendy hugged her father and said goodbye.

*   *   *

Melissa wouldn't get to face a parole board for another year and had not had a visitor in some time. Marie would visit her once a year but never Paul. He didn't cross the bridge for anyone. She was startled when the guard announced that she had visitors. *Visitors, that's plural.*

Her mind immediately went to Maggie. *She's with Conner and my grandchildren. Please, let it be them.* She was used to disappointment and promised herself that she would hide it if it turned out to be a cousin she had forgotten about.

She walked into the visitor's area and stopped in her tracks. Sitting at a table were her three children. When they saw her they all stood up.

It was Andrew who spoke for them. "Hi, Mom."

Melissa put her hands over her eyes praying that she was not experiencing a hallucination. She felt three sets of arms embrace her. The pain of a lifetime of secrets and lies vanished.

"I'm so sorry."

"Shhhhhhh," Maggie whispered.

"I love you, Mom," Wendy added.